Asda Tickled Pink

45p from the sale of this book will be donated to Tickled Pink.

Asda Tickled Pink wants to ensure all breast cancer is diagnosed early and help improve people's many different experiences of the disease. Working with our charity partners, Breast Cancer Now and CoppaFeel!, we're on a mission to make checking your boobs, pecs and chests, whoever you are, as normal as your Asda shop. And with your help, we're raising funds for new treatments, vital education and life-changing support, for anyone who needs it. Together, we're putting breast cancer awareness on everyone's list.

Since the partnership began in 1996, Asda Tickled Pink has raised over £82 million for its charity partners. Through the campaign, Asda has been committed to raising funds and breast-check awareness via in-store fundraising, disruptive awareness campaigns, and products turning pink to support the campaign. The funds have been vital for Breast Cancer Now's world-class research and life-changing support services, such as their Helpline, there for anyone affected by breast cancer to cope with the emotional impact of the disease. Asda Tickled Pink's educational and outreach work with CoppaFeel! aims to empower 1 million 18 - 24 year olds to adopt a regular boob-checking behaviour by 2025. Together we will continue to make a tangible difference to breast cancer in the UK.

Asda Tickled Pink and the Penguin Random House have teamed up to bring you Tickled Pink Books. By buying this book and supporting the partnership, you ensure that 45p goes directly to the Breast Cancer Now and CoppaFeel!.

Breast Cancer is the most common cancer in women in the UK, with one in seven women facing it in their lifetime.

Around 55,000 women and 370 men are diagnosed with breast cancer every year in the UK and nearly 1,000 people still lose their life to the disease each month. This is one person every 45 minutes and this is why your support and the support from Asda Tickled Pink is so important.

A new Tickled Pink Book will go on sale in Asda stores every two weeks – we aim to bring you the best stories of friendship, love, heartbreak and laughter.

To find out more about the Tickled Pink partnership
visit www.asda.com/tickled-pink

 Penguin
Random House
UK

STAY BREAST AWARE AND CHECK YOURSELF REGULARLY

One in seven women in the UK will be diagnosed with breast cancer in their lifetime

'TOUCH, LOOK, KNOW YOUR NORMAL, REPEAT REGULARLY'

Make sure you stay breast aware
- Get to know what's normal for you
- Look and feel to notice any unusual changes early
- The earlier breast cancer is diagnosed, the better the chance of successful treatment
- Check your boobs regularly and see a GP if you notice a change

PENGUIN BOOKS
The Housekeeper of Holcombe Hall

Maggie Campbell grew up on a rough estate in north Manchester. Exchanging the spires of nearby Strangeways Prison for those of Cambridge University, she gained a Masters in German and Dutch. Maggie has now returned to Manchester, where she writes full time and enjoys a heart-warming, uplifting ending.

Also by Maggie Campbell

The Housekeeper of Holcombe Hall

MAGGIE CAMPBELL

PENGUIN BOOKS

PENGUIN BOOKS

UK | USA | Canada | Ireland | Australia
India | New Zealand | South Africa

Penguin Books is part of the Penguin Random House group of companies
whose addresses can be found at global.penguinrandomhouse.com

Penguin Random House UK,
One Embassy Gardens, 8 Viaduct Gardens, London SW11 7BW

penguin.co.uk

First published 2025

001

Set in 12.5/14.75pt Garamond MT
Typeset by Falcon Oast Graphic Art Ltd
Printed in Great Britain by Clays Ltd, Elcograf S.p.A.

The authorized representative in the EEA is Penguin Random House Ireland,
Morrison Chambers, 32 Nassau Street, Dublin D02 YH68

A CIP catalogue record for this book is available from the British Library

ISBN: 978-1-405-96638-2

Penguin Random House is committed to a sustainable
future for our business, our readers and our planet. This book is
made from Forest Stewardship Council® certified paper

For Hilary, Victoria and Vicki.
Books and bagels are mightier than the sword.

August 1929

I

Below stairs, Florrie Bickerstaff's heartbeat sped up to match the thud, thud, thud of the big band, playing jazz in the ballroom above them. Even through thick floors fashioned from great oaks, felled in Holcombe's forests some three centuries earlier, the reverberations from drums and dancing feet were causing dust to fall from the ceiling in rhythmic puffs. Florrie looked up and frowned, wondering how on earth the old lathe and plaster survived these raucous parties.

'Ooh hey!' Sally said, side-stepping to dodge the falling dust. 'I don't fancy getting that muck in my eyes again. It makes them stream something rotten.' The tray in her hands tipped slightly so that the full glasses tinkled ominously. 'And it lands in my hair so I look grey as a badger.'

'Straighten up, will you?' Florrie said. 'Never mind your hair. If Mrs Douglas sees you've spilled a single drop of that champagne, she'll have your guts for garters, never mind promoting you from kitchen maid.' Looking down the narrow hallway towards the kitchens, she spied the butler, Mr Arkwright, marching their way, his highly polished shoes and immaculately Brilliantined hair gleaming in the gaslight. She lowered her voice to a whisper. 'And if Arkwright cops you, you'll be out of a job. We both will. Come on. Let's look lively.'

Ignoring the pain in the soles of her tired feet, Florrie led the way, carrying her own drinks-laden tray up the back staircase, praying that her hands would remain steady.

Behind her, Sally complained. 'By heck, my arms are already killing me. Lady Charlotte should have let us fill these glasses in the vestibule next to the ballroom or the cloakroom or summat.'

Florrie scoffed. 'She didn't want any servants "hanging around above stairs like a bad smell, spoiling my birthday celebrations". That's what I heard her telling Mrs Douglas.'

'Charming!'

'"A gal doesn't turn twenty-five every day of the week, Mrs Douglas."' Florrie mimicked the coquettish, upper-class voice of her employer.

Sally laughed. 'Poor Bertha.'

'Mrs Douglas to the likes of you and me.'

'Aye. Poor Mrs Douglas. I don't know how she bites her tongue.'

Not for the first time that day, Florrie thought ruefully of the trip to Rawtenstall that she was supposed to be enjoying on this, the eve of her *own* twenty-fifth birthday. It would be just her luck that Alfred Hitchcock's *Blackmail* would have stopped showing altogether by the time she eventually made it to the town's picture house.

'No rest for the wicked,' she muttered under her breath, forcing herself to climb the last couple of creaking steps up to the rarefied world of the Harding-Bournes.

With her muscles complaining at the weight of the

4

tray, Florrie almost lost her balance as a couple of tipsy, high-society flappers skittered into her on their way to the privy. They glittered like rare jewels in their fashionable beaded frocks, whispering to one another and apparently unaware that they'd almost sent one of their hostess's servants flying. Florrie caught a whiff of their heady perfume and a snippet of their conversation as they passed by.

'He's keen on you, Portia,' the taller of the two young women said, her slender arm draped around her friend. 'He was devouring you with his eyes, I swear.'

'What? Evelyn?' Portia said. She stumbled in her heeled sandals. 'Whoops-a-daisy! Oh, you are fanciful, Ophelia. Waugh's a married man.'

'Don't be naive, darling. They're to divorce, I hear.'

'Whatever would *I* do with an impoverished writer?'

Their exchange ended in a peal of giggles, and, swinging their beaded evening bags as they went, the two click-clacked around the corner and out of sight.

'Everything all right?' Sally asked.

Florrie glanced down at her friend on the steps below. 'Just some squiffy debs. On with the motley.'

Feeling the perspiration roll beneath her heavy maid's uniform, Florrie made her way into the ballroom and switched on her brightest smile for the guests, as Mrs Douglas, their beloved housekeeper, had trained them to do.

'Champagne, sir? Champagne, ma'am?' Florrie was always careful to water down her Mancunian accent when she spoke to the illustrious guests of the

Harding-Bournes. Arkwright had told them all that it didn't reflect well on Sir Richard and Lady Charlotte if their staff sounded like uncouth mill workers. Florrie had had a week's pay docked on the one occasion she'd pointed out she *was* the daughter of a mill worker. She had not made the same mistake twice.

'Young lady,' a male guest shouted above the shrill call of the big band's trumpets. He blasted her with alcoholic breath. 'Are there any more of those splendid canapés?' His black bow tie hung undone around the stiff collar of his pristine white dress-shirt. There was a greasy stain on the black satin collar of his dinner jacket that made Florrie wince inwardly. He blinked slowly at her, clearly inebriated.

Florrie looked around the ballroom to spot the other maids and the footmen who had all been corralled into serving, whether it had been their usual night off or not. She could only glimpse the young footman, Danny, on the far side of the dancefloor. 'On their way, sir.'

The guest nodded and turned away from her, as though she'd been rendered invisible.

As Florrie handed out drinks and collected empty goblets, she eyed the opulently embellished, drop-waisted evening dresses of the duchesses, starlets and politicians' wives; dresses which she knew had likely been fashioned by the finest Parisian couturiers. With their Marcel-curled or poker-straight, sleek bobbed hair adorned with precious stones and peacock feathers, they all looked like elegant exotic birds. Florrie caught her reflection in the tall windows of the ballroom and quickly turned away from the sight of her form in its shapeless black maid's dress, thick black lisle stockings and frilled white apron.

She felt a tap on her shoulder.

'I say, Florrie!' A man's voice was startlingly loud, right next to her ear.

Florrie turned to find Sir Richard leaning in towards her, smiling.

'Yes, sir?' She bobbed a curtsey as best she could, given the tray she was carrying.

Unlike the other men, who were drunkenly jitterbugging and dancing the Charleston with the women, or else standing on the periphery, smoking cigars, Sir Richard was clearly sober. He was as immaculately attired as he had been at the start of the evening, and Florrie noted that he smelled of that expensive cologne he wore – a smell that gave her butterflies in her stomach.

He laid his hand on the small of her back and leaned in so that their cheeks were almost brushing. 'Do you see that rather exuberant gentleman over there, dancing with my wife?' He pointed to Lady Charlotte and the very man who had asked her about the canapés.

Florrie nodded. 'Yes. He's rather the worse for wear, that one.' She reluctantly took a step forward to free herself from his touch.

'Well, do keep him topped up with champagne, there's a dear. He's Clarence Hatry, a *very* influential business man. He's presiding over a merger of steel companies worth millions, and HB Steelworks is one of the major players. I need to keep him happy. Holcombe Hall could do with a new roof, sadly, and Lady Charlotte's penchant for all that glitters shows no sign of letting up!' He chuckled.

'Say no more, Sir Richard.' Florrie smiled.

'What would we do without you, our Florrie?' He locked eyes with her for a moment too long, smiled with what she was sure was a wistful look in his eyes, and then walked over to a group of cigar-smoking, important-looking men.

Our Florrie, Florrie thought. *He even knows how to make a humble maid like me feel like a princess. What on earth is a smashing fellow like Sir Richard doing married to the likes of Lady Charlotte?* She sighed deeply.

Carrying her tray, she gingerly made her way across the champagne-slippery parquet through the fray towards Lady Charlotte. As she watched the birthday girl flinging her arms to and fro, dancing, laughing, carefree and commanding the attention of every man within twenty feet of her, Florrie realized why Sir Richard had chosen such a wife: not only was Lady Charlotte the daughter of an earl and a relation of King George V himself, she was indisputably mesmerising. She had the long limbs, good bone structure and lustrous hair of a woman who was descended from a long line of well-fed, well-bred nobility. *I feel like a donkey on Blackpool beach standing next to a racehorse, whenever I'm in the same room as her,* Florrie thought ruefully.

'Champagne, my lady,' Florrie shouted over the music.

Lady Charlotte turned to Florrie and pointed. 'Oh, here she is!' She beckoned Florrie over. 'Come here,

8

Florrie. Look, Clarence!' She turned to the drunken guest Sir Richard had identified as his business associate, Clarence Hatry. 'This is the maid I was telling you about. Florrie Bickerstaff.' She spoke the name with a rendition of Florrie's Mancunian accent and then reverted to her perfect King's English. 'We're practically twins, aren't we, darling?'

Florrie could feel her cheeks growing flame hot. Hatry was staring at her as though she were a novelty exhibit in a zoo.

'Her birthday is tomorrow, and she's the same age as me, Clarence. Who would believe it to look at her?' Lady Charlotte slapped Florrie playfully on the shoulder, and again, her accent changed to that of a working-class northerner. 'Hey up, chuck. What's tha getting for thy birthday tomorrow? A lump o' coal?' She turned to Hatry, and the two burst into conspiratorial laughter, snatched up fresh drinks and clinked glasses.

Biting the inside of her cheek, Florrie willed herself to smile politely and keep her humiliation to herself. She thought of Mam and her sister, Irene, at home with her little nieces and nephew, who all desperately needed the money she sent home every week. 'Ha. Yes. Very droll, my lady. I'll send Daniel over with some fresh canapés.'

'Good girl.'

Florrie turned and headed as fast as she could over to the young footman, whose platter was almost empty. His face was glum and his shoulders slouching.

Speaking close to his ear so that the guests wouldn't overhear her, Florrie said, 'Get that tray filled up and get over to Lady Charlotte. Sir Richard needs the gentleman with the bald head and moustache to have a good evening, and I've already had him asking me about grub. Where are the other lads?'

Danny looked her up and down. 'Who are *you* to give me orders?'

Straightening her back so she was as tall as possible, Florrie considered her response. 'I've served at Holcombe Hall for ten years, young man – 1919, I joined this staff. I remember His Lordship, may he rest in peace. And I am a good seven years older than you.'

'So what? You're nowt but a lowly maid.'

'I'm a *lady*'s maid, thank you very glad!'

'Poppycock. You're a parlourmaid with ideas above her station, just because that Lady Charlotte has you running after her like you're her little lapdog. But they're still paying you a parlourmaid's wage. Am I right?' The sneer slid from his face and was replaced by a smile as a guest took the final canapé. 'I've had enough of this. I'm due a break.' He turned to leave for the back stairs.

Florrie was determined not to let her hurt show. 'You can't take a break. There are two hundred guests that want feeding, and they're not going to get fed if we're not bringing them food.' She stared at his back, willing him to turn around and take his words back.

He merely shot her a glance over his shoulder. 'What are you going to do about it, eh?'

'Mrs Douglas is going to throw a hissy fit.'

He was already walking away from her. 'I answer to Arkwright,' he shouted above the band.

Florrie shook her head at the cruel and obstinate lad. 'Don't say I didn't warn you.'

With her own tray full of empty glasses, Florrie weaved her way through the dancing throng, pausing only to take in the sight of the band for the first time. She tapped her foot to the beat. The instruments of the brass section glimmered like gold beneath the lights of the ballroom's enormous crystal chandeliers. How she would like to be taken to see a big band play; to sip champagne and dance the night away with a debonair man. Yet she mused that she wouldn't even have anything to wear beyond her Sunday best – a woefully outmoded, sack-like dress that her mam had sewn up from spare curtain fabric. She stopped tapping her foot, and was just about to move on when she caught sight of Sally walking briskly towards her. The kitchen maid wore an expression of undisguised alarm.

'Sal, whatever is the matter?' she asked.

'Come quickly, Florrie. All hell has broken loose in the kitchen.'

2

'Enough!' Cook said, slapping her hand on the worktop of the large Welsh dresser with such force that the carefully arranged crockery on its shelves rattled ominously. 'Will you both just sit down and discuss this calmly over a cup of tea?'

As she reached the bottom of the service stairs, Florrie found Mrs Douglas and Arkwright shouting at one another in the kitchen, with Cook acting as referee.

Cook leaned over the large oak table where the staff all dined together and pushed towards them a slightly lopsided Victoria sponge cake that clearly hadn't been quite good enough to serve at the party. 'How about a slice of cake? Sweeten you both up?'

Neither Mrs Douglas nor Arkwright were listening, however.

'*I'm* the housekeeper of Holcombe Hall,' Mrs Douglas said, tapping her finger insistently on the table top. '*I'm* the one in charge of the staff for this party—'

'Well, I beg to differ, Bertha.' Arkwright stood to attention like a sergeant major, with his hands behind his back. 'I am the butler. I am the one with the office and the authority.'

Mrs Douglas grew even redder in the face. She folded her arms over her bosom. 'Hey! It's Mrs Douglas to you.

I don't care whether you're the butler or Sir Richard himself. *I* say who gets to call me by my Christian name.' She dug a short-nailed thumb into her chest. 'I answer to Sir Richard, not you, and Sir Richard said the *Tatler*'s here. You know what that means. There's a journalist and a photographer upstairs, watching the family's every move. Not just the family. Us too. The staff. We've been told by his nibs to be on our very best behaviour. And *your* lads aren't pulling their weight. Poor old Cook here has made enough platters full of appetizers to feed an army . . .' She pointed to a sideboard laden with silver salvers filled with enticing-looking eats. 'And all but three of them are still sitting down here, while guests are going hungry up there. Where are your lads precisely? Smoking out the back, no doubt.'

Arkwright pressed his thin lips together and touched his rigid, shining hair. 'My lads are busy filling the champagne goblets, staffing the cloakroom and organizing the parking of cars and carriages, as I instructed them to do. And I would look more closely at the tablecloths on the ballroom occasional tables if I were you, before you go throwing accusations around about my lads. I noticed *stains*.' He looked pointedly at Sally. 'You might have a word with your kitchen maid.'

Sally gasped audibly and covered her mouth with shaking hands. Tears welled in her eyes. Florrie wanted to stand up for her friend, but she didn't dare speak out of turn.

Mrs Douglas glared at Arkwright, digging her fists into her hips, every inch the ferocious and protective mother figure that all the young maids loved, relied upon and were only slightly terrified by. 'My kitchen maid can hardly be blamed for the laundress moving to Scotland, can she? Sally's doing her very best.'

'Well her best simply isn't—'

Arkwright's retort was interrupted by the thunder of hasty feet on the stairs. Sir Richard came into view, and the kitchen fell silent at once.

'What ho, ladies and gents. I hope I'm not disturbing anything.' Sir Richard was blinking fast; his handsome face unusually wan.

'Is everything quite all right, sir?' Arkwright asked, bowing slightly.

Sir Richard fingered the black satin lapel of his jacket uncertainly. He frowned. 'I'm afraid there's a bit of a ruckus between my rather silly brother, Sir Hugh, Daphne le Montford and that unbearable bore, Walter Knight-Downey. And with the chaps from *Tatler* photographing everything, one really can't afford any kind of scandal appearing in the next issue. Especially since I'm trying to woo an important business associate.'

Arkwright smoothed his moustache with his little finger. 'And how exactly might *we* assist, sir?'

Sir Richard looked at his feet. 'Well, the principal concern is that Sir Hugh and Knight-Downey are now both vying rather forcefully for Miss le Montford's attentions. These bright young things are like a keg full of gunpowder the moment you introduce champagne to the equation, they really are. And they haven't really eaten.' He smiled ruefully.

As he glanced over at the platters of food on the side-board, Florrie saw Mrs Douglas flashing an accusatory glance at an almost contrite-looking Arkwright.

'So, can we get more food in circulation, please?' Sir Richard continued. 'And I feel a subtle distraction may help. Perhaps a member of staff with a little finesse could intervene.' He turned to survey the rest of the staff, locked eyes with Florrie and pointed to her. 'Ah, could you spare Florrie, Mrs Douglas?'

Florrie could feel a nervous itch crawling its way up her neck. She held her hand over skin which she knew would almost certainly be blossoming with bright pink patches.

'Florrie, do you think you could entice Miss le Montford away from her gentlemen admirers? Send Sir Hugh over to Lady Charlotte and myself. Tell him it's urgent – for his ears only.' The furrows in his brow deep-ened. 'Tell him anything, as long as we can break up their little contretemps. If we don't intervene, I'm rather con-cerned there's going to be a fist fight in the next issue of *Tatler,* and that could ruin the Harding-Bourne rep-utation entirely.'

Florrie curtseyed. What choice did she have but to oblige?

Stifling a yawn that betrayed her dawn start, and carrying a platter full of canapés, Florrie made her way through the crowded ballroom, desperately hoping that her exhausted mind would present an easy solution. *Come on, Florrie, wake up!* she told herself. *You've been given the responsibility for sorting this out. Sir Richard's depending on you.*

What did she know about Daphne le Montford that might help her plight? The woman was a toff of some description – weren't they all? She dabbled in the theatre. Yes, Florrie had overheard Sir Hugh eulogizing about her acting abilities at breakfast only recently. Hadn't he said she'd appeared in a musical production in London's West End? Yes! Florrie allowed herself a smile. She had a plan.

Spotting Sir Hugh near to the band, Florrie hastened through the throng of dancing guests towards the three-some. Sir Hugh, she noted, was looking very much the worse for wear in his shirtsleeves, with his bow tie undone and his stiff collar hanging loose – no sign of his dinner jacket or waistcoat. He was pushing his chum, Walter Knight-Downey, roughly and repeatedly in the shoulder. Knight-Downey towered above Sir Hugh and was clearly trying to grab the smaller man's wrists. At their side, the flame-haired Daphne le Montford looked on, clutching her long string of pearls taut against her slender neck. She seemed to be asking the men to stop locking horns, and her finely plucked eyebrows arched above her heavily made-up eyes gave her a distraught appearance. Florrie noticed that a smile was playing on her ruby red lips, however.

'Sir Hugh! Sir Hugh!' Florrie shouted above the band's male crooner, who was singing the chorus to 'Tiptoe Through the Tulips'. 'Sir Hugh, might I have a word, please?'

Sir Richard's younger brother turned to face her, his eyes flashing. 'What? I'm busy, can't you see?'

'Sorry, Sir Hugh. Only I believe Sir Richard and Lady Charlotte urgently need you. They're standing over there with one of their guests . . . beneath the portrait of your mother and father.' She pointed to her employers, engaged in conversation with Clarence Hatry on the far side of the ballroom, just visible through the crowd.

She held the platter of food out. 'Mr Knight-Downey, would you care for something to eat?'

Walter's look of irritation was immediately supplanted by a look of delight. He slurred slightly as he spoke. 'Caviar! Devilled eggs! This is just what the doctor ordered, young lady.' Scooping three small appetizers into his mouth, his attention turned from Sir Hugh to the band.

Sir Hugh pushed the platter away, however. 'Not for me, thanks. And my brother doesn't need me at all. I'm no fool. He's asked you to sidetrack me, hasn't he? Hugh Harding-Bourne, the perennial family embarrassment. Ha!' He turned away from Florrie to face Daphne. 'Take no notice of Walter, Daphne, darling. He's being oafish, and I'll gladly—'

'Miss le Montford, sorry to interrupt . . .' Florrie manoeuvred herself around the three so that she was standing next to Daphne, determined not to fail in her mission. 'But Sir Richard was rather hoping you'd get up on stage with the band and sing a song for Lady Charlotte – you being a famous musical star and all.'

Daphne smiled a perfect pearly-white smile, marred only by a pronounced gap between her two front teeth. She batted her eyelashes and pressed her long-fingered, manicured hand to her chest. 'Little me? Why, it would be an honour. When?'

'Now. Right now.'

The upper-class starlet patted Sir Hugh on the shoulder and squeezed Walter's hand, dismissing both as though they were little more than schoolboys squabbling over a game of marbles or jacks. She lost no time in making her way to the stage, where she interrupted the band's singer, whispering her intentions in his ear. 'Tiptoe Through the Tulips' came to a swift end, and Daphne le Montford had the attention of every guest in the ballroom.

'My Lords, Ladies and gentlemen,' the male singer said. 'Please put your hands together for the one and only Miss Daphne le Montford, singing Al Jolson's "Swanee" . . . with a little birthday twist.'

The band struck up, and Florrie watched with bemusement as the young socialite broke into slightly flat song, replacing 'Swanee' with 'Charlotte'. *The guests are going cock-a-hoop for this nonsense,* Florrie thought, looking around at a sea of captivated faces – a couple of the younger men were wolf-whistling – *but at least I've put a lid on the pot for Sir Richard before it boiled over.*

She glanced up at Walter Knight-Downey, who still only had eyes for Daphne. Florrie made her way through the crowd, offering appetizers as she went. As she neared the top of the back stairs, she caught sight of Arkwright down the hall, answering the telephone. It occurred to her that the hour was late for telephone calls, but then she knew the wealthy had, by and large, installed telephones in all their homes, and it was, after all, Lady Charlotte's birthday party. Perhaps it was a well-wisher. When Arkwright's eyes met hers, however, she shivered involuntarily.

With no small degree of solemnity, he held the telephone apparatus and the earpiece out towards her.

Hastening into the hall, the noise of the band and the revellers fell away.

'It's for you, Florence,' the butler said.

'Whatever do you mean, Mr Arkwright? I don't know anyone with a telephone.'

'It's your mother.'

'But—'

'She's calling from the Manchester Royal Infirmary.'

Florrie felt the blood in her veins chill to ice. She set the empty platter down on a side table. Swallowing hard, she silently took the apparatus from Arkwright. She gripped the receiver tube tightly, pressed the earpiece to her ear and spoke into the mouthpiece with a tremulous voice.

'Mam? Is that you?'

'Florrie! Oh, dear Lord!' On the other end of the crackling line, her mother sounded flustered. Whatever could have befallen her?

'Why are you in the hospital, Mam? What's so wrong that you're calling me at this hour, and from the infirmary to boot?' Florrie could feel Arkwright's judgemental gaze on her. She turned away from him. 'Are you ill?'

'It's not me, love,' came Mam's voice, crackling through the earpiece. 'It's your sister.'

'Irene? Whatever's the matter?'

'It's her lungs.' Her mother began to weep. 'Pneumonia. She's badly with it, and all. They reckon she won't make it through the night. Our Reenie's going to die, Florrie. My little Reenie.'

The line went dead. Florrie set the phone down with shaking hands and felt her legs give way beneath her.

3

'Florrie? Florrie? Are you awake?' Sally's voice was timid on the other side of the bedroom door. She knocked again.

'Keep your wig on, Sal. I'm coming.'

Florrie reluctantly pushed off her bedclothes, which were damp with perspiration. She'd finally been able to hang up her apron and retire to bed in the small hours of the morning, but had been lying awake ever since, staring at the play of the moonlight on the ceiling of her stiflingly hot attic room, thinking about Irene and her mam. When the estate's cockerels had finally crowed at dawn, she'd been filled with paralysing dread. The sun rose, bringing with it the worst kind of uncertainty. Might Irene have died in the night? Would the Harding-Bournes give her permission and lend her money to travel to Manchester? What would become of her small nieces and nephew if they lost their mother?

'Are you all right, Florrie? Do you need anything?' Sally's whispers were full of concern.

Swinging her tired legs over the side of the lumpy mattress and padding to the door in her nightgown, Florrie took a deep breath. She opened the door, caught sight of her friend's face and suddenly found that exhausted tears were rolling on to her cheeks.

Sally enveloped her in an embrace. 'Oh, there, there. It'll be all right.' She patted Florrie's back.

Gently disengaging herself from the girl, Florrie shook her head and took a step backwards. She wiped her eyes on the collar of her nightgown. 'No, Sally, love. I don't think it will. But thanks for your thoughtful words.'

'Did you manage to speak to Lady Charlotte or Sir Richard last night? Have they granted you compassionate leave?'

Florrie shook her head. 'Arkwright told me in no uncertain terms that I had to wait 'til this morning. Mrs Douglas didn't contradict him, either, which was disappointing. Said I wasn't to burst Lady Charlotte's birthday bubble, when there's no train to Manchester before midday in any case.'

'Is there owt I can do?' The kitchen maid's flushed face was a picture of concern.

'Unless you can turn back time and find a cure for pneumonia, no.' Florrie swallowed hard. A memory of the argument between Mrs Douglas and Arkwright popped unbidden into her head, and she noticed then that there were dark circles beneath Sally's eyes. 'And don't you be letting Arkwright rob you of sleep over a stained tablecloth. You answer to the housekeeper, not the butler. Remember that. I'll put in a good word for you with Mrs Douglas as soon as I get the chance.'

Sally bit her lip and then smiled weakly. 'It's not everyone who would stick their neck out for a kitchen maid like me. Thank you, Florrie.'

'Mrs Douglas is a good sort. She's a widow but hasn't

got any children of her own, so she's like a mam to all us girls. I doubt she'll treat you unfairly.'

Watching Sally make her way downstairs, carefully carrying a full chamber pot covered by a cloth, Florrie made a mental note of all the things she would have to do as soon as the Harding-Bournes rose. Then, she remembered that it was her own twenty-fifth birthday. She defiantly wiped another tear away. There was no time for self-pity. Mam and Irene needed her. There was a noise further along the landing, and Florrie retreated inside her room before Mrs Douglas or Cook caught sight of her in a state of undress.

'Oh, Florrie dear. I *am* glad to see you. My head feels like I have a little man inside it, pounding away at my skull with an axe.' Late in the morning, Lady Charlotte sat at her dressing table, staring mournfully into the mirror. Her eyes were still ringed by the remnants of make-up; her satin robe hung from her shoulder. The wooden clock on the marble fireplace mantel said noon was not far off. 'Do you think you could ask Cook to concoct me one of her magic potions? I do desperately need a pick me up. A Prairie Oyster, perhaps, or maybe just a simple Alka-Seltzer? I feel utterly rotten.' She picked up her hairbrush with a slightly trembling hand. If she had remembered that it was Florrie's twenty-fifth birthday, she gave no sign of it. 'Brush my hair, will you? There's a dear girl.'

Biting back frustration that Sir Richard had been nowhere to be found that morning, and she'd had to wait so many interminable hours to speak to Lady Charlotte about her family's situation, Florrie cast a judgemental eye over the four-poster marital bed. The bedcovers were in disarray, but she could see from the perfectly plump pillow on Sir Richard's side of the bed that he had slept in one of Holcombe Hall's other bedrooms.

She took the brush from Lady Charlotte and considered her words.

'My Lady, I have something important to ask.' She started to run the brush through her employer's hair, though the waves, styled close to the scalp, were still stiff with setting lotion.

'Ask away!' Lady Charlotte slapped at Florrie's hand, her momentary scowl visible in the mirror's reflection. 'And do be a little more gentle with my delicate head. There's a good girl.'

'Well, my sister's very poorly with pneumonia.' Florrie stopped brushing. She could feel tears pricking at the backs of her eyes. 'I got a telephone call last night. She's on her last legs, I'm afraid, and I was wondering if you would allow me to go to her bedside, urgently.'

Lady Charlotte spun around to face her. 'Oh, my dear. How terrible.' She took the brush from Florrie and set it on the dressing table. She then clasped Florrie's hands inside hers. 'Why on earth didn't you say anything sooner?'

'I didn't want to spoil your celebrations, my lady.' Florrie blinked away the tears that were pooling, blurring her vision. She dabbed at her eyes with the hem of her apron.

Lady Charlotte released Florrie from her cold grip and glanced at the clock. 'And you've been waiting until this late hour to tell me? Whyever aren't you packing to make this afternoon's train?'

'Well, I need your permission to travel, for a start. I'll need to borrow some money as well. I'll pay it back, like. Only I don't have the fare for a return ticket to Manchester, and then there's the issue of . . .' Florrie bit her lip. 'If my sister dies, I'll need to help pay for her funeral.'

Lady Charlotte's sympathetic smile faltered. She placed her fingertips on her brow and winced. 'My head. Good Lord.' She blinked hard. 'Doesn't your sister have a husband to support her? Your mother, perhaps?'

'My brother-in-law abandoned my sister and her children not six months ago.' Florrie could feel her cheeks glowing hot with embarrassment. She clasped her hands together tightly over her stomach, hating every moment of having to explain her family's circumstances. 'And my mam's been out of collar for a couple of years. There's a lot of unemployment in—'

'Yes. Yes.' Lady Charlotte waved her hand dismissively. 'I know. Dreadful. Simply dreadful.' Rising from her stool, she pulled on her robe properly, slid her feet into feather-trimmed mules and paced over to her bedside cabinet. She opened a drawer and took out her purse, proffering a pound note. 'Here's a pound. That should cover it.'

'Well, actually, I think funerals are more like five pounds. Maybe twice that. I know they're not cheap.

People save for years for them, but my sister's never put anything aside for one. She could never afford it.'

Lady Charlotte frowned momentarily and pulled out a five-pound note. 'Here. You can pay me back at, say . . . a shilling a week?'

Florrie took the money, wondering if it would be even remotely enough, and bobbed a curtsey. 'Thank you, my lady.'

'Now, we'd better hurry. Once you've helped me to get ready, we'll have Thom drive you to the station in the Bugatti.' Lady Charlotte pursed her lips and frowned. 'No, no. What am I thinking? Not the Bugatti. And not the luggage car either. Both are a little ostentatious for a maid, even in her hour of need.' She glanced again at the clock and rang the servants' bell that would bring Arkwright to the bedroom imminently. 'Thom can take you in the pony and trap. It will be just as quick.'

Florrie had had only minutes to fling what few normal clothes she had into her cardboard suitcase before there was a sound of hooves clip-clopping on the gravel outside. She looked out of her attic window and waved down at the gardener, who often doubled as a chauffeur for the other members of the Harding-Bourne family when Sir Richard's driver, Graham, had taken him out in the Rolls-Royce.

Dressed in dusty old slacks and with his shirtsleeves rolled up above his elbow, as if he'd come straight from digging up potatoes in Holcombe Hall's walled vegetable garden, Thom looked up at her, smiling. He tugged at the brim of his flat cap. With a tanned arm, he beckoned her to come outside and pointedly took his fob watch out of his trouser pocket, tapping on the watch face.

'Dear, dependable Thom.' Florrie allowed herself a weak smile. 'Always there when you need him.' She shouted through the open window: 'On my way!'

Hastening down the service stairs, Florrie came across Mrs Douglas on the first floor, carrying what appeared to be one of Dame Elizabeth's black taffeta gowns.

'Ah, Florrie. I was hoping to bump into you,' Mrs Douglas said. 'She gave you permission to go, then, Lady Charlotte?'

'Yes, thankfully,' Florrie said. 'And I'd better dash, else I'll miss the train. Thom's waiting with the pony and trap.'

Mrs Douglas rolled her eyes and lowered her voice to an almost-whisper. 'All their money, and she wouldn't let him take you in a car? Honestly. The more they've got, the less they part with.' Unexpectedly, she planted a kiss on Florrie's cheek and, juggling the cumbersome old dress, withdrew something from her skirt pocket. She then pressed a ten-shilling note into Florrie's hand. 'Here. Take this. You might need it.'

Florrie gasped as she looked down at the note. She shook her head. 'That's too much. I've borrowed five pounds off Lady Charlotte. She said I could pay her back at a shilling a week.'

'Well, a fiver won't be enough, and I don't want to see you out of pocket if you've got a funeral to pay for. You told me about how your sister had been left in the lurch with all those little kiddies to look after. Consider it a sort of loan. If you don't need it, I can have it back. If you do need it, lovey, it's yours. It's not like I have kin of my own. Just don't tell the other girls.'

'Oh, that's too kind, Mrs Douglas. Thank you so much.' Florrie threw her arms around the housekeeper, overcome with gratitude to this woman who had always freely offered comfort and guidance, especially when she'd felt the absence of her real mother so acutely.

The housekeeper broke free from the embrace and winked. 'Bertha to you, and well you know it, after all these years. Now, go!'

Florrie was about to continue down the stairs when she remembered her promise to Sally. 'About Mr Arkwright and the tablecloth fiasco . . . Young Sally was right upset this morning. She's a good girl, you know.'

Mrs Douglas nodded. 'Don't you worry about Sally Glover. I can see she's a grafter, and Mr Arkwright's got no jurisdiction over my girls. Now, get cracking, or you'll miss that train.'

Hastening through the narrow servants' access to the hallway, Florrie glanced up at the galleried landing above the grand staircase. It wouldn't do to bump into one of the family members or guests who might waylay her. Seeing the coast was clear, she marched across the marble-tiled floor to the vestibule and pulled open the heavy front door. The smell of beeswax polish was supplanted by the heady scent of honeysuckle and freshly mown grass.

Thom walked up the stone steps to meet her. 'Here

you go, Florrie. Give us your suitcase. Let's get you to that station.'

He helped her up and into the trap, and they set off down the winding driveway. Florrie looked back at the great sandstone house, glowing in the late morning sun. The place was so old and opulent and beautiful – framed by ancient oaks and cedars of Lebanon; surrounded by acres of manicured grounds, landscaped by Capability Brown himself – that it looked as though it was immune to human notions of loss and sadness. Florrie sighed heavily at the thought of what lay ahead in Manchester.

'Sorry to hear about your sister,' Thom said, shaking the reins so that the horse sped up to a fair trot.

'I've got a bad feeling that I'll be too late.' Florrie swallowed.

Thom laid his hand on hers. 'It'll be what it'll be.'

Florrie didn't push his hand away. 'I've never been there for her. Ten years I've been in Holcombe, always knowing where my next meal was coming from. All the while, she's been roughing it in a Manchester tenement with a feckless husband and kiddies to feed. Now, I might not even get to say goodbye.'

'If you miss her, you mustn't blame yourself,' Thom said, shooting her a sideways glance. 'I'm from a big mining family, me. My old man lost his job back in '12, after a bad accident what left him lame. He swore he wouldn't let any of his sons go down the pit. My older brothers joined the army before I was old enough to enlist.' He tutted and inhaled sharply. 'Both killed in the Great War. That left me as the oldest lad. I did my stint in the trenches – how could I not? – and I was lucky to make it out alive. But I still didn't go home, because I then went into service at Holcombe as an apprentice gardener. All I could do was be strong for the rest of them . . . from a distance, mind. I sent money home to my mam and dad to help with my younger brother and sisters, right until Mam and Dad passed away, my younger brother got himself a job and my sisters married. I used to visit whenever I could. That sort of thing. Being in service can be very hard on everyone when a family's in need, miles and miles away. But there's nobody to blame, because you're just doing the best you can. It's just the way it is for us working folk. So, don't beat yourself up.'

Florrie squeezed his strong, rough hand. 'Thank you, Thom. Your words mean a lot.'

'Send a telegram and let us know how you get on. We'll all be here for you when you get back, whatever happens.' It was he who withdrew his hand first. He reached under the driver's seat and pulled out a small package, roughly wrapped in brown paper and string. 'And happy birthday.'

They were pulling up to the train station with barely enough time to allow Florrie to purchase her ticket.

'For me?' she said, taking the package, wondering what could be inside.

'Just a little summat.' His piercing blue eyes met hers for an instant, and then he looked away. 'Don't get excited. You can open it on the train.'

'I don't know what to say.' Staring down at the package,

32

Florrie smiled with bemusement. 'I didn't realize . . . I never thought . . .'

Thom brought the horse to a standstill, just as the billowing smoke from the chugging steam train came into view, between the two steep hills that loomed large over the valley.

'Best get a wiggle on or you'll miss your train.' He climbed down from the trap, came around to the passenger side and helped her down. Then he hefted her suitcase from the back. 'Don't forget. Keep in touch.' He carried the case to the entrance to the tiny ticket hall and set it on the ground. 'We'll all be thinking of you.' He doffed his cap. 'Safe travels, Florrie.'

Florrie waved a hasty goodbye, picked up her case and ran to the ticket booth.

Once on board the train, she took a seat in a carriage that was occupied only by an elderly woman who had her nose in a book. Only then did she start to unwrap the package Thom had given her. The delicious smell hit her the moment the paper came loose. She gasped with delight at the punnet of perfect red strawberries, laid out neatly in a heart shape. 'Oh, Thom, you daft ha'porth!' she whispered under her breath.

Though her mouth watered, Florrie knew she couldn't possibly eat one, when her family would be going hungry in Manchester. She wrapped the thoughtful package back up to give to them.

When the countryside gave way to blackened chimney stacks and mills, and the train finally arrived at its

33

destination, Florrie used some of her precious budget to take one of the hackney cabs outside Victoria Station to the Royal Infirmary on Oxford Road. If Irene was as ill as she suspected, she knew she hadn't a moment to spare.

The hospital bustled with visitors, doctors and nurses going about their urgent business. After asking where she might find Mrs Irene Eggleston and getting lost in the maze of corridors twice, Florrie eventually entered the ward where Irene was meant to be. The smell of disinfectant and fresh distemper stung in her nostrils.

She approached a stern-looking woman whose long, white cap and starched apron marked her out as a nursing sister.

'Excuse me. I'm here to visit Irene Eggleston,' Florrie said, her breath coming short and the blood rushing in her ears from sheer panic that her visit might be too late.

'Visiting hours are not until this evening,' the sister said.

'But I've travelled all the way from Holcombe in Lancashire. My mother telephoned me last night to say she's desperately ill, but I couldn't get here any sooner.' She grabbed the sister's arm. 'Please. *Please!* I must see her.'

The sister looked pointedly at Florrie's hand until Florrie let her go. Her hard features seemed to soften, then. She glanced down the ward and her eyes came to rest on curtains that had been drawn around a bed. 'Very well. Follow me.'

4

'I'm here, our Reenie. Mam's here. I'm with you, love, and your dad's watching over you. The little'uns are waiting at home. Keep fighting.' As Florrie walked down the ward full of the sick and wounded towards her sister's bed, the sound of their mother's voice, soft and encouraging, wafted towards her from behind the closed curtains. 'That's my girl. Keep breathing.'

Florrie's heart pounded harder with every step she took. She cast a nervous glance at the wiry-haired woman in the adjacent bed, slurping at a glass of water with the wayward lips of the toothless; caught sight of an old man in the bed opposite, sleeping with his mouth open, wearing the waxy pallor of the almost-dead. She shivered, and the air seemed to chill as she neared Irene's bed.

'Make sure you keep noise to a minimum.' The ward sister held a curtain back to allow Florrie entry into the semi-private cocoon.

The scene before her was desperate: beneath the crisp hospital sheets, her sister lay trembling, blank eyes almost shut but not quite, staring into some abyss, while their mother patted at the sheen of perspiration on Irene's brow with a white cloth.

Her mother sprang to her feet and wrapped Florrie in a tight embrace. 'Oh, Florrie, thank God. You came.'

Florrie felt the old lady's tears warm and wet on her cheek as her mother kissed her. 'Of course. I got here as soon as I could.' She looked down at Irene, whose chest rose and fell rapidly, her breath coming in barely audible, shallow puffs. 'How is she?'

Her mother turned to the ward sister. 'Sister, my Reenie's burning up. The treatment's not working. Can't you do something?'

The sister pressed her lips together and frowned. She took Irene's wrist and felt for her pulse, peering down at the ticking second hand on her nurse's fob watch. After a short while, she examined Irene's flaking finger-nails and then put her hand back down gently on top of the banket. 'I'm afraid she hasn't responded to the anti-pneumococcal serum therapy. The doctors here sing its praises, but I'm afraid it simply doesn't work in every case.'

'But she's young and strong,' Florrie's mam said.

The sister smiled sadly. 'Irene was already gravely ill when she was admitted. Her organs are shutting down.'

'Could you get a doctor to take another look?' Florrie asked, searching the sister's face for signs of hope.

The sister nodded. 'Of course. I'll fetch him. I'm sure you have many questions.'

With the sister gone, Florrie sat on the edge of the bed, frowning at the yellow tinge to her older sibling's skin. She took her mother's gnarled hand in hers and stroked Irene's burning hot cheek with her free hand. She felt choking tears locked inside her so tightly that her chest ached.

'Told you she was badly,' her mam said. 'She's not going to make it, is she?' Her voice had dimmed to a whisper, as though she couldn't bear Irene to hear that she had lost hope.

Florrie held her own breath, watching Irene's chest rise and fall, rise and fall, rise and fall too quickly. The phlegm rattled ominously at the back of her sister's throat. 'We're not God, Mam. Only he can know whether Irene'll—'

'She can't go,' Mam said, squeezing Florrie's fingers too tightly. 'Those kiddies. What'll they do without their mother? What will we do without our Reenie?' Her shoulders heaved with silent sobbing.

Florrie searched for words of comfort and hope. She opened her mouth to speak just as Irene inhaled sharply in with a low rattle. Startled, Florrie leaned over to examine her sister's face. Was she waking? Her eyelids were flickering but her eyes were dull and unfocussed.

'Irene? Reenie? It's me, Florrie. Can you hear me?' Florrie bit her lip and tasted the salty tang of tears she hadn't realised she was shedding. 'You're made of stern stuff, our Reenie. Hang on in there, our kid.'

Her beloved older sister responded by exhaling softly for what seemed like an age. Her chest fell still.

'I think she's gone, Mam,' Florrie said, holding the back of her hand by Irene's mouth to feel for the warmth of even the shallowest breath. Nothing. She withdrew her hand and groaned. 'She's passed. I'm sure of it.'

'No!' Mam said, smoothing Irene's hair back from her forehead. 'Don't say it. I can't bear it.' Her tears plopped on to the sheet.

Florrie pulled a handkerchief from her pocket and offered it to her mother, trying her utmost to keep her savage grief inside; to be strong for her mother. 'She looks so peaceful, Mam. It's like she fell asleep.'

At that moment, the curtain was pulled abruptly back, revealing a stern-looking, bespectacled man in a white coat. 'Hello, I'm Doctor Chalmers,' he said, looking down at Irene and frowning. He barely glanced at Florrie or her mother. 'Move aside, please, while I examine the patient.'

'You're too late!' Mam said, shooting the doctor with a venomous stare. 'My daughter's dead. You should have been here five minutes ago. Call yourself a doctor? You're neither use nor ornament.'

'I came as quickly as I could.'

Florrie took her mother by the arm, pulled her away from the bed and manoeuvred her on to the visitor's chair. 'Hey, come on now, Mam. Let the doctor do his job, eh?' She turned to Doctor Chalmers. 'She's gone, hasn't she? About a minute or two before you turned up, she just took this deep, rattling breath. Then she let it out very slowly, and that was that.'

Doctor Chalmers pressed two fingertips to Irene's neck. He took his stethoscope and listened to her chest. Then he took the apparatus out of his ears and looked at his wristwatch. 'Two minutes ago, you say?'

'Aye.'

He took up Irene's notes that were hanging on the end of the iron bedframe, retrieved a fountain pen from his breast pocket and noted down the time. Finally he turned to Mam. 'I don't believe we've met before. I'm normally on the night shift. I take it you're the patient's mother.'

Mam nodded dolefully, the rims of her eyes red-raw; tears spilling on to her cheeks. 'That's right. Mrs Bickerstaff. Matilda.'

He then pivoted to Florrie. 'And you are?'

'Her younger sister, Florrie Bickerstaff. Miss.'

'Very well, ladies.' Doctor Chalmers nodded solemnly and looked down at his shiny brogues. His mouth was a grim line, his brow deeply furrowed. Finally, he locked eyes with Mam. 'Yes. I'm afraid your daughter suc-cumbed to her pneumonia. I'm so very sorry. We tried everything we could for her, but . . .'

'But we didn't have enough money to grease your palm? Is that it?'

'Mam!' Florrie felt her cheeks grow hot.

The doctor didn't respond. He merely leaned in and carefully covered Irene's face with the bedsheet.

Mam sprang from her seat, however, clutching her handbag in front of her like a weapon. She took a step towards Doctor Chalmers, her knuckles turning white from the evident strength of her grip. 'I bet if my Reenie had been a rich woman, she'd have survived. Am I right? Three children she's leaving. Three under the age of six, with a ne'er-do-well for a father that we've not seen hide nor hair of for months and months, all living in a damp tenement.'

Doctor Chalmers stood up straight and blinked hard. He opened his mouth to speak but seemed to think better of it.

Florrie studied his face, realizing that he was not as old as he had first appeared to be, despite his hair being combed carefully over a balding pate. She felt suddenly sorry for him. 'Leave it, Mam. Doctor said they tried their best.'

'She came into hospital too late, I'm afraid,' he said.

'We couldn't afford to send her to see no doctor. We kept our fingers crossed that she'd get over it.'

He pressed his lips together. 'Mrs Bickerstaff, it grieves me to admit that, had your daughter been wealthy, not only would she have been diagnosed earlier by a doctor, but she may not have caught bacterial pneumonia in the first place. We see far too many people living in cramped, damp conditions in slum housing coming in with life-threatening respiratory conditions.' He rocked back on his heels and pushed his spectacles further up the bridge of his nose with his middle finger. 'I hear tell of experimental treatments for pernicious infection being tested under laboratory conditions – sulphonamides, the scientists call them. But until we physicians in hospitals around the country have access to such a medical magic bullet, I'm afraid patients will continue to die in unacceptable numbers.' He clasped his hands together and bowed his head. 'You have my sincerest condolences, ladies.'

As he left, he drew the curtain shut behind him.

Florrie stared down at the bed, hardly believing that her big sister lay dead beneath that sheet. 'How did this happen? I mean, last time I spoke to her . . . a couple of year ago, admittedly . . . she was full of beans. Little

Nelly was no more than two months old – Alice was still a twinkle in her mam's eye. Our Reenie had apples in her cheeks, talking about taking on some extra sewing work she could juggle with the little'uns. Her and Frank seemed happy.'

Mam stood at the head of the hospital bed, still clutching her handbag in white-knuckled fists. 'She asked me not to tell you. Not to worry you with it all.'

'With what?'

'You know that Frank left soon after Alice was born. That was the start.' The bitterness in her voice seemed to sour the air. 'I tried my best to take some of the weight off her shoulders, but my poor Reenie couldn't cope. She ran herself ragged. Got run down. Ended up potless, and moving into damp, cockroach-infested rooms above a pub.' She set her handbag on the floor and stumbled.

'Ooh, eh, Mam. Steady on.' Florrie grabbed her mother beneath the arms and levered her back on to the chair.

Her mother started to howl disconsolately, but Florrie felt her own grief stuck in her throat, choking her. *Hold it together, Florrie*, she told herself. *You've got to be strong for Mam and the kids. This is not a time for you to break down. Irene needs you to step in and be the head of the family.*

'How will I survive, raising three grandchildren when I've not a ha'penny to my name?' Mam cried. 'And that Frank drank away his wage packet as it was. Reenie said he refused to set aside burial insurance money for her and the children. How can I forgive myself for burying my firstborn in a pauper's grave?'

Florrie cleared her throat and blinked her own tears away. 'Leave this to me, Mam. We can give Irene a half decent send-off. There'll be no pauper's grave for her. I've borrowed money from my boss.'

Her mother looked at her through bloodshot eyes. 'Oh, lovey!'

'I can't afford bells and whistles, but it'll be a respectable do – something the kiddies won't be ashamed to look back on.'

'God bless you, Florrie,' Mam said, clasping her hand. 'You're a good'un.' Tears welled in her eyes afresh. She inhaled sharply, her eyebrows contracting in sorrow. 'But, oh, sweet Jesus! How am I to break the news to my little grandkids that their mam's dead and gone?' She clasped her hands to wan cheeks that were etched with deep lines. 'My house is no bigger than a postage stamp, and I can barely afford to feed myself. How am I to put a roof over the heads of three babies, let alone provide for them, when I've got no work?'

Florrie swallowed hard. Suddenly, she was faced with a conundrum almost as bad as saying goodbye to her beloved sister. The petty tribulations at Holcombe Hall seemed a long, long way away now.

5

'Is Mammy coming home from hospital tomorrow?' Irene's eldest, George, asked Florrie, swinging on her arm and skipping to keep up, still oblivious to the tragedy that had just unfolded in the infirmary.

Florrie swallowed hard, wondering how to answer the boy; when to answer the boy. At her side, Mam was pushing little Nelly and baby Alice in the squeaking old pram along the terraced streets that spanned the quarter of a mile between the house of Irene's neighbour, who had been watching the children, and Mam's place. Florrie opened her mouth to speak, but a busy street full of playing children and gossiping neighbours was no place to break such terrible news. She exchanged a glance with Mam, who shook her head decisively. Not here. Not yet.

'Let's get you back to Nana's, eh?' she said. 'You can have some more of them lovely strawberries I brought from Holcombe House, and we can get you cleaned up. What a mucky pup you are!'

George giggled, holding his juice-sticky hands up with fingers splayed like a mischievous imp. In the giant pram, the two girls were also smothered in red pulp, each grasping a piece of the fruit in their tiny fingers and babbling away blithely. The sun was shining over the slate rooftops, bouncing off the windows of the Victorian terraced houses, as if it were wholly indifferent to Irene's death. The earth was somehow still turning. Florrie smiled at her nephew, but inside, her heart was leaden.

'Here we are,' she said, as they turned into her mother's street. 'Let's cross over.' She helped her mother to negotiate the high kerb with the heavy pram, dodging the horse manure that littered the cobbles – a sign that either the milkman or the rag and bone man had visited that morning. 'Oops-a-daisy!'

'Why are we going to Nana's?' George asked. 'I want to go home. I want Mam.' He tugged at Florrie's hand. 'Nana, why's Mammy still in the hospital? Nana!'

Florrie's mother marched on in silence, pushing the pram resolutely along the pavement as if she hadn't heard the boy.

Her next-door neighbour was kneeling outside her own front door, scrubbing her doorstep with soapy water. She got off her knees with a grunt, wiped her hands on her apron and stood to greet Florrie and her mother.

'Aye-aye, Matilda. How's your older girl bearing up?' The neighbour scratched at her scalp beneath a headscarf that had been fashioned into a turban of sorts, tugging loose a rogue lock of wiry grey hair.

Mam shook her head dolefully and wiped away a tear.

Florrie watched as the smile fell from the neighbour's face. 'Ooh hey. I'm so sorry, love.'

'Why's the lady sorry, Aunty Flo?' George asked.

Florrie squeezed his hand and squatted, so her gaze was level with his. 'Let's get you inside and get you some jam on bread, shall we?' She shot the neighbour a

44

warning glance. In the street and in front of a stranger was not the place to break such dreadful news.

The neighbour reached out and put her work-worn hand on Mam's shoulder. 'Let me know if there's anything you need, love.'

Inside the cramped hallway of the Victorian terrace, Florrie struggled to squeeze alongside the pram to lift out Nelly. 'Ooh, by heck. You're getting bigger by the day, our Nell.'

Her mother lifted baby Alice out. 'Let's get you all cleaned up, shall we?'

With Nelly on her hip, Florrie took the punnet of strawberries into the damp little scullery at the back of the house, where George was already standing on a stool, trying to reach the bread bin.

'We need to tell them,' Florrie whispered to her mother. She wet a cloth beneath the tap at the cracked butler's sink.

Her mother fixed her with bloodshot eyes. 'I don't want to. I can't. I can't say the words.'

'Then I will.'

Florrie helped her mother to clean up the children and get them seated at the scratched old kitchen table. She held baby Alice on her knee, letting her teethe on a piece of stale bread and butter so that she drooled copiously.

Mam stood by the window, looking out at the yard bathed in sunlight, where dazzling white nappies, pegged on the washing line, flapped on the breeze. She turned to Florrie and nodded once.

'Now, kids. Are you listening to your aunty?' Florrie said. She caught the eyes of Nelly and George. 'I've got something important to tell you.'

'Finished!' George shouted, holding his empty plate up. 'Can I have another slice, please?'

Florrie reached out and patted the boy's forearm so that he put the plate down. 'Pay attention, Georgie, because only well-behaved boys get seconds.'

Finally, they were sitting straight and giving her their full attention. She took a deep breath. 'Now, I'm very sorry to have to tell you this, but we've got news about your mammy, and it's not good, I'm afraid.'

'Mammy poorly,' Nelly said.

Swallowing down a fresh lump of grief that seemed to stick in her throat, Florrie nodded. 'Well, your mam was so poorly that she's . . . she's gone to live with Jesus in heaven.'

Both children cocked their heads to the side and frowned at her as they tried to make sense of what she'd said.

'Mammy's not coming home?' George asked.

Florrie shook her head. 'She's with Granddad in heaven.'

'With the angels?' George asked.

'Yes.' Florrie wiped a tear away. She forced herself to smile through her sorrow. 'But she's looking down on you and watching over you, because she loves you very much. But she was so so poorly, Georgie. And that's why she's gone to live with Jesus. Do you understand?'

Nelly's face crumpled, and the little girl burst into

tears. 'Want Mammy.' She held her hands out to Florrie's mother. 'Want to go home.'

Finally, Florrie's mother approached the table and lifted Nelly from her seat. She buried her face in the child's flaxen hair and sobbed. 'I want your mammy too, cocker, but she's in heaven, now.'

George burst into silent tears, wiping them away aggressively with the back of his hand. He swiped the punnet of strawberries on to the floor. 'No, no, no! I don't want Mammy to be in heaven.' Standing abruptly, he toppled his chair, making Nelly start and cry even harder.

Florrie set the baby in her high-chair and caught George in a tight hug. 'There, there, Georgie boy. I know it's awful, but sometimes, lovely people like your mammy get sick and pass away. Even the doctors can't help. But we love you, and we'll look after you. I promise.'

'Where are we going to live?' he asked through a veil of tears. 'Will we have to go and live with Daddy?'

'Not while I have breath in my body, son,' Florrie's mother said. 'Not with that reprobate and his new harlot. No. You'll come and live here with your nana.'

That evening, after Florrie had arranged with the undertaker for the collection of Irene's body from the Infirmary's mortuary and a burial date had been booked, she helped to settle the two older children into the single bed in her mother's spartan back bedroom. The baby, swaddled in an old crocheted blanket, was already fast asleep in a drawer placed on the floor that served as a makeshift cot. The two women repaired to the back parlour and sat with jam jars of strong tea.

'The funeral's in a week,' Florrie said. 'I'll stay 'til that's done, of course. I sent a telegram to the housekeeper at Holcombe Hall. She's a good woman is Mrs Douglas. She'll understand.'

Her mother sipped her tea in silence. Presently, she spoke with a wavering voice that was almost a whisper. 'I don't know how I'm going to manage, our Florrie. Three babies in a house where there's barely room for the pram. Three mouths to feed, when I've got buttons coming in from taking on the odd bit of washing or seamstress piecework . . . *when* I can find it.'

'I'll send home as much money as I can, Mam. I promise.' Florrie thought about the children, sleeping cheek by jowl like tinned sardines in the cramped back bedroom, with its bare floorboards, peeling wallpaper and rickety sash window. She thought about the freezing winds that would whip through the cracks in the window-casing, three out of the four seasons; peasouper fogs that descended in winter, mingling with the acrid smoke from thousands of chimneys, shrouding the city's tenements in a suffocating, sulphurous blanket that left the weak – like Irene – and the old gasping their last. 'But this is no place to bring up children. Not if you can get away. Get out of the city, where the air's clean.'

Mam set down her jar. 'How can I get out? Out to where, exactly? Manchester's the only place this side of the Pennines where there's industry enough to find work, and even then, most of the mills are sacking their

48

workers off. I'm an out-of-collar loom operator, doing what she can to keep her own head above water.' She held up three fingers. 'Now, I've three extra mouths to feed and no breadwinner in the family. Where would we even go?'

'Further out. Lancashire somewhere.'

'What? Like Bury or Bolton? Blackburn? Their mills have got the same problems we have. Same in Leeds, I hear. Same everywhere. Down the mines; in the shipyards. Fellers are having it as rough as the women are.'

Florrie rubbed her face in frustration. 'Didn't you say you had a second cousin with a farm in Cumbria? Charles. What about him?'

Her mother shook her head ruefully. 'I don't think our Charlie's got much call for a milkmaid of my advanced years – especially not one missing two fingers!' She held her left hand up to reveal the stumps that bore testament to an old loom mishap in one of the city's cotton mills. 'Certainly not one with a passel of grandbabies tugging at her skirts.'

Florrie stared mournfully into the empty grate of the fireplace, picturing her sister's face. 'I wish I could have done something to help our Reenie. I didn't even get to say goodbye properly.'

Mam rose from her seat and put her arms around Florrie. When she planted a kiss on Florrie's head, her clothes still smelled of the bleach and distemper of the hospital ward. 'You were there at the end, love, and that counts for summat. Reenie knew you were by her side, I'm sure of it.'

6

'Why do I have to wear this collar?' George complained on the morning of his mother's funeral. 'I don't like it. It digs in, Aunty Flo.'

Florrie held him gently but firmly by the shoulders to stop her fidgety nephew from squirming relentlessly. 'To show respect, young man,' she said. 'You've got to wear your Sunday best to say goodbye to your mammy. She'll be looking down from heaven, so you need to look smart for her. You're the man of the house now, Georgie boy.'

She tried to stifle the sorrowful sigh that pushed its way out nevertheless, and as she fiddled with the buttons on George's stiff collar, she cast her mind back to the previous evening, when the neighbour had minded the children so that she and Mam could visit the chapel of rest, where Irene had been laid out in readiness for her funeral.

Together in the gloom, they'd stood by Irene's simple coffin, holding hands.

Florrie had stared down at her sister, searching for words that might comfort her mother. Yet such words had proven hard to come by. 'They've put rouge on her cheeks. Funny, our Reenie never wore rouge.' The figure in the coffin had looked like a facsimile of the real thing – like the ones she and Irene had seen at Louis Tussaud's waxworks on a family day out in Blackpool, when they'd been young. Florrie realized her sister had truly gone. She'd felt suddenly intensely alone; had almost been able to taste the bitterness of her mother's grief, yet she had to be strong for both of them. 'She looks bonny in that dress, Mam. Isn't that the hand-me-down from Lady Charlotte that I sent to Reenie a few years back?'

'Aye,' her mother had said, reaching out to touch the starched cuff of Irene's sleeve. 'Paris fashions. She had it hanging in her wardrobe, but I never saw her wearing it once. That reprobate Frank never took her anywhere nice enough to warrant dressing up. It looked like a dishrag pulled from the bottom of a jumble sale pile when I got it out the other day.'

'But it's come up lovely with a bit of Matilda Bickerstaff magic,' Florrie had said, squeezing her mam's hand. 'You're a dab hand with laundry. You've done Reenie proud. She'll be laid to rest looking like a toff.'

Now, as Florrie finally fastened her nephew's collar and tied his bow tie, the seed of an idea had begun to germinate in the back of her mind. She kept it to herself, though. Today was a day for saying goodbye to Irene, not for hatching plans.

'There,' she said, licking the tips of her fingers to smooth a wayward lock of his hair. 'You look very smart indeed, young man. And I want you to set an example for your sisters and be a well-behaved little gentleman in the cemetery. No wriggling. No interrupting the vicar. Do I have your word?'

George nodded.

'Now is Christ risen from the dead, and become the firstfruits of them that slept . . .'

In the dank, austere church where the service for Irene was being held, the vicar's reading from Corinthians reverberated off unforgiving stone walls and the lofty vaulted ceiling.

Sitting on the front pew, stroking Nelly's hair absently, Florrie glanced behind her. The pews were empty but for a handful of well-meaning neighbours and a few doughty old worshippers, who Florrie assumed turned out for any and every occasion to assure their place in heaven. *Is this all our Reenie has to show for her twenty-seven years?* she thought. *Poor lamb deserved so much better.* At least Irene had known the joys of motherhood, leaving children behind to tend her grave and carry on her line. Florrie suspected that if she were to die before her thirtieth birthday like Irene, the pretty church in Holcombe village or even the private chapel on the Harding-Bournes' Holcombe Estate might be full of mourners for her funeral. Before long, though, she would leave nothing behind but a hazy memory of some spinster of a maid, who had excelled in rendering herself almost invisible in her service and who had almost shared a birth date with Lady Charlotte. *I wish I would one day amount to more than that,* she mused. *There must be more to life than drudgery and an early grave.*

Florrie kissed Nelly on the head and savoured the smell of the Derbac medicated soap she'd washed the girl's hair in, to ward off headlice. She turned her attention back to Irene's simple wooden coffin, topped with a wreath of her favourite summer blooms – freesia and yellow roses. Florrie made a silent promise to keep the memory of her sister alive for her tiny children, if only by writing to them regularly with reminiscences of their mother.

Summer rain had started to fall as the five of them reached the cemetery. There had been no money for hired transport to follow the hearse – the vicar had been kind enough to ferry them there, all squeezed into his own motor car. Together, they stood in reverential silence beside the freshly dug grave – Florrie holding baby Alice, her mam clutching Nelly by the hand, and George in the middle – and watched as the undertaker and his men carried the coffin from the hearse to the graveside.

The vicar opened his prayerbook and began the burial service in earnest. 'Man that is born of a woman hath but a short time to live and is full of misery. He cometh up, and is cut down . . .'

'Is Mammy really inside that box?' George asked loudly, his chin dimpling in sorrow as the enormity of saying a final goodbye dawned on him. He wiped the rain from his face with the back of his sodden sleeve. 'Did somebody cut her down in the hospital, like the vicar said?'

Florrie's mother shushed him sharply.

The boy was undeterred. 'Are they going to put Mammy in that big hole? Won't she get cold and muddy? What about worms?'

Blowing her nose loudly and pointing at him, Florrie's

mother spoke haltingly through a veil of tears and rain. 'E-enough, George Eggleston! Behave yourself i-in front of the vicar, young man. Don't you be making a show of this family.'

Florrie realized her mother's snappiness was merely a show of intense grief. She put her arm around George and leaned over to speak softly in his ear. 'There, there, Georgie. It's just your mammy's body being laid to rest in the ground. No harm can come to her there. She's too deep even for the worms. Her soul is with Jesus and your granddad, now. She's free: free from pain and suffering.'

'Can she fly like an angel?'

'Yes, love.'

'Has she got big white wings?'

The vicar shot George a disapproving glance, and the boy finally fell quiet.

One by one, they were invited to cast earth on to the coffin, which had been lowered into the grave. Florrie felt the soil, gritty, damp and cold between her fingers. She threw her handful down, sobbing as it scattered across the coffin lid. When she saw her sombre-faced little niece and nephew throw tiny fistfuls of soil into the hole, the agony of their loss made her gasp. She shivered in the cool summer rain that mingled with her salty tears.

'We commend unto thy hands of mercy, most merciful Father, the soul of this our sister departed,' the vicar said. 'And we commit her body to the ground, earth to earth, ashes to ashes, dust to dust . . .'

'Ta-ra, our Reenie,' Florrie whispered beneath her

breath. She kissed Alice, savouring the warmth of the baby's rosy, petal-soft cheeks against her own skin. 'I promise I'll see to it that these babies are cared for. I don't know how just yet, but I swear I won't let you down.'

With Irene laid to rest, the five of them made their way in the now-lashing rain back to Mam's cramped terraced house. When her mother unlocked and opened the front door, Florrie was hit with the musty smell of rising damp.

'I'll make us a ham sandwich and a brew,' her mother said. She ushered George and Nelly in front of her. 'It's as close to a wake as our poor Reenie's going to get, God forgive me.' Her voice cracked with sorrow when she spoke. She looked up at the ceiling, sighed heavily and then pushed past the pram, through to the scullery.

With a leaden heart, Florrie carried baby Alice over the threshold. For the first time, she noted that the old Lincrusta wallpaper beneath the hall's dado rail was peeling, exposing plaster that had become spotted with black mould. The deep skirting boards that ran along the edges of the encaustic-tiled floor looked worm-chewed and flaking with rot. She had already seen the cockroaches that crawled out in their thousands overnight, scattering for cover as soon as a lamp was lit. The fires needed to be set, even in summer, belching smoke back into the rooms when her mother couldn't afford to pay the chimney sweep. She tutted at the condition of the place.

'Get changed, Georgie,' she told her nephew. 'Put on something nice and dry and comfortable. Give your nana the wet clothes to hang in front of the fire.'

She undressed the girls, though they wriggled and grizzled and yawned, rubbing their eyes. It was clear they were exhausted. After putting them in their nightgowns, she set Alice and Nelly down in the back bedroom for a nap, tucking them up in the pristine bedding that her mother had so carefully laundered down at the wash house. Florrie's thoughts returned to that seed of an idea she'd had . . .

She returned to the scullery to find Mam setting a fire, while Georgie played listlessly at the table with a spinning top. On the stove, a pan of water was coming to the boil.

'Did they settle?' Mam asked, standing with audibly cracking knees. She opened a newspaper and held it over the hearth to encourage the fledgling flames to draw oxygen from the chimney. Then she took a step back and watched as the fire started to lick over a pile of fresh coke in earnest. Only then did she turn to Florrie.

'Aye. They were fair worn out, poor little mites,' Florrie said. She took up the bread knife and started to slice the remainder of yesterday's loaf that was already somewhat stale. She took the ham and the butter from the pantry and started to spread butter thickly on to the bread with an old, ivory-handled knife. 'Look, Mam. I've been thinking again about you and the children living here . . .'

Her mother slumped into a kitchen chair at the old

table and blew her nose loudly on a snowy-white man's handkerchief. 'Unless it involves bringing our Reenie back, I don't want to hear it. Not right now. I just want a brew. And don't be making me a butty. Now I come to think of it, I can't face it.' She put her hand on her stomach.

'You've got to eat, Mam.' Florrie sliced a ham sandwich into quarters, placing them on a side plate. She set the plate before her mother. 'Starving's not going to do you any favours.'

Her mother pushed the plate towards George. 'Come on, lad. You come and eat this for your nan. You need to grow big and strong. It's what your mammy would have wanted.'

George shook his head solemnly. 'No ta, Nana. I don't want owt.'

'Blimey. Listen to the pair of you!' Florrie said, taking the pan from the stove and pouring boiling water on to the tea leaves in the old brown ceramic teapot. She moved the teapot to the table and added a small amount of milk to the bottom of two jam jars. 'We all need to keep our strength up. Reenie's gone, and we've got to have the energy to sort out what happens next.'

'What do you mean, sort out what happens next?' Mam said, taking up a sandwich quarter and curling her lip at it. She put it back down.

'I mean, you definitely can't stay in this house with these little'uns. Least, not for more than a couple of weeks. It's so damp, I'm surprised you've not got webbing between your fingers.'

'We've had this conversation already, and I told you. There's nowhere we can go.'

Florrie ruffled George's hair. 'Well, I've just lost my sister to pneumonia, and I couldn't bear it if the rest of you got sick too, because you're living in slum housing that's not fit for the rats.'

Her mam raised her eyebrows and stared blankly at the steaming teapot. 'I'm more concerned about how I'm going to feed all these extra mouths when I'm on my uppers. Maybe I can get some work charring for the local doctor. He might let me bring the kids with, if they behave. At least it would keep the wolf from the door.'

Florrie poured the tea, dropping in dollops of jam and handing a jar to her mother. 'But what if I could get you out of here and into the fresh air of the countryside?'

'Oh, miracle worker, are you?'

'Maybe I am. Time will tell.'

'What did you have in mind, exactly?'

Toying with the starched corner of her mother's white cotton handkerchief, Florrie allowed herself the flicker of a smile. 'You're a dab hand with laundry, aren't you?'

Mam nodded and folded her arms over her bosom. 'I take pride in my wash. I may be poor, but nobody can say Matilda Bickerstaff hasn't got clean sheets on the bed and clothes on her back, whether or not they've come from a jumble.'

Florrie snapped her fingers. 'Right. Well, the laundress that serviced Holcombe Hall has moved to Scotland, so there's an opening for a woman that knows one end of a scrubbing brush and washboard from another. How would you like me to put you forward for the job?'

Her mam looked at her askance. 'Where on earth would we live?'

'Well, I need to think about that. Make some enquiries. Leave it with me.'

7

'Ah, Bickerstaff. There you are,' Mr Arkwright said, as Florrie trudged the last ten yards up the long and winding gravel driveway to the servants' entrance of Holcombe Hall. Even in the heat of the afternoon, he was immaculately turned out in his butler's attire. 'About time, too. We were all beginning to think you'd absconded with some Mancunian ne'er-do-well.' The most fleeting of smirks twitched at his lips.

Florrie stopped short and glared at the butler, too tired to be deferent. 'You do know I just buried my sister, don't you?' After walking the five or so miles from the train station, carrying her cardboard suitcase in the late summer sunshine, all she wanted was to drink a large glass of water and kick her shoes off.

Yet here was Arkwright, checking his fob watch as though she was late. 'Time waits for no man, Miss Bickerstaff. Mrs Douglas needs you in the kitchen straight away.'

'I did send a telegram to say I'd be on today's train from Manchester. Did nobody pass it on to Thom? Only it's a long walk on a hot day. Do you mind if I—'

'Kitchen. Right away, please. Duty calls.' He turned on his heel and marched back inside, holding the door open for her pointedly. 'Chop, chop.'

In the cool gloom of the labyrinthine servants' quarters below stairs, Florrie drank in the familiar smells of cooking, carbolic soap and boot polish. Even though her case weighed heavy as though she carried all of her grief inside it, Florrie felt her spirits lift. The place was buzzing with life. Three of Arkwright's valets marched past her on some errand or other, greeting her as they went. Gladys, one of the housemaids, bustled past her, carrying a bucket and mop. She was closely followed by Sally, carrying a basket containing bedlinen.

'Hey up, stranger! Good to see you're back.' Sally set down her basket and abruptly embraced Florrie, planting a kiss on her cheek. 'Mrs Douglas told us you sent a telegram . . .' She flicked her gaze to the wall and then looked awkwardly down at Florrie's feet. 'I'm so, so sorry for your loss.'

Florrie rubbed her colleague's upper arm. 'Thanks. Yes. Well . . .' She sniffed and willed herself not to burst into tears at the keenness of her grief and the kindness of her friend. 'We gave her a respectable send-off.' The sound of hammering, coming from above stairs, broke the uncomfortable silence. 'What's going on up there?' she asked. 'Did the house start falling down without me?'

Sally's eyes widened with obvious excitement. 'Ooh, it all went on while you were away. The day after Lady Charlotte's birthday party, the place were a right mess. Me and big Gladys had to mop and buff that ballroom floor 'til our knees were red-raw and twice their normal size.'

'That was the day I left,' Florrie said.

'Well, it were *plastered* in champagne and cigarette dog-ends, were that parquet. *Covered.*' She wrinkled her nose. 'Dirty ha'porths. The richer they are, the worse they behave. Anyway, Sir Hugh eventually gets out of feather in time for dinner. You'd gone by then. And him and that Walter Knight-Downey start brawling in the dining room over that Daphne le Montford bird, and Hugh . . . well, you'll never guess what he did.' Sally was getting quite red in the face. 'He picks up a dining chair and flings it at Walter. Except he misses, and it goes straight through the stained-glass window. The big bay, smashed to smithereens. Sir Richard hit the roof. I've never seen him fly into such a rage. He's normally so collected and gentlemanly. And you should have seen Dame Elizabeth's expression. Black like thunder, I tell you. What a to-do!'

At that point, Mrs Douglas's voice rang out down the corridor. 'Sally Glover! Is that you I can hear gossiping? Sound travels, you know.'

Florrie started at the sound of their superior's commanding voice. 'Best get going, eh?'

Sally nodded and winked. 'You'll soon see the damage for yourself. Welcome back, eh?' She picked up her basket and turned back towards the kitchen.

Florrie grabbed her by the shoulder. 'Hold your horses, Sal!' She lowered her voice. 'Before you dash off, tell me, are you still getting it in the neck from Arkwright?'

Sally turned around, her brow furrowed. She bit her lip. 'Mrs Douglas has been fighting my corner, when she can. I'm managing.'

Florrie nodded and patted her on the forearm. 'Good on you. I'll watch your back as much as I'm able.'

Life at Holcombe Hall had continued while she'd been in the midst of death. It had been incredibly hard to leave her grieving, impoverished family behind, but it was time to resume her own life, especially if she were to earn enough money to send back to Mam and the children. She knew her mother was strong and resourceful – she would cope at least in the short term. Florrie also privately acknowledged that it felt good to be away from Manchester's claustrophobic terraces and damp slum dwellings; back in the fresh air of the countryside and the pristine beauty of the Hall. Yet what sort of chaos had she returned to?

'Florrie! Lovey!' Cook stopped rolling out pastry as soon as she saw Florrie emerge from the warren of corridors that led down from the servants' entrance to the kitchen. She held floury hands out. 'Give us a hug, you poor girl.'

Florrie barely had time to set down her suitcase on the well-scrubbed terracotta tiles before she was folded in the embrace and homely smell of Holcombe's cook. She exhaled with relief and then broke away. 'Ooh, it's good to be back. You wouldn't believe the time I've had.'

Florrie was just about to tell Cook all that had gone on in Manchester, when Mrs Douglas emerged from the pantry, carrying a notepad.

'Florrie Bickerstaff, there you are!' She stuffed the pad and pencil into her skirt pocket, and took Florrie's hands in hers. 'I've been thinking about you all this while, dear girl. We got the telegram, saying your sister had passed.' She released Florrie from her grip. 'Such a tragic loss. I do hope she didn't suffer too much.'

Behind the large kitchen table, Cook crossed herself and looked upwards. 'The Lord giveth and the Lord taketh away. What a terrible to-do. Your sister's at peace now, lovey.'

Feeling hot and sticky and exhausted to her very bones, Florrie rubbed her face and sighed. 'Thank you. Both of you. I barely made it to the hospital in time to say goodbye. It's been truly dreadful.' She forced back the tears. 'But to add insult to injury, I've had to leave my mam behind in a dump of a house, coping with my sister's three tiny children. I feel like I've left my own babies in a pram outside the Co-op and walked away.' She shook her head. Was it too soon to bring up the laundress vacancy?

'Mrs Douglas!' Breaking up their reunion, Arkwright strode through to the kitchen from the direction of the back stairs that led up into the main house. 'Sir Richard has asked that afternoon tea be served to him and his guests in his study, while the window in the dining room is being replaced. He's asked for it early, because they're going on a walk through the woods before dinner.' He checked his fob watch. 'And they're breaking from their meeting in half an hour, so Cook had better hurry up with whatever it is she's concocting.' He waved dismissively at the half-rolled dough on the table.

Mrs Douglas raised an eyebrow.

With narrowed eyes, Cook had picked up her rolling

pin and was now pointing it at Arkwright. 'I'll thank you not to use that tone with me, Mr Arkwright.'

'Sir Richard is our employer, need I remind you?' Arkwright had already turned his back to Cook and faced Mrs Douglas, wearing a sour expression. 'He's entertaining *very* important heads of rival steel companies that are involved in this merger. What sort of an impression would it make if he can't feed such esteemed guests after their negotiations?'

'My raised game pie will be ready *when it's ready*,' Cook said.

Arkwright didn't even deign to glance at Cook. He was still glowering at Mrs Douglas. 'You need to get your kitchen in order.'

'Sir Richard and his business associates have never starved yet, have they?' Mrs Douglas winced suddenly and gasped. She pressed a hand to her bosom and frowned. 'Just you remember who's the butler and who's the housekeeper, here, Mr Arkwright. Cook's under my jurisdiction, not yours, and I run a tight ship. You need to keep your nose out of my affairs.'

'Are you all right, Mrs Douglas?' Florrie asked.

The housekeeper nodded. 'It's him.' She glared at Arkwright. 'He gives me heartburn.'

'You'll have more than heartburn if Sir Richard and his guests have nothing to eat.' Arkwright smoothed his Brilliantined hair with a manicured hand and headed back to the stairs.

Mrs Douglas was quite red in the face. She steadied herself on the corner of the table and then manoeuvred herself on to one of the dining chairs. 'One of these days . . .'

'Take no notice of him, Bertha,' Cook said. 'He's just trying to rattle your cage, that one. You leave afternoon tea to me.' She winked. 'Even if the raised pie and the cupcakes won't be ready in time, us lot can have them later for us tea. I've always got something I can knock up at short notice.' She gestured to several golden-brown loaves that were standing on cooling trays on top of a sideboard. 'This morning's batch of bread came out lovely, and one of the lads has just brought us up a fresh ham from the cellar. I've got two big egg custards in the pantry, left over from Lady Charlotte's ladies' lunch yesterday, because her pals are all watching their waistlines.' She rolled her eyes. 'So don't you let that Arkwright get to you.'

Rummaging in her pocket and retrieving her pad and pencil with a shaking hand, the housekeeper started to scribble down a note. 'Right, Cook, before we were so rudely interrupted, we were making a list of supplies the pantry's running low on, weren't we?'

'Are you sure you're quite all right, Mrs Douglas?' Florrie asked.

'Fine.' She didn't look up but continued writing. 'Ten pounds of sugar, you say? And you're short of tea and cocoa?' Mrs Douglas finished her list and got to her feet. Her cheeks were still flame-red and she seemed a little breathless when she spoke. 'If there's anything else you've missed off, do let me know before I telephone the order through to the supplier.'

Florrie exchanged a concerned glance with Cook. 'Do you need me to do anything, now I'm back? Once I've put my case in my room and changed, like.'

The flustered-looking housekeeper's brow furrowed deeply. She narrowed her eyes momentarily at Florrie as though she were a stranger. Then the fog seemed to lift and she smiled. 'Ah, yes. If you'll serve afternoon tea in Sir Richard's study, that would be fine and dandy. Now where's that Sally Glover gone?'

Mrs Douglas hastened away from the kitchen towards the back stairs, leaving Florrie with Cook.

'Is it just me, or did Mrs D just have a funny turn?' she asked.

Cook rolled her pastry into a ball, covered it with a muslin and popped it to one side. She walked over to the sink and started to wash her hands in the basin full of suds, scrubbing at her nails with a small scrubbing brush. 'No, I think you're right. She's been complaining of indigestion for a while. I've made her up some Andrews Liver Salts, but it doesn't seem to do the trick.'

'Perhaps she's overwrought,' Florrie suggested.

Cook turned back to Florrie, lowered her voice to a near whisper and mouthed her words with no small amount of drama. 'She struggles with her monthlies, does Bertha.'

'Oh?' Florrie felt a blush heat up her already clammy face.

'Suffers terribly, though you'd never know by looking at her, would you?' Cook rinsed her hands beneath the cold tap.

'She's always seemed unflappable to me.' Florrie picked up her case, her skin itching with embarrassment at such personal talk about a woman she held in great esteem.

'Exactly.' Cook dried her reddened hands on a tea towel. 'Well, Bertha's nerves must be bad, like, because she lets herself get right het up by *him*. As long as I've been here, it's been a battle of wills with those two, over who rules which bit of the roost. And you know what Arkwright's like. He's a right little sergeant major. Always has been. Fancies himself as one of them upstairs.'

Florrie bit her lip, wishing Cook hadn't ensnared her into one of her famous gossiping sessions. 'If you don't mind, Cook, I'm going to go and freshen up and get into my uniform.' She glanced at the clock, picked up her case and started to head off towards the back stairs.

'Before you go!' Cook shouted. She dipped into the pantry and emerged with a tin. Pulling the lid off, she held the tin out towards Florrie. 'Chocolate? We had a Belgian pastry chef come up to cater the pudding for a dinner last weekend, and by heck, but he could whip up a belting chocolate. Go on, lovey. Have one.'

Popping a delicate and beautifully decorated chocolate into her mouth, Florrie smiled. 'Ta.'

She was taken aback when Cook planted a smacking kiss on her cheek. 'Lovely to have you back, flower. I'm very sorry about your sister, and that, but welcome home. We're all here if you need us.'

Florrie's room was stiflingly hot and smelled dusty. She threw open the window and looked down at the grounds of Holcombe Hall. From this high up, she could see the vegetable garden. She smiled at the sight of Thom, hoeing the beds. Beyond them was the walled rose garden, and beyond that was the orchard. Nestled at the far end, she could just about make out a tumble-down cottage that was covered in roses, wisteria and ivy – the old gamekeeper's cottage, abandoned for decades to the elements. She allowed herself a moment to imagine her mam, living in the cottage with her little nieces and nephew. Was that a possibility? She was due to serve afternoon tea to Sir Richard and his guests in some forty minutes. Dare she go over Mrs Douglas's and Arkwright's heads and ask the lord of the manor himself about the cottage and the laundress position?

'No time like the present, Florrie,' she said.

Once she'd taken her maid's uniform from the small wardrobe in the corner of her attic room and hung it on the door, she carefully retrieved a photograph from her suitcase, laid open on the bed. It was a portrait of Irene on her wedding day, her smiling face full of hope and joy. Florrie set it on the little table at the side of her lumpy single bed, next to her battered old copy of *Wuthering Heights* – a gift from Irene when she had first left Manchester to begin service at Holcombe Hall.

Wiping a tear from her eye, she traced her index finger along the veil that framed her sister's beautiful face. 'I'll not forget my promise, our Reenie. I'll make sure everyone's looked after and loved. Georgie, Alice, Nelly and Mam. I miss you.'

*

Once Florrie had collected silver platters of sandwiches from the kitchen, she made her way into the study, where Sir Richard's boardroom table had been laid for a meal. Around the table were twelve sombre-looking business men, smoking cigars and all wearing grey pinstripe suits, as if they too had their own uniform. Sir Richard sat at the head of the table, and having spent weeks away from Holcombe Hall, the sight of him suddenly made Florrie's legs feel like jelly.

'Ah, gentlemen. Let us adjourn from our difficult business. Afternoon tea is upon us.'

Arkwright was already pouring wine from a carafe into the guests' crystal goblets. He eyed Florrie suspiciously.

'Florence here is one of our longest-serving maids,' Sir Richard said. 'She's practically my wife's twin, born the following day in the same year. Ha ha.' He beckoned her to bring the platters over. 'How we've missed you, Florrie.'

Willing her feet to move, Florrie reluctantly found herself rooted to the spot, unable to stop staring at Sir Richard, whose incandescent smile seemed to brighten the dark green walls and dark wood panelling of the study. She bobbed a curtsey for want of something better to do, and then felt instantly silly. Arkwright's judgemental gaze bored into her, silently insisting she do her duty and serve the food. Finally, she snapped out of her reverie, flushed of cheek and feeling perspiration roll down her back. One thing she knew for certain, in that room full of earnest multi-millionaires, busy discussing the steel merger, the question of Mam and her nieces and nephew coming to Holcombe Hall would have to wait.

8

'Slice of game pie?' Cook asked, holding her hand out for Florrie's plate. 'New potatoes?'

With a stomach rumbling with enthusiasm in the kitchen full of delicious smells, Florrie nodded. 'Yes, ta. I could eat a horse after the day I've had. I don't think I've stopped since five o'clock this morning. My baby niece's eyes open as soon as the sun's up, and once she's up, you can wave goodbye to kipping.'

The rest of the Holcombe Hall staff who had gathered around the large table for the late staff dinner murmured in agreement that their feet hurt, their backs ached and their shoulders were tied in knots.

'Those glaziers in the dining room made a right mess,' Sally said. 'I mean, the window's fixed, and it looks bonny and all that, but my knees are like squashed dumplings after cleaning and rewaxing that dining room floor.'

Florrie rubbed her friend's upper arm in solidarity. 'It's a murderous job. Make sure you put a few folded towels under your knees, else you'll be hobbling round with a stick by the time you're forty.'

'It would be a good start if the towels young Sally washed actually came out white,' Arkwright said, pointing at Florrie's friend with a potato, skewered on the end of his fork. 'Only the other day, Sir Hugh threw his fresh towel on to the landing outside his bedroom door in disgust. And I can't say I blame the man. The towel was *grey*.' He curled his lip and then shovelled the potato into his mouth whole.

Mrs Douglas let her cutlery clatter on to her plate. 'Mr Arkwright! What have I told you about criticizing my girl?' She pointed to a giant steel cooking pot that was bubbling merrily on the stove. 'How easy do you think it is to boil a manor-house's worth of whites to snowy white satisfaction when you've also got to spend the day cleaning up other people's muck? Eh?'

The two engaged in yet another round of bickering, each accusing the other of managing staff who weren't pulling their weight. Florrie had heard it all before, many times.

At her side, Sally set her own cutlery down quietly and pushed her plate away.

Florrie saw tears standing in her friend's eyes; her chin dimpling. 'Take no notice,' she whispered in Sally's ear. 'And try not to cry. Come on. Stiff upper lip, eh?'

Sally turned to Florrie, keeping her voice low enough to evade the attentions of either Arkwright or Mrs Douglas. 'It's been bad as ever, while you were away. I hate it, Florrie. I'm just about ready to throw in the *dirty* towel and go home.' A tear dropped on to the bib of her maid's apron.

'Don't give him the satisfaction.'

Florrie looked around at the other junior staff, all of whom were eating in silence while the butler and the housekeeper argued. Even Cook had turned her back to the table and was studiously slicing a fresh cucumber to top up the dwindling bowls of salad.

Now's the time, Florrie thought. *They might be your elders and betters, but you need to speak up. Be brave. Think of your family. What have you got to lose?*

She cleared her throat. 'Actually, I might have a solution to the laundry issue.'

Mrs Douglas and Arkwright fell silent. All eyes were on Florrie now. She caught sight of Thom, sitting at the far end of the table, smiling expectantly at her. Feeling the heat blossoming in her cheeks, she looked away to focus on Danny, the footman, and then turned to Ethel, one of the other parlourmaids.

'Go on, dear,' Mrs Douglas said. 'We're all ears.'

'Impertinence!' Arkwright said. 'You and I were in the middle of a conversation, Mrs Douglas. This young upstart shouldn't have interrupted. Know your place, miss!'

'Oh, do stow it, Mr Arkwright,' Mrs Douglas said, waving dismissively at him. 'We were having an entirely usual set-to about owt and nowt. Nothing that couldn't be interrupted.' She turned to Florrie. 'Go on.'

Florrie dabbed at her mouth with her napkin and set it carefully on her lap. 'My mother. Matilda. She's a cracking washer. Even with the most basic of facilities, her wash is as good as it gets. White as lightning, never mind snow. And she's a dab hand with a darning needle.'

'But your mother lives in Manchester,' Arkwright said.

'Leave this to me, please!' Mrs Douglas held her hand up to the butler. She locked eyes with Florrie. 'Didn't you say your mother was now looking after your sister's children? How would that work?'

'Well, they'd all have to come with her, naturally. They'd have to live in Holcombe. Fresh air would do them the power of good. Not sure there's anywhere in the village to rent, though – certainly nowhere cheap enough and big enough for a woman and three children. And I'm not sure how my mother could work here in the Hall's laundry without bringing them with her.'

'How old are these children?' Arkwright asked, stabbing at some lettuce leaves with his fork. 'Are they old enough to be in service here? We can always use stable lads and chimney sweeps.'

'Child chimney sweeps were outlawed fifty-odd year ago, Mr Arkwright,' Cook said, distributing the sliced cucumber among the three salad bowls. 'I should know. Both my uncles were sweeps. Aged eight and ten when that became law, and they lost all their wages overnight. Family would have starved if my aunty hadn't left school and gone straight into service for the old Lord Harding-Bourne and Dame Elizabeth. So don't you be getting big ideas about sending little boys up no chimneys at Holcombe Hall. Sir Richard would have your guts for garters.'

Arkwright shot her a venomous glance. 'We live in soft times, Cook.'

'Well, half our lads got killed in the Great War not ten year ago, so I wouldn't call these soft times,' Albert, the old head gardener, said, thoughtfully extracting soil from beneath his fingernails. 'Old timers like me are lucky if we've got any young gardeners coming up through the ranks to replace us. Even Thom here nearly lost a leg in the trenches, didn't you, son?'

Thom nodded. 'Aye. Happen I'm a toe short thanks to frostbite. Started to look like gangrene. Lucky they didn't amputate my leg from the knee down.'

Florrie gasped in horror, as did the other young women around the table. She noted that the young footmen were all looking at Thom with undisguised admiration.

'Such unsavoury talk at the table, Thomas,' Arkwright said, eyeing the game pie on the end of his fork with disdain. 'Can we change the subject, please?'

'He's a war hero is our Thom!' Cook said. 'Fighting for King and country against the Hun. Nowt unsavoury about that. Gangrene in a good cause, eh?' She chuckled to herself.

Mrs Douglas grimaced and turned back hastily to Florrie. 'How old are the children, dear?' Her grimace softened into an encouraging smile.

'Our George is five. Nelly is two and a bit, and the baby, Alice is . . . well, she's a baby. Eight month old.' Florrie could see from the way the smile on Mrs Douglas's face had evaporated, leaving behind only a flinty look of disappointment, that her boss's enthusiasm for her mother becoming the new laundress was dwindling fast. 'They're delightful. Never any trouble.'

Arkwright shook his head. 'Much as we need a reliable washerwoman to keep the linens et cetera shipshape and Bristol fashion, unless they are the progeny of the Harding-Bournes, we can't have children running amok in the Hall – especially not snotty little nippers in nappies.'

'I'm afraid it's true, Florrie. We can't have infants living in the servants' quarters, keeping everybody up all hours with crying and jibber-jabbering.'

'I wasn't suggesting they live in the big house.' Florrie's heart grew leaden in her chest as she thought of Mam, forever consigned to that grey, damp, prison-like tenement in Manchester, eking out an unhealthy existence with the three children. How soon before one of those three babies succumbed to tuberculosis or polio; measles, mumps, whooping cough? Or pneumonia like their mother? With no money for a doctor, any number of illnesses could carry one of them off at any time. She balled her fists beneath the table. 'There's the old gamekeeper's cottage at the far end of the orchard.'

'That place?' Cook cried. 'It's haunted!'

'Rubbish,' said Albert, the head gardener. 'You don't half talk some codswallop, woman.'

Cook shook her head vehemently, got to her feet and opened the oven door, heating the kitchen by several degrees on a balmy evening that refused to cool down, even though the windows had been thrown open. She donned a pair of charred oven mitts, took out a tray full of biscuits and left them to cool on top of the range. 'It's true. I heard from Thora Cartwright in the village. She knows two lads what got over the estate walls and went scrumping in the orchard last October. They were nearly frightened out of their own skins by . . . a *ghoul*.' Her eyes widened with intrigue.

'Shouldn't have been scrumping then,' said Fred the gamekeeper, picking at his already rotten teeth with a chicken bone. 'If I'd have caught them, I'd have filled their backsides with shot. Who was it?'

'Shan't say,' Cook said. 'I'm no gossip, me. I promised Thora her brother's secrets were safe with me.' She treated Fred to a mischievous wink and grinned.

At that moment, the servants' bell rang. All eyes turned to the wall to see from which room the summons had come. It was Dame Elizabeth's bedroom.

'Florrie, dear, can you go and see what she wants?' Mrs Douglas asked. She looked at the clock on the wall. 'She's normally asleep by now. Perhaps it's her gout playing up.'

Trying to hide her frustration that the conversation about Mam taking up the laundress's position had come to nothing, Florrie got up from the table. 'Yes, Mrs Douglas. Of course.'

She left the heat of the kitchen, the camaraderie of her colleagues and the mouth-watering smells of Cook's wares to head up the back stairs to the ground floor of Holcombe Hall. She found the place eerie at night, even though the hallways were adequately lit with recently installed electric lights. Because of her gouty disposition, Dame Elizabeth's quarters were on the ground floor, beyond Sir Richard's study and the library. Florrie had to walk past the open doors of the dining room (which smelled of glazier's putty and wood polish), the drawing room and the music room. All were unlit, this close to midnight, but the glow from the midsummer-blue night sky streamed through the tall windows, casting long shadows that seemed to stretch on purpose right to the doorway, as if they were trying to grab at her.

She walked on to the library, just as the silence was broken by a man's voice coming from within:

'Well, I said to Gerald, I've made and lost so much money over the years – three times I've been bankrupt, and three times I turned stone into gold. Even the war made me richer. So, *now* I know when a deal is a sure thing. Take my Photomaton Parent Corp. Who'd have thought photographic machines in railway stations and amusement parks could make so much money? But, Dicky, I know a good business opportunity when I see one.'

Florrie recognized the voice as belonging to the entrepreneur in charge of the steel companies' merger, Clarence Hatry.

'The Photomaton success is indeed a feat of genius, Clarence. And I was only too happy to invest in your General Securities. The Marquess of Winchester speaks very highly of your acumen . . .'

Florrie could hear Sir Richard talking, now, though his voice was hoarse, as if it had been a long day of discussions. There was the sound of whisky or perhaps brandy glugging from a bottle into glasses.

'Cheers.'

The clink of crystal tumblers somehow made Florrie draw closer to the part-shut door. What were two such eminent men celebrating?

'This steel merger is going to make us forty million. Maybe more. We're making history, Dicky.'

'Though I do worry about getting into bed with my competitors, Clarence. What of my company's existing commitments? The Chrysler Building? Locomotives for India?'

Forty million? Indian locomotives? Didn't Pathé News say the Chrysler Building is in New York? What on earth . . .? Florrie felt suddenly that she had no appetite for eavesdropping on business talk that was so far beyond her personal experience as to be meaningless. Millions were but an abstract concept to the likes of her and Mam, struggling to make ends meet. She backed away from the library, looking around to check nobody had seen her with her ear pressed to the door, and continued on her way.

When she got to Dame Elizabeth's quarters, she knocked quietly, but there was no answer. She knocked again, wondering if Dame Elizabeth was busy with her toilette in the bathroom.

'Dame Elizabeth.' She knocked a third time, but again, there was no answer. Wondering if the old lady had fallen ill, Florrie pushed the door open. She raised her voice a little, this time. 'Dame Elizabeth? You rang?'

She crept forwards through the small salon, where the old lady sometimes received guests, noticing that all the cushions on the settee were in disarray, as though there had been a visitor.

'Hello?'

She advanced into the little vestibule beyond, glancing in the bathroom to find there was nobody there.

Florrie's pulse picked up when she poked her head into the bedroom, imagining the grande dame of the house lying stricken on the bed. The bed was empty. Florrie jumped when she spied a figure in a voluminous black dress in the corner of the room, but she took a moment to steady herself when she saw that it was merely Dame Elizabeth's gown, hanging on a tailor's dummy for the night. Where was the old lady?

There could be only one place, for there was only one place left – Dame Elizabeth's dressing room, filled with colourful gowns from the time before Lord Harding-Bourne's death; before she had gone into mourning. This room, tucked away at the back of her apartments, also doubled as a private study where she wrote her correspondence and, it was rumoured, poetry. Florrie knew that it looked out over the fountain at the rear of the house and the formal, terraced rose garden, but few staff ever went in there. Dame Elizabeth was a private woman.

'Ma'am,' Florrie said quietly. She pushed the door and peered inside.

Dame Elizabeth was in her nightgown, with her grey hair in a loosely tied braid that hung over her right shoulder. Seemingly oblivious to Florrie's presence, she was sitting at her bureau, reading a letter written on light blue paper that was clutched in her shaking hand.

'Ma'am. You rang?' Florrie said, curtseying.

Clearly caught unawares, as though she'd forgotten she'd rung for assistance, Dame Elizabeth quickly folded the letter and stuffed it into one of the many drawers in the bureau. The old lady's face was drawn and pale.

'Florence. There you are. Would you bring me a camomile tea, please? I'm afraid sleep evades me tonight.' The Dame's voice seemed thin and reedy.

'Are you feeling all right, Your Ladyship?' Florrie asked, noting how the old lady trembled and seemed to struggle to get up from her stool. Florrie reached out to steady her. 'Is your gout playing up? Maybe I can ask Mrs Douglas to fetch the doctor in the morning.'

'Yes. My gout. That's right.' Dame Elizabeth smiled weakly, though her eyes darted back to the bureau. 'It's proving quite the challenge, today.'

'You're pale too, if you don't mind me saying,' Florrie said, taking her by the elbow and steering her back towards the bedroom. 'You look like you've seen a ghost.'

'Ha ha. Dear Florrie, you are so fanciful!' Dame Elizabeth patted Florrie's hand and allowed herself to be helped into bed. 'I'm just a tired old lady in need of a cup of camomile tea. Fetch me one, will you?'

'Of course, ma'am.' Florrie steeled herself not to wince when she caught sight of her employer's red, swollen feet and ankles. She lifted them carefully on to the mattress. 'Oops-a-daisy. There we go. All tucked up.'

Dame Elizabeth smiled at her, though the smile didn't quite reach her eyes. 'And do pass me my novel before you go. There's a good girl.' She pointed to a book that sat on the top of her tallboy. 'I'm reading the new Agatha Christie collection, *Partners in Crime*. Though don't tell anyone, will you? I shall never live it down if it becomes known that I'm rather partial to a humble murder mystery!' She chuckled to herself.

As Florrie ended her first shift back at Holcombe Hall with a mission to find some camomile tea, she realized that not only was she beyond exhausted and disappointed not to have remedied Mam's situation, but also that Dame Elizabeth had clearly been upset by that letter she'd been reading. The old lady was hiding something.

Later, as Florrie lay in bed, overtired and struggling to settle, she pondered what that could possibly be.

9

'Now, when Lady Charlotte returns from her Paris travels, I want you lined up at the bottom of the steps ready to meet and greet her. Is that clear?' Arkwright said, standing behind his desk in his butler's office like a sergeant major issuing orders to the troops.

The high windows in Arkwright's partially subterranean office stood wide open, but with the nearby kitchen range still emanating hellish heat from Cook's four o'clock batch of bread, even the early morning breeze did little to cool the warren of rooms and corridors that comprised 'below stairs'. Florrie fanned herself fruitlessly with her hand, crammed in as she was against the warm bodies of Sally and one of the footmen.

'Not meaning impertinence, like, Mr Arkwright, but since when do we need to stand on ceremony like that for Lady Charlotte?' Danny the footman asked, fingering his wispy moustache. 'She's always gadding here, there and everywhere. We normally only stand on ceremony when the whole family comes back from one of their foreign sojourns, like.'

Arkwright nodded. 'Good question, Danny. Well, this time, she's bringing some dignitaries back from Paris, by all accounts. Some lady that's big in fashion circles, and a German nobleman. Lady Charlotte telephoned ahead, saying she wants to make a good impression.' He took his fob watch from the top pocket of his waistcoat and checked the time. 'And they're due in an hour. So look lively, you lot.'

Heading back to the kitchen, lost in thoughts of her mother and Irene's children, stuck in that godforsaken hovel in Manchester, Florrie started when Mrs Douglas placed a hand on her shoulder.

'Is anything the matter, Mrs Douglas?' she asked.

The housekeeper shook her head. 'Not at all, dear. Only, I've got a personal appointment I have to keep in the village.' She placed a hand on her chest. 'So I'm leaving you in charge of making Lady Charlotte's guests as comfortable as possible.' She winked. 'Housekeeper for a morning, eh? How do you fancy it?'

Florrie nodded enthusiastically. 'Sounds smashing, Mrs Douglas. Don't you worry. I'll not show you up.'

'Now, I'm just going to slip out quietly. I'll be back as soon as I can.' The housekeeper patted her arm.

The very notion that she had been given such a responsibility – even just for a couple of hours – seemed to take the sting out of Florrie's tired feet and washed away the fatigue that came with a restless night.

In the kitchen and the scullery, house and parlour-maids were all gathered, taking the opportunity to hastily down a glass of Cook's lemonade before returning to their duties. Bright red in the face with exertion, Cook was chatting away to them all, while beating a mixture in her giant baking bowl with a wooden spoon.

Florrie covered her mouth with her hand, suppressing

a nervous smile as she wondered how the others would receive her temporary promotion. *Come on, now,* she counselled herself. *You can do it. Mrs Douglas believes in you, so* you *must believe in you. Stand up and be counted, Florrie Bickerstaff.* She cleared her throat and clapped her hands until the other women fell silent. 'Can I have your attention please, ladies?'

All eyes were on her.

'What's got into you, Florrie?' Cook asked. 'Making an announcement? Has Thom finally asked you out?' She exchanged a meaningful glance and a raised eyebrow with Sally, who merely giggled.

Feeling her cheeks burn, Florrie steeled herself to continue. 'Enough of that nonsense, Cook. We've got work to do. Mrs Douglas has had to nip out, leaving me in charge.'

The other women all looked at one another. A murmur of intrigue rippled around the kitchen . . . or was it disbelief?

'What's she "nipping out" for?' Cook asked, setting her bowl down.

'A personal errand,' Florrie said simply. 'She'll be back after lunch.'

'Bertha never neglects her duties. Must be something up.' Cook leaned in towards Florrie, dropping her voice to give an air of secrecy, though there were ten or more women gathered nearby. 'Is she seeing a quack?' Cook pursed her lips, clearly ruminating over the possibilities. 'Happen her indigestion must be bad if she's forking out to see a doctor.'

'Let's not idly speculate, eh?' Florrie said, crossing her arms over her bosom. 'How about we get on with our tasks? Now, Sally, I want you to go up to the blue bedroom and get it ready for Lady Charlotte's Parisian guest. Get the windows open, take the dust sheets off and put on clean bedlinen. You're to tend to her needs.'

'What? I don't have to scrub anything down or spend the day in the laundry?' Sally asked, beaming.

'Let's not get carried away, Sal,' Florrie said. 'You still have to do those things, but Mabel here can give you a lift for an hour.' Florrie noted that young Mabel's face fell. 'It's only for today, Mabel,' Florrie told the girl. 'I know you were promoted to Dame Elizabeth's lady's maid back in the spring, but we're a team, remember? We all pull our weight together. And this gives Sally a chance to show us if she can succeed in doing more than just wash and clean. Sal deserves a chance, just like you were given a chance.'

Sally beamed at Florrie. 'I won't let you down.' She linked arms with a clearly reluctant Mabel. 'Come on, Mabel. Let's show Florrie and Mrs Douglas what we're made of.'

Mabel rolled her eyes but eventually smiled. 'Well, if you put it that way.'

'Well, you might be ordering them around, but I'm not taking no orders from a young whippersnapper like you, Florrie Bickerstaff,' Cook said, chuckling. 'And Arkwright won't either. Sure as eggs is eggs.'

'No need. You already know what you're doing. I'm

only filling Mrs Douglas's boots for a couple of hours – *her* orders, not mine. But let's get on, shall we?'

'Hey! How do you like? Arkwright said Lady Charlotte's bringing back a Parisian *and* a Hun,' Cook said.

Florrie nodded. 'A chance to show these continental types how it's done in Blighty.'

Cook took up her mixing spoon and pointed it at her. 'Well, if you put it like that . . . I'd better put on something a bit fancy for lunch and dinner.'

'*That's* the spirit.' Florrie clicked her fingers emphatically and grinned.

With orders given to the various maids and everyone dispatched to perform their duties as quickly as possible in anticipation of the visit, just shy of an hour later, the staff lined up by the grand stone steps at the entrance to Holcombe Hall.

Arkwright marched up and down, inspecting their uniforms, repeatedly checking the time on his fob watch. 'Any minute now, ladies and gentlemen.'

He stopped short at Florrie. 'Where's Mrs Douglas?' he barked.

Florrie explained the housekeeper's private appointment. 'She'll be back in a jiffy. Honest.'

'How dare she not ask my permission first?' Arkwright's brows drew together, casting his eyes – beady at the best of times – in shadow.

Florrie bit her lip, trying desperately to think before she spoke out of turn. She had Mam's prospects to think of now, not just her own. Dare she remind

Arkwright that Mrs Douglas answered only to Sir Richard? 'I'm sure Mrs Douglas would have said something if she'd thought it necessary.'

Arkwright opened his mouth to respond, but everyone's attention was caught by the roar of an engine. Florrie turned to see the Rolls-Royce advancing along the sweeping, gravel drive that led up to the Hall. It gleamed in the high-summer sunlight. When it swept to a halt in front of them, she peered through the windows, trying to catch a glimpse of the occupants. Lady Charlotte was instantly recognizable, of course. Today, she wasn't wearing her hat, but it seemed she'd bleached her bobbed hair to a platinum blonde while in Paris.

'By heck,' she heard Danny the footman mutter to Arkwright. 'She looks like a harlot.'

Arkwright slapped the young footman on the back of his head. 'Bite your tongue, young man. It's not your place to judge your betters.'

The butler's frown instantly switched to a winning smile. He walked to the car and opened the door for Lady Charlotte, bowing. 'My lady! I trust your trip was successful.' He offered her his gloved left hand and clicked the fingers of his right at Danny to open the other door for the guests.

Lady Charlotte took Arkwright's hand and stepped out of the car. 'Thank you, yes.' She gestured to the trunks and cases that protruded from the half-open boot of the car. 'As you can see, my trip was a little bit too successful. Ha! But I blame all those fashion houses in Paris.

I'm like a giddy gal in a sweetshop. Most of all, I blame this lady. Allow me to introduce Mademoiselle Chanel.'

Florrie gasped at the name, as did some of the other maids who, like her, had never lost an opportunity to read Lady Charlotte's old, discarded copies of *Vogue* during their breaktimes. Could this really be Coco Chanel? *The* Coco Chanel? Florrie looked down at her old, highly polished but oft-repaired shoes and her sack-like uniform, feeling suddenly incredibly frumpy, like a relic of a bygone era.

Coco Chanel stepped out of the car on the far side and turned to Holcombe Hall. She inhaled deeply and sighed. 'Ah, what a beautiful home you have, Charlotte.' Her English was heavily accented. 'Why, I do declare I like it almost as much as Bendor's Eaton Hall.' When she stepped out from behind the Rolls-Royce, she was wearing a knitted two-pieced skirt suit, with a striped top beneath and long multiple strings of pearls. Like Lady Charlotte, her hair was styled in short waves, though decidedly not platinum blond. She seemed aloof.

Florrie cast her mind back to the magazine articles she'd read about this feted couturière, and soon remembered that Bendor was none other than Hugh Grosvenor, the Duke of Westminster, who had infamously taken Chanel as his mistress. *What a rum bunch these toffs are*, she thought.

Finally, the male guest stepped out of the car. He was tall and blond. Florrie didn't recognize him, but Lady Charlotte introduced him to Arkwright as His Royal Highness Hans von Grunwald, a Prussian prince.

Just as Florrie was musing that von Grunwald looked rather forbidding, Cook elbowed her. 'Go on! You're up!' she whispered.

Privately wishing Lady Charlotte could have stayed away for longer, Florrie approached her employer and curtseyed. 'Good to have you home, my lady,' she said. 'I love your new hair.'

Lady Charlotte patted her platinum locks and stroked Florrie's cheek. 'Dearest girl. You are so kind. I'm very glad to see you back. It was so dreary without you – especially with my husband doing all that *boring* business entertaining with those dreadfully *tedious* old men. I simply had to run away to Paris for a while.' She looked up at the entrance to the Hall, ignoring the line of staff waiting to greet her; failing to mention Irene's death. 'Where is that dratted husband of mine? He knew I was coming home this morning.'

Arkwright, who was overseeing his lads carrying the mind-boggling amount of luggage up to the house, turned to her. 'Sir Richard is working in his study, Your Ladyship. He's asked not to be disturbed. He will see you at dinner, as I understand.'

Lady Charlotte's smile faltered. 'I see. Where on earth is Mrs Douglas?'

Florrie cleared her throat. 'She has a medical appointment. She'll be back shortly. I'm standing in for her until then.'

Holding her hand to shield her eyes from the sun, Lady Charlotte peered in the direction of the rose garden. 'It's such a beautiful day, and we've been cooped up for simply *aeons*. We took the Flèche d'Or from Paris to Calais and then that new Canterbury ferry, which is *supposed* to be first class, but . . . ugh.' She wrinkled her nose. 'So tiresome. They couldn't fix a decent Tom Collins. And *then* we had to get the Golden Arrow into London. And *then* . . . well, poor Graham had a long drive back.' She flapped her gloved hands dramatically as she spoke. 'Really, we should have flown with Imperial Airlines.'

'They wouldn't have taken all our luggage, *ma chérie*,' Mademoiselle Chanel said, laughing.

'Quite.' Lady Charlotte tittered. She turned back to Florrie. 'Well, we are entirely "bushed", as the Americans might say. And I certainly don't want to be inside for one moment longer on such a lovely day. So, would you organize a picnic lunch in the rose garden for us? There's a good girl.'

Lady Charlotte and her guests climbed the stone steps up to the front door, seemingly oblivious to the servants' smiles and respectfully muttered greetings. Florrie ordered the women temporarily under her authority to return to their duties.

10

By the time the three new arrivals emerged from their rooms, having changed their clothes, Florrie had organized lunch to be served in the walled rose garden. She stood at the bottom of the grand staircase, waiting to accompany them outside.

'Lead on, Florrie,' Lady Charlotte said, linking her couturière friend halfway down the stairs. 'Mademoiselle Chanel here *adores* flowers.'

'*C'est vrai*,' Coco Chanel said. 'I happen to think that the pure white camellia is the most perfect of flowers. So chic.'

Lady Charlotte gasped. 'Then we must find you one! No. We'll find you a roomful!' She turned to Florrie. 'She makes the most divine perfume, you know.'

'*Ah, oui*. But roses are very important in making scent.'

The women led the way into the entrance hall towards the open door, their voices echoing off the highly polished marble floor and the vaulted dome of the ceiling. Florrie was acutely aware of von Grunwald walking behind them, however. He came to a halt in front of a large oil painting of the late Lord Harding-Bourne – a refreshingly informal portrait painted towards the end of his life, where the great man had sat for the artist in the library, his increasingly brittle frame cosseted by a battered old leather armchair, with his beloved red setters at his feet. It took pride of place in the hallway, and Florrie liked it much better than the more formidable portrait of him as a younger man in his naval uniform that hung in the drawing room.

For a while, von Grunwald stood and contemplated the painting in silence. Then he turned to Florrie, his brow furrowing. He pointed to Lord Harding-Bourne.

'He has a big nose. Tell me, did he have Jewish blood in him?' His blue eyes were ice cold and seemed to chill the warm summer air by several degrees.

Florrie opened and closed her mouth, shocked at the brutality and bluntness of the observation. She started to shake her head but felt uncomfortable answering, as if she'd be colluding with von Grunwald's unpleasantness to clarify Lord Harding-Bourne's racial pedigree. 'Shall we . . . ? The wine will be warming in the sun.'

In the rose garden, blankets had been laid on a circular patch of pristine lawn that had been cultivated in the centre of the walled enclosure, specifically for the purpose of holding picnics. Florrie had arranged for a hamper to be carried there containing sandwiches, pork pies, salad and a bowl full of summer berries that had been freshly plucked from Holcombe Hall's strawberry patches, blueberry bushes and raspberry canes. The wasps knew a late August treat when they saw one and were buzzing around the fruit.

'Ugh, picnics always seem a better idea than the

reality,' Lady Charlotte said, batting a wasp away while trying to spoon salad on to her plate.

Von Grunwald took the bottle of chilled Lanson champagne from the hamper. 'I know what will cheer you up, Charlotte. How about a little fizz?' He popped the cork and passed the bottle to Florrie.

As Florrie poured the champagne into flutes on the little folding wooden table from which the servants could more easily serve drinks, she eavesdropped on the conversation.

Coco Chanel was nibbling on salad leaves, ignoring the sandwiches and pies that von Grunwald piled on his plate.

'I do so love Britain in summer,' she said. 'Paris is the best, most beautiful city in the world, but it is unbearably hot in August. Yet here you have rolling green fields and woodland. It's dreadful for fashion but so much better for sleeping, no?'

Florrie passed out the filled flutes without speaking. She knew her job was to remain as invisible as possible.

Lady Charlotte took a hearty gulp of her champagne. 'Oh, how could you say that? It's so dreary here in the northern countryside. I do so wish I were living in Paris or Mayfair or Belgravia. Anywhere but Lancashire, with its constant rain and the flat vowels of the dough-faced locals. It's quite the antithesis of chic.' She turned to von Grunwald. 'Tell me Berlin isn't a thousand times more stimulating than this bucolic hell on earth?'

Von Grunwald bit into one of Cook's pork pies and made approving noises. 'We Germans value nature. East

Prussia is not dissimilar to here. Rolling fields and agriculture. Forests.' He dropped crumbs into his lap as he chewed and spoke at the same time. 'But the Vaterland is sick. We are overrun with vermin.'

'Rats?' Lady Charlotte asked, balking.

He shook his head. 'Jews, of course. Germany will return to its former glory once Hitler has implemented "Lebensraum" – More room for true German Aryans,' he explained.

Coco Chanel rubbed his ankle affectionately. 'Weren't you just in Nuremberg for the big National Socialist gathering? I read in the newspaper that it was a triumph. Almost thirty thousand supporters, *non*? Am I right?'

Von Grunwald nodded. 'It was a rousing spectacle. Our men marched through the streets wearing their smart brown stormtrooper uniforms. It brought a tear of pride to my eye. Even among the crowds, you could not move for NS Partei members, standing shoulder to shoulder, saluting and cheering.' He smiled wistfully. 'I was one of the dignitaries asked by Herr Hitler himself to lay a wreath at the new Ehrenhalle monument to honour our fallen heroes.' His cold blue eyes became glassy. 'He is such a charismatic leader. I feel certain he will lead us to power and turn the German fortunes around.' He turned to Lady Charlotte. 'Did you know we are at almost one hundred and fifty thousand members, now? Every time we have a gathering in Nuremberg, support for Hitler's ideas grows. He knows the inept, corrupt Weimar government must fall.'

Coco Chanel smiled at him. 'We all do. The Weimar

Republic is rotten to the core. Herr Hitler will do great things, Hans. I know it.' She raised her glass, waiting for Florrie to top it up. 'And hopefully, France will then follow suit and deal with its Jewish problem. Why, I was fleeced by that bandit of a Jew, Wertheimer, when he licensed my parfum, Chanel No. 5. Now I only get a miserly ten per cent, while he gets rich off my invention. If we had our own Herr Hitler in Paris, I could get back what is mine. Germany for Germans. France for the French, *non*?'

As Florrie topped up the couturière's glass, she watched Lady Charlotte carefully to see if she joined in with the frightening talk. Her employer merely looked confused by the international politics and studied her fingernails.

Out of the corner of her eye, Florrie noticed a tall, broad figure appear at the arched entrance to the rose garden. It was Thom. He was pushing a wheelbarrow before him, whistling, clearly oblivious to the fact that Lady Charlotte was entertaining her guests close by. Florrie found she was smiling at the sight of him, with his shirtsleeves rolled up to reveal tanned, muscular forearms, and his caramel-coloured hair, never Brilliantined and always streaked through with gold in the summer months. Today, it hung loose in his eyes. Dear Thom.

Lady Charlotte had clearly spotted him too, since she grinned, got to her feet and beckoned Florrie over. 'I need to speak to that gardener,' she said. 'Walk with me, Florrie. I have a question to ask him.'

Together, they approached Thom.

Thom nodded his head. 'Lady Charlotte.' He turned his attention to Florrie, smiling warmly. 'Miss Bickerstaff. Lovely afternoon.'

Florrie noticed how Lady Charlotte raised an eyebrow and smirked at the sight of Thom's large, calloused gardener's hands.

'Thom, isn't it?' She patted her hair. 'Do tell me where we can find camellias for my good friend, Mademoiselle Chanel. She simply loves white camellias, and I'd like to surprise her with a nice arrangement for her guest room. Maybe one for her to wear in her hair.'

Thom set the wheelbarrow down. He grabbed the braces that held up his trousers. 'No can do. Sorry.'

Lady Charlotte looked affronted by the refusal. Her eyes flashed dangerously. 'Whyever not? I *want* white camellias. Surely you can procure them for me.'

Shaking his head, he leaned a broad shoulder against the brick archway, scratching at his stubble. 'Afraid you won't find any of those at Holcombe right now, my lady. Not in August, you won't.' He crossed his arms. 'Camellias are out late February, March time. Spring blooms.'

'I don't believe you.'

Thom chuckled. 'I wouldn't lie to you. I'm a gardener, not a miracle worker. We got plenty of camellias growing on the estate, but they're done 'til next spring. The bushes are what we call dormant in August. Sleeping, like.' He caught Florrie's eye and she was sure he was blushing, though perhaps it was just the hot sun reddening his skin.

'Yes, I know what dormant means.' Lady Charlotte rolled her eyes. She turned to Florrie. 'Well, while we're eating, can you two at least gather a floral arrangement that will impress Mademoiselle Chanel? She's very discerning, you know. She makes unrivalled French perfume, so make sure you gather the best that Holcombe Hall's gardens have to offer.'

The disgruntled Lady Charlotte left them to return to her guests.

Florrie looked first at the mossy paving stones and then forced herself to look up at Thom, though she met his enquiring blue eyes for only a moment before embarrassment forced her to focus instead on the small cleft on the tip of his nose. She smiled uncertainly, toying with the cuffs of her dress.

'Thought gardeners were the closest thing to God,' she said. 'That's what Albert reckons.'

Thom laughed. 'Aye. Happen Albert's got a bit of a ticket on himself. But even he couldn't make camellias bloom in high summer.' He rubbed idly at his cheek and left a streak of dirt there. 'Come on. Let's get a basket and get snipping. Got some late lilies flowering in a bed round the way. I bet Madame French Perfume would like them.'

'Shouldn't we collect some roses first?' Florrie asked. 'Seeing as we're *in* the rose garden.'

Thom looked over at Lady Charlotte and her guests, quaffing champagne and laughing loudly at each other's witticisms. 'Roses can wait 'til last. You might be in service, but you don't have to spend every waking moment under someone's watchful eye. They don't need your help to polish off that champagne.'

As soon as they had left the rose garden, he held his arm out for Florrie to link.

'Are you being forward with me, Thomas Stanley?' Florrie asked, grinning.

'Wouldn't like you to trip and get your apron dirty, would I?' His expression became serious. 'You know, I were thinking about you, while you were in Manchester. I said a prayer for your sister, and I'm sorry to hear it weren't answered.'

Florrie merely shook her head in response, remembering the strawberries that Thom had arranged in a heart shape for her birthday, which she'd given to her malnourished nieces and nephew. 'I don't know what I'm going to do, Thom. I need to get my mam and the children out of Manchester. She's got to get that laundress's job.' She turned to the orchard, where the apples, pears and plums were beginning to grow fat in the summer sunshine. Glimpsing the tumbledown cottage in the distance, she sighed. 'But there's nowhere for them to live, unless . . .'

Thom followed the line of her gaze and nodded. 'Are you thinking about that old gamekeeper's cottage?'

'I haven't seen it up close in five years, maybe. Even back then, it had gone to the dogs.'

'Let's scout it out, shall we?' He started to pull her away from the flower beds and in the direction of the orchard.

'Now?' Florrie looked back at the old flint walls that

separated the Hall's main flower beds from the enclosed rose garden. 'But she'll wonder where I am if I'm not back soon.'

'Won't take long.'

'But what if Albert comes looking for you?'

Thom shrugged. 'My job is to look after the grounds – the dirty, heavy stuff. Albert's getting on in years. He's happy to let me crack on, while he gives the younger lads orders and tends the tropical stuff in the warmth of the greenhouse. Can't say I blame him.'

Feeling like a naughty schoolgirl skiving off lessons, Florrie allowed Thom to lead her through the orchard. She couldn't help but glance back once or twice to check Lady Charlotte wasn't calling for her, and she trod gingerly through the long grass, hoping she wouldn't step in a pat of animal droppings, left by the estate's grazing deer. Once the cottage loomed large through the trees, however, her misgivings about abandoning her duties were forgotten. She came to a stop as the brambles became an impenetrable thicket and any notion of a path was lost.

11

'It's like something out of a fairy tale,' she said, taking in the squat, part-timbered house that looked far older than the Hall itself. Wisteria and rambling wild roses had wrapped themselves around the place, concealing half of it almost completely in a shroud of green leaves and burgeoning rose-hips. Ivy covered the end wall and spread out on to the mossy roof slates.

'Aye, well, apparently it's been empty since the new gamekeeper's cottage got built in 1869. And it's had a hole in the roof for the last ten year, after a tree come down in a storm. Couple of the beams'll be rotten inside, I'd say.'

'Oh, so it's uninhabitable?' Florrie asked, feeling her ambitions for Mam dampened by Thom's observations.

As if Thom had read her mind, he put his arm around her and squeezed her shoulder. 'Chin up, Florrie. Albert said this place were built in the 1500s with granite from the Lake District . . . good local grown hardwood and lime plaster on the top half; walls nearly three foot thick. Apart from being overgrown and having a hole in the roof and the odd beam that wants replacing, she's solid as a rock.' He took a machete from a sheath that hung from his belt and hacked a way through the under-growth. 'Let's have a proper look. Windows'll be dirty, but you can still see inside, I'll bet.'

Treading carefully over the roots and shoots that could so easily snare her feet and scratch her legs through her stockings, Florrie followed Thom until they reached a window at the front of the cottage. She almost didn't see it, hidden as it was behind a huge hydrangea bush, festooned with giant blue and purple mophead flowers. Thom pushed the hydrangea aside, but still, tendrils of wisteria hung down from the eaves, as if protecting the inside of the cottage from prying eyes. Beneath the leaves of the vigorous climber, Florrie could see the glass was covered in a yellow-green haze of pollen and algae, and the window itself sat in an old grey timber frame where any paint had long since peeled away.

'It's lost to Mother Nature,' she said. 'I've never seen anything like it. My mam can't live here.'

'Just neglected, is all,' Thom said. Taking his secateurs and snipping the wisteria away, he took a rag from the pocket of his trousers and rubbed at the window until he'd cleared a patch of glass the size of his face. He peered inside. 'By heck! Come and look!' He beckoned Florrie close.

She peered through the clean patch and glimpsed an empty parlour, where the yellowed plaster of the walls was speckled with mould. A giant stone fireplace took pride of place on the right, the ornate carving of the stone mantel still visible. Above it, the ceiling was low and beamed, but already, Florrie could visualize the place repaired, redecorated and furnished simply, perhaps with oddments borrowed from Holcombe Hall's large store of spare furniture. She stepped away from the window and looked around at the overgrown site, imagining the cottage garden cleared of brambles – a grassy place with deep flower beds in front of the windows and the roses tamed, where George, Nelly and Alice could play safely.

'How could they neglect such a charming place?' she asked.

Thom shrugged. 'When a house stands empty that long . . . Sixty year of damp getting in unabated. Albert says it really started to go to wrack and ruin after the tree came down in that storm and damaged the roof.'

'But the rain! Surely all the timbers are rotten now. How could anyone let that happen to such a lovely old house, when there are families living in slums in Manchester? All for the want of a few roof slates.'

'Lord Harding-Bourne and Dame Elizabeth were grieving over Sir James. They got the telegram that he'd been killed in the trenches the same weekend as the storm.' He shook his head and pressed his lips together solemnly. Then he looked at Florrie and his stern expression softened. 'It were a week before you started. I remember like it was yesterday.' He beamed at her. 'A young girl standing at Holcombe train station in the pouring rain, clutching a cardboard suitcase that had all but fallen to bits from the wet.'

Florrie smiled and felt her cheeks heat up. 'Should have arrived on time to pick me up, then, shouldn't you?'

'You looked like a drowned rat.'

'Charming.' She pushed him playfully in the shoulder.

Thom grabbed her hand and kissed it. 'The prettiest drowned rat I ever saw.'

'Get away, you rum pig. Good job you're as good at growing things as you are at idle flattery.' The tension in the air seemed to crackle. Her heart pounded so hard, she felt certain it would beat its way out of her chest at any moment. More alarmingly, she felt certain Thom was about to lean in and kiss her, and she wasn't ready for that. Florrie looked back through the trunks of the fruit trees to the walled rose garden. 'We'd better get back.'

The tension seemed to lift as they made their way to the gardeners' shed on the other side of the orchard. Thom disappeared inside for a moment and returned holding two handled baskets for collecting cut flowers. He passed one of the baskets and a spare pair of secateurs to Florrie.

'Ta.'

As he locked up, she listened to the chirruping birds that played in the nearby hawthorn hedgerows and the call of the peacocks further away, strutting and preening on the front lawn of the Hall. The world was still turning, even though Irene was no longer in it. It felt wrong, somehow, and Florrie felt like she was failing her sister. 'Now I've seen that gamekeeper's cottage, I realize having my mam and the kids living on the estate is just a pipe dream,' she said with a sigh. 'What am I going to do, Thom?'

'Ask Lady Charlotte to get the cottage fixed up. If she says no, you could ask Dame Elizabeth. Ladies'll be more likely to understand your mam's predicament.'

They walked back to the flower beds, where bumble bees buzzed lazily from bloom to bloom. She snipped a pale pink lily that was just about to open and laid it in her basket.

'What if they say no?'

'Cross that bridge if you come to it.'

With half-full baskets, they returned to the rose garden, where Lady Charlotte and her guests seemed oblivious to them having been gone for a while.

'See? They don't care,' Thom said. 'They're drunk, judging by the way they're laughing like drains. I reckon there's no better time to ask her nibs about the cottage than when she's had a few.'

Once Florrie had assembled and installed the impressive floral arrangements in Mademoiselle Chanel's bedroom and also in the dining room, she ordered one of the young footmen, who was smoking by the servants' entrance, to retrieve the picnic hamper and blanket from the rose garden.

By the time she caught Lady Charlotte alone in her room, Mrs Douglas had returned from her appointment, leaving Florrie to resume her normal duties, which included helping Lady Charlotte dress for dinner.

'I really ought to wear one of Mademoiselle Chanel's creations tonight, oughtn't I?' Lady Charlotte held a black strappy dress with a tiered long skirt against her, admiring her reflection in the cheval mirror. 'What do you think, Florrie? Yay or nay? Do you think all black drains me of colour?'

By now, Florrie knew that if she answered honestly, even if she were as tactful as possible, Lady Charlotte would sulk for the rest of the evening. 'You look like a film star in whatever you wear, my lady. Especially with that new hair. You're positively radiant.'

Lady Charlotte hiccupped and giggled. She smoothed the curl that wound its way across her forehead. 'Oh, you are a tonic! Thank you, dear Florrie. You know, I stopped by Sir Richard's study when I came in from the rose garden, and all he managed to say was, "What's wrong with your hair?"' She put the Chanel dress back on the hook and held a dark green gown close, pouting in the mirror. 'I hadn't seen him for ten days, and that's all he had to say for himself. Men!' She hung the green gown up and tried the black one again. 'If you ever attract the attentions of a man, Florrie, be prepared for their intolerable lack of tact. Honestly, you're far better off being a spinster. Sometimes, I wish my life was as simple and straightforward as yours, instead of keeping an important man happy and keeping the wheels of this old pile turning.'

Florrie bit her lip and swallowed down the variety of spiky responses that tried to jab and scratch their way out. Perhaps most irritating of Lady Charlotte's tactless comments was the notion that she played any part whatsoever in the running of a household that relied solely on a huge, hardworking and highly experienced staff. 'Definitely the black one,' Florrie said.

Lady Charlotte beamed at her and shoved the dress into Florrie's hands. 'You're right. Help me on with it?'

Florrie helped Lady Charlotte to climb into the dress, noticing that she was wearing new silk chemise-pantalons – French undergarments trimmed with the finest lace, which must have cost a small fortune; entirely unlike the shapeless, utilitarian slip that Florrie was forced to wear beneath her uniform, Florrie mused ruefully. She fastened the dress.

'Ow, you're pinching my skin,' Lady Charlotte said. 'Do be careful!'

'Sorry, my lady. It's fiddly.'

Lady Charlotte reached back and smacked her hand away. 'Stop it. You're all fingers and thumbs. I'll do it.' She was scowling into the mirror, now.

Florrie wondered if she could garner the support of Lady Charlotte before her champagne-fuelled effervescence went entirely flat.

'When me and Thom were picking flowers for Mademoiselle Chanel earlier, we found ourselves walking by the old gamekeeper's cottage.' She swallowed hard and crossed her fingers behind her back.

'Oh? Whatever were you doing out there?' Lady Charlotte swept over to her dressing table and took the stopper from her bottle of Chanel No. 5. She dabbed a little behind her ears and on her wrists. 'Was Thom trying to woo you? He is terribly rugged.'

Florrie shook her head. 'No. But I wanted to ask about the cottage. It's my mother, you see. We desperately need a new laundress at Holcombe Hall, and Mrs Douglas said my mother could have the job, except there's nowhere for her and my sister's children to live, so—'

Lady Charlotte looked at her askance. 'You want to install your mother and your dead sister's children at Holcombe Hall?'

'No. Not *in* the Hall. But maybe they could rent somewhere handily close by. Like, on the estate itself. I notice the gamekeeper's cottage is just standing empty.'

'But that place is derelict.' Lady Charlotte's red lips thinned to a hard line. 'It would cost a fortune to fix up. Are you seriously asking me to pay a king's ransom to restore that old pile of rubble just so we can get a new washerwoman?'

Florrie saw Lady Charlotte's look of disgust and already knew the answer to her question.

12

'Ah, dear Florrie. I rather fancy a change this morning,' Sir Richard said, holding his hand over his cup at breakfast.

A fortnight had passed since Lady Charlotte's return from Paris, during which time Florrie had written to her mother as often as she could, sending moral support and whatever money she could spare. Today, it was the first time in a while that Florrie had served her employer breakfast in the dining room, along with other members of the family. At the opposite end of the long dining table was Dame Elizabeth, already dressed in full widow's weeds and tackling a boiled egg with some ferocity. Next to Sir Richard was Sir Hugh, reeking of stale alcohol, dressed in his pyjamas and dressing gown, looking forlornly down at the bacon sandwich he'd requested. Lady Charlotte was still sleeping, of course, and Florrie knew she would only emerge in time for lunch, as was her wont.

Now, Sir Richard treated Florrie to a winning smile, though she noticed shadows beneath his sharp grey eyes. 'I've been burning the midnight oil in preparation for this merger, you see,' he said. 'So would you be so kind as to procure me a nice strong coffee, please? There's a good gal.'

Florrie bobbed a curtsey, privately hoping that Dame Elizabeth wouldn't notice her smiling back rather too enthusiastically or blushing. 'Of course, Sir Richard. Right away.'

'Yes, coffee for me too, I think,' Sir Hugh said, grimacing and clutching his head.

Dame Elizabeth set down her teaspoon. 'Hugh, you really must tackle your excessive drinking. It's entirely unseemly in a man of your social standing. Where were you last night?'

Sir Hugh coughed with a rumbling chest. 'The Nag's Head.'

Always keen to see the wayward and spoiled Sir Hugh receive a dressing-down from his mother, Florrie hung back a while, pretending to check the milk jug so that she could witness Dame Elizabeth's reaction.

'I beg your pardon? Am I right in hearing that you've been *supping ale* with the locals in Holcombe village?' Her words dripped with undisguised disdain. 'My son, rubbing shoulders with the working-class hoi polloi in a tavern?' She pushed her egg away. 'Small wonder my appetite is poor and sleep evades me. What is to become of our family legacy when my daughter-in-law can't even be bothered to attend breakfast, let alone bear her husband an heir . . . ?'

'Mother!' Sir Richard said. 'That's hardly fair. You know Charlotte gets awfully fatigued.'

Dame Elizabeth glowered at her elder son. 'What is the point of you marrying the daughter of an earl – a relation of the King himself – if you cannot produce a boy to carry on the Harding-Bourne name and inherit the Holcombe Estate and our family business interests? Was your father's toil for nothing?'

Florrie watched as Sir Richard opened his mouth to speak, yet no retort emerged.

Turning to Sir Hugh, Dame Elizabeth merely shook her head and tutted. 'And my youngest son would rather fritter away his inheritance in a public house, or brawl with his fascist best friend over some theatrical floozie—'

'Steady on, Mama! Daphne's hardly a floozie, and Walter's not *really* a fascist.'

'He's a known associate of Oswald Mosley, isn't he, that idiot friend of yours?'

Hugh took a bite from his bacon sandwich and spoke as he chewed. 'Mosley's a Labour man, mother. An MP in the Midlands. It's all quite respectable.'

'I hear Mosley has some rather unpalatable ideas and an ego that rather outstrips his intelligence.' Dame Elizabeth drummed her fingers on a folded letter she'd been perusing at the table, and Florrie noticed then that it was written on the same pale blue paper as the one the old lady had been furtively reading at her bureau not so long ago. 'When are you going to find yourself a suitable wife, Hugh? You're not going to find one in the Nag's Head. *Nag's Head*, indeed! Your father, may he rest in peace, will be turning in his grave.' She got up from the table, snatching up the letter and clutching it against her middle. 'And being a little judicious with your expenditure won't do you any harm, young man. Our funds are not limitless.'

'Oh, Mother, you do worry excessively,' Sir Richard said. 'We're about to make a fortune from this steel merger that will mitigate any losses we've been making from the mills and the mines.'

Dame Elizabeth placed a hand on his shoulder as she made her way to the door. 'At least we have a steady hand on the tiller of the Harding-Bourne business empire. Though you must be sure not to count your chickens before they're hatched, Richard. That Hatry man has a rather ferrety look to him. He's terribly nouveau riche, and your father never trusted that lot.'

Sir Hugh burst out laughing. 'Oh, Mama, you are so droll. What are Richard and I if not third-generation nouveaux-riches?' He turned to his older brother. 'The family's baronetcy was only conferred on Grandpapa some seventy years ago, which pegs us rather low in the rankings of high society. Isn't that why you married Charlotte? They needed the money, and our family needed the kudos, what?'

Sir Richard folded his arms tightly across his chest. 'Hugh, need I remind you that it takes two generations to make a fortune and one idiot generation to lose it. Just as well I inherited and not you, eh?'

'You only inherited because James succumbed to the Hun, so pardon me if I don't worship at your eminently sensible size tens, your godliness.'

'Boys!'

Leaving Sir Richard to parry with a hung-over Sir Hugh, Florrie slipped away to the servants' back stairs before the distraught Dame Elizabeth could cross her path. She hastened down to the warren of servants' quarters below stairs and came across Arkwright, who was standing inside his office with the door wide open. Wearing an apron, he was ensconced behind an ironing board, ironing the *Financial Times* so that Sir Richard would not get newsprint all over his hands.

'Ah, Florence, just the girl,' Arkwright called out to her.

Florrie came to a halt, registering a sinking feeling. 'Mr Arkwright, I'm just about to—'

'You're looking rosy cheeked this morning, may I say?' He beckoned her inside.

'Oh. Am I? Thanks.' Florrie reluctantly stepped over the threshold into the office, wondering why Arkwright was at once so ashen-faced yet also so uncharacteristically friendly.

She noticed his hand trembled as he smoothed the iron over the paper. 'In fact, your colour is a little high, actually. Is everything quite all right in the dining room?' He narrowed his eyes.

'Nothing that a pot of coffee for Sir Richard won't cure.' Where was Mrs Douglas when she needed her to intervene? The last thing Florrie needed at such a busy hour was a curious tête-à-tête with Arkwright. 'Now, if you don't mind, I've got coffee to procure and Sir Richard's eggs order to pass to Cook.'

Arkwright took the impeccably flat newspaper and deftly bound the pages together with a wooden newspaper stick. He held the *Financial Times* out to her and retrieved from a side table both *The Times* and the *Daily*

Telegraph, which he'd also prepared for reading. 'Would you mind taking these up to Sir Richard, Florence? Only I have difficult business to attend to with one of the footmen.'

'I don't mean to be disrespectful, Mr Arkwright, but I'm going to have my hands full as it is. Can't you get Danny to do it?'

'I'd rather you did it, Florence. I'm sure Sir Richard will welcome the morning's news from you.'

Florrie felt goosebumps erupt on her arms, and the fine hairs stood to attention. 'Oh?'

Arkwright smiled encouragingly at her. 'I know you're Sir Richard's favourite maid. You'll just be cheering up a very busy man and doing me a favour to boot. Please?'

Nonplussed and wholly mistrustful of the butler who was behaving very oddly, Florrie relented and took the papers. Distracted by her numerous responsibilities, she passed by the kitchen to leave a list of required items with Cook and then she made her way back to the servants' stairs. It was only as she got to the top, where the light improved, that she glimpsed the headline above a story in the *Financial Times* – a major story that was accompanied by a photograph of a familiar face. Only then did she realize why Arkwright had blanched and tasked her with delivering not just bad news, but terrible news.

'You conniving old . . .' she muttered beneath her breath, scowling at the predicament Arkwright had put her in.

Wondering if she should hold the newspapers back

until Sir Richard had breakfasted, Florrie jumped at the sudden appearance of Mrs Douglas at the top of the stairs, returning from her morning inspection of the housemaids' efforts. 'Oh, blimey. You gave me such a fright. I wasn't expecting to bump into anyone.'

Mrs Douglas smiled uncertainly at her. 'Sorry, dear. I didn't mean to startle you. Why aren't you in the dining room?'

Florrie showed the *Financial Times* to the housekeeper. 'I wondered why Mr Arkwright had fobbed this job on to me.'

The housekeeper balked at the news. 'Oh, good Lord. That doesn't sound at all promising.'

'What should I do?' Florrie asked.

Mrs Douglas took Florrie by the hand and marched her back down to Arkwright's office, where he was idly sipping from a cup of tea. She grabbed the newspapers from Florrie's hands and slapped them down on Arkwright's desk. 'Don't use my girl as your stooge.'

Arkwright set down his cup and sat up straight. 'I beg your pardon!'

'You heard,' Mrs Douglas said, her face rapidly turning beetroot. She laid a hand on her chest but ushered Florrie back towards the kitchen before Arkwright could start an argument. When they were out of the butler's earshot, Mrs Douglas spoke quietly. 'I've got a nasty feeling about this,' she said. 'Sir Richard's likely going to hit the roof when he reads that story, but there's no reason for Arkwright to manipulate you. If he ever tries it again, you tell me straight away. And if I'm not around for whatever reason, stand up to him. I've absolutely had it with that man.'

Cook leaned towards them, her eyes glittering with intrigue, as she served scrambled egg on to a plate. 'Hey, what's all this about?' She slid a silver dome over the food and put the plate on to a tray.

'Just give Florrie the tray for Sir Richard. This is not time for idle gossip – especially not for my kitchen staff.' Leaving Cook open-mouthed, Mrs Douglas marched off towards the laundry.

Before Cook could probe her about the matter, Florrie took the tray and headed back to the dining room, where Sir Richard was now reminiscing with Sir Hugh in a rather more amiable fashion about their deceased father and brother. She set the tray down and slid the plate in front of Sir Richard, lifting the dome to reveal the steaming scrambled eggs. She poured his coffee and left the pot within reach. 'Cream or sugar, Sir Richard?'

'Neither, thank you, Florrie. I'll take it black today.' Beaming at her, Sir Richard laid his napkin on his lap. 'Please pass my thanks to Cook. The eggs look divine this morning. I've already polished off two sausages, and they were spiffing too. But I do think having it all served by the maid with the loveliest of smiles makes everything taste all the better!' He winked.

Desperate to conceal her blushes, Florrie set about tidying the serving table. Out of the corner of her eye, she saw Arkwright march in and shoot her a venomous glance.

'Your newspapers, Sir Richard.' He laid the newspapers

within reach of their employer, gave a short bow and left rapidly.

Holding her breath, Florrie watched as Sir Richard forked some eggs into his mouth, still wearing the remnants of the warm smile with which he had greeted her. Then his gaze transferred to the *Financial Times* and the smile slowly turned to a frown as he read.

'I don't bally well believe it.' He slammed his cutlery down and snatched the paper up, stalking over to an occasional table by the newly reglazed stained-glass window, where the sun streamed through in a kaleidoscope of colour.

'What is it, old chap?' Sir Hugh asked.

Sir Richard turned to his younger brother, his colour visibly drained. 'Clarence Hatry. He's blown the steel companies merger out of the water.' He turned back to the paper, his eyes darting from side to side as he read the details of the story. 'He's . . . he was refused funding for the deal by Monty Norman at the Bank of England; Lloyds Bank too.'

Sir Hugh lit a cigarette and blew blue smoke rings into the air. 'And? What of it? Surely a bunch of steel magnates could club together if he needs a boost.'

Sir Richard shook his head and closed his eyes. His Adam's apple rose and fell. 'You don't understand. He's been caught issuing fraudulent stocks to raise a million-dollar loan. The chairman of the London Stock Exchange has declared the Hatry Group bankrupt. They've suspended trading all shares in it.' He threw the newspaper down. 'Damn, damn, damn and blast!'

'What does this mean for us?' Sir Hugh asked, leaning on the back of his dining chair impassively as he turned to face his brother.

'Well, the man in charge of the steel merger – *our* steel merger – has been arrested for fraud. *Fraud*, Hugh! A man in whose group of companies I'd invested significant sums of money. What do *you* think that means for us?'

13

'I've asked you once, and I'll ask you again. Kindly turn that off, will you?' Sir Richard barked at his brother and Lady Charlotte, who were both in their stockinged feet, practising their Charleston together by the gramophone in the drawing room by way of after-dinner entertainment. The music issuing from the horn was tinny and crackling. 'I can't hear the news for that blasted din.' Sitting in the far corner of the drawing room, bathed in the golden glow that came from the sconces mounted either side of the enormous Georgian portrait of his grandfather as a bewigged young man – the man who Florrie knew had laid the foundations for the Harding-Bourne business empire – Sir Richard put his ear next to the wireless's speaker. He frowned with such vigour that his brow cast his eyes almost entirely in shadow.

'Oh, Richard, you are a terrible killjoy,' Lady Charlotte shouted over the music.

'For heaven's sake, Charlotte! This is important. This is about our family's fortune.'

'But we're rich, Dicky! Our fortune lies in us being fortunately filthy rich!' Sir Hugh burst out laughing.

Florrie had been watching the tense exchange as she poured port into glasses for the three of them. Ordinarily, serving port would be Arkwright's job, but the butler had retreated to his office after dinner, complaining of sciatica, and Mrs Douglas had ordered Florrie to attend to the family's post-dinner refreshments. Dame Elizabeth was also absent, given she had taken to dining alone in her quarters of late, suffering from regular but unspecific maladies. Florrie suspected that both she and Arkwright were avoiding Sir Richard's uncharacteristic foul moods, brought on by mounting financial uncertainty since Clarence Hatry's arrest for fraud and the implosion of the steel companies' merger.

'Anyway, I thought you said the markets had rallied since the debacle with Hatry,' Hugh shouted, somewhat out of breath as he engaged in some energetic waving and kicked his legs behind him.

Sir Richard got to his feet and stalked across the drawing room. He pushed his brother aside, glared pointedly at his wife and lifted the stylus off the gramophone record, which brought the music to a squawking, scratching end. Exhaling hard once silence ensued, he turned to face his brother. 'That was over a fortnight ago, and in the last week, things have gone from bad to worse. The merger's been blown out of the water, for a start. And didn't you read this morning's papers?' He clasped a hand to his forehead. 'Oh, silly me. That would be far too boring for *you*, wouldn't it?'

'Steady on, Dicky. No need to be unkind,' Sir Hugh said, clearly nonplussed by the attack.

'There's every need,' Sir Richard said.

'You're being such a spoilsport, Richard,' Lady

Charlotte said, flinging an arm around her husband. 'Hugh and I were only practising our steps, weren't we, Hugh? We've both decided that we will all go to the Chelsea Arts Ball this New Year's Eve. We're invited every year, of course, but you're always such a stick in the mud about New Year's Eve. It sounds like *such* a good wheeze, and everybody wears fancy dress. Couldn't you fancy a New Year's shindig at the Royal Albert Hall, darling? Just for once?'

Sir Richard looked despairingly at his wife and extricated himself from her embrace. He turned back to Hugh and locked eyes with him. 'Yesterday's Wall Street prices collapsed. The *Financial Times* is trying to talk things up as it being just the end of a five-year bull market, but in the same breath it's reporting that the *New York Times* is calling yesterday "Black Thursday". Now, do shut up, both of you, and let me listen to the news.'

Lady Charlotte and Hugh merely shrugged at each other and rolled their eyes, stifling giggles like schoolchildren, while Sir Richard returned to the wireless and turned it high enough to drown out their silliness.

Florrie passed Sir Hugh and Lady Charlotte their drinks and then carried Sir Richard's port over to him. 'I'll just set this down here,' she said quietly, placing the drink on to a crocheted doily that sat on a side table Mrs Douglas had said was one of the Hall's many Louis XIV pieces. She thought about the old orange box that her mam used as a sidetable in her slum dwelling. Then she pictured in her mind's eye the short and brutal letter she'd received that morning from Manchester.

Dear Florrie,

I know you said we should move to the country, and you were right, love. As I write, Nelly is badly with a whooping cough that just won't shift, even with pan after pan of boiled water steaming the air in the back bedroom. She's been lying in bed much of the day, coughing to the point of sickness. I am so worried, I can barely breathe. Tuberculosis has found its way on to the street — her at number 57 — and I am praying every night that it won't get as far as this house. The cockroaches are getting more and more brazen now the nights are colder, as are the mice.

Luckily, I've found work one morning a week, charring for the local doctor, and her next door takes the kids for a couple of hours. By the time I pay her, though, I find I've earned barely enough for an extra loaf of bread and a pack of bacon. The children take up too much of my energy for me to work longer hours away from the house, but piecework as a seamstress is hard to come by, what with everyone being laid off at the factories and mills.

We desperately need to get away from here, Florrie. I feel like I'm sinking fast. Maybe when you get this letter, some bright idea will occur to you, or that laundress's job at Holcombe Hall will be more than just a pipe dream.

Please write as soon as you can. I feel so alone.

All my love
Mam xxx

Florrie stood by the wireless gazing into space, not listening to the news about the volatility of Wall Street trading and the concerns of multi-millionaires, but thinking about the contents of the letter; the desperation in her mother's words; their grinding poverty.

'Are you quite all right, Florrie?' Lady Charlotte asked.

Florrie turned away from Sir Richard, who was still glued to the inauspicious tidings of the BBC newsreader. She bobbed a curtsey. 'Yes, my lady. It's a terrible to-do, isn't it?'

'Oh, don't you start,' Lady Charlotte said, holding her port glass out for a top-up. 'Sir Richard is being melodramatic. Anyone would think we live in New York, not the wilds of the Lancashire countryside. Honestly! I doubt this nonsense will affect us materially at all in Britain – especially not here at Holcombe Hall. You really mustn't worry.'

Florrie carefully poured more port into her glass from the decanter, wondering that upper-class young women drank so much and so frequently. 'Oh, I'm not worried for myself, Lady Charlotte.' Might she say something now? Might this finally be the window of opportunity to address her mother's needs within earshot of Sir Richard? 'It's just my mother, actually. I am worried for her. I had a letter from her today, and she's in a desperate fix with my sister's children and no work. All the while, I know there's a laundress's job going at the Hall that she could do in her sleep . . . If only we could somehow sort out accommodation for her and the children. It's very frustrating not being able to help and knowing, with this stock market business, that things could get even worse for them in Manchester. And all the while, there's that empty gamekeeper's cottage . . .'

Lady Charlotte lowered her voice and spoke with an air of conspiracy. 'Lord, don't mention the plight of Manchester's great unwashed within earshot of my husband right now! Look at him. He's a tormented soul. Clearly believes *we're* about to lose our shirts, so the last thing we need is to get him thinking about the poor and needy. He spends far too much time thinking about them as it is.'

Either Lady Charlotte hadn't heard her comment about the cottage, or she was deliberately ignoring Florrie. *Great unwashed? Is that all you think my family amounts to?* she thought.

'He's going to be intolerable for weeks,' Sir Hugh said, staring morosely into his empty glass. 'Top me up will you, Florrie dear. There's a good gal.'

Florrie bit back frustrated tears and forced herself to smile. 'Of course.'

After her shift, Florrie trudged down to the kitchen with a growling stomach and a heavy heart. Ten or more people were sitting around the big table, eating a late dinner. Florrie was surprised to see Thom among them, leaning back on the hind legs of his chair, puzzling over the crossword in one of Sir Richard's old copies of *The Times*.

'Hey up, love,' Cook said to her. 'You look like you've lost a tanner and found a ha'penny.'

'Have you been crying, Florrie?' Sally asked, slapping the empty chair next to her.

Florrie took a seat next to Sally, shaking her head, but the tears that rolled on to her cheeks betrayed her words.

'What's all this now?' Cook asked. She edged her way around the table, stood behind Florrie and wrapped her meaty arms around her. 'Tell Cookie what's the matter, love.'

'It's my family,' Florrie said. 'I can't bear it.' She told everyone the story of Mam, the children and the futility of trying to ask the Harding-Bournes to renovate the gamekeeper's cottage so Mam could take up the position of laundress and put a roof over their heads. 'Lady Charlotte made it very clear I was to drop the subject. I wanted to say Mam could pay rent on the place if it was done up, but she didn't give me the chance. I've tried to drop hints since, but . . .' She shrugged. 'And if I end up losing my job because I keep opening my mouth, then where will my family be? Mam'll have nowt coming in. I'm caught between the devil and the deep blue sea.'

Thom slapped his newspaper down on to the table. 'I swear to God, Florrie,' he said. 'If they won't do owt to help your mam and those kiddies, we'll have a whip-round, and I'll fix that gamekeeper's cottage up with my own two hands in my spare time.'

Albert, the head gardener, dragged on his pipe and chuckled. 'What spare time might that be, young Thomas? And which of the folks round this table do you think has got money to chuck in a pot for Florrie?' He turned to Florrie. 'You're a grand lass, love, but we've all got family back home, what rely on us earnings here. No rich servants round this table, that's for sure. Not with what the Harding-Bournes are paying us. The rich get richer . . .'

A chummer of agreement rippled around the kitchen.

Thom leaned forward so that he caught Florrie's eye. 'Well, stuff this lot.' He thumbed himself in the chest. 'I haven't got any family alive that I still need to support, so I'll fix that cottage up for your mam out of my own pocket.'

'You're talking out of your backside, Thom,' Cook said. 'You're forgetting that it's not your property to go tampering with. Frustrating though it might be, because God knows we need a good laundress . . .' She turned to Florrie and gave her an apologetic smile. 'You've *got* to get Sir Richard to give the go ahead and the money for this. It's his land; his staff payroll; his cottage.'

14

'Where's Arkwright with the dratted newspapers?' Sir Richard said at breakfast on the last day of October – a week after the 'Black Thursday' that had set him on edge so. He got to his feet, marched to the threshold of the dining room and yelled into the hallway. 'Arkwright! Arkwright, where are my papers?' With obvious irritation, he pressed the servants' bell twice, three times, then returned to stand expectantly in the doorway.

Florrie shrank as far as she could into the corner of the room, stacking the spent crockery on to a tray. Sir Richard's recent outbursts were so out of character that she wondered if he'd suffered some kind of apoplexy in his sleep that had left him a changed man – an abrasive Mr Hyde forever replacing the unflappable and charming Dr Jekyll. For the first time in her ten years at Holcombe Hall, she felt somewhat uncomfortable being alone in her beloved employer's company. She certainly hadn't dared bring up the subject of the gamekeeper's cottage since the announcement on the wireless, two days earlier, that Wall Street had crashed entirely. Much as she didn't understand high finance, she could intuit from Sir Richard's pallor and foul mood that a stock market crash was not good news.

'Oh, there you are,' Sir Richard said. 'At last.'

Florrie fully expected Arkwright to enter the dining room, so she was surprised when instead, Dame Elizabeth swooped in. Florrie noted she was wearing a scowl that could sour milk.

'Charlotte says you're being a curmudgeon,' the old lady said, taking her customary seat at the head of the dining table. 'I thought I'd better investigate.'

Sir Richard seemed to calm somewhat in his mother's presence. 'And you've been acting like a hermit of late. You haven't dined with us in days. I've been worried about you, Mama.'

'We are living in worrisome times.' Dame Elizabeth cleared her throat and held her tea cup out to Florrie.

As Florrie dutifully poured the tea, Arkwright appeared bearing the day's newspapers on their reading sticks and handed them to Sir Richard.

'Will that be all, sir?' he said.

Sir Richard waved him away. 'Yes, yes. Though actually, you could try to be a little more punctual with the papers. Your standards are slipping lately, Arkwright.'

Arkwright's demeanour stiffened. 'My apologies, sir. I have been a little unwell.'

Lowering the *Financial Times* to study his butler in earnest, Sir Richard's stern expression softened. 'I'm very sorry to hear that, Arkwright. I hope it's nothing serious. Do see the doctor if you need to. We can't have the staff dropping on us.'

Arkwright pressed his lips together, bowed and left in haste, exchanging a meaningful glance with Florrie.

Florrie was privately relieved to see a little of Sir

Richard's normal bonhomie return, though his composure was only momentary.

'Listen to this, Mother,' he said. He read aloud from the paper. '"The crash has come with dramatic suddenness."' He turned to Dame Elizabeth with a raised eyebrow. 'Well, pardon me if I don't agree with that naive appraisal. This nonsense started when Hatry's stock was frozen. It's been a race to the bottom ever since.'

'Go on,' Dame Elizabeth said, taking a piece of toast from the rack and buttering it slowly.

He resumed reading. '"Stocks of many established companies have had one-half or more lopped off the highest of their inflated market prices, amid scenes of excitement to which Wall Street has known no parallel."' He looked up at her. 'Well, I can tell you now, my phone is ringing constantly with calls from the shareholders complaining that Harding-Bourne steel has slid drastically.'

'Do we still have the contract for the Chrysler Building?' Dame Elizabeth asked. 'And what of the locomotives bound for India?'

Sir Richard shook his head with his eyes closed. 'Yes, all of that is safe. I have to go to New York imminently to placate the architect of the Chrysler Building and the construction company he has working on it, but they have a contractual commitment to use our steel. Our solicitors tell me the contract is watertight. And the Indian deal's fine.'

'Then why are you worried, dear boy?' Dame Elizabeth smiled sympathetically at him. 'You, of all my sons, have always been the least prone to panic and unnecessary drama. This is but a temporary blip, darling. Harding-Bourne has diversified interests, and this is a catastrophe of the Americans' making. You should concentrate more on providing that heir.' She gave him a knowing look.

Sir Richard held the paper up in front of his face. Florrie could see he was watching her from the corner of his eye. She noticed that his cheeks had coloured. 'Not in front of Florrie, Mother. I'm sure she doesn't need to hear chat like that.' He cleared his throat. 'In any case, I fear you're wrong in your optimism. The journalist says this: "The full effect of the slump on American industry, and therefore the confidence which formed the basis of the boom remains to be seen . . . a curtailment of consuming power seems inevitable."' He lowered the paper to look at his mother once more. 'Even this hopeless optimist admits a Wall Street Crash is going to have a knock-on effect in Britain.'

'No, dear,' Dame Elizabeth said, sipping her tea. 'He said, "It remains to be seen." He's equivocating for good reason. Here is not there. We have the Atlantic in between, mercifully.' She set her cup down and stood, smoothing her skirts; she looked out into the grounds of the Hall at the autumn sunshine. 'I might take a turn around the grounds this morning. The trees are turning, and the colour is simply beautiful.'

As she left, she stopped at Sir Richard's chair, squeezed his shoulder and kissed the top of his head. 'I know you carry the weight of this family on your shoulders,

Richard, but I do wish you wouldn't wear it quite so heavily.'

When they were alone together, Florrie cleared the table and watched Sir Richard push away the newspapers with a heavy sigh. She could hear the telephone ringing down the hall. Would Arkwright return to the dining room imminently to announce yet another call from one of his distraught business associates?

For once, and surely not for long, she had her employer to herself. In her head, a battle raged between the side of her that wanted to discuss the gamekeeper's cottage and the side of her that knew now was the worst possible time to bring up a matter that required expenditure, even though she knew the sums required for getting the cottage back to a liveable standard were mere pocket change to the likes of the Harding-Bournes. Lady Charlotte probably spent more on a pair of shoes.

Sir Richard cocked his head to the side and locked eyes with her. 'You are very lucky not having such grave responsibilities, Florrie. How I envy you right now.'

Florrie froze with a stack of plates in her hands. Suddenly, she could no longer hear the telephone ringing. She was no longer aware of the late October draught coming from the enormous, many-paned windows that whipped around her ankles. She couldn't see anything but Sir Richard's faltering smile. 'You envy *me*?' Where on earth were these brave, confrontational words coming from? Tears were pricking the backs of her eyes, but she willed them away. 'You don't think I have responsibilities that match yours?' She put the plates down on to the table and turned to face him, desperation making her brave. 'My sister's not long since died from pneumonia, and I've had to leave my ageing mother looking after three babies under the age of six in a slum tenement full of cockroaches and damp. My mam hasn't got a bean to her name because she got the push at the mill where she'd worked for donkey's years – a *Harding-Bourne* mill, I hasten to add – after an accident that weren't even her fault. She lost two of her fingers in a loom, and now she's got nowt coming in and three extra mouths to feed.'

Sir Richard stood before her wide-eyed and blinking hard. He opened his mouth, then closed it again, as if words failed him. His eyebrows drew together, his face the picture of contrition. 'I say, Florrie, that's terribly tragic. I had no idea.'

Florrie inhaled sharply. 'Sorry to speak out of turn, but if I don't work and send as much money home as I can spare, my mam and those kiddies will end up starving to death. That's if pneumonia or TB don't get them first. And they'll have to go into a paupers' grave because I only managed to bury my sister after your wife kindly lent me five quid.'

Sir Richard opened his mouth to respond but fell silent when Florrie spoke again.

'But . . . and here's the cherry on the cake . . . I wouldn't be able to ask to borrow more because I have to pay Lady Charlotte back at a shilling a week. I'm already going to be in debt to her for years as it is. So do you really still envy me?' She stopped, a little startled by her own daring.

Sir Richard rubbed his face with his hands and made a strange growling noise. Had Florrie pushed it too far, she wondered? Was she about to be dismissed? 'Florrie, Florrie, Florrie,' he said, putting his hands together in supplication. 'How can you ever forgive me for being so insensitive? It had completely slipped my mind that you're recently bereaved, and I didn't know the circumstances of your family. That sounds truly dreadful.'

'It is,' Florrie said, defiantly wiping a tear away. 'I can barely sleep with worry. My infant niece has whooping cough, and my mam keeps sending these dreadful, heart-breaking letters . . .'

Leaving his chair, Sir Richard approached her and took her hands in his. He looked into her eyes. 'Tell me how I can help, dear Florrie.'

Taking a deep breath, amid flowing tears, Florrie managed to stutter and stumble her way through the details of the laundress vacancy and the gatekeeper's cottage and how Thom had offered to do the restoration work himself out of his own pocket, if only he could get permission. 'It would be the most wonderful home for those children,' she said. 'If it could be fixed up, I honestly think it would save their lives. And Holcombe Hall would be getting the best laundress this side of the Pennines.'

Sir Richard stroked her cheek, wiping a tear away. His face was so close to hers, she could feel the warmth of his breath, and he was looking into her eyes intently. Florrie wondered if he could hear how hard her heart was beating. For a fleeting moment, she wondered if he might even kiss her.

'Florrie, my dear, you won't need a penny of Thomas's money.' His words were fleetingly laced with derision. 'And we don't need a *mere gardener* tampering with such a fine old building, no matter how dire its state of repair may be. That cottage belongs to the estate. It is *my* responsibility and mine alone. Of course, your mother must have the job. I wish you'd told me all this sooner, dear Florrie.' With a look of regret on his handsome face, he squeezed her hands and let them go, taking a step backwards. 'Renovations will begin straight away, and I will pay for the finest craftsmen to restore it to its former glory as quickly as possible. You have my word. Consider it done. And please, accept my humble apology for being such a thoughtless prig.'

15

Dear Mam,

As I write, the gamekeeper's cottage is being done up. Sir Richard is footing the bill happily, and the place will be safe, comfortable, clean and dry by the time you move in, in December. Thom, our head gardener's right-hand man, is currently clearing the garden. It was a terrible tangle of brambles and Lord knows what before, but he's going to plant it up with herbaceous borders, so that George, Nelly and Alice can watch the bees and butterflies all summer long!

Looking out of her bedroom window, Florrie realized the sun had already risen on her day off, and there was much to do. Completing the letter would have to wait. She screwed the lid on her father's old fountain pen, yawned and pulled on the gardener's overalls Thom had given her.

Hastening down to the kitchen, where Sally was standing in for Cook on her morning off, Florrie poured herself a cup of tea from the oversized steel pot that the servants used.

'How's the tea?' Sally said uncertainly.

Florrie forced herself not to grimace at the weak brew. 'Wet and warm, Sal. Just how I like it. And how are you managing, frying up eggs and bacon for the landed gentry? Quite a step up from scrubbing floors.'

Sally beamed at her. 'Arkwright blew his top when he found out Mrs Douglas was giving me a go at doing breakfast, but do you know what? I haven't had a single plate sent back!'

'Good on you!' Florrie said. 'Well, today's my turn to scrub floors, and I can't wait!'

'Aren't you going to church?' Sally asked.

Florrie shook her head. 'Cleanliness is next to godliness, Sal. I'll honour the Lord by cleaning some windows and scrubbing out the new privy what's been installed at the cottage. My mam's not going to believe her luck. Inside facilities. Fancy that! They'll be living like royalty.'

Shoving a piece of cold toast in her mouth, Florrie made her way to the equipment store and pulled out the mop and the metal bucket. She filled the empty bucket with the scrubbing brush, some rags, some vinegar, some bicarbonate of soda and all manner of other cleaning accoutrements. 'Right. See you later.'

Though winter was approaching, heralding its arrival with a late November nip in the air and an early light frost, Florrie was warmed by the prospect of her family being installed in their new home before Christmas. Trudging through the long, crisp grass of the orchard, beneath the bare branches of the fruit trees, she mused on how her impassioned outburst at the end of October had galvanized Sir Richard to have the cottage renovated by a team of craftsmen – a team that had turned up at Holcombe Hall only days later, and had been crawling all over the place daily ever since. It felt like a miracle.

Setting down her bucket by the new gate that had

been installed at the end of the cottage's front garden, Florrie took a moment to inspect the place now that it had been cleared of foliage.

'Pretty as a picture,' she said, admiring the new slate roof and the repaired lime plaster on the part-timbered upper half of the house. The plaster had been repainted in its original fetching shade of blush pink. She sniffed the air, savouring the smell of fresh paint and putty and sanded wood.

Hearing sawing coming from the back garden, Florrie pushed open the gate and made her way down the recently excavated old garden path, marvelling at the short grass of the lawn and the deep borders that had already been cleared of weeds and planted up with winter-bare shrubs. The old hydrangeas beneath the windows were bare now and had been cut back hard, but she was pleased to see they hadn't been removed.

She dropped her bucket and mop by the front step and made her way round to the back garden to see who was working at such an early hour on a Sunday morning.

'Morning, Florrie,' Thom said, smiling. He was standing by a makeshift workbench that he'd erected on the grass. Sawn planks were stacked in a neat pile beside him. With his wood saw still in hand, he straightened up and nodded at her. 'Nice to see them overalls fit.' He chuckled. 'Happen you look like Gertrude Jekyll.'

'Who?'

'Woman what planned the rose garden here.'

'Oh aye?' Florrie said, wondering if that was a good or a bad thing. She felt her cheeks flush hot and hooked a stray lock of hair behind her ear. 'What you doing here? I thought you'd finished the garden.' She appraised the tidy lawn, enclosed by shrubbery that had been cut back hard. A square of bare earth had been dug in a sunny corner. 'It certainly looks well. Is that a veg patch I see?'

'Aye. Thought the little'uns might like to help your mam grow stuff. Potatoes and tomatoes and that.' He set down his saw and wiped his brow with the sleeve of his ragged woollen jumper. 'I've already put in some seed spuds for an early crop of King Edwards. Never too early to start young'uns on gardening.'

'That's such a good idea, Thom. Ta. So, what you sawing?'

Thom inclined his head towards an A-frame of steel poles that had been erected in the middle of the freshly mown, yellowed lawn. 'Thought I'd make a swing. No sense in having a garden like this if the little'uns can't play in it. Especially when they've come from the city.'

At that moment, Florrie was so tempted to throw her arms around him in gratitude that she had to put her hands in the pockets of her overalls to stop herself. 'You're a thoughtful man, Thomas Stanley,' she said.

Thom looked at his work boots. 'Anything for you, Florrie Bickerstaff.'

Momentarily, she studied his handsome face, marvelling that such a rugged-looking man should be so gentle and considerate. Did Thom have feelings for her? Yes, it was likely he did, though Florrie wondered what he could possibly find attractive in her well-scrubbed face, with her dowdy, unfashionable hair, dressed as she always was in something utilitarian and shapeless. *You should let him court you,* a voice inside Florrie said. *He's a grand feller, a grafter and an honest soul. You could be happy together. Don't let the chance of love slip through your fingers.* She silently shushed her inner voice of reason, knowing that it would be unfair to begin a romance with Thom when she had so little to offer. Thom deserved far better. 'God bless you.' She looked back at the cottage. 'Right. Them floors aren't going to scrub theirselves.'

She was just about to make her way inside when Thom spoke again.

'I got the new range fired up for you, by the way.' He pointed to the chimney that was merrily puffing out smoke. 'I reckoned you'd need some hot water for your bucket, like.'

Ignoring the warring thoughts inside her head, Florrie marched up to Thom and gave him a peck on the cheek. 'You're a belter, what are you?' Then she hurried inside before the fleeting kiss could turn into something more.

It was a week since Florrie had last set foot inside the house. Placing her bucket and mop in the blissfully warm scullery, she eyed the brand-new, gleaming range that Thom had mentioned. At the side was a basket of freshly split logs. She opened the door to the fire box and smiled at the flames that crackled away inside. Using iron tongs, she popped an extra beech log on top, to keep the fire blazing. She shut the fire box door and lifted the lid off the hot water tank that sat at the side of the cooking rings. Thom had filled the tank already, and a cloud of steam billowed up to greet her.

'Magic. Mam won't believe her luck.'

Taking out her cleaning equipment, she scattered soap flakes into the bucket, half filled it with a little cold water from the butler's sink and then opened the tap on the front of the new range to top up the concoction with boiling water.

Wondering where to start, she carried the sloshing bucket of hot suds up the creaking old staircase, heading for the brand-new bathroom that had been created from one of the four original bedrooms. When she got to the top, she heard a strange scraping sound, followed by a crack and then a clatter, coming from the direction of the bathroom.

'Hello? Is anybody there?'

Thom hadn't mentioned that anyone else was due to work inside the cottage that morning, but clearly she wasn't alone. With the blood rushing in her ears and clutching the mop in her right hand, Florrie crept down the landing straight to the bathroom. The door was ajar. She pushed it open too hard, and the handle smacked loudly against the wall.

'Steady on! What's all this?' A startled-looking man, perhaps in his forties, was kneeling on a sheet of plywood that covered the newly tiled floor of the bathroom. He was surrounded by piles of tiles and held a scoring device in his hand.

'Who are you?' Florrie asked.

'Patrick,' he said. 'The tiler.' He looked at her mop. 'Were you going to mop me to death?'

Florrie laughed with relief. 'Sorry if I gave you a start.

I'm one of the maids from the big house. I've come to clean through and I wasn't expecting anyone else to be inside today. I thought you might be an intruder!' She took in the splendour of the fully fitted bathroom that sported an indoor toilet in an alcove of its own. 'Crikey, this is posh.' The floor was covered in a mosaic of black and white miniature porcelain squares, while the walls were beautifully tiled to waist height in pistachio green, topped with an unbroken border of shining slimline black tiles. The scheme extended to the low ceiling above an enormous curved cast-iron bath – the type Florrie had seen described in Lady Charlotte's fashion magazines as 'Art Deco'. The tiling was all finished but for a patch of naked plaster that remained behind the gleaming silver bath taps.

Patrick pointed to the patch. 'I'm just finishing off, but I wouldn't clean in here yet, love. You need to let the grout dry. Give it a few days to go off, if you can.' He put a tile down on the plywood and, using a metal rule, measured it and marked it with a pencil. 'Who's moving in here, then? Member of the family, I'm guessing, because His Lordship told my gaffer there was to be no expense spared.'

Florrie opened her mouth to respond, but Patrick continued, barely pausing for breath.

He pointed to the smooth plaster of the ceiling. 'See that? There was a great big hole in that just over a month ago. I've never seen a roof redone that quick. Joiner replaced a load of rotten joists and floorboards too . . . like *that*.' He clicked his fingers to indicate immediacy.

'That's what happens when you've more money than sense.'

Florrie bit her lip. 'Actually, it's my mam what's moving in. She's the new laundress.'

Patrick looked at her with wide eyes. 'You what? All *this* for a washerwoman? Your mam secretly got blue blood?' He wedged his pencil behind his ear. 'Or maybe she's the most beautiful washerwoman in the world, because you'd have to love someone to lavish this much attention and money on such a wreck of a house.'

Florrie merely shrugged. 'My mam's whites are something to behold. What can I say?'

Keen to avoid any further interrogation, she left Patrick to his tiling and walked past each of the bedrooms, drinking in the smells of recently applied distemper and freshly sanded floorboards. The eaves came low and the windows were small and leaded with the diamond-shaped panes that were typical of such an old house, meaning it would be gloomy except in full sun. The bedrooms were all dry, fresh and cosy, however, each one sporting a small, working cast-iron fireplace. All the rooms needed was a sweep of the floorboards, and they would be ready for the rugs and the furniture that Mrs Douglas had allowed her to pick from the basement store full of Holcombe Hall's spare, long forgotten and unloved pieces.

'Well, if I can't make a start on the bathroom, I'll mop downstairs and get all these windows clean,' she told herself.'

After she'd been working for some three back-breaking hours without a rest, there was a knock at the front door.

'Florrie! Anybody home?' Florrie recognised Thom's gravelly voice.

'In the parlour,' she shouted. 'Take your boots off if you're coming in. I've just cleaned all the floors.'

Seconds later, Thom appeared at the threshold of the parlour, brandishing a battered tin lunchbox and a Thermos flask. 'Fancy a bite to eat? I've got enough for two.'

'I'll say! You're heaven-sent, you are,' Florrie said, dropping the rag she'd been using to clean the dirty window panes back into the bowl of white vinegar solution.

'Smells like a chip shop in here,' Thom said, wrinkling his nose. 'Fancy sitting in the garden? It's warmer out now.'

Together, they sat on the new swings, gently rocking back and forth as they polished off his cheese sandwiches and strong tea.

'Do you think this stock market business will mean Sir Richard will have to lay off staff?' Florrie asked, gazing at the cottage that now looked more like a handsome country home.

Thom shook his head. 'I don't know much about money because I've never had any, but I do know his type cry poverty when they're still sitting on a king's ransom. The rich get richer, Florrie.'

'And the poor get poorer,' she finished. She pointed to the cottage. 'But it was right kind of him to do this, especially with his steel merger going to the dogs and that Wall Street Crash.'

Thom nodded. 'I suppose. But when houses like this are standing empty in the countryside, with all those desperate people sleeping four, five to a bed in city slums, because they've been laid off by mill owners like the Harding-Bournes—'

'Mam *was* laid off from a Harding-Bourne mill!' Florrie said.

'Well, only right his nibs should put his hand in his pocket for your mam, then. About time that lot did something right, with all the money they squander on high living, while honest working folk are starving not fifteen mile away. I bet your mam'll be paying rent and all.'

Florrie nodded. 'Oh aye. She won't be living here for free. Lady Charlotte wanted to offer her the job with just a small allowance for food in return for a roof over her and the children's heads, but Mrs Douglas intervened with Sir Richard and insisted my mother still gets paid the going rate—'

'Good old Bertha. Good for her!'

'Mam still has to pay rent – cheaper than what she'd pay in the village, but still . . .'

Thom tutted and sighed.

They spent the rest of their break in companionable silence.

'Right, best get on,' Thom said presently, getting to his feet. 'I've got quite a bit of spare wood, so I'm going to knock together a bench for your mam.'

'Oh, you don't have to do that, Thom,' Florrie said. 'It's your day off!'

'I want to do it. It's no trouble at all.'

For the rest of the day, as Florrie methodically worked her way from room to room, scrubbing and rubbing and buffing the windows until they gleamed, she stole glances outside at Thom. She thought about his acts of kindness and his clear affection for her. Yet she also found herself puzzling over the reasons why Sir Richard might have incurred such enormous expense in renovating the cottage. Perhaps Thom's inference – that it was to assuage the guilty conscience of a rich man – was right, and the bill would simply be pocket change to a man of Sir Richard's considerable wealth. Or could it be that Sir Richard had wrested the gamekeeper's cottage back from Mother Nature's fierce grip out of fondness for her?

16

'Will you ask Cook to prepare me some eggs Benedict? There's a dear.' Lady Charlotte treated Florrie to a sickly smile. In the white light emanating from the frosty December scene outside, her skin appeared pasty and wan. 'I do feel rather horrid this morning.' She held a hand to her forehead.

'Of course, my lady,' Florrie said, curtseying.

Sir Richard entered the dining room at that moment, wearing a thick jumper, patched at the elbows, and rubbing his hands together. He made straight for the soup tureen that contained Cook's hearty broth. 'First of all, darling, it's already past noon,' he said, ladling some soup into a bowl. 'And second of all, perhaps you wouldn't feel quite so dismal if you didn't stay up until the small hours, drinking champagne and dancing with my idiot brother.' He carried his bowl to the table, batting Florrie away as she tried to intervene and take the bowl from him. 'I'm quite capable of serving myself soup, Florrie dear. But I'll happily let you procure me a slice of bread and butter, if you'd be so kind.' He smiled at her. 'Thank you so much. And do get my wife's eggs before she expires on us.'

Florrie studied her employer's face, looking for signs that he'd remembered today was a momentous milestone for the Bickerstaff family: Mam and the children were finally coming to live on the Holcombe Estate. She looked at him expectantly for several beats of her heart, but then realized from his furrowed brow and the faraway look on his face that his mind was elsewhere.

'Oh, and could you tell Arkwright I'm urgently expecting a telephone call from New York?' he said. 'The architect of the Chrysler Building – William Van Alen. They're five hours behind over there, but tell Arkwright to come and find me the moment he rings. Don't forget, will you?'

'William Van Alen,' Florrie repeated. 'I'll remember.'

Sir Richard turned to Lady Charlotte, who was idly looking at her nails. 'The scoundrel has been trying to undercut us by bringing in Pennsylvanian steel from that Carnegie lot.'

'Oh, you are *so* boring, Dicky. Do shut up. You're giving me a headache.'

Florrie was so consumed by thoughts of greeting her family at the train station later that afternoon, however, that she'd completely forgotten the architect's name by the time she found Arkwright.

While Cook prepared the eggs Benedict, she sought out Mrs Douglas to ask if she'd be able to take a few hours off to help her family settle in. She found the housekeeper in the music room. Spying her through a crack in the door, Florrie could hear she was in the middle of upbraiding Mabel for having neglected her duties.

'But I'd already done everything,' Mabel protested. Though she was out of sight, the defiance in the maid's voice was audible. 'Dame Elizabeth said she didn't need owt.'

'She didn't need *anything*,' Mrs Douglas said, her hands laced together in front of her, reminiscent of a stern schoolmarm. 'Speak properly, girl! Stand up straight! And even if you felt there was nothing else to do, that did not give you carte blanche to spend the rest of your shift smoking and getting up to Lord-knows-what with the stableboys behind the stables. You should have come to me and asked for extra duties.'

'Yid.'

Florrie had raised her fist to knock at the door, but breathed in sharply when she heard Mabel utter the slur. Had she imagined it?

'*What* did you call me?'

'You heard,' Mabel said. 'You're a dirty Yid, Bertha, and you can find some other mug to skivvy for that fussy old bag, Dame Elizabeth, with her mood swings and secretive ways. I've had it with Holcombe Hall!'

Mabel stormed out of the music room, red in the face. She glared at Florrie. 'You heard enough, goody-two-shoes? Get out my way!' She pushed past and ran down the hallway.

'I heard how you spoke to Mrs Douglas, Mabel Woolley!' Florrie called after her. 'You should be ashamed of yourself.'

She turned her attention back to the music room and the housekeeper, who she could hear was quietly sobbing inside. Finally, she steeled herself to knock quietly. 'Mrs Douglas? Are you all right?' She pushed the music room door open and saw the housekeeper pressing her fingers to her eyes, wearing a wretched expression.

'Ooh, hey. There, there, Mrs Douglas.' Florrie produced a clean handkerchief from her pocket and held it out.

Mrs Douglas took the handkerchief and smiled sadly. 'How much of that did you hear?'

'Enough,' Florrie said. 'I'm really sorry Mabel said those hateful things. She couldn't possibly mean them. I'll get her to apologize.'

Dabbing at her eyes, Mrs Douglas seemed to regain her composure. 'Don't bother, Florrie, love. I'd rather she just went. It's bad enough hearing Sir Hugh and Lady Charlotte consorting with their fascist pals, but I don't need it from my girls.'

'I had no idea you're Jewish,' Florrie said. 'Douglas isn't a typically Jewish surname.'

Mrs Douglas exhaled hard. 'Aye, well. My surname's actually Demsky. My father came over from Poland at the turn of the century . . . escaped the pogroms over there. You know what those are?'

Florrie shook her head.

'Best you don't.' Mrs Douglas squeezed her arm. 'Violence the likes of which I hope never to see in England. But if Sir Hugh's pal, Walter Knight-Downey, and people like that big German who came to visit Lady Charlotte . . . if their ilk have their way . . . But anyway, my poor father risked life and limb to get here. He sailed over on a leaky cattle boat. Thought he was disembarking at New York.' She chuckled sadly. 'He got quite the surprise when he realized he'd got swindled by the captain and dumped off at Liverpool docks. But turns out, he wasn't much welcome here, either. He changed our family name so we could keep our heads below the parapet.' She placed a hand over her chest and coughed.

'How did Mabel know? I've been here ten year and I didn't have a clue.'

Mrs Douglas shrugged. 'Folk like her are taught hatred at the knee. They sniff Jews out.' She cleared her throat and smiled. 'Anyway, never mind that. What was it you wanted, dear?'

'Well . . .' Florrie considered how Mabel had been chastised for shirking her duty, and suddenly thought better of requesting time off. 'It's nothing.'

'No, go on.'

Florrie bit her lip. 'Well, my mam and my nieces and nephew arrive on the afternoon train from Manchester. I just wanted to ask if I could take a couple of hours off to help them settle in, if I make it up another day. But then I overheard you giving Mabel a dressing-down for taking liberties, so . . . Honestly, forget it.'

'You're not Mabel,' Mrs Douglas said. 'You go above and beyond your duty, and you carry more responsibility than you're being paid for.' She stroked Florrie's cheek. 'Once lunch is over, you take the rest of the day off, chuck. I insist. Today's special. You've made a minor miracle happen, getting Sir Richard to renovate that cottage so that someone deserving can have a fresh start in it. Be with your family. Enjoy every minute of it. I'll ask that Cook sends Sally over with a hearty meal for you all, and I'll look forward to meeting my new laundress tomorrow morning!'

'It's late,' Florrie said, looking at her battered old wrist-watch. 'I hope there isn't a problem.' She had changed into her Sunday-best frock and wore her woollen winter coat and a thick scarf that Cook had knitted for her as a Christmas gift the previous year, but on the rural station platform, which offered no shelter from the bitter-cold elements, she shivered and stamped her numb feet.

Thom smiled at her. 'What problem could there be?'

Florrie shook her head, imagining all sorts of woeful scenarios. 'Ice on the line? Maybe they missed the train.'

He laughed. 'Train isn't even here yet, and you're worrying they missed it? By heck, Florrie, stop fretting! It'll arrive soon enough. It's not like it's coming all the way from Portsmouth.' His breath steamed on the air. He nudged her playfully. 'You're as wound up as that watch you keep checking!'

'I've been waiting months and months for this moment,' she said, wistfully hoping to see a plume of smoke billowing up from between the trees, where the train track cut through a swathe of forest. She turned to Thom, feeling warmed by his smile. 'If it weren't for you, they'd still be stuck in Manchester on their uppers.' Daring to take his large gloved hand, she squeezed it affectionately. 'You're a bobby-dazzler.'

Suddenly her words were swallowed up by the chug-chug of a steam train, carried to them on the freezing wind. She looked up to see that longed-for plume of smoke, trailing behind the train from Manchester. 'At last!'

With squealing brakes and the rattle of its wheels on the track, the train appeared as a black and red smudge emerging from the treeline, its locomotive engine growing ever larger until its colossal metal bulk loomed above them, and the choking stink of burning coal and smoke that drifted down on to the platform was almost overwhelming. Florrie covered her ears against the deafening squeal as the train slowed at the platform's edge. She peered through the slowly passing windows set in the doors, hoping to spot her mother. 'I can't see her. Oh, you're kidding. She's not there. She must have missed her train!'

The train came to a standstill.

'Stop fretting, Florrie,' Thom said. 'Can't be many getting off at Holcombe. I bet she's wrestling with those little'uns and their baggage.'

The blood rushed in Florrie's pounding ears. A uniformed member of the train's staff stepped off the footplate, checking his fob watch. She watched as several hands slid through opened windows to unlock the doors from the outside. Travellers emerged into the cold afternoon. Instantly recognizable were the town's butcher and a schoolteacher whom she'd once met at church. There also appeared a man whose impeccably shiny, two-tone brogues, felt hat and suitcase marked him out as a possible travelling salesman. Where was Mam, though?

17

Florrie ran the length of the platform, desperately peering through the windows. Finally, she spotted her mother struggling at the last door.

'Mam! Mam! I'm here!' she called out. She beckoned Thom over to help.

'I can't get this blinking door open while I'm holding the baby,' Mam said.

The train conductor blew his whistle once. 'All aboard who's coming aboard,' he shouted.

'Wait!' Florrie shouted. 'My mother's stuck. She needs to get off. Don't leave without letting her off!'

The conductor hastened over, and between him and Thom, they managed to bundle Mam, the children, four cardboard suitcases and Alice's pram safely on to the platform.

As the conductor stepped back on to the locomotive's footplate and blew his whistle twice, Florrie flung her arms around her mother and baby Alice. 'You made it! I was so worried.' She kissed Alice's florid cheek and noticed the baby had a streaming nose and watering eyes. 'Is she poorly?' Taking out a handkerchief, she gently wiped the baby's nose.

'Aye. Nelly and all. They caught it from her next door's lot.'

Florrie knelt to greet her tiny niece and noticed how inflamed her cheeks also were. Nelly tugged at the sludge-green knitted pixie hood that was tied beneath her chin, working herself into a frenzy of irritation that she couldn't remove the hat.

'Itchy, Nana! Itchy!' she cried.

Only George seemed in fine fettle. He was staring up at Thom, sucking his thumb.

'Pleased to meet you, young man. I'm Thom. I work with your Aunty Florrie.' Thom bent down and stuck his hand out to shake George's hand, and the little boy giggled.

Yet when the train's deafening whistle sounded, all three children started and then burst into tears.

'Oh, dear, what a to-do!' Florrie said, taking Alice and holding her tightly, while Mam set up the pram and adjusted the blankets inside. She then lifted the baby into the pram and popped Nelly in beside her, moved by the sight of the three hysterical children and an evidently panic-stricken Mam. The dark circles beneath her mother's eyes and the way that her clothes hung loose on her spoke to months of struggling to make ends meet and tending to such tiny children under the most difficult of circumstances. 'Looks like we got you into the fresh air of the country in the nick of time, I'd say.'

The children soon cheered up when they caught sight of the two enormous chestnut horses that were pulling the Harding-Bournes' old bow-fronted carriage.

'How's about that for transport?' Florrie said, taking George by the hand.

'Can I pat the horsies?' George asked.

''Course you can, pal,' Thom said. He hefted George into the air and allowed him to stroke one of the horse's flanks. 'Fancy riding with me? I'll let you hold the reins.'

George clapped his hands with glee. 'I'll say!'

Once Thom had loaded the carriage with Mam's belongings and the pram had been safely stowed, Florrie watched with no small degree of satisfaction as he helped her little nephew up to the cab.

'Look, Aunty Flo! I'm driving the horsies.'

'You're doing a cracking job, Georgie boy.' Florrie gave him the thumbs up and proceeded to clamber into the carriage alongside her mother and nieces.

Her mother ran her hand over the claret leather studded upholstery. 'This is fancy.'

'Thom reckons it's a good fifty years old, this carriage,' Florrie said. 'But when you've got a team of stable lads and valets and that, and when no expense was spared in the first place, it's easy to keep things looking tip-top. You should see the family's cars.' She raised her eyebrows above wide eyes, knowing Mam would scarcely believe the standards of luxury that the Harding-Bournes were used to.

The girls soon settled with the clip-clop of the horses' hooves and the rhythmic rumble and rattle of the carriage's wheels on the cobbled road. Florrie observed with delight how both Nelly and Alice sat on hers and Mam's laps, staring outside at the small, picturesque village, with its charming sandstone houses and church, all set against the backdrop of farmland on one side – ordinarily green, but today, everything was dusted in a thick layer of white hoar frost – and the moorland of Holcombe Hill the other.

'Ooh, what's that tower?' Mam asked, pointing to the landmark that sat on the hill's summit.

'Peel Monument, it's called,' Florrie said. 'After some old Prime Minister, I'm told.'

'Sir Robert Peel?'

'Aye. That's the one. He was from round here. Bury, I think. Certain times of the year, the hill's covered in purple heather. It's lovely, isn't it?'

Mam nodded and tutted wistfully. She pointed to some sheep in the distance. 'It's a different world.'

Thom drove the carriage beyond the village, deep into the forested countryside where the bare branches of the deciduous trees were clothed in feathery white. Everything shone like diamond dust in the winter sun, dazzling Florrie so that she had to shield her eyes. They emerged finally from the forest into the undulating bucolic paradise that Florrie knew as home. Passing between the tall stone gateposts that marked the entrance to the estate, each topped with a stone raven and carved with the family's crest, she saw how her mother's mouth fell open.

'Is this it?' Mam asked.

Florrie nodded. 'Welcome to the Holcombe Estate.' She grabbed her mother and planted a kiss on the old lady's cheek. 'This is where you live, now.'

As the horses clip-clopped along the winding drive and they rounded a corner, she delighted in George's excited squeal coming from the cab. He had clearly just spotted what they could not yet see from the windows in the carriage, but they rolled around another bend in Capability Brown's sculpted grounds and suddenly, the sprawling golden sandstone glory of Holcombe Hall came into view.

'Flaming heck,' Mam said. 'Sweet Jesus! Is *this* where you've been in service the last ten years?'

Chuckling, Florrie nodded. 'Aye. Lovely, isn't it?'

'Lovely's an understatement. Look at those pillars and that dome over the middle and the stone lions either side of the steps! *That's* their front door? The size of it all! It's like it was built for giants.'

Florrie pointed to the small windows, just visible behind the decorative stone parapet that partly concealed the uppermost floor. 'See those attic windows . . .? The one four from the left is my room.' She felt a ball of warm pride swell within her, banishing the chill of the December day. 'I'll take you over to the big house tomorrow so you can meet Mrs Douglas, the housekeeper – your new boss. But first, let's get you into *your* house.'

Mam gazed out at a picturesque Holcombe Hall, drenched in the sunshine of a fine winter's afternoon, and for the first time since she'd stepped off the train – perhaps the first time for some years – Florrie saw her mother smile.

Thom drove the carriage past the orchard to the gamekeeper's cottage and brought it to a halt.

'We're here,' Florrie said.

When they had all disembarked from the carriage, they stood together, admiring the blush-pink Tudor cottage that glowed welcomingly in the sun. The recently retiled roof looked as if it had been dusted in icing sugar.

Clutching a now-sleeping Alice to her chest, Florrie nuzzled the fluffy hair on her niece's head. 'It's like the gingerbread house in *Hansel and Gretel*,' she said softly to her mother. 'Remember when Dad used to read that to me at bedtime, when I was little? Ooh, I did love the pictures.'

Mam nodded, looking around at the neat, recently tamed and replanted garden. She gasped. 'Are those hydrangeas under the window?'

'I see you've got an eye for plants, Mrs Bickerstaff,' Thom said.

'Call me Matilda, son.'

He grinned and touched his cap. 'They're lovely old blue mopheads, Matilda. They were big as Florrie by the end of the summer. I cut them back hard so the joiner could get to the windows to fix some rot on the frames, like. But they should flower nice in a couple of years' time.'

'I *love* hydrangeas!' She turned back to Florrie, tears standing in her eyes. Then she grabbed Florrie's hand and kissed her knuckles. 'You are so . . . What did I do to deserve you? My cup runneth over.'

Florrie took the key to the cottage out of her pocket and pressed it into her mother's palm. 'There you go. Go and see if you like the furniture I picked out. I got the range going earlier, so it should be nice and warm in the scullery, at least.'

Mam gasped and stared at the key in her hand as though it were a precious jewel. Then she looked up at the sky, held the key to her chest and said, 'What I'd give for our Reenie to be here, sharing in this good fortune.'

'I wish we could have saved her, Mam,' Florrie said, shaking her head dolefully, visited by the bitter memory of Irene breathing her last in the hospital bed. 'I wish I could have arranged all this before she got ill, so she could have moved out here with you. She'd still be alive now.' She swallowed her sorrow and guilt, not wanting to upset the children by weeping. 'But . . . She'll be watching from up there, smiling down on us all, knowing our Reenie. She'd want you and the kids to have a fresh start.'

Mam nodded thoughtfully, walked determinedly to the front door and unlocked it. She went inside, leaving the children in the garden with Florrie.

'Happen I'll bring some logs in, then,' Thom said, blowing on his fingertips which poked through the holes in his woollen gloves. 'It's cold enough to freeze the balls off a brass monkey. So let's get a nice fire going in the parlour and bedrooms, eh?' He gathered up a large stack of logs that had been split and left neatly piled against the side of the house.

'Will I have a bedroom all to myself?' George asked, looking up at Florrie, his wide eyes shining with curiosity.

'Let's go inside and see, shall we?' Florrie said, winking. She took Nelly's hand and carried Alice over the threshold into the cottage's boot room.

She found her mother in the parlour – now furnished with a grand old brocade settee and a comfortable if old-fashioned winged armchair. There was everything a family might want from a parlour: paraffin lamps set on sturdy oak side tables and an old, jewel-coloured Persian rug covering the cold floor. Mam was turning slowly on the spot, wearing an expression of wonder as she took everything in.

'I feel like I'm in a dream,' she said, coming to a halt and clasping her hands beneath her chin.

'There's no electricity in here yet, but there's a coal boiler upstairs what'll give you hot water for the indoor bathroom.'

'*An indoor bathroom?*' Mam asked, her voice high-pitched with apparent disbelief.

Florrie nodded and chuckled. 'You should see it. It's the height of modern glamour, I'll have you know. Sir Richard said he'll get electric lighting in here as soon as he can. Maybe in the new year.' Florrie gently rocked Alice in her arms. 'Do you like it, then?'

Thom strode across the parlour, carrying some logs. He got to his knees and started to place the logs in the fire basket. 'Soon get it toasty in here, Matilda.'

Mam walked to the window and looked out at the front garden. She turned back to Florrie. 'I don't like it. I *love* it.'

18

'Pass us the red bauble,' Florrie said, holding out her hand. She glanced outside at the flakes of snow that were falling gently. It was cold enough to have started settling on the ground, though there was not more than an inch of the stuff. Shivering, Florrie grimaced and then turned her attention back to Sally. 'If it's going to snow, I do wish it would snow properly. I like fat snow, me. Christmassy snow – deep enough to squeak when you walk in it. I can't wait for our George and Nelly to be able to play in proper Holcombe snow.'

Sally shifted her position at the base of the spruce pine from sitting cross-legged to kneeling. Her knees cracked audibly. 'Ooh, hey. That doesn't sound right, does it? That's scrubbing all them floors, that is.' She selected one of the red glass baubles and handed it up to Florrie. 'Tree's a reet big'un this year, isn't it? Must be twenty foot.'

Florrie chuckled. 'Well, it's not quite that high, but it didn't half take some ingenuity from Thom, getting it through that door.' She nodded her head towards the doorway that connected the drawing room to the dining room. The door had been left slightly ajar. 'First, Lady Charlotte wanted it in there to brighten up mealtimes. Then Dame Elizabeth insisted it go in here.'

'That lot could afford fifty Christmas trees if they wanted. Don't they normally have about five? One in the hallway, one in't ballroom, upstairs, downstairs and in my lady's chamber!'

Florrie hung the red bauble, found she was dissatisfied with the placement and moved it a couple of branches lower. 'Yellow bauble, please.' She held out her hand again and idly looked out of the window as she did so. 'They're tightening their belts, apparently. Not that chopping down a tree or three costs them anything. Mean-spirited so-and-sos!' She caught sight of her mother, trudging across the grounds from the direction of the orchard, pushing a pram full of Alice and Nelly, piled high at the feet-end with what appeared to be ironed bedding. Florrie knew she'd opted to do the ironing in the gamekeeper's cottage rather than in the Hall's laundry, if only so that the children could safely busy themselves in their playpen or the garden, rather than being cooped up and on their best behaviour in a spartan tiled room that contained only the mangle and a washtub for entertainment. Now, George ran on ahead through the thin smattering of snow, rolling a hoop with a stick. He was dressed in sensible long trousers and a thick woollen coat – hand-me-downs that had once belonged to Sir Hugh, donated by Dame Elizabeth, so Mam had cooed with gratitude. Florrie was pleased to see that only a fortnight after their arrival, her family were already looking much better for a life in the countryside with good, fresh food on the table every day.

'Bauble!' Sally shouted, clicking her fingers. 'Wake up, daydreamer.'

Florrie took the yellow bauble from her, and in companionable silence, they continued to dress the tree. The peace and quiet was broken only by the sudden sound of people in the dining room. She frowned down at Sally questioningly and pointed to the doorway that linked the two rooms.

Sally merely shrugged, then cupped her hand behind her ear and winked.

'Do sit down, Hugh. You're always late. You'll be the last to arrive at your own funeral, no doubt.' It was Dame Elizabeth's voice.

'Should I apologize for not jumping to attention, Mama? And there was me thinking I was a grown man!' Florrie recognized the indolent tones of Sir Hugh.

'For heaven's sake, Hugh, show Mama some respect. This is about the family's future.' That was clearly Sir Richard speaking.

'Funny. I thought you were now the head of the family, Dicky. Has our mother stripped you of your authority?' Sir Hugh laughed. 'It's like that Kafka novella about the young chap being trumped by his decrepit father. What was it called again?'

'It's called *Das Urteil,* and I sincerely doubt *you* could have read it, let alone understood it.'

'My German's jolly good, I'll have you know.'

'It's just about adequate if you're in Berlin and need to order another bottle of champagne. Do stop pretending to be an intellectual, Hugh, just because you consort with the likes of that idiot scribbler, Waugh. I can tell when you're parroting their opinions.'

'You are very mean to poor Hugh, Richard.' Lady Charlotte was clearly also in attendance.

There was the sound of hands being clapped together. 'Boys, do stop locking horns,' Dame Elizabeth said. 'I need you to listen to what I have to say, but I can't speak if you're behaving like infants.'

At the base of the tree, Sally started to snigger. Florrie held her finger to her lips, impressing on her how important it was for them to keep quiet.

'Do go on, Mama. We're listening. *I'm* listening. What's preying on your mind?'

Dame Elizabeth lowered her voice so that Sally crawled across the floor and sat with her back against the drawing room wall, close to the door. Florrie tiptoed over to join her, careful to bring with her a box of decorations to look busy in the event that Mrs Douglas or Arkwright caught them eavesdropping.

Dame Elizabeth began to speak. 'Now, I wanted to speak to you all away from the staff, because I am very concerned that the Hatry trial is going to bring our family into disrepute.'

'Don't worry, Mama,' Sir Richard said. 'There's been something of a whip-round to fund his defence. The poor chap says it was all an error of judgement to save the steel merger. He only had our best interests at heart.' There was a superficial confidence to his tone of voice, but Florrie could hear underlying doubt.

'There is *no* excuse for being a fraudster.' Dame

Elizabeth said. 'I'm surprised at you, Richard. I had always thought your judgement to be sound.'

'It *is* sound. I am inclined to believe him, and I contributed a respectable sum to his defence pot, which runs to almost one hundred thousand dollars.'

'What a preposterously large sum,' Dame Elizabeth said. 'Should you be frittering away our family's money on this con man, Richard?'

'I'm not the only one who believes him, Mama. We're hopeful he'll be acquitted.'

'That's not what I've heard,' Sir Hugh said. 'I've heard the odds are strong that he's facing a long spell in prison.'

'What the hell do you know about the world of business, you fop?' Richard asked. 'Monkey business, perhaps! You've never done a day's work in your life.'

'I have friends in all the best circles, including the judiciary. Socially, my dear brother, you have always been entirely eclipsed by the brightness of my star.'

'Hugh, I understand it was you who originally introduced Richard to this good-time Hatry fool, so I wouldn't be so cocksure.'

Florrie clasped her hand to her mouth, trying desperately to stifle a giggle. Sally's shoulders were shaking with mirth.

'And Richard, you would do well to distance yourself from Hatry once and for all,' Dame Elizabeth said. 'I *will not* have this family's name being dragged into disrepute. And the principal reason I wanted to talk to you all is the American financial chaos causing ripples here in Britain. How are the businesses coping since the Wall Street debacle?'

Sir Richard spoke. 'It's not the best, I'm afraid. We're hanging on by the skin of our teeth to our steel interests across the pond. Fortunately, India shows no sign of its appetite for locomotives waning, so that should shelter us from some of the storm. But our mining and shipbuilding interests are suffering.'

'We are in peace time,' Dame Elizabeth said. 'Your father always said war was terribly good for business. Sadly, we amassed a considerable sum from naval shipbuilding during the Great War but paid for it with the life of our darling James. Let us pray we do not see Britain at war again in our lifetimes. I could not bear to lose another son.' She sighed deeply and the family fell silent for a moment. Then she sniffed and spoke again. 'You have lost money though, haven't you?'

'I'm afraid I lost rather a large investment in Hatry's company,' Sir Richard said. 'And our company's shares lost a good deal of their value, which I fear they may never regain. The mills are also doing badly. Nobody wants our fabric at the moment. Demand is down across the board. I've been laying staff off for a while, and I fear the situation will only deteriorate, sadly.'

'Are you quite certain you need me here?' Lady Charlotte asked. 'Only, I have a pheasant shoot and a soirée this evening, and it won't do if my guests arrive and find me looking like a charlady.'

Sally nudged Florrie and rolled her eyes.

'You and Hugh, of all people, need to listen most

closely to what I'm about to say,' Dame Elizabeth said. 'I heard the phrase uttered on the wireless the other day that people must, "tighten their belts". I thought that particular metaphor rather apt. We too at Holcombe Hall must tighten our belts if we're to weather this dreadful downturn in international fortunes. I will not lose Holcombe Estate, do you understand?' She spoke quietly, though her tone was ferocious. 'And I will not tolerate sliding into genteel poverty, keeping up appearances while the roof leaks. Richard, I'd rather you prioritized maintaining the fabric of the Hall itself before you go spending large sums on refurbishing outbuildings for the servants, however good they might be at their jobs.' Her tone was castigatory. Florrie felt her cheeks heat up like Cook's steamed puddings. She pressed her lips together, cringing with embarrassment.

When Dame Elizabeth uttered the next admonition, Florrie imagined that she was glaring pointedly at Lady Charlotte and Sir Hugh. 'That means no more balls, no more profligate entertaining, no more costly shooting weekends that end in drunken revelry and banquets fit for a Roman emperor. You are not Caligula, Hugh. And Charlotte, I would rather you reined in your ostentatious couture habits and your frequent trips to Paris.'

'But *Tatler*'s readership has certain expectations that a close relative of His Majesty King George V should—'

The sound of someone thumping the table came from the dining room. Dame Elizabeth spoke with an air of grim finality. 'Young lady, while you're my daughter-in-law, living under *my* roof, I expect you to worry less about appearing in *Tatler* and more about curbing your expenditure to ensure that when you eventually *do* produce an heir, he will have something worth inheriting.'

Florrie breathed in sharply. Sally had formed a perfect 'O' with her lips and then burst into another fit of silent giggles. Florrie shushed her friend once again.

'Are you going to let her speak to me like that, Richard?' Lady Charlotte asked, clearly affronted.

'Mother, steady on!' Sir Richard said. 'We are trying to conceive.'

'I shan't steady on, young man, and I am levelling this advice not just at Charlotte but at you too, Hugh. Your father was a highly respected peer, as was his father, as am I. *You* consort with types unbefitting of a Harding-Bourne. Until this financial fiasco blows over, our priority is to keep our costs down – and that precludes lavishing any more money on renovating old outbuildings to house waifs and strays related to your favourite staff members, Richard . . .'

Florrie felt a rash itch its way up her neck. Sally clearly sensed her discomfort, laying a placatory hand on her arm.

'I'm rather glad the gamekeeper's cottage is restored to its former glory,' Sir Richard said. 'And I think it's delightful that there are children on the estate again. I make no apology for materially improving a family's life at the same time as gaining a laundress, which I understand from Mrs Douglas that we desperately needed. But I take your point, Mama. We may well have to shed some staff, and we should certainly watch the pennies.

Switching lights off, if we're not in the room. Only heating rooms when necessary.'

'And no more parties,' Dame Elizabeth said.

'Except for this evening,' Lady Charlotte said, sounding affronted. 'I can't possibly cancel at this late stage.'

'Kindly ensure this is the last one.'

'Will you be coming on the shoot this afternoon, Dicky boy?' asked Sir Hugh.

'Certainly not,' Sir Richard said. 'I have important matters to attend to in my study.'

Hearing movement in the other room, Florrie and Sally scrambled back over to the Christmas tree and resumed their decorating task – not a moment too soon, since Sir Richard popped his head into the drawing room and gave them a merry wave.

'What ho, girls! Didn't realize you were beavering away in here. It's looking jolly festive. Keep up the good work.'

Once they were alone, Sally locked eyes with Florrie. 'Are we going to get the order of the boot?'

19

'Now, you make sure you collect the ladies' coats when the guests return from the pheasant shoot,' Mrs Douglas told Florrie and Sally, once the table had been laid for dinner. 'Mr Arkwright has ordered Danny to wait on the gentlemen.' She glanced out of the window. 'They'll be coming in any minute.'

Florrie nodded. 'Yes, Mrs Douglas.' She spotted a wine goblet that had a watermark on it. She snatched it up and polished the mark away on the skirt of her apron. 'The ladies will need help dressing for dinner, won't they?'

Mrs Douglas straightened the cutlery on Sir Richard's place setting at the head of the table. 'Sally, I do wish you'd pay attention to detail, dear. You've put the fish knife in the wrong place and the main course knife and fork are crooked.' She sighed. 'It's really not good enough.'

Sally curtseyed. 'Sorry, Mrs D. I am really trying.'

'Yes, you are trying!' Mrs Douglas's stern expression softened. 'Practice makes perfect, eh?'

Casting her mind back to the conversation she'd overheard between the Harding-Bournes, Florrie wondered if she shouldn't tip Mrs Douglas the wink that Sir Richard would be looking for opportunities to cull domestic staff. *Last in, first out.* She rubbed her fingers against her thumbs nervously. *Mam and the children rely on me fighting their corner.* There was nothing else for it but the truth. 'Mrs Douglas, could I ask you something delicate in nature?'

Sally's eyes narrowed and she shook her head at Florrie as if she'd anticipated the subject Florrie was about to broach.

'Out with it.' Mrs Douglas was distracted by a large silver tureen stand that wasn't standing quite central in the table.

'I might have overheard Dame Elizabeth saying something to Sir Richard about tightening belts because of this Wall Street Crash thing.'

'Very sensible. If they drank less champagne and Lady Charlotte bought fewer dresses and furs, they'd save a king's ransom.'

'Only there was mention of maybe cutting back on staff to save money, and I'm worried, like . . . Especially with my mam being the latest addition to the domestic side.'

Mrs Douglas froze and turned to face Florrie. 'Losing staff?'

'Are we going to get the boot, Mrs D?' Sally asked. 'Because my family would starve without the money I send home.'

'Nobody's getting the boot.' Pink appeared in Mrs Douglas's cheeks, quickly turning to beetroot red. 'Not while I've got breath in my body. *I'm* the housekeeper of Holcombe Hall. Anybody comes for my girls, they'll have to come through me. And that includes Sir Richard.'

Feeling buoyed by Mrs Douglas's assurances, Florrie stood shivering in the entrance hall with Sally, Danny and another of the footmen, waiting to receive the shooting party.

Arkwright opened the door just as the group of seven appeared at the bottom of the stone steps. He bowed, and when he spoke, his tone was as obsequious as ever. 'A successful shoot, I trust.'

'Terrible.' Sir Hugh flung his coat at him with such vigour that Arkwright stumbled backwards. 'All the birds had gone to ground. I need a drink. Fix me a Tom Collins, will you?'

Lady Charlotte wriggled out of her tweed coat, not even glancing at Florrie as she took it. 'Daphne, darling, you really are a crack shot. I don't think Hugh is ever going to recover from you being the only member of the party to bag a bird.' She trilled with laughter.

Daphne le Montford slapped a territorial hand on Sir Hugh's shoulder and batted her eyelashes at him. 'Can you ever forgive me, Hugh?'

Sir Hugh slid his arm around the starlet's waist. 'I'll forgive you anything, Daphne.'

Among the guests, Florrie recognized Walter Knight-Downey, Sir Hugh's perennially badly behaved best friend, and the Prussian prince, Hans von Grunwald, who had made her feel decidedly uncomfortable when he had picnicked in the Hall's rose garden. There was another couple – an eccentric-looking man who wore a paisley silk cravat, and a dour-looking woman with an overly short fringe to her black bobbed hair. Florrie could not be entirely certain if they were writers or artists, but she recognized their faces, either from one of the balls that Lady Charlotte had thrown or else from inside the pages of one of Lady Charlotte's high society magazines.

Though her arms ached from decorating the Christmas tree's upper branches and fatigue made her eyelids heavy after staying up with a teething Alice so that Mam could sleep, Florrie performed her duties without complaint. She helped Lady Charlotte to dress for dinner, checked that Sally was coping with the female guests' demands, and then made her way down to the kitchens to collect the individual starter plates that Cook had lovingly prepared. With two of the other serving staff in bed with the flu, Mrs Douglas insisted she would also pitch in.

In the dining room, the guests gathered and Sir Richard finally appeared, wearing black tie and smiling but seeming somewhat distracted. As she set the starter plates down unobtrusively, Florrie listened to the guests' conversation.

'I think it's all jolly depressing,' Sir Hugh said, forking ruefully at his prawns. 'We've all been having a high time, and now the bally Yanks have ruined it all, and everyone's going to stop having fun.'

Walter Knight-Downey held his wine glass up to the candlelight so that it glowed golden-yellow. He narrowed his eyes. 'How do you think a Labour Prime Minister like Ramsay MacDonald is going to cope with even longer queues for the labour exchange? They're little more than Bolsheviks, the Labour Party. I tell you, they're going to build poky little boxes all over our beautiful green countryside to rent out to ne'er-do-wells, and who is going to fund these jobless types in an island that's bursting at the seams with forty million people crammed on to it?'

'It is no better in Germany,' von Grunwald said, chewing on a prawn. 'The Weimar Republic is crumbling because the Americans have withdrawn all their investments, and we have over three million without jobs. Hindenburg is way out of his depth. He couldn't control the country if he tried.' He raised an eyebrow. 'Hardly surprising since the Jews control everything.'

'I'm sure that's not the case,' Sir Richard said, raising an eyebrow.

Florrie almost gasped at the German's comment. Standing by the serving table, she shot a sideways glance at Mrs Douglas. They locked eyes, but Mrs Douglas shook her head and pressed her index finger to her lips.

Unaware that he was commenting in earshot of a Jewish woman, von Grunwald went on. 'Oh, but it is. Jews caused the inflation in the first place. It is their greed that has brought about the crash, and now the whole world is destabilized. And the Communists . . .' He smirked and aggressively bit his prawn in half. While he chewed in silence, Lady Charlotte, Sir Hugh and their guests seemed to wait with bated breath to hear his next nugget of wisdom. 'Every week they take over Berlin with their demonstrations, as if they have the solution, but they are nothing but Stalin's pawns.'

'Not *prawns*, though, eh?' Lady Charlotte laughed at her own joke, looking to the others for a reaction.

Daphne le Montford joined in, leaning coquettishly towards von Grunwald, who sat opposite her. 'I rather like your Herr Hitler. I'm not sure about his moustache, though.' She giggled. 'And he seems a terribly serious chap.'

'I don't trust Hitler's national socialism one bit,' Sir Richard said. 'He's little more than a bully-boy, with his brownshirt thugs.'

'Nonsense. He's a jolly good orator.' Walter Knight-Downey took another gulp of his wine, loosened his bow tie and left it hanging freely around his neck. 'My pal Mosley thinks him deeply charismatic. And he's completely correct about the Jews. Why, they run the banks, don't they? Rothschild and his ilk.'

'Don't you think such talk is a little crass for the dinner table, Walter?' Sir Richard asked.

'There are Rothschilds everywhere,' Hans said, undeterred. 'Britain, Austria . . . Nowhere is safe.'

'Hans is right,' Daphne said, toying with a lettuce leaf. 'The Jews are responsible for this crash lark.' She raised her glass. 'Down with those party-poopers!'

'Such vermin,' Walter said. 'Corrupting our upstanding Christian ways with their oriental strangeness and unfettered breeding – worse than the Catholics!' He wrinkled his nose.

'Walter!' Sir Richard turned to Sir Hugh. 'Hugh, kindly ask your guests to behave like the gentlemen and ladies they supposedly are.'

Sir Hugh merely shrugged and chuckled. 'I'm not their keeper, Dicky.'

Florrie stood by the serving table, her toes squirming inside her shoes, aghast at the undisguised loathing that tripped off the tongues of these so-called dignitaries. Until she'd discovered that Mrs Douglas was Jewish, the only Jew she had ever come across had been the Cheetham Hill tailoress who had made Irene's wedding dress. Yet she had never heard that kind of vitriol at home from her parents, and her gut had always tightened when she'd heard fascist talk at the Harding-Bournes' table. Now, she studied Mrs Douglas for her reaction to the dreadful talk, but ever the professional, the housekeeper was merely making her way round the table, surreptitiously collecting empty starter plates. Her expression was inscrutable.

How can everyone apart from Sir Richard be acting like this is normal; like nothing bad is going on here? Florrie thought. *Do they realize Holcombe's housekeeper is Jewish? Won't Sir Richard put a stop to this terrible talk?*

Turning her attention to Sir Richard to gauge his reaction, she started when she realized he was staring right at her. The tendon in his jaw was flinching, and his eyebrows were drawn together in a frown above melancholy grey eyes.

As if he'd read her mind, he rose suddenly from the table. 'Will you excuse me?' he said to the gathering. 'I seem rather to have lost my appetite for this conversation, and I suggest you stop before you curdle the cream for the coffee.' He threw down his napkin and turned to Florrie. 'Would you be so kind as to bring me a plate to my study, please?'

Florrie bobbed a curtsey, trying desperately not to smile with satisfaction as Sir Richard stormed out. She met Mrs Douglas's gaze, expecting the housekeeper to wink at her, but Mrs Douglas remained grim-faced. She had paled visibly.

Having collected the starter plates, Florrie, Mrs Douglas and Sally left the dining room and, carrying their laden trays, descended the back stairs.

Sally was the first to break the tense silence, halfway down the stairs. 'Well, what a bunch of—'

'Not here!' Mrs Douglas snapped.

Once safely in the kitchen, Florrie set down her tray next to the sink and unloaded her plates and cutlery. She turned back to Mrs Douglas. 'I don't know how you bit your tongue in there, I really don't.'

Mrs Douglas deposited her own tray and leaned heavily on the old wooden worktop. 'I'm not in the business of washing my dirty linen in public, Florence,' she said quietly. She sounded breathless. 'There's nothing I can do about the opinions of my employer's brother and his chums. If I lose my job over opening my mouth, I'm the only one who suffers. Just let it lie.'

'Let what lie?' Cook asked.

Florrie hadn't realized Cook had been standing so close, yet there she was, arms folded and with an expectant glint in her eye – the sort she always got when gossip was in the offing.

'Nothing,' Florrie said, intuiting that Cook was the last person Mrs Douglas would want to confide in.

She glanced over at Mrs Douglas, who had lowered herself on to a kitchen chair and pressed a hand to her stomach.

Sally was not aware of the sensitivities at play, however. She slid her dishes, one by one, into the sink full of suds, chatting animatedly. 'You should have heard them upstairs. They were coming out with some right rum stuff about Jews. That Walter Knight-Downey and the German one. They were all hanging on his every word, weren't they, Florrie?'

'The rich say what they like because they don't have to bite their tongues,' Cook said, leaning on the large Welsh dresser that held the servants' crockery. 'They think every word what comes out of their mouths is a work of genius.'

'Well, I don't think it's nice,' Sally said, shaking her head vehemently and wiping her hands on a tea towel. 'They were saying horrible stuff about Catholics, too. I'm a Catholic. My old mam would have given them what for, if she'd heard them going on about breeding like vermin. Cheeky beggars!'

Not wanting Cook and especially not Mrs Douglas to think she'd agree for one minute with the likes of Knight-Downey or von Grunwald, Florrie couldn't help but comment. 'It *was* a disgrace. I was shocked. And Sir Richard clearly didn't like it neither, because he pulled them up on their ghastly chat, and when they wouldn't listen, he just got up and stormed out.'

Cook grinned, wide-eyed. 'Get away! He never!'

'Aye. Said he'd lost his appetite for the conversation.'

'Cook, do you think you might attend to the oven instead of tittle-tattling about our betters?' Arkwright's voice shattered any illusion of the four of them enjoying any measure of privacy. He had slipped into the kitchen unobserved while they chatted. Now he was standing by the range, pointedly sniffing the air. He had clearly overheard everything. 'And need I remind you all that it is not our place to comment on the political views of the nobility?' He smoothed his moustache with a white-gloved finger. 'Particularly when their opinions are educated and worldly and ours, by and large, are not.'

Unexpectedly, Mrs Douglas got to her feet and strode briskly towards Arkwright, pointing. 'Who are you to tell my girls — moral women, with their hearts in the right place — that they're wrong, and them upstairs are right, eh? What kind of a spineless excuse for a man are you, that you doff your cap and look for rain, when that lot's pissing on you from a great height?'

'Mrs Douglas!' Arkwright stiffened and took a step backwards. 'What unnecessary foul language! I've never heard . . . I can't condone . . .'

Undeterred, Mrs Douglas poked him in the chest. 'We have to keep our gobs shut when we're above stairs, because servants are meant to be seen and not heard, but below stairs, if we want to express concern in the privacy of the kitchen that them lot are entertaining fascists . . .'

She pointed to the ceiling. 'That's our right. They buy our services, not our souls.'

Arkwright blinked hard, clearly flustered by Mrs Douglas's impassioned outburst. 'We are an army at Holcombe Hall. The Harding-Bournes are our superior officers, while we . . . *you* are merely a lowly housekeeper; a foot soldier in the trenches.'

Mrs Douglas's eyebrows shot towards her hairline. She gasped. 'What did you just call me? *Lowly?* I'm a "lowly housekeeper"? How dare you?' She grabbed at her left arm. 'How *dare* you lecture me on my position in this house. I run this house! And how dare you tell me that my values and opinions are worth less than theirs, because they have money and are high-born, while I'm just vermin.' She had colour to her cheeks again – too much colour, Florrie thought. 'Yes, that's right. Because *I'm* a Jewess. Me.' She thumbed herself angrily in the chest. 'Bertha Douglas is Bertha Demsky, and all these years, I've kept my mouth shut while the likes of Hugh Harding-Bourne pronounce over how the Jews control the world and bring disease and misery to good Christian souls, wherever they go. So don't tell me . . .' She winced now and clasped her hand to her chest. 'Don't . . .' She squeezed her eyes shut and gasped. She reached out to Arkwright to steady herself.

'Mrs Douglas!' Florrie cried.

Arkwright grabbed hold of her. 'Bertha! Oh, good Lord! Cook, grab a chair!'

Cook merely stood stock-still, her hand over her mouth, staring in horror at the unfolding scene.

Florrie snatched up a chair and rushed it over to where Arkwright was standing by the range, clearly struggling to support Mrs Douglas's weight. Their efforts came too late, however, and Florrie watched in dismay as Mrs Douglas slid to the floor, arms splayed awkwardly and eyes open yet unseeing.

'No! Mrs Douglas!' Florrie shouted. She couldn't tear her eyes from the housekeeper's supine body and vacant gaze. 'Give her mouth-to-mouth resuscitation or something. Quickly, Mr Arkwright!'

Arkwright knelt over Mrs Douglas and held the back of his hand over her mouth. 'I can't feel any breath.' He shook his head, pressing his fingers to his forehead. 'I . . . I . . . I think she's dead.'

'Is there a pulse?' Cook asked. 'Feel for a pulse, man!'

Arkwright seemed paralysed. He merely stared at Mrs Douglas's lax features.

Florrie had no idea how to breathe life back into a person, but she knew if she didn't at least try, Mrs Douglas could never be revived. Shaking with shock, she pushed Arkwright out of the way and then she too knelt down and leaned over the housekeeper, trying not to look into her disconcertingly unfocussed eyes. She prised her mouth open gently, placed her own lips on top and exhaled sharply. Dimly aware that Cook was now also on her knees, reaching out to feel the side of Mrs Douglas's neck with two fingertips, Florrie broke the seal between hers and the housekeeper's lips and looked to see if her chest had started to rise and fall once more. There was no movement. *Come on, Bertha.*

Don't leave me! Florrie inhaled deeply, poised to try the resuscitation again.

'Time to give up the ghost, lovey,' Cook said eventually, grunting as she got to her feet.

She pulled off her mob cap and Sally did likewise. Both women crossed themselves.

Florrie looked up at her. 'What do you mean, give up?'

Cook shook her head. A tear leaked from her eye, rolled off her cheek and splashed on to the floor by Florrie's knee. 'She's beyond our help now, chuck. Mrs Douglas has gone.'

20

'Close her eyes, for heaven's sake,' Cook said, sniffing hard and looking away.

Florrie was still kneeling on the floor beside Mrs Douglas, holding her long-time champion's hand, wishing fervently that she and Sally had insisted they'd be fine without extra help in the dining room. If only Mrs Douglas hadn't been privy to that terrible conversation . . .

'Close 'em! I can't bear it!'

Remembering how her mother had slid Irene's eyelids shut after her sister had taken her last breath, Florrie now did the same for Mrs Douglas. She didn't try to stifle the sob that escaped her lips. 'Sleep well, Bertha,' she whispered. 'And thank you for everything.' The pain of losing another woman who had meant so much to her, so soon after Irene's death, was almost unbearable.

'What do we do now?' Sally asked, seemingly transfixed by the sight of Mrs Douglas's body. 'Should we fetch a doctor or summat?'

'Doctor's for the living, Sal,' Cook said, blowing her nose loudly.

'No, Sal's right,' Florrie said. 'We'll need the doctor to establish why she died and issue a death certificate. And I'm sure we'll need a bobby to attend and all, to confirm nothing suspicious has seen her off.'

Sally's face was a picture of horrified intrigue. 'Ooh, like poison?' She turned to Arkwright. 'Are you going to tell them above stairs and then telephone the police station? Mr Arkwright?'

The butler didn't answer. He was sitting in the chair Florrie had drawn up for Mrs Douglas. His hands covered his eyes and his shoulders shook. Florrie was fairly certain he was crying – a sight she'd never imagined possible in one so cold – yet she could barely contain her wrath.

'I blame *you*,' she said, pointing to the butler.

He removed his hands to reveal bloodshot, watery eyes. 'I beg your pardon?'

'You! You riled her up so badly with all that talk of her being a lowly housekeeper . . . You insulted her, and you had to keep digging, digging, digging, didn't you?' She clawed at the air repeatedly to mimic Arkwright's unwillingness to let the matter drop. 'Until she had a heart attack or an apoplexy or whatever it was that's seen her off.'

Arkwright shook his head. 'I never meant to . . .'

'Why didn't we see it before?' Florrie said, looking round at the others. 'Why in God's name didn't we realize how ill she was? We could have spared her this, if we'd known.'

'She were a very private woman,' Cook said. 'A closed book. I could never get nowt out of her. Never knew she were a Jew. Never knew she were ill, though come to think of it, she went to the doctor not long ago.'

'She never said a word,' Arkwright said forlornly. 'And

now we've lost one of the finest women I ever met.' Head in hands, he wept openly. 'The Harding-Bournes aren't fit to wipe her shoes. But she's dead and it's all my fault.' He hiccoughed loudly. 'Why did I insult her? I didn't want to hurt her!' He beat himself in the chest with his fist. 'And now she's gone, and I never told her anything. I never said . . . She never knew . . .'

Florrie observed the outpouring from the normally inscrutable Arkwright and suddenly realized what lay at the root of his grief. He had been in love with Mrs Douglas. She exhaled hard and closed her eyes. 'What a bloody waste,' she muttered beneath her breath, imagining just for a moment a different fate, where the bachelor butler and the childless, widowed housekeeper of Holcombe Hall had shelved their sense of duty to the Harding-Bourne family, just long enough to allow romance to blossom between them. Might they have married and had a family of their own?

She shook her head and got to her feet, reluctantly letting go of Mrs Douglas's already cooling hand. 'Right, here's what we're going to do. We can't just leave her on the floor in front of the oven like this. It's not right. So, you three move her carefully to the bed in Mr Arkwright's office; cover her with a tablecloth, keep the other staff out of the room, and then telephone the doctor and the police. I'll get Sir Richard. He'll have details of Mrs Douglas's family, and he can send a telegram. They can make necessary arrangements.' She turned to Cook and Sally. 'Get the dinner out for them lot upstairs, before it's burnt to a crisp. Everything must carry on as normal until the doctor and the police have told us what to do next.'

Wiping her own tears away, she took a deep breath and steeled herself to leave the kitchen. Above stairs, as she walked past the enormous gilt-framed mirror in the hallway, she caught sight of her red-rimmed eyes and looked away abruptly.

She found Sir Richard in his study, sipping whisky from a crystal tumbler and reading some typed document by the light of his desk lamp. In an ashtray on his desk, a Havana cigar smouldered. His bow tie hung loose; his dinner jacket was draped over the arm of the green leather chesterfield by the window. 'Ah Florrie, there you are.' He laid his document down, giving her his full attention. His smile quickly turned to a frown. 'My dear, have you been crying? Whatever is the matter?'

Florrie stood on the other side of his large leather-topped desk, lacing her fingers together in front of her. 'I'm afraid there's terrible news.' As she explained the circumstances of Mrs Douglas's collapse, she found herself unable to keep her anger inside. 'It wasn't just the argument with Arkwright that caused her collapse,' she said. 'Did you know she was Jewish?'

Sir Richard balked. 'Jewish?' He shook his head. 'I had absolutely no idea.' He picked up his tumbler and swilled the whisky around absently, the furrows in his forehead deepening. Then he set it down again. 'And she was privy to that disgraceful talk around the dinner table, wasn't she? Good Lord! That's unforgivable.'

'Yes. It is.' Hot tears leaked on to Florrie's face. She wiped them hastily away with the back of her hand.

Getting to his feet, Sir Richard walked around the desk. 'Poor Mrs Douglas. And my poor, dear Florrie.' He reached out to put his arms around her.

At first Florrie flinched at his touch, but then she realized that a hug was what she needed most of all. She allowed his embrace and wept heartily into his chest, taking comfort in the familiar smell of his sandalwood cologne and cigar smoke.

When she heard laughter drifting along the hallway from the dining room, she broke away from him and looked awkwardly at the floor. 'The doctor and police should be on their way. I asked Arkwright to telephone them. Will you contact her family?' she asked.

Sir Richard strode over to a filing cabinet by the window. 'Let's shed a little light on the subject, shall we?'

Florrie switched on the main light, wincing at the sudden brightness. When Sir Richard took out a file and turned to face her, she averted her gaze, keen that her employer shouldn't see the unsightly extent of quite how bloodshot and red-rimmed her eyes were.

'Here we go,' he said, brandishing the folder. He took it to his desk and opened it. He donned his spectacles and read the scant contents. 'How extraordinary. Mrs Douglas came to work at the house when I was but a boy – shortly before I was sent away to Eton. Even after my father passed away, and I inherited the estate, I've never once looked at her file . . . until now.' He looked up at her. 'Can you believe it, she had no next of kin listed whatsoever?'

'What?' Florrie asked. 'Nobody at all?'

He shook his head. 'And she was only forty-five years old. I thought she was *decades* older than me. What a tragic soul. I would have paid for the best specialist to see her, if only she'd told me she had a condition.' He sighed.

'What are we going to do about burying her if she's got no family?'

Sir Richard closed the file and patted it gently. 'Leave it with me. If she was Jewish, perhaps there are different arrangements to be made. I do believe there are a number of synagogues in Manchester and Leeds. I'll call them tomorrow. And as for my brother and his beastly friends, you can rest assured I'll be having a stern word with them all. This untimely death of a good woman is a stain on my family.'

'She died from a massive heart attack,' Dr Bridgford told the police sergeant, drawing the tablecloth back over Mrs Douglas's face and straightening up.

Florrie had only ever seen the sergeant once before. It had been a year or two after she'd entered service at the Hall, when one of the footmen had been caught red-handed by Cook trying to steal a large silver candelabra from the locked silver cabinet in the butler's office – a rare occasion when Arkwright had been away, visiting relatives in Blackpool. Now, Sergeant Wallace's jacket was rather too tight for his gut – surely the sign of a sedentary job in a village where little happened beyond the odd altercation outside the pub on a Saturday night.

Wallace scribbled in his notepad with a pencil. 'You sure about that?'

Dr Bridgford nodded and pushed his tortoiseshell spectacles up his bulbous nose. 'Oh yes. She'd been to see me several times about suspected angina – breathlessness, pain in the chest, et cetera. Her blood pressure was elevated to a worrying degree. It was clear she had heart disease, sadly, but she refused to see a specialist.' He shook his head. 'Perhaps the issue of cost was involved, but she did tell me she "couldn't abide fusspots". I do wish she'd made more of a fuss about getting treatment for her condition. Her sudden death tells a salutary tale.'

At the foot of the bed, Arkwright was ashen-faced and looked to have aged by ten years at least. Florrie noted that he hadn't taken his eyes off Mrs Douglas's body – certainly not since Florrie had returned below stairs.

'Could cross words have killed her?' Arkwright asked, his voice almost a whisper.

Dr Bridgford returned his medical instruments to his leather doctor's bag and closed the clasp. 'Extreme aggravation can bring on a heart attack in those with high blood pressure.'

'So, does that make me a murderer?' Arkwright asked.

Sergeant Wallace chuckled sadly and shook his head. 'If having a barney was intent to kill, Mr Arkwright, prisons would be full to bursting every time someone's husband got his ear bent for staying too long in the pub, or someone's missus forgot to put the Christmas turkey in the oven on time. God knows, people who work together for a long time – close, like – can drive each other up the wall. Like a marriage. But what's happened here looks like the tragic death of a sick woman on the back of an argument and nowt else.' He looked at the supine form of Mrs Douglas beneath the tablecloth and then turned his focus back to Arkwright. He retrieved his hat from the butler's desk. 'A word of advice: try to dwell on any fond memories you have of your friend; agonizing over harsh words you exchanged just before she passed won't do anybody any good.'

When the doctor and the sergeant had gone, Florrie insisted Arkwright come to the kitchen, where she asked Cook to serve the staff's dinner, as was the usual custom.

'We have to keep the home fires burning,' she told everyone, once they'd taken their places around the table. 'It's what Mrs Douglas would have wanted, and it's what the Harding-Bournes need.'

In a reflective silence that even Danny observed without objection, the staff members all nodded soberly. Florrie watched how the valets, footmen and stableboys looked to Arkwright for comment, yet the butler sat at the table like a statue, deathly pale and mute in his grief. Albert, the head gardener, placed his hand wordlessly on the butler's shoulder.

'I assume that until Sir Richard updates us about Mrs Douglas's replacement, we're all to carry on with our duties, exactly as Mrs Douglas would have instructed us?' Florrie asked.

'Aye,' Cook said. 'But someone'll need to do all the

ordering in of supplies. Bertha kept a ledger in the sideboard.'

'I'll do it,' Florrie patted Cook's hand. 'Me and you have been here longest, so we'll take up the reins on practical matters like that.' Studying the faces of the younger maids, Florrie felt far older than her twenty-five years. It suddenly occurred to her that Arkwright had nowhere to sleep, since Mrs Douglas was taking up his bed until an undertaker took her away. 'Mr Arkwright, you must sleep in the spare servant's room tonight in the attic.'

Arkwright's answer was so softly spoken, he was barely audible.

'Right, that's settled,' Florrie said. 'Let's eat.'

When her shift was over, Florrie trudged through the orchard in the falling snow to the gamekeeper's cottage, where she found her mother ironing in the scullery, with the children tucked up in their beds. They moved to the parlour, and sitting in one of the armchairs, clutching a hot cup of tea, she told her mother all that had happened in the last few hours.

'That poor woman,' Mam said, putting a blanket around Florrie and tucking it in around her. She kissed Florrie on the forehead. 'She was ever so kind, and straight as a die in her dealings with me, God bless her. It's her I've to thank for us being given a fresh start.'

Florrie reached up to stroke her mother's face. 'I thank God she lived long enough to bring you to Holcombe Hall by offering you your job. But oh, it was dreadful, Mam. One minute she's giving Arkwright a piece of her mind, which I *always* loved to see. The next, she's gone.'

She clicked her fingers. 'Just like that.' She stretched her feet out so her toes might thaw in the warmth of the dwindling fire. 'And now I can't help feeling like death is following me around.'

'How do you mean, death is following you around?' Mam asked, sitting on the old brocade settee. 'Why should Mrs Douglas's passing have anything to do with you? She was a good woman, but she wasn't your flesh and blood, love.'

In the glow of the firelight, Florrie affectionately observed the lines in her mother's ageing face, her dishevelled greying hair and her puzzled smile – loved, but less familiar to her than the wrinkles, grey hair and smile of Mrs Douglas, who had been a constant daily presence in Florrie's life for the last ten years. New to the world of domestic service as she was, would Mam ever understand how perfect strangers could come to feel like family over time, when they spent every waking hour together, ate together, wept together, laughed together; all in the service of the same employer? Had Mam ever realized how terrifying and isolating it had been for her fifteen-year-old daughter to leave her family, her home and everything she had ever known, with no money for a train ticket to visit occasionally, even if she'd had time for one; no communication beyond a weekly letter? Might Mam then understand how important the housekeeper had become to Florrie as a buffer to all that loneliness and upheaval?

'Mrs Douglas was very supportive and I was very fond of her. I just wish people would stop dying on me. That's all.'

Mam slapped the empty space beside her on the settee. 'Come and have a cuddle, love.'

Florrie joined her for a hug. Together they watched the muted dance of the dying flames in the fireplace. Though Florrie revelled in finally having her own mother close by, she also wept silently at the loss of her surrogate mother, Bertha Douglas.

'By heck, look! They've come to collect her,' Cook shouted, early the following morning.

A windowless black van with gold Hebrew lettering on the side pulled up at the back entrance to Holcombe Hall. Two suited men stepped out of the van into the thick snow. Both wore skullcaps, partly covering hair that was closely cropped other than the curled sidelocks that hung behind their ears. They carried with them a stretcher. One rang the bell of the servants' entrance.

'That was quick! Sir Richard must have got through to a rabbi last night,' Florrie said, registering a feeling of dread. She thought of Mrs Douglas in Arkwright's room. It was strange and so very sad to think that the housekeeper would be leaving Holcombe Hall for good within the half-hour.

Letting the undertakers in, Florrie sent Sally to fetch Sir Richard. When he appeared, dressed against the winter cold in double jumpers and thick tweed trousers, the men were already carrying Mrs Douglas out of Arkwright's office.

'Oh, I say,' Sir Richard said, looking crestfallen. 'Is this the last we'll see of our Mrs Douglas? Is this where we say goodbye for good?'

Florrie could see tears welling in his eyes and felt an entirely inappropriate urge to squeeze his hand as a show of support. She resisted it, however, swallowing a lump in her throat. 'Will we be able to go to her funeral?'

One of the undertakers turned back to her. 'She's being buried at two o'clock this afternoon, miss,' he said. 'Jewish cemetery in Rainsough. That's near Prestwich Village in north Manchester.'

'So soon?' Sir Richard asked. 'By Jove, she only passed away last night.'

'It's our custom to bury our dead before sundown the following day, wherever possible, if they've died after sunset or on the Sabbath or a holy day.'

'But won't she be laid out proper and put in a chapel of rest?' Cook asked. 'Shouldn't I find her a nice frock?'

The undertaker shook his head. 'We come into this world with nothing, and we go out with nothing too. A simple shroud is all our dead need. She'll be looked after by some religious ladies, don't worry. We have men from the synagogue who say the necessary prayers at the graveside.'

'Do you need payment for the funeral?' Sir Richard asked the man. 'Mrs Douglas had no next of kin that I could find, so obviously, as her employer, I'll be happy to settle any bill.'

'Mrs Douglas paid into a funeral plan at the synagogue you contacted, so the burial costs will be covered, sir. We'll be in touch nearer the time of her stone-setting . . .

that's not for another twelve months. Someone here *will* have to pay for her headstone, if she had no living relatives.'

'I'll cover any costs, of course,' Sir Richard said.

Florrie noticed Arkwright standing by the door. For the first time in all the years she'd known the butler, he wasn't wearing his tailcoat. He was dressed in a black cardigan over a shirt and black tie with black corduroy slacks, looking most unlike his usual immaculate self. His hair hung loose and limp over his pale face. Wordlessly, he followed the men carrying the stretcher out to the van.

'Should we go out and say our goodbyes?' Sally asked.

Florrie watched Arkwright through the window. She shook her head. 'No. Leave him to it. We've said all we need to Mrs Douglas. She knows we're thinking of her.'

Sir Richard dabbed at his eyes with the heel of his hand and gasped. 'Oh dear. What a sad day. And we can't even say our farewells properly with a normal burial. No matter though. We must respect her heritage. I think what we might do, though, is plant a new tree in her memory.'

'That's a smashing idea,' Florrie said. 'She loved magnolias in spring.'

Sir Richard smiled sadly. 'Then that is exactly what we'll plant . . . I'll speak to Albert. We can have a little memorial thing and all say a few words.' He turned to leave.

Before he passed over the threshold into the vestibule that led to the back stairs, Florrie called after him. 'Sir

Richard, I know it's a little soon, but when will you be interviewing for a new housekeeper? We're keeping the home fires burning down here, but . . .'

Sir Richard had stopped and he now turned to face them, leaning against the door frame. 'Ah, yes. Well, I've given it some thought. We already have our new housekeeper.'

'Oh?' Cook asked, straightening her apron and smoothing her hair. 'Who might that be, then?'

Sir Richard smiled at Cook and then wafted his hand in Florrie's direction. 'Meet the new housekeeper of Holcombe Hall . . . assuming she'll take the job.'

21

'I don't mind taking orders from a girl half my age,' Cook said, spatchcocking a pheasant with something bordering on brutality. 'But just don't start fiddling about with my menus. All right?'

A week had passed since Mrs Douglas's death, and Florrie was sitting at the kitchen table with a notebook open in front of her. 'Well, first of all, Sir Richard gave me a couple of weeks to think about it, and being as Mrs Douglas's body isn't even cold yet, I'm still mulling his job offer over. It's a lot of responsibility, with even longer hours and the stress of managing the staff – enough to kill Mrs Douglas off.'

'You're not wrong there.' Cook's eyebrows shot up towards her mob cap.

'So as far as I'm concerned, I'm still just standing in as housekeeper. But second of all, whether I take this job or someone else comes in from outside, Sir Richard wants economies made. And that's going to affect your menus. It's unavoidable.'

Cook rolled her eyes and shook her head. 'It's bad enough our Bertha's gone and we're having to plant a flipping tree instead of having a proper funeral, like sensible Christian folk, but all this talk of cutting back seems like hysterical stuff and nonsense to me.'

Shrugging, Florrie gave Cook her most apologetic face. 'Who are we to question the likes of Sir Richard? I'm no expert on business and stock markets. If he says a storm's coming, well, you're going to have to cut expensive items out. He's already said no more banquets or balls until further notice.'

'I'm going to end up out of a job, aren't I?' Cook said, skewering the pheasant angrily with two wooden sticks. 'Four days 'til Christmas, and I'll be out on my ear by the second of January – you watch. They'll bring in some slip of a girl, barely out of school, who can just about make a stew, but she'll work for half my wages.'

'Listen, if I take the job of housekeeper,' Florrie said, 'I'll see to it that you won't get replaced. Sir Richard has told me he wants staff culling . . .' She lowered her voice to a whisper. 'But I'll recommend it's some of Arkwright's boys that go.' She jerked her thumb in the direction of Arkwright's office. 'He's got way too many layabouts on his staff, like Danny. This Hall would be rat infested within a fortnight without maids, the gamekeepers, the tenant farmer, the gardeners . . . We keep everything shipshape and make sure the larders are full.'

'Aye. You're not wrong there.' Cook pointed to the pheasants she'd plucked that morning and looked over at the sink full of brown feathers. 'That lot above stairs wouldn't take kindly to me serving up barley broth. If they want to watch the pennies, they'd do better with cellars full of hanging game and hams than that fancy French champagne they guzzle like it's water.'

'Exactly,' Florrie said, feeling that she'd at least

got Cook on her side. Yet Cook was the least of her challenges.

At that moment, Danny walked through the kitchen, coming from the direction of Arkwright's office. As he passed Florrie, he tutted slowly.

'Is there any particular reason you're tutting at me, Daniel Phillips?' Florrie asked, getting to her feet and raising herself to her full height so that they were almost eye-to-eye.

'Arkwright's not happy. That's all I'm saying.'

'Of course he's not happy. We're holding a memorial service for Mrs Douglas this afternoon.'

Danny treated her to an unpleasant yellow-toothed grin. 'It's *you* he's not happy with. Ideas above your station. He knows a climber when he sees one. That sort of thing doesn't go down well with *my* boss.'

'Show some bloody respect, you!' Cook said, pointing at him with a wooden skewer.

Laughing, Danny merely offered a rude hand gesture in response and headed for the back stairs.

Realizing that this would be her fate for weeks to come if she were to accept the housekeeper position, Florrie sighed. 'Anyway, the food for Bertha's memorial wake sounds lovely. You'll do her proud.' She chewed the inside of her cheek ruefully, remembering Danny's nasty grin. 'I'd best go and check on the bedrooms, now Lady Charlotte's and Sir Hugh's guests have finally gone.'

En route to check on the other maids' progress in cleaning the bedrooms, Florrie stopped by the laundry. She poked her head into the large room and was immediately hit by a humid fug that smelled of bleach and washing detergent. 'Everything all right, Mam?'

Her mother, who was scrubbing something at the sink with a long-handled brush, waved merrily. 'Morning, Florrie, love.'

Out of the corner of her eye, partly obscured by the mangle, Florrie noticed Nelly and George playing with a pail of soapy water, blowing bubbles at one another and squealing with delight. Alice was crawling around on the tiled floor, gurgling away happily to herself, pausing only to bite down on a makeshift doll that Mam had fashioned from an old, balled pair of white socks with roughly stitched eyes and a mouth.

'Is it safe for them to be playing in here?' she asked. 'You haven't got any windows open.'

'It's still nippy, even though the snow's gone. And where else am I going to put them?' Mam asked.

'George should be in school, for a start. Maybe Nelly in nursery school, too.'

'They've just lost their mam, Florrie, and they've been wrenched from everything they've ever known. What they need is to be around family, not strangers. Plenty of time for school. Besides, little'uns love playing with water – you and Irene always did – and the floor's spotless in here.' She set down her scrubbing brush and wiped her reddened hands on her apron. 'Is this how it's going to be, now you're housekeeper? Checking up on me every five minutes?' She winked, but it was clear she was sincere.

Florrie walked over to the children and kissed them

each on the head. 'I haven't taken the job yet. And to be honest, Mam, I don't know if I should.' She felt tears prick the backs of her eyes and couldn't be sure if they came from the deep sense of loss she felt at her champion having passed away suddenly, or if it was Danny's unkind behaviour and the prospect of a permanent clash of wills with Arkwright. 'I'm treading on too many toes. I'm going to have a mutiny on my hands, I know it. Small wonder poor Bertha dropped dead from a heart attack.'

Her mother led her to a chair, on which freshly laundered, dry bath towels sat in a neat pile. She removed the towels and pushed Florrie to sit. 'Hey! Enough of this defeatist talk. Did I raise you to pass up the chance of a better life, just so you'd never face the discomfort of challenge or change?'

Taken aback by her mother's candour, Florrie blinked hard, opened her mouth to answer but found she had no words. She merely shook her head.

'Opportunity knocks but once, Florence Bickerstaff. You grab this promotion with both hands. We've still got three children to raise between us, and even though Sir Richard has been generous, sorting us out with a lovely house and turning a blind eye to my grandchildren knocking around, what he's paying me won't cover everything they need. So, think on. Battle's not won yet, and the only side you need to be loyal to is us Bickerstaffs'.'

'Well, now that we're all standing here, I – I'm not entirely sure what to say,' Sir Richard said, his breath steaming on the freezing air. Standing next to Lady Charlotte at the spot in front of the Hall, where Thom had dug a hole in the only-just-thawed ground, he stamped his feet and rubbed his gloved hands together. At his side was a strappy magnolia sapling, its root ball covered by a hessian sack. Sir Richard scratched his reddened nose and sniffed. 'Arkwright, perhaps you'd like to say, er, a little something about our dearly departed Mrs Douglas.'

Florrie could see that Arkwright had regained a little of his vigour over the last few days, but his skin was still pasty, and there were dark circles beneath his eyes.

'Actually, I have prepared a few words.' He took a piece of folded paper from his pocket and opened it out. From the inside pocket of his black woollen coat, he took a pair of metal spectacles and hooked them over his ears.

Excepting only Mam, who had stayed in the gamekeeper's cottage to look after the children, the entire domestic staff of Holcombe Hall stood shivering in the darkest Sunday-best clothes they'd been able to find, staring expectantly at Arkwright.

He cleared his throat and started to read. 'Mrs Douglas was the housekeeper of Holcombe Hall, queen bee of our *below-stairs* hive. Where I am the lungs, she was the beating heart of this complex beast; where I am the hands of the clock, she was the pendulum that kept me ticking; where I am the captain responsible for all souls on board, she was the engine powering our great ship through all weathers.' A fat tear bypassed the lens of his spectacles to splosh on to his sheet of paper. Florrie could see where the black ink dissolved into a rainbow smudge. The butler's lips trembled. His chin dimpled. His voice wavered. 'I worked with Mrs Douglas – Bertha – for twenty-four memorable years.' He smiled weakly, looking wistfully at the sapling. 'She came to the house a young, childless widow, and she eschewed the chance of remarrying to make the people of Holcombe Hall her family.' He looked at Sir Richard and Lady Charlotte. 'She was utterly dedicated to serving the Harding-Bournes.' He regarded his colleagues. 'She treated the junior staff as if they were her own children. And to me . . .' He exhaled hard. 'She was in many ways . . . in all but the biblical sense . . . my other half; my better half.' By now, Arkwright spoke only haltingly, and his tears flowed.

Florrie felt so sorry for the forlorn butler, with his heartfelt metaphors and misspent longing, that she had to dig her hands deep into her coat pockets to stop herself from reaching out to comfort him. Peering around at the gathering, she saw there was not a dry eye among them, apart from Lady Charlotte, who was gazing blankly back at the house and yawning, absently stroking the fur pelt of her mink coat. Florrie's attention came to rest on Thom. He looked dapper in his Sunday-best suit, worn with a black armband. The fine lines around his eyes softened as he returned her gaze. She turned then to Sir Richard, who looked down at his brogues, his face a picture of dignified sympathy as he listened to Arkwright.

'My deepest regret was that Mrs Douglas and I locked horns with such regularity.' Arkwright smiled again, blinking away tears. 'Mainly because she always turned out to be right.'

Cook and Sally chuckled, and for once, Florrie saw the butler exchange friendly smiles with them. Her toes and fingers were warmed by the thought that Arkwright harboured a secretly poetic soul and a tragically unrequited love for a woman she'd greatly admired. *Perhaps I'll be able to work with him after all,* she thought. *He can't be all that bad.*

'It will be *impossible* for any woman to fill her shoes adequately,' Arkwright said, saving a withering glance for Florrie.

Who am I kidding? This leopard won't change its spots.

Arkwright folded his piece of paper back up solemnly. 'Mrs Douglas was the grandest of women, a credit to the fairer sex. I shall think of her every day that I have left on this earth.' He looked up at the heavy clouds that were white with the threat of fresh snow. 'Goodbye, Bertha Douglas.'

Thom planted the magnolia, firming the earth around the stem with the heel of his shoes. 'It's a sturdy sapling, this,' he said, dusting compost from his hands. 'I reckon we might even see a few blooms in its first spring.'

'It's a fitting tribute. Thank you, Thom.' Sir Richard removed his glove and adjusted his black armband. 'And thank you to Arkwright for those heartfelt words.' He glanced momentarily at Florrie and then looked to Lady Charlotte, his melancholy expression inscrutable. 'Very moving.' When he offered his wife his arm, Florrie was certain she heard him sigh.

*

'I've made up my mind,' Florrie said quietly to Sir Richard, when they were standing side by side next to the kitchen table on which Cook had laid out a generous spread. She took a slice of pork pie from a platter and carefully laid it on her side plate. 'I'll take the job. I'll be the new housekeeper.'

Sir Richard turned to her and grinned. He kept his voice low. 'Excellent news. I knew you would.' He nudged her playfully. 'Our Florrie's a force to be reckoned with, eh? Not even the truculent words of Mr Arkwright can dampen her spirit. Ha!'

He was standing so close to her that she could feel the heat from his body almost as acutely as she could feel the eyes of her colleagues boring into them. Could they see that she was blushing? 'He's going to give me a run for my money, isn't he?'

'Don't worry about him. He forgets who's head of this estate. And he has to work with you *in loco parentis* for a large staff – a rather too large staff. Listen, I'll draw up a new contract immediately and your increased pay will be backdated to when Mrs Douglas passed away.' He helped himself to a salmon sandwich. 'You've already been doing a sterling job.' He bit into it and chewed thoughtfully, taking a merciful step to the side, away from Florrie. 'I may spend much of the day in my study, but that doesn't mean I don't know what's going on below stairs.' He tapped the side of his nose and winked. 'You'll be a first-rate housekeeper, my dear. I'm sure you'll keep us all on our toes. In fact, I'm rather looking forward to it.'

Florrie was relieved when her employer moved off to chat to Albert about the crops he'd be growing in the vegetable garden. She was unsurprised when Cook sidled up to her. Brandy fumes and a hunger for gossip seemed to ripple off her.

'That looked very friendly. Good job Lady Charlotte wouldn't grace us with her presence below stairs, eh?' She scooped up a pickled onion and bit into it noisily. 'What was he saying?'

'We were just discussing the terms of my employment.'

'So, you're taking the job, then?'

'Aye. I'm officially the housekeeper of Holcombe Hall. I don't know how, and I don't know why, but—'

'I'll tell you why,' Cook said knowingly. 'It's because he's sweet on you, Florrie Bickerstaff. Always has been. You'd better keep your hand on your ha'penny, now you've not got Bertha to look out for you no more.' She started to cackle.

Florrie could feel irritation prickling beneath her skin. 'Come on now, Cook. You can't come out with stuff like that. He's our employer – *married* to the King's second cousin. It's not right, chat like that. And it's not true.'

'And then there's young Thomas. He's definitely got the glad eye for you.' Cook put her arm around Florrie and squeezed tightly. 'I never thought our little Florrie would have two fellers beating a path to kiss her under the mistletoe. This is going to be a Christmas to remember, chuck. I can feel it in my waters.'

22

'Are you sure you don't want me to help with that?' Florrie asked Thom, who was struggling to drag a fat, newly felled pine tree through the narrow doorway of the gamekeeper's cottage.

'You just get your mam to put a brew on,' he said. 'I can manage this by myself.' He grunted with exertion, but the tree finally yielded. From there, he was easily able to pull it through to the parlour, leaving a trail of pine needles and a heavenly pine smell behind.

'Are we having a Christmas tree?' George asked excitedly. Florrie's small nephew was wearing Mam's red headscarf as a neckerchief and an old, wide-brimmed sun hat that Thom had found in the gardening store and had convinced him was as good as a real cowboy hat. In his hand, George held a thick, gnarled stick that was almost the shape of a pistol. 'A giant Christmas tree on Christmas Eve, like in the films?'

'Aye,' Thom said. 'Big enough to make Santa Claus want to make this his first stop tonight, when he's out delivering presents to all the good little girls and boys.' He started to wrestle the tree into an upright position in the corner by the playpen he'd fashioned out of old wooden clothes horses for Alice. 'You'll have to get your nana to listen out for the tinkle of reindeers' bells and Santa's sleigh, landing on your roof.'

Florrie laughed at the sight of George jumping up and down with glee, pretending to shoot his pretend gun in the air. Nelly copied him, though she almost certainly didn't understand why she was doing so. Florrie got down on her knees so that she was closer in height to the children. 'Are you going to help me decorate it with posh spare baubles from the Hall?'

'You betcha bottom dollar!' George yelled. 'Nana! Nana, guess what?' He tore out of the parlour down the hallway towards the kitchen.

Nelly flung herself into Florrie's arms. Cuddling the little girl, she glanced up at Thom, who was propping the tree against the wall. When she realized he was watching her with a wistful look on his face, she picked Nelly up and walked over to the window with her. 'Can you see Father Christmas yet?'

There was some hammering as Thom nailed the trunk of the felled tree to a flat wooden base. Alice started to cry in her playpen, and soon Florrie found herself sitting on the settee, consoling an alarmed baby and trying to calm down an over-excited toddler. She couldn't help but giggle at the situation. 'Come on, girls! Santa only gives out presents if you've been good, and Aunty Florrie's got to be back at the Hall in a bit to serve Christmas Eve dinner. I need you to be good.'

'George thinks he's Gary Cooper, doesn't he?' Thom shouted above the noise of Alice's wailing and Nelly's squealing. 'He makes me laugh, that lad. I'd love to have a son.'

'Oh, yes. Children are a delight.' Florrie rolled her eyes

and chuckled, narrowly dodging an accidental punch from the distraught Alice. She took a bauble from the box that was on the settee and distracted the baby with its bright blue colour and the distorted reflection that appeared in the teardrop-shaped glass.

'Would you like your own one day?' he asked, testing the strength of the base so that the tree's branches shook, emitting that wonderful smell again.

Florrie realized then that there was a strong possibility Thom was sounding out her maternal credentials. She had suspected for a while that the strong, handsome, honourable gardener had a soft spot for her. The very thought made her cheeks glow, and she covered her blushes behind Nelly's head.

'I've never given it much thought,' she said, not daring to make eye contact with him. 'There's been so much going on . . . I mean, I've only just taken on the job of housekeeper. And me and Mam have got our hands full with my sister's lot.'

'Oh, of course! I didn't mean . . . I mean . . .' Thom scratched awkwardly at his neck and loosened his collar. He turned to the tree. 'Right. I think it's nice and stable now. All ready for your baubles, and just in time for Christmas Eve.'

'Are you ready for that brew and a mince pie, Thomas?' Mam called through.

He rubbed his hands together. 'You know the way to a man's heart, Matilda,' he shouted back.

George pelted back into the parlour, pretending to shoot Thom in the gut. Thom clutched at his stomach and groaned, joining in the game. Meanwhile, Florrie carried a calmed Alice back to the playpen. She set Nelly down by the tree and retrieved all the baubles.

'You've got to be very, very careful with these . . .' she told Nelly and George, taking a pink and gold bauble out of the box, 'because they're glass. If they break, they'll cut your little hands to ribbons.'

George nodded earnestly, though Florrie wasn't convinced her five-year-old nephew appreciated how much care was required for flimsy Victorian tree decorations.

'Here we go!' Mam carried a tray through to the parlour and set it down on the ornate yew coffee table that had once – perhaps over a hundred years ago – sat in some reception room in Holcombe Hall. She stirred the tea in a large pot that was decorated with flowers and gold-leaf flourishes. A number of freshly baked mince pies were stacked on a plate steaming merrily. 'Look how posh this is,' Mam said, pouring milk into the dainty cups from a small jug. 'No more jam jars for *us*, Florrie! It's cups all the way, now. China ones, at that.'

'My own mam always served tea in jam jars,' Thom said.

He was about to sit on the brocade settee, when Mam hastily slid a towel beneath him. 'Hey! Don't you be getting gardener's muck on my nice settee. Look after your furniture, and it'll look after you. And you can get them work boots off in here, and all.'

Florrie smiled at the pride she saw in her mother's face at having a home she could call her own, albeit only as long as she held the post of laundress. 'You tell him, Mam. The gardeners are the worst for leaving trails of muck below stairs after Sal's mopped through.'

She focussed her attention on the tree and started to hang baubles with the children, guiding their hands to avoid mishap. All the while, she listened to the easy chatter between Mam and Thom about his life in service and what it was to be a poor manual worker, living in the North West in a decade that had seen the rich get richer and the poor slide further into poverty.

'I don't miss those mills,' Mam said. She held up the hand that was two fingers short. 'They're death traps, and the owners do nowt to protect their workers when profits are down. In fact, I never thought I'd say it, but I'm glad to have left Manchester behind me.' Reflected in the shining glass bauble she held in her hand, Florrie watched her mother pick up her cup and saucer and sip her tea, gazing absently at the tree. 'I just feel so badly that my sister's still there; still struggling to make ends meet since she's had her hours cut right down and all. Not much different from me, a couple of week ago.'

'Were it a Harding-Bourne mill, where you worked?' Thom asked, biting into a mince pie.

Mam nodded. 'Don't get me wrong, love – Sir Richard's generosity has given our family a Christmas miracle.' She set down her cup and sighed. 'But that's because our Florrie, here, is right under his nose every day. She made it bloody hard for him to ignore her family's plight, if I know my girl.'

Florrie repositioned herself so she was now facing

the two of them. 'I didn't nag him at all. He did it out of the kindness of his heart, Mam.' She untangled the gold thread at the end of a red bauble.

Thom crossed his right leg over his left knee and regarded his large, sock-clad foot with a raised eyebrow. 'I'm not being funny, but Sir Richard only coughed up once he'd heard I'd said I'd renovate this place in my own time, with my own money. Not meaning to burst anyone's bubble, like.'

Mam reached out and squeezed his arm. 'You're a good'un. What is he, our Florrie?'

'He *is* a cracker,' Florrie said, feeling torn between her loyalty to Sir Richard, with his grand gestures, and her acknowledgement of Thom's quiet heroism. Though she hated to admit it, Thom was probably entirely accurate in his appraisal of Sir Richard's motives for fixing up the cottage. The men had been two stags, competing to claim ownership of the largest set of antlers.

'Well, here we are, tucked up and warm on a Christmas Eve, living the life of Riley,' Mam said. She raised her cup. 'And whatever his reasons were for giving us such a grand home, thank you, Sir Richard. But handsome is as handsome does, in my book.' She treated Florrie to a stern, sobering look. 'There are still hundreds if not thousands of destitute families in Manchester, Leeds and Liverpool who won't even have enough coal to put on their fires this Christmas because some millionaire industrialist kicked them off the payroll without so much as a thanks. And all the while, the Harding-Bournes are living high off the hog, and that Lady Charlotte's got more couture clothes than I've had hot dinners. I should know. I'm washing them!'

'It's not right, is it, Matilda?' Thom said. He drained his cup and set it back on to the tray. He got to his feet and nodded at the tree. 'It's looking well. Just needs a few presents underneath it from Father Christmas.' He looked at Florrie and winked. Then he checked his fob watch, pressing his lips together. 'I do believe dinner is almost served. Would Madame Housekeeper like me to escort her back to the main house?' He offered her his arm.

Florrie kissed her family and wished them a Merry Christmas, making the children promise they'd go straight to sleep and not lie awake listening out for Santa. Then she took Thom's arm and they left for the Hall in the twilight.

'I like your mam,' Thom said on the walk back.

'I do too!'

'She's a good woman. Like you.'

Florrie nudged the gardener, feeling his warmth banish some of the wintry cold and damp from her bones. She sensed that he was looking down at her, but kept her focus on the path through the grassy orchard.

'I've got some gifts for the children,' he said. 'Nothing fancy. Only, it's their first Christmas here . . . without their mother . . . and I thought they'd need all the cheering up they could get.'

'That's so thoughtful, Thom. You shouldn't have! What have you got them?' Florrie felt suddenly guilty that she'd not had time to organize anything more than some chocolate angels, pilfered from Cook, though she had at least contributed the wool that Mam had used to knit them new sweaters.

'It's a surprise! I'll make sure I get them to you after we've had our staff dinner.'

'Smashing. I'll drop them off at Mam's before I start tomorrow's shift. At five in the morning, I might just about beat our Alice waking up!'

He cleared his throat. 'Before we go back, can we stop by the greenhouse? I've something for you.'

Aware that she was already delayed in her return to the Hall to supervise dinner, feeling like Thom might be preparing to execute some romantic overture that she wasn't certain she wanted, Florrie hesitated to answer.

'Well?'

'Aye. But after that, I must get on, Thom. You can guarantee Arkwright will be watching my every move now I'm the housekeeper. He'll be looking for reasons to run with tales to Sir Richard about my timekeeping.' Was she being too ungracious with this considerate man? Did she deserve for her brusqueness to be rewarded with a gift?

Uncertain, she followed Thom to the greenhouse, which was illuminated by a bright moon.

'Close your eyes,' he said.

Shivering, Florrie covered her eyes. 'They're closed.' She heard the squeak of the greenhouse door as it opened and then again as it shut. Presently, it opened and shut again.

'Merry Christmas, Florrie,' Thom said.

She opened her eyes to see Thom was holding a flowering plant in a porcelain pot. 'Oh, very nice.'

'It's a Lenten rose – a hellebore. I forced it in the greenhouse so it would flower for Christmas. You can't really see the lovely pink in this moonlight . . .' He looked up at the bright sky, where the icy clouds had parted to reveal a dazzling moon that was surrounded by a magical halo. The contours of his strong features were picked out in the moonlight, as though he'd been painted with quicksilver. 'But I bred it specially for you. I've called it *Blushing Florence*.'

Holding the pot in her hands, Florrie opened her mouth to respond but found she couldn't articulate how flattered she was or how her heart was gladdened by the gesture, and how intensely awkward she found it that she couldn't bring herself to reciprocate Thom's evident feelings for her with either words or actions. 'By heck,' she said. 'It's . . . it's a darn sight prettier than the real blushing Florence! Ha. Thank you, Thom. That's quite . . . something. I'm deeply honoured.' She was tempted to kiss him on the cheek, but the fear of it becoming more and the blood rushing in her ears paralysed her. 'I must get back.'

23

'Oh, darling, don't be a spoilsport! Do come and dance with me. You can't always expect Hugh to keep a gal company. Especially on Christmas Eve!' Lady Charlotte held out her hand to Sir Richard, batting her eyelashes at him coquettishly.

Florrie set down the tray of petit fours and coffee, which the Harding-Bournes had requested be served in the drawing room. She watched how Sir Richard switched from gazing dolefully into his brandy to looking forlornly at his wife. *How can that be a happy marriage?* she thought. *And why on earth didn't Lady Charlotte just marry Sir Hugh and have done with, if they're that good a match?*

'No, Charlotte. I'm afraid you'll have to kick up your heels with my rather more exuberant brother. I'm feeling quite un-festive, and I don't want to poop your Christmas Eve party.'

'Oh, you are such a stick in the mud, Dicky,' Sir Hugh said. He turned to Charlotte, his face a picture of disappointment. 'I do wish Daphne were here this evening. It's such a shame she's spending Christmas with her family in Gstaad.' His woeful expression gave way to a smile. 'But I suppose you'll just have to do as my dancing partner.' Shouting over to his brother, he took a record off the gramophone's turntable and put on a new one.

'Dicky, boy, you don't know what you're missing!' Jazz music filled the drawing room – rather too loud and crackling.

'Oh, but I do,' Florrie heard Sir Richard say.

She poured the coffees from the tall pot and set Sir Richard's on his fireside occasional table, along with a side plate containing several delicious-looking petit fours that Cook had lovingly topped with festive decorations. 'Will that be all, sir?'

Her employer looked up at her. His eyes softened to a languid grey. 'Dear Florrie. You are very kind to attend to us personally, even though you're now above such humble duties.'

'It's my pleasure, Sir Richard. I like to see you're looked after properly, and anyway, I wanted to give my maids an earlier start to their dinner, it being Christmas Eve and all.' She looked at the ornate clock on the mantelpiece and saw it was almost ten. 'They want to go into the village for midnight Mass.'

Sir Richard frowned as if the thought of going to church hadn't occurred to him. 'I suppose we ought to show our faces, but I feel my religious zeal has all but left me with this dastardly Wall Street business. Ah well. We'll go to the Christmas Day service in the Holcombe Estate chapel, like the dutiful Christians we are.' He laughed mirthlessly, but then his face brightened up. 'You must be very excited to have your mother and your nieces and nephew spending their first Christmas at Holcombe.'

Florrie nodded. 'It's a Christmas miracle.'

His penetrating gaze was unwavering. He spoke

almost in a whisper. 'It's the least I could do for our most dedicated staff member. You spread joy wherever you go. Always have.'

Looking down, she felt her face flush hot and thought of Thom's gift – *Blushing Florence*. How keen the gardener's observation was! 'You're too kind.'

Sir Richard glanced over at his wife and brother and then turned back to Florrie. 'As usual, I'll be handing out staff Christmas gifts tomorrow, but before you retire for the night, there are a couple of extra ones under the tree – one for you and a couple of little somethings for your nieces and nephew. They're wrapped in different paper, each labelled with the recipient's initials, so you'll know which are for you and which are for the children. Do make sure you take them and open them when there are no prying eyes.' He shot another pointed glance towards Lady Charlotte and Sir Hugh. 'I wouldn't want to be accused of favouritism.'

'I don't know what to say . . .'

'I hope you like them.' They locked eyes for a moment too long. He opened his mouth to speak, but whatever it was he wanted to say remained a mystery. After a few agonizing seconds, he merely said, 'Merry Christmas, Florrie.'

'Are you coming to church, Florrie?' Cook asked, once the staff dinner was over.

Florrie shook her head. 'I'll give it a miss this year,' she said. 'I've got to be up with the lark to put presents under the tree at the cottage, before the children are awake.'

She exchanged a glance with Thom and smiled, thinking of the bag of presents he'd given her for Alice, Nelly and George – wrapped in brown paper, but beautifully packaged nevertheless. Then, she clapped her hands together to attract the attention of the maids. 'And I want all of my girls up bright and early to make sure Christmas Day runs like clockwork. No oversleeping!'

'We won't, Florrie,' Sally said.

The others chimed in with their agreement, though Florrie noted that nobody had yet started to call her Miss Bickerstaff. She wondered if that was something she should insist on, now that she was housekeeper. Her new uniform fit well, but she reasoned it would take her a while to grow into the new responsibilities and authority that came with it. She decided that she would ponder the name conundrum in the New Year. In the meantime, she was itching to sneak back into the drawing room to retrieve the clandestine gifts from Sir Richard.

Getting to her feet, she collected Thom's bag of gifts from the sideboard, wished the rest of the staff who were still sitting around the table a Merry Christmas, and climbed the back stairs to the main house.

Padding softly along the hallway, Florrie checked that the dining room was empty before tiptoeing through the darkness to the door that connected it with the drawing room. Pressing her ear to the wood, she was surprised to hear silence, but for the thudding of her own heart inside her chest. Could it be that Lady Charlotte and Sir Hugh had retired before midnight for a change?

Daring to push the door open a fraction, she realized

the drawing room was also in darkness. Setting down Thom's bag, she put on a lamp and hastened over to the tree. When she found the differently wrapped gifts, her heart leaped. Sliding them into the bag, she then turned off the lamp and ascended the back stairs to her room on the top floor.

She perched on the edge of her bed and took out Sir Richard's packages. Three were large, but the one labelled 'F' was a small, unyielding rectangular box.

What could it be? Tearing off the paper with trembling hands, she found a hard leather case. Jewellery? Surely not! Perplexed, she opened it to find a beautiful tortoiseshell fountain pen with a gold nib, trim and clip. She gasped. She lifted the expensive-looking pen out and realized when she unscrewed the barrel to reveal the ink pump that there was a note tightly curled inside. Florrie stifled a giggle, biting her lip at the subterfuge. *What in God's name is going on here? This is a rum do.*

She set the pen and its case down on her bed and unfurled the note. It had been written in Sir Richard's tight, cursive hand and simply said:

Dearest Florrie,

Whenever you write the lists, letters and entries in the house-keeperly ledgers that keep Holcombe Hall ticking; whenever you pen your triumphs, woes and the closely guarded desires of your heart in a journal, let this pen remind you of my gratitude.

Yours always,
Richard

Florrie gasped and clasped the note to her chest. Flipping heck. *Closely guarded* what? She re-read the note, which seemed to say everything and nothing at the same time. *Yours always*? Was it normal for him to bestow such a fine and elegant gift on a newly appointed housekeeper? She shrugged, reasoning that Mrs Douglas and Arkwright had taken up their positions at a time when Lord George Harding-Bourne, Richard's father, had been in charge, so Florrie's appointment was a novel experience for him. Yet the tone of the note was hardly what she would have expected from her employer. *Let this pen remind you of my gratitude.* She smiled and covered her mouth with her hand, noticing how the fine hairs on her arms stood to attention.

Looking over at the plant that Thom had specially bred for her, its rich pink double flowers brightening up her spartan room, Florrie marvelled that she had received such gifts from two fine men. Yet one must have been at least a year in the making – a unique and personalized present, given by an unmarried man of excellent character from her own social class. The other was an easy purchase by an incredibly wealthy peer of the realm, perhaps picked up on a whim during some business trip to Manchester or London – a pen accompanied by a furtive note from a member of the upper class, who happened to be her employer and also, crucially, married.

'Florrie Bickerstaff, what on earth have you got yourself into?' Florrie said, placing the pen in its box beside the hellebore.

*

'Merry Christmas!' Florrie whispered, when Mam cracked the front door open on Christmas morning. It was still dark as night at just gone five in the morning, with a bite in the air, and a crisp frost that had crunched underfoot as she'd walked over from the Hall. 'Are they still asleep?'

Mam pulled her inside and hugged her tightly. 'Merry Christmas, love. Yes, all still snoring in their beds, bless them.'

'Did you manage to finish knitting all them jumpers what I bought the wool for?'

'All three of them. Finished them yesterday.' Mam rummaged in her knitting bag and pulled out the darling pieces that she'd knitted for the children: a pink smocked cardigan for Alice, a yellow pullover with a lamb on the front for Nelly and a pale blue pullover with a dog on the front for George. 'I'll wrap them and put them under the tree.'

Florrie reached inside the bag full of presents she'd brought and pulled out three small Christmas stockings she'd fashioned from her old woollen socks, embroidered in a rudimentary fashion with a simple Christmas tree silhouette. 'These stockings full of chocolate are a little extra from me, so you might try to hang them from the fireplace.' She then passed her mother the bag. 'I wish I could see their little faces light up when they open these, but I'm up to my eyes in it today. You'll bring them over for the staff Christmas lunch, won't you?'

Kneeling down to lay the beautifully wrapped presents under the tree, Mam nodded. She looked over her shoulder. 'I wouldn't miss it for the world. George is *so* excited to go to the big house, though I don't think our Nelly really understands any of it yet, and Alice . . . Well, she's just a babe in arms, isn't she? But I can't wait to try some of Cook's festive grub, and there's other staff I've still not even met yet.' She turned back to the presents, took a pair of reading spectacles out of her pocket and put them on. 'Now, who are all these from?'

Florrie knelt next to her mother, careful to keep her voice low, lest the children hear them speaking and spoil their own surprise. She pointed to each of the gifts. 'The ones in brown paper are from Thom. The ones in fancy wrappings are from Sir Richard.'

She could tell Mam was scrutinizing the side of her face. 'Lovely of Thom. What a grand lad. Very generous of Sir Richard. *Again*. Did he get *you* a present?'

Florrie looked sheepishly at her mother and pulled the pen case from her skirt pocket, though she'd hidden the note inside a shoe in her wardrobe.

Her mother took the case and opened it. When she saw the pen, she breathed in sharply. 'Jesus wept! He must have paid a mint for that.' She frowned and shook her head. 'You've got to give it back.' She thrust it back at Florrie. 'A gift like that has conditions attached, believe you me. He'll expect something in return, and there's only one thing a girl like you has got what's worth a gift like that.'

'He give it me as a token of his appreciation. For doing a good job.'

Her mother scoffed. 'Oh, aye? Pull the other one, it's got bells on.'

Florrie stuffed the pen case back into her pocket, irritated that her mother should take the shine off Sir Richard's generosity with such abrasive and, she had to admit, seemingly astute observations. Yet she didn't want to think of Sir Richard as being so manipulative. 'Sir Richard's not like that.'

'Rubbish! He's got the same thing in his trousers as every other man.'

'Mam!' Florrie heard Alice start to fret upstairs.

Her mother was no longer whispering. 'You know what happens to young female domestic staff who succumb to the charms and advances of their amorous bosses, don't you? They end up out on their ear with a bun in the oven. No job; no husband; no money to feed a baby born the wrong side of the blanket.' Without warning, Mam gripped Florrie by the wrist and pulled her close. 'Is it too late to give that pen back?' Her mother looked at her through narrowed eyes as though she were scrutinizing her beneath a magnifying glass. 'Have you already forfeited your good reputation, Florence Bickerstaff?'

Florrie shook her off, affronted. 'Don't be so . . . bad-minded, Mam. I'm twenty-five years old and I've never so much as kissed a man. Chance would be a fine thing! I bet you didn't give our Irene this lecture.'

'No, I didn't. Know why? She beat me to it. She was already carrying George the day she got married. I never liked that dead-leg she wed, but she made it so she had no choice.' Mam's scowl softened and she stroked Florrie's cheek. 'I don't want you to make the same silly mistakes she did. I want better for you, love.'

'It's Christmas! Merry Christmas!' George's excitable shouting resounded through the cottage, drowning out even Alice's cries. 'Nana! Nana! Has Father Christmas been?' There was the sound of small feet thundering across the floorboards above them, then Nelly's burbling started up.

'I'll slip out back,' Florrie said, getting to her feet. 'Let them think Santa left this lot.'

Mam stood, folding up the large bag that had contained the gifts. She gave it back to Florrie. 'Remember what I said, love. Give him the pen back. Don't be beholden to him. It's just a game to men like that – fun and games at your expense.'

Florrie nodded ruefully. She slipped silently into the scullery and out of the back door.

'Pass us a bit more of that turkey, will you?' Albert asked Cook. 'It's right moist this year.'

Cook looked at him askance. The Christmas cracker paper crown she'd donned was slipping low over her eyebrows. 'What do you mean, *"this* year"'? What you trying to say about my cooking, you cheeky beggar?'

Albert chuckled and held his plate out towards her. 'Nowt. Stop looking for insults where there are none and get us fed, will you?'

'Save some seconds for me,' Thom said.

'And me!' George said, holding his plate up so that his knife and fork almost fell off.

'George!' Mam said. 'Manners at the table, young man!'

Thom smiled and reached behind Florrie to ruffle

George's hair. 'Good lad. Put hairs on your chest, will Cook's Christmas dinner.'

Across the table, Arkwright shovelled a roast potato into his mouth thoughtfully. Today, full of uncharacteristic festive cheer and wine, he had colour in his cheeks and had smiled more than once. 'Did you get anything from Father Christmas?' he asked George.

With a forkful of food stored in his cheek like a squirrel, George ignored Mam's admonitions not to speak with his mouth open. 'Ooh, I got a cowboy hat and a holster and toy pistol and a sheriff's badge, just like Gary Cooper, and I got a new woollen pullover with a doggy on it, and I got some chocolates and a posh leather book with nice pictures in it. I can't read it yet, but Nana's going to read it for me, aren't you, Nan?'

Arkwright cocked his head to the side. 'Are you not starting at the village school in Holcombe? You've grown like billy-oh just in the few weeks you've been here. Surely a big boy like you should be learning to read for himself, in class.'

'I haven't had time to register him yet,' Mam said.

Arkwright smiled benignly at George. 'Well, until you do, I could manage a half-hour a day to start him on some simple reading. There are some old picture books in the library, bought by the old governess, from when Sir Richard and Sir Hugh were small boys. I'm sure there would be no issue in my using them to teach George.'

Florrie exchanged amused glances with Cook, Sally and Thom. Was this the Arkwright they'd known for a decade or more? Had the passing of Mrs Douglas really changed him for the better, or was it just the wine? 'Thank you, Mr Arkwright. That's very thoughtful.' She raised her glass to him.

When the meal was over, everyone was replete, and Mam took the children back to the cottage. With the Harding-Bournes already catered for, Florrie remained at the table, talking with her colleagues about the mills shutting and the financial chaos in America. Eventually, tired and stiff and in need of a nap, she got up, took her leave and was heading for the back stairs when she heard a hissing sound.

'Psst.' Thom was beckoning her into the shadows.

'What's with all the secrecy?' she asked.

It was then that she noticed he was standing on the threshold of Cook's pantry, twirling a piece of mistletoe between his fingers. Her heart froze.

'Kiss under the mistletoe, Miss Bickerstaff?' He grinned at her, his face flushed.

Florrie had a choice to make. Should she rebuff Thom, knowing she had feelings for Sir Richard, however misplaced, and needing to maintain some distance as the housekeeper of Holcombe Hall, or should she kiss this loveable, sweet, handsome man, at long last?

1930

24

'Darling Florrie, you really must help me decide what to take to New York in such relentlessly bitter weather,' Lady Charlotte said, peering into the largest of her four wardrobes, which housed her collection of furs. In the other three were stored sparkling gowns, silken outfits, hand-lasted shoes and hats from the finest milliners — a collection that had almost certainly cost more than the entire domestic staff of Holcombe Hall earned in a decade.

'I'm sure my opinion will be of little use, my lady. All of your clothes are exquisite.'

Florrie thought about her two Sunday-best dresses hanging in her wardrobe in her attic room. One for winter and one for summer. Both woefully out of date. Then there was her uniform, which was marginally better now she was the housekeeper but which still made her look like an Edwardian governess. As for her shoes, she only possessed two pairs, one of which was the hiding place for the note from Sir Richard. It was the 6th January, and she still hadn't found the right moment to return the fountain pen, but she would. As it was, Florrie had felt she had no option but to gently resist Thom's attempts to kiss her beneath the mistletoe. She could not in all fairness toy with his feelings when she was not even certain of her own. She would not start a romance with an honourable man who clearly wanted a family, while she was committed to a job that required her to remain a spinster.

'But you have an excellent eye for common sense clothing, Florrie.' Lady Charlotte's thinly disguised insult brought Florrie back to the here and now. 'Even on a Sunday, I don't think I've ever seen you wearing anything that couldn't be described as "comfortable".' She looked Florrie up and down, wearing a sympathetic smile.

Florrie forced a smile in return. How she wished that her promotion would preclude her from having to double as Lady Charlotte's lady's maid. Yet Lady Charlotte was still insisting with regularity that Florrie should act as her confidante, hairstylist and dresser, even though Florrie had assigned a new lady's maid to cater to her needs.

'Here! Hold these, will you? I'll try them on.' Still clad only in her negligée and a silk dressing gown, Lady Charlotte had pulled out a full-length mink coat as well as a silver fox and now pushed both on to Florrie.

Florrie laid the fox on the bed and held open the mink for her employer to try on. 'I've always loved this coat on you, my lady.' She relished the feel of the lustrous fur between her fingers. 'It feels so luxurious to the touch; so heavy and well made with such a lovely satin lining. I'm sure you'd be very warm.'

Lady Charlotte slid the coat on and started to fasten it. She got halfway down the furrier's hooks when she frowned. 'Oh dear. This is a little tight.' She pulled the edges of the coat together, but the hook wouldn't quite meet the eye. 'Drat, Christmas over-indulgence! You must tell Cook to prepare me only light soups until we leave.' She took it off and flung it at Florrie. 'Let's try the fox. We'll keep going until I have the perfect wardrobe to last me a month, sailing the high seas and braving Fifth Avenue.'

Realizing that tending to Lady Charlotte's wardrobe conundrum was eating into her housekeeping duties, Florrie was relieved when Sir Richard entered the bedroom. Unlike his wife, he was fully dressed, and Florrie knew he'd been served breakfast in his study at seven o'clock, some four hours earlier.

'Florrie! There you are.' His gaze rested on the open trunk that his wife had already filled with coats and his nostrils flared ever so slightly. 'Darling, do you think I can steal Florrie from you on actual housekeeping business?'

Lady Charlotte rolled her eyes and growled. 'If you must.'

Sir Richard pointed to the trunk. 'Do go easy on the baggage, dear. We're only going on a business trip, and I rather think, given the straitened circumstances over the pond at the moment, arriving with the finest Paris fashions in five trunks might look rather crass. Don't you think?'

Lady Charlotte pooh-poohed him and waved him away. 'Go on. Take my Florrie, but don't blame me if my appearance has the whole of New York high society gossiping behind our backs that the British are a shabby lot.'

Florrie was at once relieved to be freed from the demands of Lady Charlotte and also nervous that Sir Richard clearly wanted to speak to her in private. She'd said a polite, 'thank you for the gifts' on Boxing Day, but neither of them had broached the subject further. *His over-familiarity is making me so darned uncomfortable. Is it flirtation or is it just favouritism? How I wish I had the pen in my pocket right now,* she thought. *I could have drawn a line in the sand before he goes away. Darn it, Florrie Bickerstaff! You're your own worst enemy!*

She followed Sir Richard down to his study, where he closed the door firmly behind her. He placed his hand lightly on the small of her back and indicated that she should take a seat in the visitor's chair by his desk.

Flinching at his touch, while at the same time realizing her skin tingled beneath his fingertips, she took her seat. Would he proposition her, as her mother expected?

'Now, Florrie. I wanted to talk to you about your priorities while we're away in New York.' He opened his notebook at a page where he'd written out a list in that familiar, cursive hand. There was no glint in his eye or any other signs of flirtation in his mannerisms. 'I'm going to need you to instigate some economies.'

Florrie took out her notebook and pencil, poised to write down his requests. 'Fire away.'

'Right. First, could you please ensure that no lights are left on and no fires are lit in rooms that aren't in use?'

'Of course, Sir Richard.'

'My brother and my mother will remain here, of course. I don't anticipate Mama will be throwing raucous parties . . .' He flashed her a knowing grin. 'But Sir Hugh, on the other hand . . .' He raised his eyebrows. 'He's been told not to indulge in expensive soirées, of course, but my brother seems to think budgetary restraint beneath him.'

'What would you like me to do if Sir Hugh does have guests to stay?'

Sir Richard pressed his lips together and thumbed his freshly shaven chin. 'There's nothing you can do, realistically. Just ask Cook to roll out the cheapest food and wines, if he does entertain while we're away. I'll tell Arkwright to water the booze down. I don't need any more smashed windows, costing me a small fortune to replace, and I can't have my brother quaffing the Harding-Bourne estate into dereliction. We must, must, must watch the pennies.' He listed some other areas in which housekeeping might save money, then he narrowed his eyes at her. His brow furrowed. 'Now, there is one other major request that I have of you. This will undoubtedly save us the most money, but it's going to be the least popular, I'm afraid.'

Florrie anticipated what he was about to say. She had known this would come with the territory of being housekeeper, but that did nothing to quieten her pounding heartbeat or quell the sense of dread that now filled her. 'Go on.'

'We need a leaner domestic staff, and that means letting non-essential people go.' He steepled his fingers and tapped his fingertips together, never taking his eyes from her. 'There. I've said it. Is this something you think you can tackle while we're gone?'

Knowing she ought to say yes to please him, Florrie blurted out, 'Well, I'm not sure, actually.'

He blinked repeatedly and cocked his head to the side. 'Sorry. I – in what way?'

Florrie took a deep breath. 'Well, I appreciate your conundrum, but have you seen the size of this place? If you don't maintain the same number of kitchen maids, chambermaids, ladies' maids . . . all of those girls under my jurisdiction who are up at the crack of dawn and don't see their beds 'til near midnight . . . this place would be quickly eaten by the woodlice, silverfish, damp and mould. We struggled with the laundry 'til my mother started. We've just lost one maid, who had to be sacked just before Mrs Douglas passed, and three have since been laid up for a fortnight with influenza.'

He shook his head. 'The cuts have to come from somewhere, Florrie. I'm having to shed staff at the mills, the foundry and shipyards, too.'

'Of course. I promise I'll do my level best to see where we can economize with household expenditure. Cook can definitely give more thought to costly ingredients for meals – things like lobster and foie gras are a terrible drain on the budget. We can certainly exercise caution with lighting and heating, as long as the pipes don't freeze in a very cold snap.' Thinking about the impoverished mill workers in Manchester like her aunt, whose employment was precarious at best, it was all Florrie could do to bite her tongue about Lady Charlotte's and Sir Hugh's profligacy in any given month, which cost sums that would keep ordinary families fed for years. 'If I may, I suggest you'd do better to look at Mr Arkwright's man-servants. He has a lot of lads that seem to do little apart from smoke out by the stables. And I understand stocking the wine cellars is a significant drain on finances . . . Maybe you could ask Mr Arkwright to negotiate with the vintner?'

'Right. What about the gardeners?' Sir Richard asked, looking out of the window.

Was Sir Richard testing her loyalty towards Thom? Had Cook been right in thinking Sir Richard saw him as some kind of competition for her affections? The very thought made her gut tighten, and she renewed her resolve to give the pen back as soon as possible. 'I only ever witness the gardeners working exceedingly hard,' she said. 'You've about a hundred acres of land, just inside the estate walls. Farmland beyond that. I sincerely doubt you could spare a gardener, unless you want the deer eating Capability Brown's best efforts.' She smiled resolutely. 'But I would encourage you to have this conversation with your butler about his lads. Beyond Mr Arkwright himself, your driver, a couple of stable boys and the handyman, I'm afraid I can't really see the need for most of them.'

Sir Richard frowned, nodding slowly and chewing his bottom lip. 'But you'll try to make cutbacks where you can? And if you can see an opportunity to let a girl go, you'll do it? Please?' He leaned in towards her, his face a picture of sincerity. 'I've been very supportive of your family lately, and I'm just asking you to help me in this book-balancing endeavour in return.'

'You *certainly* have. I promise, I'll do my best,' she said, smiling. 'This place will be in safe hands while you're away.'

'Stand up straight and smile,' Florrie told her staff as they lined up outside Holcombe Hall two days later to bid bon voyage to Sir Richard and Lady Charlotte. In the freezing cold of a day that was wavering between icy wind, driving sleet and hail showers, she walked past Cook and along the row of maids, inspecting each one. 'I know it's flipping freezing, but you'll not have to be out here for more than five minutes, as long as her ladyship gets her lipstick on straight first time.'

The maids giggled, even as their teeth chattered.

On the other side of the steps, Arkwright had lined up the valets and footmen and now strode up and down the row like a sergeant major, batting a glove at any man who wasn't standing perfectly as if it was a military parade. 'Stop your fussing over the weather!' he said. 'Any man caught whingeing or slouching gets his wages docked a shilling.'

At the bottom of the stone staircase, the gleaming Rolls-Royce awaited the Harding-Bournes – their chauffer, Graham, impeccably clad in his smart livery and hat, standing to attention, though his nose was bright red and his eyes streamed in the wind. He checked his watch and looked to the heavens, clearly muttering beneath his breath.

Lady Charlotte was the first to emerge, pulling on her gloves and already wearing a dark grey cloche hat. She had on an ankle-length chinchilla coat, rather than one of the furs she had tried on in the bedroom with Florrie. Sweeping down the staircase, she didn't even glance at the staff, who were braving the biting cold to see the travelling couple off.

Graham opened the rear door for her and she stepped gracefully into the Rolls-Royce and was out of sight in an instant, without a backwards glance.

'Charming,' Sally said out of the corner of her mouth. 'Love you, too.'

Florrie shushed her and shot her a stern look.

Sir Richard appeared next, smartly clad in a double-breasted tweed coat and homburg hat. He was followed by Arkwright's lads, who were carrying the copious amounts of luggage out to a separate vehicle – a Ford – that was to be driven by Thom to the Liverpool docks where their liner awaited.

'Hello, everyone,' Sir Richard said, taking off his hat and waving it merrily at the staff. 'Good Lord, you didn't have to stand to attention out here in these Arctic conditions, just to bid us farewell. Do get back inside where it's warm.' He made his way down the stairs and came to a standstill by Florrie and Arkwright. 'For heaven's sake, you shouldn't be out in these elements without so much as coats. Whatever will become of Holcombe Hall if you're all frozen to death? My mother will starve and my brother will almost certainly become feral . . . even more feral, I should say.' He looked around, smiling at the laughter that rippled among the staff. Then he clapped his hands together. 'Inside, the lot of you. Go on! Go and get yourselves some tea and cake. If Mr Arkwright tries to deny you, remind him I said you could.' He winked at Arkwright, then turned to Florrie, treating her to a dazzling smile. 'Miss Bickerstaff, I entrust my humble home to your careful stewardship.' Much to her surprise, he bowed. 'We will write, though no doubt, our letter won't reach you until we're home again, in four weeks' time. Do think of us, Miss Bickerstaff, as we are forced to rub shoulders with Americans and drink a poor facsimile of tea.'

Florrie couldn't help but chuckle at his playful good-bye, yet she found her heart was already aching at the thought of him being away for so long. All thoughts of the fountain pen were pushed aside by her imaginings of how empty the house would feel without him. Worse still, for the first time as housekeeper, she was being abandoned to the vagaries of Arkwright's moods.

25

'Budgets?' Arkwright asked, scowling. 'What do you mean, we need to discuss budgets?'

Standing in the butler's office, feeling rather like a scolded schoolchild sent before the headmaster, Florrie steeled herself to broach the subject of culling staff members. 'Sir Richard said that while he's away, we're to make savings.' Not wanting any of the staff to over-hear their conversation, she kept her voice so low that Arkwright was cupping his ear.

'I can't hear a word you're saying, girl.' He clicked his fingers at her. 'Close the door, for God's sake.'

She complied and repeated Sir Richard's request.

'And? You're in charge of switching off lights and the like. That's a housekeeping concern. Look, can't you see I'm busy?' He poked the ledger that stood open on his desk. 'Can this wait?'

'No.' Florrie pulled up the visitor's chair, which Arkwright notoriously always set at the far end of the room because he didn't like to encourage visitors. She sat down decisively, only to discover she was now lower than him and was forced quite literally to look up to the butler. 'Sir Richard wants a leaner staff, and I really can't see how we could manage without any of my girls. So, Sir Richard suggested you have a think about the lads you need on the payroll and which ones you might be able to let go.'

Arkwright's mouth fell open. He got to his feet and started to bellow with such ferocity that spittle flew out with every word he uttered. 'I am the butler of Holcombe Hall, and I've been serving here a damn sight longer than you, young lady. Almost three decades longer, in fact.' He started to point, point, point. 'How dare *you* tell *me* how to run *this* house and run *my* staff, when you were nothing but a glorified housemaid until last month?'

'Whether I'm too youthful for your liking or not, Mr Arkwright, the fact remains that I am the new house-keeper. The ladies are under my jurisdiction and the fellers are under yours. I am your equal, and we must discuss the staff wages bill like adults.' She placed one hand on top of the other on her lap and looked at him expectantly, determined not to buckle at the sight of his enraged, beetroot-red face. 'Sir Richard demands it.'

'"Sir Richard demands it!"' He mimicked her high voice. Spreading his hands along the desk, he leaned over towards her. 'Your champion isn't here to defend you now, sweetheart, and I'm not softened by a pretty young face and a perky bosom.' He thumbed himself in the chest. '*I'm* in charge, and if you want to make cuts, I suggest you give the order of the boot to that useless dishrag of a girl, Sally Glover. Better still, how about you send your mother back to Manchester where she belongs, because she's cost this estate so much money, I expect her to be spinning the bedding and towels into gold thread, never mind washing them.'

Florrie sat bolt upright and laced her hands together tightly. 'I beg your pardon, Mr Arkwright,' she said, her tone so icy, the room seemed a few degrees colder. 'I would rather you *didn't* slander one of my maids, just because you're faced with the uncomfortable prospect of accounting for the many, many lads under your jurisdiction and letting one or two of the more useless ones go. We *all* need to make savings. And yes, the family has been very generous to my mother, but she works long, hard hours, her work is impeccable, and she's saving money now by repairing clothes that were being thrown away or sent to the jumble sale.' She took a deep breath and continued, emboldened by Arkwright's open-mouthed silence. 'Need I remind you that before my mother arrived, you were complaining mightily that we needed a laundress, post-haste?'

Arkwright glared at her, his nostrils flaring with indignation. 'I don't need reminding of anything, you cheeky young whippersnapper. I am the butler! And this is my office. I can say what I bloody well want in my office.' He thumped the desk. 'Your mother's had preferential treatment because Sir Richard unfathomably has a soft spot for you.'

'I don't see you complaining when my mother returns your clothes to you in immaculate condition.'

'Well, she has no right living in that gamekeeper's cottage with those snot-nosed infants. Holcombe Hall is not the Salvation Army.'

Florrie gasped. Her frosty composure melted and evaporated in an instant. 'How dare you say such unkind things about my nieces and nephew? And to think, you're supposed to be teaching George to read! If this is the way you talk to him when he's in your care, I shudder to think how fondly he'll feel about reading as he grows up.' Willing the lump in her throat and the tears in her eyes not to betray her, she shoved the chair out of the way, scraping its feet noisily along the wooden floor, and marched to the door. She turned back to Arkwright, balling her fists and steeling herself not to let him have the last word. 'I don't know how on God's good earth Mrs Douglas put up with you for twenty-five years, but all I can say is I'm not surprised that poor woman dropped dead of a heart attack if this is how you spoke to her. You, Mr Arkwright, are a beast. A beastly, bullying, fickle little man, and I shall await your apology.'

She slammed the door closed behind her and fled into the kitchen, rushing past a curious Cook and up the back stairs. She marched at a brisk pace to the library, feeling certain that, at this time of the day and with Sir Richard gone, she would be alone there.

'That nasty, nasty, horrible . . .' She thumped her palm. 'Bully of a man.'

Florrie knew that she could not face any of the maids until she'd collected herself. Breathing deeply to slow her thunderous heartbeat, she slipped into the library and hid between two bookshelves that housed collections of very old-looking leather books. Slumping to the floor, she sat, head in hands, willing herself to stifle the dry, wracking sobs that tried their best to tear their way out of her chest.

It was only as her pulse started to slow that she realized she could hear voices coming from the mezzanine above her. A woman's and a man's.

'All these years you've kept me at bay, Elizabeth,' the man said. Clearly not Sir Hugh. He sounded older.

'With good reason! My family's reputation comes before everything, but you are notoriously persistent. If you weren't, we wouldn't be sitting here now, would we?' That was undoubtedly Dame Elizabeth speaking.

Florrie wondered that this gentleman caller was being received in such apparent secrecy. She didn't recall anyone arriving at the house. Had he somehow slipped in without announcing his arrival?

'Don't tell me you've never wanted to look upon my face again.' The man's voice softened. 'I've yearned to see yours, Lizzie.'

'Don't call me that! Lizzie was a foolish girl, and I am now an old woman. A *wiser* woman.' Florrie could hear Dame Elizabeth's skirts rustle. 'And your letters have been intolerable enough as it is. They have to stop, do you hear me?' She sounded vehement, frightened even.

Their voices then dropped so low that Florrie could only hear the odd snippet of conversation. The visitor sounded like someone who exerted some kind of pull over Dame Elizabeth. Might she be in some sort of danger? Yet Florrie's inclination to rush up and ask if the old lady needed help felt like uninvited intrusion. The two were likely out of sight for a reason. Although she desperately wanted to know what was being discussed so furtively, if only for the sake of Dame Elizabeth's safety, she did feel like she was turning into Cook. Dare she at least creep closer to lay eyes on this male visitor?

All thoughts of Arkwright's cruel words now banished to the back of her mind, Florrie looked around to see if there was some way of getting a look at the mezzanine discreetly, other than climbing the stairs, where she would be instantly spotted.

She caught sight of a wheeled library ladder, designed to be moved along the stacks to provide ease of access to the uppermost bookshelves. Perhaps if she silently moved the ladder to the start of the stack, she could somehow crane her neck to see through the wooden balustrade that edged the mezzanine.

Pushing the ladder along as quietly as she could, she reached the outermost reaches of the bookshelf that protruded beyond the boundary of the mezzanine. Good. She started to climb, wincing when a rung squeaked. She froze. Yet the subdued chatter continued.

'. . . asking after Richard's wellbeing. How could you think I wouldn't want to know how the boy . . .' The man's speech passed frustratingly in and out of earshot.

The boy, Florrie thought. *Richard? Not,* Sir *Richard. That sounds very familiar.*

Hanging on to the ladder, she strained to hear Dame Elizabeth's response. All she caught was the word 'presumptuous' and 'familiarity you haven't earned'. She climbed a little higher – a little too high, because as Florrie craned her neck to see over the dusty top of the bookshelf, through the balustrade, she could feel herself beginning to tip backwards. She looked down at the floor, which felt suddenly like too steep a drop. The room seemed to swim and her hands were slick with sweat. *I'm going to fall and break my flaming neck, and then everyone will know Florrie Bickerstaff was eavesdropping on her boss's mother.*

Managing somehow to regain her balance, Florrie gingerly climbed back down the ladder, shaking from the near miss she'd had. It was no good. She would have to catch whatever she could of the conversation from the safety of the stacks.

The voices from above became raised and more heated, but their words were partly drowned out by noise coming from the hallway – laughter from a man-servant and a maid.

'I want you gone from my home and my life, do you hear me? Get out!' Dame Elizabeth exclaimed. There was the sound of her skirts rustling again and the scraping of a chair.

'Please, Lizzie. Try to see it from my perspective. All I want is . . .' The man's wishes were obscured by the laughter and a bawdy exchange between what now sounded very much like Danny and Sally.

Florrie wished fervently that the two servants would get back to their duties or at least quieten down. She cupped her ear to hear more.

Dame Elizabeth spoke. 'If it ever becomes public knowledge that . . .'

Her cryptic words were swallowed up by the sound

of Danny's foghorn of a voice: 'Hey, Sal. Gordon in't stables reckons Cook's got bigger knackers than His Lordship's stallion. She's got a moustache, and all.'

Be quiet, for heaven's sakes, Florrie yelled in the confines of her head.

There were footfalls from above, now, and Dame Elizabeth started to shout in earnest. 'Get out, I say, or I'll call for assistance! There are servants outside. I can hear them. I'll call them.'

Two sets of footsteps resounded on the stairs that led from the mezzanine to the lower floor of the library. They were both coming down. Florrie shrank into the shadows between the stacks, praying she'd get a glimpse of the visitor, yet her subterfuge would remain undiscovered.

'I'll be in touch,' the man said.

'Kindly don't bother,' Dame Elizabeth said. 'If you do, I shall telephone the police.'

They came to a halt just within sight. Dame Elizabeth stood in front of the man, obscuring him, but when she moved a step to the side, Florrie got a good look at him. He was indeed an older man – somewhat older than Dame Elizabeth, in fact. He was smartly dressed, though not as elegant as a man of the Harding-Bournes' social standing would be; perhaps a professional of some sort or a man from the lower echelons of nobility. He did look strangely familiar, though, and Florrie rifled through her memories to pinpoint where she might have seen him before. So many people came and went at Holcombe Hall, and it was possible that if this man was now persona non grata, he'd been involved in Dame Elizabeth's life long before Florrie had begun service there.

Outside, Danny and Sally had fallen quiet. Had they gone?

'I regret deeply that we have come to this, Lizzie,' the visitor said, reaching out to take Dame Elizabeth's hands. His face was a picture of contrition, but there was a glint in his eye. 'Squabbling over something we have a mutual interest in.'

'Get out.' Dame Elizabeth pushed him away and pointed to the door. 'And make sure you leave with as much discretion as the manner in which you arrived. Do me at least that much of a kindness.'

'This isn't the last you'll hear from me.' The man bowed curtly and marched out.

Dame Elizabeth remained standing in the middle of the library for a moment. She sobbed only once, dabbed at her eyes with a lace handkerchief. Then she inhaled sharply, lifted her head, looking as regal as ever, and exited the library in a swoosh of black skirts.

Florrie emerged from her hiding place, trembling with trepidation and intrigue. 'By heck,' she said softly to herself. 'I wonder what all that was about.'

26

'Just leave the tray there, dear,' Dame Elizabeth said a week later, pointing to the green velvet ottoman at the end of her bed.

She lay on the chaise longue, clutching a novel that Florrie was certain she hadn't been reading in earnest, since it was upside down. Her eyes seemed unfocussed and her manner distracted, as if her thoughts were elsewhere.

'It's seven days now that you've been taking your meals in here,' Florrie said, setting down the tray that held a simple egg sandwich and a glass of water at Dame Elizabeth's request. She studied the old lady's face, noting that the lines in her forehead were etched deeper than usual and her mouth had an even more downturned appearance. 'Will you not dine with Sir Hugh, my lady?'

Dame Elizabeth shook her head. 'No, no. He'll only want to bend my ear about the joys of fascism and jazz. I feel in rather low spirits at the moment, the kind that cannot be remedied by my son's inane twittering.'

'Is there anything you need me to fetch? A tonic? An aspirin? Cake!'

Waving her away with the book, Dame Elizabeth answered by turning to face the window. 'Leave me be, Florence. I will "come round without water", as the locals say.'

As Florrie walked back along the wing of family bed-rooms, popping into each to ensure the housemaids had left them sparkling clean, she pondered Dame Elizabeth's low mood. It was almost certainly down to her mystery visitor.

When she'd finished her inspection, she made her way back to the kitchen, where Cook was slicing vegetables and her kitchen maid was scrubbing huge steel pans at the sink.

'Cook, you've been here longer than me,' Florrie said.

'Aye.' Cook didn't look up from aggressively chopping the largest carrot Florrie had ever seen.

'Do you remember Dame Elizabeth ever having a gentleman companion? Like, a close friend.'

Cook stopped chopping immediately and sidled up to Florrie, lowering her voice. 'Whyever do you ask, Miss Bickerstaff?' Her face flushed with naked enthusi-asm and her eyes glittered. She grinned. 'Go on! Tell us. What's she up to, the old lady?'

Florrie knew immediately that she'd asked the wrong person. Of all the people in the Hall, what had possessed her to ask Cook? Mrs Douglas might have known and would surely not have responded with quite such unfet-tered glee.

'Never mind,' Florrie said. 'Forget I asked. Get on with your chopping.' She shooed her back round to her side of the table.

Cook returned to chopping the carrot and blew a wayward strand of hair out of her eyes. 'Out with it, Florrie. Has she been gambling and run up debts?

Opium addiction? Come on. You must have asked for a reason.'

Florrie shook her head. 'It's nowt. Forget it. Just a weird dream I had last night, where Dame Elizabeth had a male confidant,' she lied. 'It felt very real. That's all. I just wanted to check I wasn't losing my marbles.'

'A dream? Oh really?' Pointing the knife's blade at Florrie, Cook narrowed her eyes. 'You're stringing me a line and sitting on gossip, you big spoilsport. I can smell it.'

Feeling instinctively that she needed to extricate herself from Cook's interrogation, Florrie made her way to the laundry to see how her mother was getting on, freshening up Lady Charlotte's spring wardrobe in readiness for her return from New York and the warmer months ahead.

She heard the children before she'd even opened the door. The sight that greeted her was enough to bring on a migraine. Alice was sitting in the middle of the tiled floor, bawling and red-faced, drooling on to her dress and gasping for breath intermittently, making the sorts of ominous burping noises that might preface her bringing her lunch back up. Nelly and George were screaming at each other, each hurling a wet sponge at the other's head. Mam was at the far end of the room, standing behind the ironing board, pressing some garment belonging to Lady Charlotte with tears streaming down her face.

'What in God's name is going on in here, Mam?' Florrie asked. She forcibly parted the wringing wet

Nelly and George, restraining them by their wrists. 'Stop your fussing right this minute, you two, or I'll put you over my knee.' She glared at them until they fell silent. Letting them go, she then picked Alice up and started to rock her softly so that her tears subsided almost immediately.

Mam set the iron upright and wiped her eyes on her sleeve. 'This is what looking after three babies looks like when you're fifty years old and you've got to work 'til all hours.' She shook her head ruefully. 'I'm at the end of my tether, love. We might have food on the table and a grand roof over our heads, but . . . I can't control them.' She pulled her cardigan off agitatedly and flung it on to the top of a laundry basket by the ironing board. 'I can't control *me*! I'm freezing cold one minute, boiling hot the next. My knees crack, my hips ache, I'm sleeping terrible. I know it's just my age, but I'm expected to be a young mother to those babies, and I'm not. I'm their Nana. *And* I'm the laundress in a stately home.'

In a household that was currently quiet, given Sir Richard and Lady Charlotte were away and the remaining occupants' requirements– at least for the moment, in Sir Hugh's case – were simple, Florrie realized dealing with her mother's predicament was her most pressing responsibility.

Carrying Alice on her hip, she pressed her free hand to her forehead and mulled over the options. 'Right. This is what we need to do. First, I'll get these kids changed out of their wet clothes. I can't leave the big house to go to the cottage, but there's a trunk of old children's clothes in a box room on the servants' floor, left over from when Sir Richard and Sir Hugh were small.'

Mam blew her nose loudly. 'Whatever are they doing keeping children's clothes from a good thirty years ago?'

'The rich like to save them as hand-me-downs for the next generation,' Florrie explained. 'Dame Elizabeth's desperate for Sir Richard and Lady Charlotte to produce an heir, so I reckon some of that is wishful thinking. But in the meantime, I can put these little mischief-makers in fresh, dry clothes.'

Transferring a pile of freshly laundered bath towels from the top of a wooden stool to the windowsill, Mam sat down with a weary sigh. She held her arms out to Nelly, who toddled over to her willingly, her argument with George seemingly already forgotten. Mam stripped off the little girl's wet clothes and wrapped her in one of the clean towels.

Taking her mother's cue, Florrie set Alice down at her feet and did the same for George – by far the wettest of the three children. 'Come on, you cheeky little tinker.' She rubbed him down briskly with his towel and then wrapped it around him, tucking it in beneath his armpits to protect his modesty. 'What are we going to do with you, eh? You can't behave like this for Nana. You've been very naughty.'

'Sorry, Aunty Flo. Sorry, Nana,' George said, clearly contrite.

Florrie held George close and rested her chin on the top of his head. 'He has to go to school, Mam. That's a priority.'

'I know! I know!' Her mother sounded dismissive.

'I mean it, Mam. Having Arkwright teaching him to read is no replacement for a proper education, and Arkwright's a pig at the best of times. He might have been full of bonhomie and port on Christmas Day when he offered, but . . . George won't do well being taught by a resentful teacher that doesn't actually like children!'

Mam nodded. 'I know all that, but it's a two-mile walk just to get out of the estate, and the school's another five mile away. How am I supposed to get him into the village of a morning, when I have to start washing at the crack of dawn and there's no bus?'

Florrie chewed the inside of her cheek. She shook her head. 'We'll find a solution. Let me think on it. Maybe one of the lads that Arkwright sends on errands into the village can run him down there in the pony and trap. Either way, you've got to use your day off to take him to the schoolhouse and get him registered.'

'You're right. I will. I promise.'

'I'll watch Alice and Nelly while you go.' Florrie pondered how she could alleviate some of her mother's caring duties, not just to enable her to get on with her work in peace but also to give the poor, still-grieving woman some sanity back. Yet without getting her mother either some childcare or a laundry assistant, both of which would cost money, she realized she couldn't hope to make any material difference. 'Right, well, I've got some room inspections and stock-taking to do, but I suppose that can wait an hour or so. While I'm mulling

264

your situation over, I'm taking this lot off to get dressed and maybe play some hide and seek, given the house is so empty.' She brought her face down level with Nelly and George. 'Fancy a game of hide and seek?'

The children cheered, waving their little arms in the air and jumping up and down.

'Can I put on the coat of armour like a knight?' George asked.

'Er, no. Don't touch the armour.' Florrie realized the foolhardiness of what she'd suggested, but there was no going back on the offer now.

She kissed her mother, swung Alice on to her hip and marched the children up to the box room at the top of the house.

It didn't take long to locate the trunk and find clothes that would fit. Even Sir Hugh's baby clothes were still pristine and neatly folded. Florrie laughed at the sight of the three of them all dressed in outfits that had last been worn at the turn of the century.

Nelly twirled around in her knickerbockers, fingering the delicate lace collar of the blouse she wore beneath a stiff woollen waistcoat. George craned his neck to see the square collar of his sailor suit.

'These clothes are funny,' he said. 'Alice looks like she's in a pillowcase!' He started to laugh loudly at his own joke, pointing at his baby sister.

Florrie straightened the silk and lace of the Christening gown Alice was wearing and chuckled. 'Flipping heck. I hope Dame Elizabeth doesn't find out I've borrowed some family heirloom intended for her future grandchild.' She rubbed noses with Alice. 'You'd better not be sick on this gown, little lady!'

Feeling certain that Sir Hugh and Dame Elizabeth were strolling in the grounds, Florrie led the children down to the guest bedroom wing. Holding Alice, she stood on the landing by the grand staircase, keen to ensure her wobbly, toddler niece didn't try to navigate the stairs on her own. 'Right. I'll count to ten. No hiding in dangerous places, now. No going downstairs. No cheating. One, two, three . . .'

George and Nelly hared off in a fit of giggling, heading for the guest bedrooms.

'Ten! Here I come!' Relishing the freedom from her normal duties and responsibilities, Florrie crept forward and tried the first guest bedroom. She immediately spotted Nelly's little foot protruding beyond the bed. 'Found you!'

Nelly squealed with delight. 'Found you! Found you!' she repeated. 'Find Georgie now!'

Holding her niece's hand, Florrie searched the next bedroom and the next until she got to the fourth guest suite – the chinoiserie room, which was decked out in black lacquered, inlaid furniture from the orient, with thick patterned rugs on the floor. The walls had been decorated with eggshell blue wallpaper that sported delicate hand-painted cherry blossom. On almost every surface stood either intricately patterned, blue and white Chinese pottery that Lady Charlotte had once mentioned was 'Ming' – Florrie couldn't be certain what 'Ming' was – or deep fuchsia and mauve orchids that the maids misted regularly. Florrie loved the room. She felt sure that George was lurking in here. She sniffed the air. He'd carried a whiff of washing detergent in with him from the laundry.

'Oh, Georgie! I'm coming to find you . . .'

She spotted that one of the doors to the red-and-gold-painted Chinese wardrobe was ever so slightly ajar and she felt certain he was in there. Reaching out to grab the handle, she flung open the door. 'Found you!' George was revealed, hiding among some old moth-balled furs, covered with white cotton garment-bags. He cackled with laughter.

'What on earth is all this brouhaha?' Dame Elizabeth's voice cut through the frivolity. Florrie turned to see her standing in the doorway, beyond which was a little reception room-cum-study, which she knew opened on to the suite's dressing room and bathroom. Dame Elizabeth held on to the door frame – a commanding presence in all that black taffeta. '*Children?*'

Florrie flinched, instinctively holding Alice close. 'Oh, Dame Elizabeth. I'm so sorry, I . . . er . . . We were . . . it's just . . .' What could she say that wouldn't get her immediately dismissed?

27

'We were playing hide and seek,' George said. 'Do you want to play too, Mrs?'

Dame Elizabeth glowered down at him. 'Hide and seek, eh?' Then with cracking knees, she crouched down. 'And who might you be, young man, wearing a sailor suit I haven't seen in aeons . . . not since my youngest son had his fifth birthday party?'

'George Eggleston, Mrs.' He saluted and then grinned.

'Well, actually it's *Dame* Elizabeth, but you can call me Lizzie if you like.' Her face was still stern but the skin around her eyes wrinkled with amusement. She turned to Nelly. 'And who is this bonny little boy with rather long locks?'

'I'm not a boy. I'm a girl! My name's Nelly,' Nelly said. 'I got wet.'

Dame Elizabeth fingered the lace of Nelly's collar and inhaled sharply. She let out a long, shallow sigh. 'This belonged to my eldest son, James.' She smiled sadly and seemed to look beyond the here and now to her past. 'He wore it for the family portrait that hangs in the music room.' She tutted, straightened up and leaned in to examine Alice's peach-like complexion. Stroking her downy cheeks, she asked, 'And who is this delightful baby, wearing my middle son's christening gown?' She reached out to take her from Florrie.

Florrie saw how the old lady's face had lit up now that she was holding a baby. The ravages of age seemed to fade to give her a youthful glow and an air of vitality that Florrie had never seen in her before. Though Florrie had always supposed Dame Elizabeth was in her mid-sixties, she now had her pegged as only slightly older than Mam. 'This is Alice. These are my nieces and nephew, Your Ladyship.' She curtseyed. 'My mother's the new laundress, and she brought the children to live with her in the gamekeeper's cottage on account of their mother – my sister – dying a couple of months ago.'

Dame Elizabeth wiggled her fingers in front of Alice's eyes and made cooing noises. 'Yes. So tragic. Richard told me of your terrible loss.'

'Thank you. I'm ever so sorry for disturbing you, ma'am. I hadn't realized anyone was in here.'

'Nobody ever expects me to be in here, do they?' Dame Elizabeth told Alice in a high-pitched, babyish voice. 'I can enjoy true solitude, can't I? Yes!' Her voice returned to normal. 'I also rather like the décor, but it seems today, my hidey-hole has been discovered by my housekeeper, who is playing nursemaid to the laundress's charges.'

Florrie felt a trickle of cold sweat roll down her back. 'I know how it looks, ma'am. It's just that my mother was struggling to refresh Lady Charlotte's spring wardrobe, with the children under her feet. I'd done all my work until before dinner, and what with the house being very quiet and all . . .'

By now, Dame Elizabeth was swaying from side to

side, talking gibberish at an Alice who was completely transfixed by an unfamiliar face. 'My, don't you have beautiful blue eyes?' She looked up at Florrie. 'They all have blue eyes when they're born, even if they turn brown later. Did you know that? It's quite disconcerting when they change.' She peered back down at the baby. 'Isn't it, sweet girl? Yes! It is!' Walking over to the bed, she sat on the end and cradled Alice, who was getting far too big for such constriction and started to fret. Dame Elizabeth was unperturbed, though. 'Oh, how I wish Richard and Charlotte would give me a grandchild.' She looked over to where Nelly and George were whispering mischievously in each other's ears and giggling. 'It is so wonderful to have small children in the house again.'

'So you're not going to sack me?' Florrie bit her lip.

Dame Elizabeth got to her feet and handed Alice back. 'Don't be ridiculous, dear! Let them explore while there's so few people around. My boys adored playing hide and seek and running amok on the landings.' She pulled a pocket watch from her skirts and gasped. 'How can it be so late? I have affairs to attend to. You'll have to excuse me.'

'Will you be wanting to take dinner in your rooms, my lady?'

Dame Elizabeth eyed George and pursed her lips. 'No. Actually, tonight I think I'll dine with my son.' She smiled, then ushered Florrie and the children out of the chinoiserie room. 'We are fortunate to have so many wonderful hiding places in this wing, children,' she said to George and Nelly. 'Explore them with my blessing.'

Once Dame Elizabeth had descended the grand stair-case to the ground floor, Florrie followed the children along the hallway from room to room, but the further they got towards the large, bright window at the end of the wing that faced on to the side gardens, the more Florrie wondered why a woman with a suite of her own, located on the ground floor, would be lurking in a guest bedroom on the floor above. Liking the solitude and décor didn't convince. Yet again, Dame Elizabeth was behaving oddly, but it wasn't Florrie's place to pry.

For a further three quarters of an hour or so, Nelly and George ran and giggled themselves ragged, while Florrie and Alice went in search of them. Having exhausted almost all of the nooks and crannies of the hitherto unexplored guest bedrooms, they agreed to hold one more round before abandoning the game, so that Florrie could return to her duties.

'Here I come!' she shouted. 'Last chance!'

Flagging, with Alice growing heavier and more fidgety on her hip, Florrie was relieved to find Nelly straight away, hiding under the bed in the bedroom at the end of the wing. Where was George though?

'I'm coming to find you!' she said in a sing-song voice.

Yet he wasn't anywhere in the adjacent bedroom, or the next, or the next. The very thought of having to go back through all the bedrooms palled. She was relieved when she heard a giggle coming from a bedroom much closer to the grand staircase, where the game had begun. Another giggle drew her directly to the chinoiserie suite again, and Florrie registered a tingle of anticipation.

Pressing her index finger to her lips, encouraging Nelly to be as quiet as possible, she entered the room for a second time. George was not in the bedroom. She ventured into the reception room-cum-study, but at a glance did not see him in there, either. When she didn't see him in the dressing room or bathroom either, she felt irritation prickle.

'Come out now, Georgie. I've got to get back to work. This is getting ridiculous, son.'

She jumped when there was a loud bang within the suite. George started to cry. With a beating heart, Florrie ran back into the reception room-cum-study to find George emerging from beneath the desk, rubbing his head.

'What on earth are you doing under there?' she asked.

'Hiding!' He rubbed his head. 'But I found something sticking out under the desk, and when I pulled at it, a box thing fell on my head, and all these letters fell out.'

He pointed to a wooden contraption that now lay on the floor and a sheaf of letters, all penned on pale blue paper in the same neat hand, signed by a Miles T. Brooke Esquire.

Florrie rubbed her nephew's head and kissed the burgeoning bump better. As she did so, she surreptitiously studied the wooden contraption, and realized it was a false bottom or compartment to the desk. Dame Elizabeth had been deliberately concealing the correspondence.

'I'd best see whose these letters are so I can give them back.'

Florrie was relieved George could not yet read more than the most basic of sentences. Sitting on the floor by the desk, careful to remain concealed from anyone who might walk into the bedroom beyond, she shelved her misgivings about prying and read a small selection of the letters. They were addressed to Dame Elizabeth, dating back six months or so. It seemed to be ordinary correspondence, where Miles T. Brooke Esquire updated Dame Elizabeth about his life, trials and observations. Apart from the romantically inclined sign-offs of 'yours with unwavering devotion . . .' or 'thinking of you with fondness, always', they were the sort of letters that one would expect to receive from any friend. It was not impossible that this was just a gentleman admirer, writing to a lonely widow. There was one, however, that piqued Florrie's interest. It was dated the day after Dame Elizabeth's tryst in the library with the mystery male caller.

Dear Lizzie,

Following my visit to Holcombe Hall yesterday, I felt I must write to say I am so appalled by the way you have treated me, as if I am nothing more than an irritant. All these years, I have guarded your secret closely, wishing only to occupy a small corner of your heart, by dint of our shared interest, if nothing else.

Now, however, I feel it is time you acknowledged the importance of my continuing discretion to the Harding-Bournes' secure position within the uppermost echelons of British society. There you sit, enthroned in your stately home, a veritable dowager queen, enjoying the sort of riches even heads of industry and minor royals can only dream of. Yet here am I, a man of modest means, who could so easily bring your house of cards tumbling down, were I to tittle-tattle to the Tatler. I am privy to such delicate matters as would make headline news on the front page of The Times or the Daily Telegraph. After your appalling display of lack of faith in me and disregard for my feelings, Lizzie, I feel I must lay my noble intentions and discretion aside finally. Unless there is a way you could convince me to keep my lips sealed . . .

With perennial love from your enduring confidant,
Miles

Florrie re-read the letter and then stared at it momentarily, absorbing the contents. Dame Elizabeth was being blackmailed. What was their 'shared interest' and what could this 'closely guarded secret' be? The tone of the letter was sinister. Small wonder she'd been so taciturn and withdrawn since the mystery visit.

Examining the underside of the desk to see how the secret compartment had been attached, Florrie put the letters back into a bundle according to date order, hoping Dame Elizabeth wouldn't spot that they had been read. To the best of her ability, she left everything as it likely had been before George had tugged it out of place. She then gathered the children together.

'Right, let's get you two back to Nana, shall we?' She kissed George's head and then looked him in the eye. 'I don't want you to mention finding those letters to anyone. All right? Can you promise?'

George nodded. 'Cross my heart and hope to die, Aunty Flo. I won't even tell Nana.'

'Because I'd get into a lot of trouble and then we'd have to leave Holcombe Hall. You don't want that, do you?'

George shook his head vehemently. 'Never ever. The man in the stables said he was going to let me ride a horsey next week, and I like all the animals in the park and I love the ducks on the lake and I like our house because we've got swings and I like Thom because he's friendly and gave me a cowboy hat and pistols. I never want to leave here, Aunty Flo.' He pretended to zip his mouth closed and put his hands together in supplication. 'Swear to God.'

His childish enthusiasm almost melted her heart. She said a silent prayer of thanks that relocating her mother and the children to Holcombe Hall had worked out so well, despite the pressures of Mam having to raise them alone and in later life. Had they remained in Manchester, she was certain they would all have fared far, far worse.

'You're a good lad, what are you?' She treated each of the children to a smacking kiss on the cheek. 'I love you little tinkers with all my heart. Do you know that? Your mammy will be watching you from heaven and she'll be so proud of you all.'

Delivering the children back to her now markedly calmer mother, Florrie went about her afternoon house-keeper's duties of ordering in fresh supplies, careful to cut back on any excess and needlessly lavish ingredients for meals. As she did so, she pondered what to do with the information that Dame Elizabeth was being blackmailed. She could hardly confront the woman and offer moral support – it was none of her business and as a lowly domestic staff member, she couldn't help in any material way in any case. Should she tell Sir Richard on his return? If she didn't tell him, and the blackmail resulted in disaster further down the line, would she ever forgive herself for remaining silent? Might the family even sink into disrepute and penury, meaning she'd lose her job? On the other hand, if she did tell him, would she incur the wrath of Dame Elizabeth and end up being dismissed for being an untrustworthy gossip? Burdened with this terrible conundrum, Florrie knew that sleepless nights lay ahead for her.

28

'Hey! There's a car coming up to the house,' Florrie said, peering out of the music room window that faced on to the long, winding driveway. 'Is that them?' She squinted and recognized Sir Richard's Rolls-Royce, followed by the luggage vehicle. 'By crikey, it is. They weren't due back 'til tonight. Thom must have known. Why on earth didn't he tell me their ship had docked early?' She checked her watch with a sinking feeling. 'Oh, blast! There's at least another four hours in this spring clean. I'd planned it so we'd be finished by dinner time – not mid-morning!' She turned to Sally, who was trying to dust beneath the strings of the grand piano, and clicked her fingers. 'Come on. Leave that. We'll all need to gather by the entrance.'

Sally pulled her feather duster out of the grand piano's innards and coughed at the cloud of dust it sent billowing into the air. 'Well, that were a flipping waste of time. Bet the piano's out of tune now, and all.'

Just as they'd waved the Harding-Bourne couple off a month earlier, during which time Florrie had started to settle into her role in earnest, making economies where she could, as well as discovering the mysterious blackmail of Dame Elizabeth, the staff of Holcombe Hall mustered quickly to greet Sir Richard and Lady Charlotte on their return from New York.

'Ah, this is exactly what I've missed,' Sir Richard said, sipping his tea in the drawing room. He set his cup and saucer down on the side table by his armchair. 'You simply can't get decent tea in America. They either drink coffee, or they insist on serving you some ghastly stuff masquerading as tea, poured cold over ice with lemon and sweetened with absurd amounts of sugar, if you can believe it.' He wrinkled his nose.

'Sounds disgusting,' Florrie said, serving him with a slice of Cook's freshly baked angel cake.

'I rather like iced tea,' Lady Charlotte said, kicking her shoes off and flexing her toes. 'But I prefer champagne, of course.' She smiled winningly, shaking her flaxen curls.

'Shall I ask Mr Arkwright to prepare you a gin and tonic, my lady?' Florrie asked.

'No. I'd rather have a glass of champagne, actually. Fetch up a bottle! I'm sure Sir Hugh will help me with it.'

'I'm afraid we haven't ordered any champagne in, my lady,' Florrie said. 'As a cost-cutting exercise.'

Lady Charlotte balked. 'No champagne? *Cost*-cutting? How very tedious!'

'Perhaps temperance is a good idea, darling,' Sir Richard said.

Something unspoken passed between them, and the smile slid from Lady Charlotte's perfectly made-up face. She beamed up at Florrie, though this time, the smile failed to reach her eyes. 'I'm sure a cup of tea will be simply copacetic.'

Florrie frowned. 'Copa-what?'

Sir Richard swallowed his mouthful. 'My wife here has come home having learned every piece of American slang going. I think she now counts as being multilingual.'

Lady Charlotte trilled with laughter. 'They are so terribly amusing over there, you know. So very, very different to the British,' she explained to Florrie. 'Why, even a servant like you can rise to the very top of high society.'

'Darling!' Sir Richard's expression was stony and disapproving.

'I'm not being mean, Richard. I'm talking about the likes of Helena Rubinstein and Elizabeth Arden.' She looked at Florrie, wide-eyed with excitement. 'I visited both of their beauty salons in New York, and they were *excellent*.' She stroked her cheeks dramatically. 'I mean, Rubinstein is a Polish immigrant Jew, and she goes to all the most glamorous parties. Arden mixes in even more rarefied circles. That's the land of the free for you! Anything goes.' She laughed at her own wit and then looked disappointedly at the tea Florrie handed to her.

Florrie stood to attention, lacing her hands together in front of her. 'Will that be all, sir?' In truth, her heart sang that her employer was home, but the information she harboured about Dame Elizabeth weighed heavily on her. The issue of the fountain pen Christmas gift still niggled away at her too.

Sir Richard looked at her quizzically. 'Don't you want to hear how New York was?'

'Oh, course. I just—'

'Why would you want to bore our housekeeper with

lurid tales of the unemployed queuing five-men deep for anything and everything?' Lady Charlotte rolled her eyes at Florrie. 'Honestly, there were times when our car couldn't even get through the crowds. Our driver had to sound his horn on more than one occasion, and there were a couple of instances where it got rather nasty, and we were swamped by these oiks.'

'Darling, I wouldn't call them oiks. Those were desperate men, newly out of work with no prospect of employment; companies are shuttering their businesses; a lot of ordinary people have "lost their shirts", as the *New York Times* is phrasing it. They were queuing for soup kitchens and government assistance to feed their families. The crash is starting to really bite over there.'

Lady Charlotte scoffed. 'The great unwashed! Just because a group of layabouts decide they want free doughnuts, doesn't mean they have a right to thump on the bonnet of our car and slap at the windows. I found it *intensely* intimidating. What did they hope to achieve?'

'I think they were angry. They have nothing, and we were being chauffeur-driven in a rather smart car. You can see how it must look to them, can't you?'

'I'm afraid I can only see that they wanted to climb in and steal my jewellery and fur coat. Those policemen were right to crack down on their antics. When they can't behave and queue like civilized beings and they start swamping cars, it's rioting.'

Florrie was so tempted to say something in defence of those hungry men that a retort started to trip off her tongue. 'Haven't you considered . . . ?' She bit her tongue.

Lady Charlotte cocked her head to one side, defiance in her steely stare. 'Haven't I considered what?'

Florrie glanced at Sir Richard, who merely looked on with obvious curiosity. She cleared her throat. 'Erm . . . taking English teabags with you on your next trip, my lady?'

With wide eyes, Lady Charlotte pointed at her and clicked her fingers. 'Jolly good idea, Florrie. *Tha's a clever lass.*' She laughed at her own impression of the local accent.

'What ho, you two!' Sir Hugh strode into the drawing room at that point, still dressed in his tweed plus fours, with a broken-open shotgun draped over his arm. In his free hand, he clutched a brace of pheasant. Thrusting them idly at Florrie, he didn't even look in her direction as he addressed her. 'Give these to Cook, will you? There's a good girl.' He opened his arms to embrace Lady Charlotte. 'I thought you were never coming home.'

'Oh, Hugh. Don't come anywhere near me with your dead bird hands. You are positively disgusting!'

Florrie held the birds aloft, at once horrified by having to handle such messy objects, but also relieved that she could finally escape Lady Charlotte's insensitive commentary.

On her way back down to the kitchen, Florrie heard the doorbell ring at the main entrance. Walking past the various reception rooms, by the time she reached the grand staircase, the bell sounded again. Where was Arkwright or one of his footmen?

From her vantage point at the foot of the stairs, she

peered through to the vaulted marble entrance hall, but the front door was still shut. The bell was now ringing insistently, with not a footman or the butler to be seen. 'I wonder what Sir Richard's paying you all for,' she muttered beneath her breath. 'I suppose *I'll* answer the door, shall I?'

Marching indignantly to the door, with the dead pheasants swinging from her enclosed fist, she opened up to find an official-looking man in the sort of double-breasted suit that said this was no society friend, casually dropping by on their way up to Edinburgh or down South to the Cotswolds. His trousers were shiny at the knees, and there was the ghost of perhaps some bird droppings on his sleeve; dandruff on his shoulders.

'Can I help you?' she asked.

The man looked down at the dead birds, blinked twice and then took out some kind of identification card that he flashed too quickly before Florrie's eyes for her to be able to read the words inscribed there.

'I'm here from His Majesty's Inland Revenue . . .'

He made mention of so many different departments and titles in relation to corporate tax that his words sounded to Florrie's ears like the static that came from Cook's wireless whenever she tuned into the news. Florrie did notice the man's lower teeth were badly nicotine stained, though, and his index finger looked like an old piece of amber.

'Sorry, what was your name again?' she asked.

'Mr Neil Fitzpatrick. I'm an auditor.'

Florrie didn't know much about tax affairs beyond

what she paid on her modest earnings, but she was certain Sir Richard would not be pleased to see this man – particularly not the moment he'd stepped off the boat from New York. 'Wait there, please.' She closed the front door on the man and ran back to the drawing room, still clutching the brace of pheasant.

'Sir Richard,' she said, bursting in, struggling to catch her breath. 'There's a tax man at the door. Said something about an audit of Harding-Bourne Enterprises' books.'

Sir Richard blanched instantly. 'Oh. Why hasn't he gone to our head office, then?'

Florrie shrugged. 'Well, he's on the doorstep, and he's asking for you. Name's Neil Fitzpatrick.'

'This will be about the Hatry fraud,' Sir Richard told Sir Hugh. 'He's just been sentenced.'

Sir Hugh, who was lounging against the fireplace, nodded. 'Yes. It's been in all the papers while you were away, old chap. I was absolutely right when I predicted he'd get a long stretch – fourteen years at His Majesty's pleasure. And now the tax man's on our doorstep. Guilt by association and all that.' He raised an eyebrow.

Stubbing out his cigar, Sir Richard stood and marched over to Florrie. 'Thank you, Florrie. Please show him to my study. Offer him a drink and cake or something. Offer him the world, if it will keep him happy.' He looked down at the pheasants and frowned. 'Hang on.' Wrinkling his nose, he took the birds by the necks and thrust them back at Sir Hugh. 'For God's sake, man, if you must insist on hunting, deal with your own revolting kill. Honestly!'

He marched off to his study.

Wishing she could wash her hands in hot soapy water before doing anything else, Florrie reluctantly returned to the front door and ushered the disgruntled-looking tax man inside. 'Sorry to keep you waiting. Sir Richard will see you in his study. Can I bring you a cup of tea? Some cake, perhaps?'

Mr Fitzpatrick's mouth remained downturned at the corners. 'A glass of water will suffice, thank you.'

She showed him to Sir Richard's study, noting how he seemed to scrutinize everything as he walked through the house – every suit of armour, every oriental rug, every oil painting, every vase on every gilt Louis XIV half-moon table. As they passed open doors, he seemed to slow deliberately, clearly trying to catch sight of what lay beyond. Outside the drawing room, he actually stopped, peering in at Lady Charlotte, who was chatting animatedly to Hugh.

'Er, this way, please. There's nowt in there to interest you.'

'Sir Richard Harding-Bourne is a public figure, and his company is listed on the stock market as being *public limited*,' Mr Fitzpatrick said.

'Yes, well, public his company may be, but this is his private home, so kindly keep your eyes in your head and follow me.'

'Excuse me, but what is your name?'

Florrie's heart started to knock insistently inside her chest like the hammer inside an alarm bell. Did this man have the same investigative powers as the police? Surely not. Did he have grounds to interrogate her? Was she obliged to answer him? No. She didn't want this man, who smelled like an ashtray, knowing anything about her. 'I am the housekeeper of Holcombe Hall and I pay my taxes. That's all you need to know, Mister.'

'There's no need to be like that, miss. I'm only being friendly.'

Mercifully, they had reached Sir Richard's study. 'I'll bring your water presently.' Florrie showed him in.

Behind the desk, Sir Richard was fidgeting with the pencil sharpener. The tendon over his jaw flinched, and he was blinking too fast. Florrie could see that when he smiled, it belied fear she could almost smell on the air, and for the first time in her life, it occurred to her that being wealthy wasn't always the blessing she imagined it to be.

Once she'd closed the door behind her, she overheard Mr Fitzpatrick introduce himself.

'I'm here to forewarn you that the Inland Revenue is to audit your companies' financial records, effective immediately. We will particularly be looking for evidence of irregularities in light of the failed United Steel Companies merger and any dealings with businesses owned by convicted fraudster, Clarence Hatry.'

Florrie swallowed hard. The business empire of the Harding-Bournes didn't fall within a humble housekeeper's remit, and heaven knew she'd relish Lady Charlotte and Sir Hugh having to pare back their champagne-fuelled excesses, but suppose Sir Richard was found out as a fraudster? Could she have been wrong about him being an honourable man all these years?

'What's going on?' Cook asked, when she entered the kitchen to find a clean glass. 'You're white as a sheet.'

Florrie told her what she'd witnessed above stairs. She filled the glass, but her hands were shaking so violently that she sloshed water on to her feet. 'If that Fitzpatrick finds evidence of fraud, what might happen to us?'

Cook scratched at her chin, looking sober and thoughtful. 'Well, I've been following the write-up in the papers—'

'About Sir Richard?'

'No. Just generally, about steel owners what got involved with that Hatry's merger thing. And from what I've gleaned . . .' She leaned in and dropped her voice, speaking with a secretive air, though with none of her usual mischievousness. 'Sir Richard would be arrested, they'd freeze his assets or whatever they call it, and we could all be out of a job. That's just for starters. And even if he's just been fiddling his tax, they might send the bailiffs in if he can't repay them and he gets heavy fines and that. I don't really know. Maybe they'd even have to sell Holcombe Hall, and then we'd all be destitute too. Imagine that!'

Florrie shook her head. 'No. I don't want to.' She'd only just saved her family from destitution and she couldn't bear the thought of the four of them landing back at square one.

29

'Heavy boxes, coming through!' one of the inspector's audit assistants shouted several days later, carrying three stacked boxes from Sir Richard's study into the hallway.

He was not alone. In a bid to reach her employer, Florrie was forced to manoeuvre her way past numerous Inland Revenue staff members – ants on the march, moving to and from Sir Richard's study, carrying boxes of 'evidence' through to the ballroom. There, the afternoon sun shone on the contents of every file ever compiled on one of the Harding-Bourne companies or the Holcombe Estate itself, now spread out on the vast floor to be forensically examined by Mr Fitzpatrick.

Florrie found Sir Richard clutching a tumbler of either whisky or brandy, staring dolefully out of his study window, while the tax workers ransacked his banks of filing cabinets in the adjacent room.

She drew close. 'Can I get you anything, Sir Richard? It's past lunchtime and you've eaten nothing.'

He shook his head. 'No thank you, Florrie. You're very kind to think of me. But I'm afraid I have no appetite with all this going on.' He nodded towards the assistants. 'They're quite a machine, aren't they? And hard though it may be to believe, I'm actually sheltering here at home from the real onslaught at my head office in Manchester, where I understand they're also going through every receipt, every ledger and every piece of correspondence with a fine-toothed comb.' He exhaled hard, looking out at the thick snow that had covered the Holcombe Estate since the evening of his return from New York.

'When will it be over?'

'Your guess is as good as mine, my dear. I've always insisted my companies operate scrupulously, but when these fellows descend after a crisis to pick over your carcass, even the most honest man must feel a peculiar guilt that he perhaps committed some mortal accounting sin that has slipped just beyond memory.'

'Well, let's hope they'll be satisfied quickly and then leave you in peace. The staff below stairs are all feeling very uncomfortable with these fellers coming and going.'

Sir Richard drained his tumbler and stared ruefully at the dregs. 'Well, even if in some nightmare scenario they find something they can use to make an example of me, Holcombe Hall will still need staff. My mother has lived here for forty years of her life and my ancestors are buried in the grounds of the estate chapel. They won't take Holcombe Hall from the Harding-Bournes while my mother has breath in her body. Can you imagine trying to force the indomitable Dame Elizabeth to do *anything* she doesn't want to?' He chuckled, but there was no conviction in his light-hearted fighting talk.

Florrie thought about the blackmailing letter Dame

Elizabeth had received from Miles T. Brooke Esquire and marvelled at how little Sir Richard knew about his own mother. *So many secrets under one roof!* she thought.

Taking her leave, Florrie was headed back below stairs to supervise the delivery of new cleaning supplies, when she overheard heated voices by the front door. Surely they weren't being inundated by yet more Inland Revenue officials?

'I'm afraid you may not come in. Absolutely not.' Arkwright was speaking. 'And get that flashbulb out of my face this instant.'

Florrie picked up her pace until the butler was within sight. Beyond the front door, she saw a familiar-looking man in an overcoat and trilby. He was accompanied by a younger man who was trying to photograph Arkwright.

'We just want to take some photos of Sir Richard and Lady Charlotte,' the photographer said.

'Can you tell us about the fraud investigation?' the older man said.

It was then that Florrie realized where she recognized the older man from. In her mind's eye, she recalled Lady Charlotte's twenty-fifth birthday celebration ball: the minor royals, the politicians and heads of industry, with their bow ties hanging loose as they quaffed champagne by the magnum and danced the Charleston like financial disaster was but a bad dream; the celebrities, the flashing lightbulbs, the servants' desperate efforts to steer *Tatler* journalists away from the first signs of breaking scandal on the dancefloor. 'You're from the *Tatler*,' Florrie said, approaching.

Arkwright looked back at her, and his pained expression gave way to visible relief. 'Ah, Miss Bickerstaff. These gentlemen are here uninvited. They're clearly only interested in seeking disrepute where there is none to be found.'

The journalist put his foot on the top step. 'But we just want to speak to Lady Charlotte.'

Arkwright put his hand out to stop the journalist's progress. 'You're trespassing. Kindly leave, right this minute, or I will telephone the police and have you escorted beyond the estate boundary.' A flashbulb went off in his face again, causing him to squint and take a step backwards.

'Are you saying the Harding-Bournes aren't being investigated for fraud?' Even as the journalist was poised to write down some quote in his notepad, he was still trying to mount that uppermost step and push his way into the entrance hall.

Florrie could see that Arkwright was uncharacteristically struggling to fend these intruders off. She positioned herself next to the butler so that they formed an impassable wall. 'Sling your hook, pal. Go on!' she said. 'You're not welcome. *There's* a quote for your magazine.' She stepped forwards, spreading her arms wide to intimidate the journalist and force him back down the steps. 'That's right. Down you go. Don't trip and break your neck, will you?'

'Miss Bickerstaff, I have this in hand. Kindly come back inside and send for the police,' Arkwright said, pulling her back. 'Right this minute! Tell them that two trespassers are trying to gain entry by force to Holcombe Hall in a bid to defame the Harding-Bournes.'

Florrie retreated, and together they managed to shut the door on the insistent men. Though the arrival of *Tatler* on the doorstep, sniffing around for a story, was problematic, Florrie's heart was thumping wildly with exhilaration. Only months earlier, she wouldn't have had the courage to confront those men. Now, she revelled in her daring. Arkwright, conversely, was whey-faced and seemed to have shrunk in stature. His hands were shaking. It was clear the butler had lost a lot of his swagger since Mrs Douglas's death, and now he seemed to have lost any youthful vigour he'd been clinging to as well.

'Are you quite all right?' she asked him. 'You look peaky.'

Arkwright smoothed his Brilliantined hair with an unsteady hand, straightening up, clearly desperately trying to restore his usual imperious air. 'Why aren't you telephoning the police, woman? Must I do everything myself?' He turned on his heel and strode deeper into the hallway, where the telephone sat on a side table.

'What a Jekyll and Hyde,' Florrie muttered beneath her breath. 'I don't know why I bother trying to be nice.'

Walking briskly back to Sir Richard's study, she beckoned her employer to abandon his desk and follow her to the relative privacy of the music room.

Sir Richard stood by a cello that had belonged to his older brother, James. Now it was displayed in perpetuity in the room, with the order that it be dusted religiously every week. He stroked the scroll at the top of the pegbox. 'Whatever is the matter, Florrie? You look positively flustered.'

'It's the press. Me and Mr Arkwright have just had a journalist and a photographer from the *Tatler* at the front door.'

'Good Lord, no!' Sir Richard peered out of the window, squeezing his lower lip thoughtfully between his manicured fingertips. 'Good heavens, it's going to be all over the news that I'm being investigated. Readers won't care if I'm guilty of fraud or clean as a whistle – which, I assure you, I am. The damage will already have been done. The share price of Harding-Bourne Enterprises is going to go through the floor.' He pressed his hands to the sides of his head. 'I can't bear it. We're going to lose everything because of my . . . naivety; my greed; my ego. Why on earth did I get involved with that blasted merger when my steel interests were already doing well?'

Florrie was torn. Though she felt sorry for her beleaguered employer, who seemed to be a fair man in all things, she was well aware of the privations of poor folk in towns and cities like Manchester. She knew that, if they were lucky enough to be working, they had to endure dangerous, dirty working conditions in the Harding-Bourne mills, mines and shipyards. That knowledge made it difficult to sympathize too readily with a man who had never wanted for anything. Yet the fate of his workers – the fate of her Aunt Edna, who was still living in penury in Manchester – rested with his business fortunes. 'As long as your accounting passes muster with the Inland Revenue, this'll all blow over. You'll see.

What do you want me to tell them if they come back or if other newspaper types turn up on the doorstep?'

Sir Richard folded his arms and looked down at his brogues. He frowned and ran his tongue over his teeth. Then he locked eyes with Florrie. 'Send Arkwright in, will you? We need to arrange some security; get some sturdy lads manning the estate entrances. These hacks shouldn't be able to set foot on the property, let alone come right up to the front door. It's absurd.'

'Mr Arkwright has already telephoned the police.'

'Good, good. The *Tatler* idiots have probably cleared off by now, but the police need to know we're being targeted by journalists.'

'*Tatler*? Journalists?' Lady Charlotte appeared behind Florrie and pushed past her to sit at the piano. 'Have they come for me?' She played the first few notes of a familiar tune and looked around at Sir Richard, batting her eyelashes. 'Perhaps they want to do a feature on my winter fashions.' She got up from the piano and looked out of the window. 'Where are they?'

'Long gone, with a bit of luck,' Florrie said. 'It was all Arkwright and I could do to keep them out.'

'Oh, what a shame.' Lady Charlotte looked crestfallen. Then she smiled. 'They love me at *Tatler*.'

'They aren't after coverage of some society ball or your extensive collection of millinery, darling,' Sir Richard said, his consonants clipped, his delivery impatient. 'They're trying to dig up dirt. They can smell a scandal a mile off with all these tax investigators hanging around like a bad smell.'

'I think you should have let them in, and I'd have charmed them into writing a lovely story.'

Sir Richard turned to Florrie. 'Don't let them in. Nobody's to come in. Is that clear?'

'Crystal clear, Sir Richard.' Florrie bobbed a curtsey. 'I'll send Arkwright in.'

'Oh, you are such a stick in the mud, Richard!' Lady Charlotte slammed her fingers down heavily on the piano keys.

'No, Charlotte. I am an adult, with some very adult responsibilities towards my family, my shareholders and my employees.'

Over the coming weeks, the gardeners and the footmen reported that newspaper reporters had regularly been huddled at the estate entrances in the snow, slush and sleet, waiting for a photo of the Harding-Bournes or some damning or salacious comment from a staff member, if not a response from the man himself.

As March rolled in and the snow had cleared, Florrie had gone for a walk with Thom along the periphery of the estate, where the woodland floor was studded with pearly-white snowdrops. She had seen for herself the gathering of journalists who banged on the windows and side panels of even a truck delivering a chandelier that had been taken away and cleaned. Lightbulbs flashed as photographers pointlessly took photos of the occupants, who had nothing at all to do with the Harding-Bournes.

'It's mayhem,' Thom said. 'I caught one of them

trying to get over the wall the other day. In fact, there's one, now! Cheeky beggar.' He pointed to where a man's head and hands had popped up over the top of the thick estate boundary wall. His shoulders and trousered leg followed as he tried to scramble over.

'Hey! You!' Thom sprinted over to the man.

The man quickly dropped out of sight on the road side of the wall.

'And stay off this land!' Thom shouted after him. 'It's private property.'

Florrie couldn't quite believe the audacity of the press. After that, the footmen who were guarding the gates were accompanied by the gamekeeper's dogs as extra deterrents.

'Oh! Morning, Sir Richard. You gave me quite the surprise, there!' Florrie said the following morning, when her employer entered the dining room earlier than usual. She had been checking the table had been laid properly after Dame Elizabeth had complained a spoon had been missed from her place setting the day before.

'Good morning, Florrie.' Wearing his jumper with the holes in the elbows and a pair of old corduroy trousers, it wasn't the first time that Sir Richard had resembled a gentleman farmer more than the lord of a manor and a captain of industry. With his pallor and the dark shadows beneath his eyes, however, Florrie thought he simply looked unkempt and full of cares.

'Would you like me to have Cook prepare you anything in particular for breakfast?' she asked.

'Just a strong cup of tea and a piece of toast for me, thanks.' He started to rummage around by the table beneath the large stained-glass oriel window that Sir Hugh and his pal Walter Knight-Downey had broken in the autumn. 'Er . . . any sign of the papers, Florrie? I came down early so I'd have time to read them before these blasted Inland Revenue people show up for another day of death by a thousand paper cuts.'

'I thought Mr Arkwright had already brought them up,' she said. 'Aren't they there?'

Sir Richard reached down and picked up the pink *Financial Times*. He waved it at her. 'It had slid behind. Wish me luck.'

When Florrie returned with Sir Richard's tea and toast, Sir Richard was sitting at the table with his head in his hands. She set the breakfast items down quietly. Just as she was about to speak, Dame Elizabeth swept into the dining room.

'What on earth is the matter, Richard?' she asked. She took her usual seat at the head of the table. 'You look like you've lost a shilling and found a penny.'

Sir Richard lowered his hands and groaned. 'The share price has halved.'

'*Our* share price?' Dame Elizabeth snatched the newspaper from under his nose. Holding it close, she muttered inaudibly beneath her breath. 'Wish I'd brought my blasted spectacles. Can't see a thing . . . Oh. Oh dear.' She pushed the paper back on to the table. 'You're going to have to let staff go, Richard. Economize, and hope that after this dreadful audit is over, our share price will bounce back.'

Florrie knew she ought to get back to the kitchen to check Cook was busy preparing the porridge that Dame Elizabeth ate daily, without fail. Given her Aunt Edna's reliance on the Harding-Bourne mill in Manchester, however, she was keen to hear any information that might affect her directly. She pretended to count candles in the drawer of the sideboard.

'We're halfway to ruination, Mama,' Sir Richard said. He thumped the table three times. 'Damn Clarence Hatry, and damn the Wall Street Crash and damn this unsalvageable, interminable financial crisis.'

Dame Elizabeth helped herself to a piece of toast and started to butter it. 'But the steel business had picked up, you said. Your trip to New York was a success.'

Sir Richard sipped his tea. 'Ironically, yes. The Americans are going so cock-a-hoop for skyscrapers, they're having to look to Britain for extra materials. The steel business sparked this chaos, but it's the only thing keeping us afloat. Everything else is on its knees. Was the Industrial Revolution nothing but a fever dream?'

'Just close another mill or a mine. Streamline, boy! It's what your father did during the war. And get these auditors out of your hair. It's the scandal that's killing the share price. You have to believe the Harding-Bourne empire can weather the storm or it will be broken up on the rocks of the great depression.'

At the end of the week, Florrie was walking from room to room, checking which chimneys needed to be swept, when she overheard Sir Richard talking with Mr

Fitzpatrick. She paused outside the door of his study, hoping one of the other servants wouldn't spot her eavesdropping.

'You'll be glad to hear the audit is complete,' Mr Fitzpatrick said.

'About time. It will be jolly nice to have my home back. And?' Sir Richard's voice was tight and reedy.

'Well, I'm afraid we have found evidence of irregularity.'

'I beg your pardon,' Sir Richard said indignantly. 'Whatever do you mean, "irregularity"? I've bent over backwards to give you access to everything. Laid my soul bare for the Inland Revenue. What irregularity could you possibly have found, man?'

Florrie breathed in sharply. Was Sir Richard about to be prosecuted for fraud?

30

'So how's life in the countryside, our Tilly?' Florrie's Aunty Edna asked her mam a couple of weeks later. She dragged sharply on her cigarette and then stubbed it out in an old tin ashtray. 'I didn't know whether to hug you or curtsey when you lot got off the train. Holcombe Hall, indeed! You've come up in the world, Lady Muck.'

'Best decision I ever made,' Mam said, opening the newspaper-wrapped package on her knee to reach the greasy chips inside.

'I've missed proper chips, Nana!' George said. He shovelled three at once into his mouth. 'But it's dirty in here. When can we go home?'

Florrie shushed her nephew and tried to silence his outburst with a stern look.

'Take no notice of him,' Mam said, shooting George a warning glance.

Aunty Edna looked around at the room she was renting in the Lower Broughton tenement. 'He's right. It is dirty. It's a fleapit, but what option do I have? I can't just up sticks and move in with a bunch of toffs like you did. I haven't got two ha'pennies to rub together, Tilly. And you're washing dirty underwear for them same toffs what put me in the dole queue.'

'I'm sorry you've lost your job, our kid. I really am.

But they've been very good to me and my grandchildren,' Mam said. 'I know what it's like to be out of collar. I couldn't for the life of me make ends meet before Florrie got me this laundress job.'

'Get you! Not a washerwoman. A *laundress*! All high and mighty now?'

'Give over, will you? We've come all this way to visit you on our day off.'

Aunty Edna swigged from her jar of tea, never taking her judgemental eye from Mam. She wiped her mouth on the back of her hand. 'Want a flaming medal?'

'Don't be like that,' Mam said. 'I'm just saying, the Harding-Bournes aren't all bad, are they, Florrie?'

'Sir Richard's a good man.' Florrie saw the disappointed disbelief in her aunt's expression. 'As industrialists go, at any rate.' She looked down in embarrassment at her chip wrappings. Putting two chips into her mouth, she noticed the headline of one of the stories in the old copy of the *Manchester Guardian* in which the chips had been wrapped. It said,

Owner of Harding-Bourne Enterprises
exonerated by Inland Revenue

Florrie cast her mind back to the jubilant mood that the auditor's verdict had left Sir Richard in. With the only irregularity being that Harding-Bourne Enterprises had underpaid tax by twenty-two pounds, seven shillings and three pence, Sir Richard had given everyone an extra day off that month with full pay. Now she was making use of that day off to visit her aunt in a part of Manchester she wasn't overly familiar with – Lower Broughton. It served as the border between the outskirts of Salford and Cheetham Hill, home to Manchester's recent Jewish immigrants. Aunty Edna had only recently moved to the area, and judging by the diatribe she had launched into earlier against her neighbours, Florrie wondered if she and Mam might have better spent their precious day off by taking a train to Windermere in the Lake District.

'Don't talk to me about industrialists,' Aunty Edna said. 'They're all cut from the same I'm-all-right-Jack cloth. I've been trying to get a job at one of the raincoat factories in Cheetham. But them Jews only give work to their own.'

'That's not true,' Mam said. 'I've done piecework for a couple of raincoat factories. After I lost my fingers in the loom.' She brandished her stumps, which made George giggle with horrified delight.

'That's why this country's on its knees,' Aunty Edna said, ignoring Mam's observation entirely. 'It's them Jews. They've taken over Manchester, with their factories and sweatshops. They're taking up all the housing. Half of them don't speak English. They speak Russian or some gibberish. Worse than the Chinese.'

Florrie picked up Alice, who was merrily chewing on a giant chip, clutched tightly with both chubby, increasingly greasy hands. 'Shall we go for a walk to that nice little park I spotted on the way here?' The squalid room, with its cracked plaster, mildew-sharp stink and dirty floorboards felt suddenly too small for all six of them, and her aunt's bitterness seemed to make air that already stank of cigarette smoke, lard and vinegar wholly unbreathable. 'I think the children need some fresh air.'

'Albert Park?' Aunty Edna asked. She looked out of the grimy window. 'But it's raining.'

Already pulling on George's coat, much to his chagrin, Florrie winked surreptitiously at her mother. 'Bit of rain won't kill us, will it, Mam? It's good for the lungs.'

Mam seemed to read Florrie's mind. 'Good idea, love. You can show us around, our Edna.'

In the Manchester drizzle, with a complaining Nelly who wanted to be picked up every few steps, the six of them walked past slum dwellings – built in the Victorian era as fine townhouses for large families and a servant or two, but more recently split into squalid lodgings – over to the nearby park. On a Saturday, people were strolling along the pathways, lined with daffodils and the suggestion of tulips, though the rose bushes were still bare skeletons.

'Ooh, by heck,' Mam said, gawping unselfconsciously at two men who walked past, wearing large circular fur hats, beneath which hung long ringleted side-locks, tucked behind their ears. Both sported large, bushy beards, and their unusual attire comprised black silk frock coats and thick white stockings. Under their arms, they clutched large, leather-bound prayer books, embossed with gold lettering that Florrie recognized as Hebrew. 'Look at them!'

Aunt Edna curled her lip at the sight of the men. 'It's their Sabbath. They're on their way to their church.'

'You mean a synagogue?'

'Suppose so.'

Behind them came a family, dressed smartly and out for a stroll: a father, a mother and six or seven children, ranging from a baby in a pram to much older girls, who wore their red hair in thick plaits. They chatted to each other excitedly in a Germanic-sounding language Florrie wasn't familiar with.

She smiled at them. 'Morning!'

The man raised his hat to her. 'How do you do?' he said with an accent. She caught sight of a skull cap, worn beneath the hat.

Intrigued, she watched as the family moved off, heading for the park's exit. Noticing a group of young men loitering on the wall near to the exit, smoking and laughing but watching the family intently, she realized her hands had become clammy with a sense of foreboding. Sure enough, as the family approached, the youngsters jumped down from the wall and started to walk to meet them, flicking their spent cigarettes aside with an air of menace.

As they drew level with the family, two of the young men spat in the mother's face.

'Oh, I say!' Florrie shouted. She watched, dumbfounded, as a third and fourth pelted stones at the father. 'Hey, you!' she shouted. 'Leave them alone, you brutes! I'm fetching the police!' She shielded George's eyes. 'Look away, children.' Tempted as she was to run after the gang of young men, she was carrying a baby and holding the hand of a five-year-old boy.

Realizing there were concerned witnesses to their assault, the young men ran off, laughing, shouting terrible insults at the family.

Florrie looked at Mam, aghast. 'Did you see that?'

'Not nice, was it?' Mam picked Nelly up and kissed the girl. 'We've only been gone a couple of months, and it seems to have got worse in Manchester.'

Florrie looked at her aunt.

'What?' Aunt Edna asked.

'Those lads, starting on that family!'

Aunt Edna shrugged.

Outraged that respectable folk could be attacked in broad daylight without a single person rushing to their aid, Florrie left Mam and Aunt Edna with the children and walked over to the family.

'Are you all right?' she asked.

All colour had drained from the mother's face. She was wiping the spit from her cheek with a handkerchief. Her red-headed daughters shed tears quietly at her side. The smaller children had started to cry in earnest. 'Fine, thank you.' Her voice was tremulous but she stood straight in a dignified manner.

'It's very kind of you to ask. We're fine,' the father said, picking up one of his small sons. 'Those boys are uneducated idiots. All they know is fighting.'

'Would you like me to fetch the police?'

The father shook his head. 'They will do nothing, miss. Thank you. We will just go home. It's fine. I wish more people were brave like you.'

Florrie smiled sympathetically.

With a heavy heart and a pounding pulse, she returned to her family. She took Alice back from her mother. 'I think we'd better get to the train station, Mam.'

'You've only just arrived,' Aunt Edna said.

'Well, the trains don't run that often, and we don't want to get stranded.' She withdrew an envelope from her pocket that contained a pound note, and pushed it into her aunt's hand. 'Here. It's not much, but it should help. Best of luck finding work.'

They said an abrupt farewell and started the mile walk back to Victoria train station.

'Well, we've had better days out, haven't we?' Mam said. 'I don't honestly know what's got into my daft sister. She never used to be like that – all bitter and twisted.'

'You two have got nowt in common,' Florrie said.

'Maybe I'm just outgrowing her, at the grand old age of fifty.' Mam chuckled. 'Maybe I've outgrown Manchester.' She sighed heavily. 'You outgrew this city years ago.'

Florrie nodded, observing the way the people were dressed in ragged, dirty clothing, walking in the drizzle with their backs bent. They were thin. Most adults' mouths were concave where their rotten teeth had all been yanked out. Even the youngest looked older than their years. 'I didn't outgrow it. I escaped to a better life.' She felt thankful for the warm beds and food on the table that the five of them enjoyed at Holcombe Hall. The destitution that she saw could so easily have been her fate or that of her mother and Irene's children. 'There but for the grace of God go we, eh, Mam?'

In the city itself, with its grand Victorian buildings, now blackened with soot and recent neglect, the cobbled streets smelled of rotten cabbage; the River Irwell reeked of putrefaction, its banks seeming to move with the scurry and scrabble of rats. Nearing Victoria Station, they opted to stroll by Manchester cathedral, as their train wasn't due for some three quarters of an hour.

Florrie caught sight of a queue of people outside the Corn Exchange, shuffling forward towards a trestle table that was manned by two wealthy-looking women and a vicar. On the table were oversized tureens, and the Good Samaritans were doling out either soup or some thin stew, together with a hunk of bread.

Nelly pointed. 'Buns! I'm hungry.'

'Can we get some food?' George asked. 'I'm starving too. I didn't finish my chips.'

'That food's not for you, my darlings,' Florrie said. 'That's what's called a soup kitchen. Those people have got no money for food, so the vicar and those ladies are giving out free dinners.'

'Don't you worry, Georgie, love. We'll get something lovely to eat when we get back to Holcombe,' Mam said. She reached out to Florrie and squeezed her hand. 'Blimey, if we hadn't moved to Holcombe before Christmas, that could have been us queuing for handouts. Talk about a lucky escape!'

'I just can't get over the speed of change,' Florrie said. 'It's so sad.' She felt tears welling in her eyes. 'When we get back, I'm going to speak to Sir Richard about what we've seen today. It's shocking, and half those people will have been laid off from Harding-Bourne mills. There must be something Sir Richard can do to help the people that helped make him rich.'

31

'Do get on with it, Dicky!' Sir Hugh sat in the orangery, drumming his fingers on the games table, where the chessboard had been set up. Bright sunshine streamed in through the south-facing windows and the lantern roof, though there was still a frost outside where the ground lay in shade. 'Must we take all afternoon over this dratted game?'

His opponent was Sir Richard. Though she was cleaning out the old Moorish brass brazier that made Sir Hugh's spur-of-the-moment whim to sit in the room possible, even in a freezing spring, Florrie was watching her employer beat his younger brother at chess with amusement. She shovelled the old coals out of the brazier, dumping them into a coal scuttle.

'Good Lord, come on, man! You're so slow, even the plants are bored.'

'Patience, dear Hugh.' For the last ten minutes, Sir Richard had been frowning down at his chess pieces, intermittently picking up a knight or a bishop, only to set them down again. He finally made a move and knocked Sir Hugh's queen off the board. He put up the collar on his coat with a satisfied smile. 'That's the difference between you and me. You are impulsive, where I am considered. That's why I run the businesses and you run up the bills.'

'Oh, very droll.' Sir Hugh made a swift move and then lit a cigarette. He blew a plume of smoke up to the glazed roof. 'If I choose you over Walter to be my best man at Daphne's and my wedding, will you be this ponderous in handing over the rings?' With a cigarette dangling from the corner of his mouth, he rubbed his hands together. He glanced over at Florrie. 'Do hurry up with that fire, Florrie. We're freezing to death. Chop, chop! There's a dear.'

Seated by a sunny window, Dame Elizabeth looked up from her embroidery. 'It was you who insisted we sit in here after lunch, Hugh. You know, I had hoped you'd find a wife who would tame your puerile tendencies . . .' Wearing a sour expression, she looked through the window at Lady Charlotte and Hugh's new fiancée, Daphne le Montford, who had rushed off after Sunday lunch to 'practise Daphne's new part' in the garden, and who now appeared to be pretending to stab one another by the budding lilac bushes. 'But all you've succeeded in doing is attaching yourself inadvisably to a two-bit actress just as infantile as you, but with fascist sympathies that are not fit for anyone in this family to hold.' She shook her head.

Florrie placed fresh coal in the brazier, remembering the unpleasant scenes she'd witnessed in Manchester the previous day. Poverty was providing fertile ground on which fascists were sowing their seeds of discord, taking advantage of working-class folk who were looking for someone to blame for their misery. Given the Harding-Bournes were still millionaires many times over (if the papers were to be believed), even at a point where their business empire was being squeezed, Florrie wondered how she might broach the subject of them helping the people they'd inadvertently made destitute. Yet inserting herself into Dame Elizabeth's conversation with her sons wasn't an option. *Speak when spoken to* had been Mrs Douglas's motto, and Florrie recognized that even though she was now housekeeper, that rule hadn't changed. She continued her work in silence.

'Don't you think you ought to have a longer engagement to Daphne?' Sir Richard asked, thumbing his chin as he pondered his next move. 'A May wedding seems a little soon. It's only a few months since you and Walter were fighting over her affections. The bill for the replacement of the oriel window bears testament to her fickle ways and penchant for playing one man off against the other.'

Sir Hugh regarded the glowing tip of his cigarette. 'Ah, but I've won the fight, haven't I? A gal like Daphne . . . she has admirers everywhere. Dukes, earls, statesmen – Walter swears Oswald Mosley has taken a shine to her – stars of the arts and literature world. I need to nail my colours to her mast, as it were, before she changes her mind.'

'Hugh, you do talk such balderdash,' Dame Elizabeth said. 'The fact of the matter is that you are marrying beneath you. When you have as much as we have at stake, there is far more to a match than a pretty face and a pair of shapely legs.'

'She makes me happy, Mama.'

Dame Elizabeth looked at him over the lenses of her spectacles. 'Need I remind you that for people like us, Hugh Harding-Bourne, marriage is about securing a family's legacy? Our social status. Our fortune.' She turned to Sir Richard. 'Legacy is forever. Happiness is but a fleeting, trifling boon.'

Florrie studied Sir Richard's face for a reaction to the pointed comment. Sure enough, his amused smile dissipated, leaving him looking positively forlorn.

'Let's change the subject, shall we?' He made a move and took another of Hugh's pieces from the chessboard. He looked over at Florrie. 'I say, Florrie. There's been so much excitement this weekend, what with my brother and his new fiancée announcing their engagement and all, that I forgot to ask you . . . How was your trip to Manchester?'

Florrie started to place fresh coal in the brazier. Now was her chance. She locked eyes with Sir Richard. 'Thank you for asking, sir. I wish I'd never bothered, if I'm honest.' She proceeded to tell him all about her aunt's dire circumstances, the attack on the Jewish family in the park and the queues of the jobless for the soup kitchen. 'These people are starving. It's horrible, and the streets didn't feel safe because . . . well, I suppose they're desperate and they're angry.' She wiped her hands on a cloth and lit a fire-lighter.

'How perfectly dreadful,' Sir Richard said, never taking his eyes from her. 'And how concerning that fascism is getting a grip in our cities.'

'Rubbish! Fascism is no cause for concern,' Hugh

interrupted. 'I have it on authority that Herr Hitler and his National Socialist party are not far off seizing power in Germany. A couple of years, maybe, and he'll be Chancellor. Fascism seems to be the recipe for progress.'

'Don't say that like it's a good thing, Hugh,' Sir Richard said. 'I despise that man with his beady little eyes and that absurd moustache.'

'You underestimate him. It's as bad over there as it is over here since the crash, but Hindenburg is on his last legs. You mark my words, once Hitler finally sees off Hindenburg and his merry band of industrialists—'

'*We're* industrialists, you fool!'

'Fascism will take Germany out of the doldrums. And the same is true here. What we need is national pride and protectionism. Economic self-sufficiency and a sense of true British identity.'

Sir Richard threw his head back and laughed. He caught Florrie's eye. 'Have you heard my brother, the great strategist and political thinker?'

Florrie grinned, wiping the flaming fire-lighter over the coals until they caught and a blaze sprang merrily up. She hefted the heavy brass lid on to the brazier, satisfied that heat was already starting to emanate through the fretwork.

'Go on, Florrie,' Sir Richard went on. 'Hugh rudely interrupted you just as you were about to say something undoubtedly more sensible than his fascist babble.'

Hugh scoffed. 'As if a simple maid would know more than me.'

'More than *I*, Hugh, and Florrie is our esteemed

housekeeper, with a far better command of grammar and understanding of how the world works than you, my simple brother.' Sir Richard surreptitiously shot Florrie a collusive glance.

Florrie stifled her laughter and started to clear up the sooty mess. In her peripheral vision, however, she noticed how Dame Elizabeth had laid her embroidery down on her lap and was now quite clearly appraising the rapport on show between her elder son and her housekeeper. Her downturned mouth and narrowed eyes revealed her barely disguised suspicion.

'Do go on, Florrie,' Sir Richard said.

Florrie knew she might not get another chance to tell Sir Richard her ideas. She sat back on her heels. 'So, I was thinking . . . How about your company or your family or whatever does something for the people you've laid off?'

'Do what exactly?'

'You could . . . I don't know . . . raise money from your wealthy friends, maybe.'

'Like set up a charitable foundation?'

'Anything to help lift them out of destitution and stop them from being lured into fascism.'

'Or Bolshevism, for that matter,' Sir Richard said, nodding. He pointed at her emphatically. 'I like it. But it's not that easy, I'm afraid. We've had to cut down our workforce for a reason.' He must have seen the disappointment in her eyes, because he gave her a sympathetic smile. 'Let me look at the mechanics of how a charitable trust might work. I do know my grandfather ran one in the 1850s.' His brow furrowed. He turned to his mother. 'Mama?'

'He closed it down during the Long Depression for sound financial reasons,' Dame Elizabeth said. 'As an idealistic young man, your father complained bitterly. But one can't run an empire into the ground for the sake of philanthropy.'

Sir Hugh wriggled out of his coat. 'Ah, finally, I can feel the blood flowing back into my extremities. Thank you for your *unparalleled* insights into urban poverty, politics and philanthropy, Florrie.' He didn't bother to hide the sarcasm in his voice. 'Could you ask Arkwright to bring in some port, please?'

'Yes,' Dame Elizabeth said, picking her embroidery back up. 'I think we've kept Miss Bickerstaff from her duties below stairs for quite long enough.'

Summarily dismissed, Florrie made her way back below stairs. She headed directly to Arkwright's office to issue the port request.

'How's your mother, Florence?' Arkwright smiled benignly. 'I was thinking about her the other—'

'Fine.' Florrie was in no mood for pleasantries. 'She's over at the house tomorrow morning. You can ask her yourself then.'

Retreating to the kitchen, she was relieved to find Cook sitting at the table, chatting amiably with Thom, who looked as if he had been wrestling in mud, with a twig caught in his hair.

Florrie flopped into a chair at Thom's side. She plucked the twig free and proffered it to him. 'You'll never guess how that Sir Hugh and Dame Elizabeth just spoke to me. They made me feel so small.' She related the details of the conversation about a charitable trust. 'How do you like? Weren't they rude?'

Thom shoved his chair back and stretched his long legs out before him. He folded his work-worn hands behind his head. 'If you ask me, I reckon you get too involved in matters above stairs.'

Cook inhaled sharply and watched Florrie for a reaction.

'I do not!' Florrie said.

Thom raised an eyebrow. 'Are you sure about that? What housekeeper of a stately home gets dragged into a lady's maid's duties, for a start? That Lady Charlotte *still* has you running round after her like a blue-arsed fly.'

'Thomas Stanley!' Cook clapped her hands together and wheezed with laughter.

Florrie frowned. 'That's hardly my fault. I do as I'm told.'

'It's not just her though, is it?' Thom lowered his arms and started to examine the soil beneath his fingernails, glancing up every now and then as he spoke. 'You're too involved with Sir Richard. He's always asking you this and that. I've seen it with my own eyes. "Florrie, what do you think I should do about the tax man? Florrie, what's your opinion on the journalists? Florrie this. Florrie that. Florrie, I'll just spend hundreds of pounds doing up a gamekeeper's cottage, just so your mother can wash my socks."' He shook his head. 'You let yourself get too close to these people. One day, they'll tire of you or move on to the next obsession, and you'll be cast aside like a broken toy, or you'll say the wrong thing and you'll go from being Sir Richard's favourite to just another hungry woman in the dole queue.'

Cook's eyebrows shot up. She drummed her fingers on the table. 'Sailing close to the wind, there, Thomas. That's all I'm saying.'

Florrie could feel the indignation turning the very tips of her ears red hot. 'Is that all you see me as? A sounding board or a plaything for them upstairs?'

He nodded. 'That's not all *I* see you as. But that's how *they* see you.' He pointed to the ceiling.

'I've been here a decade! Ten years of my life under this roof. Aren't I more than just a servant? Don't I count as a human being with feelings? When they ask how I am, I tell them how I am. Same when they ask for my opinion. I give it, because I presume they're interested in my view of the world. Are you saying it's just idle entertainment for them, rather than any genuine interest in me?'

'That lot didn't get rich by being genuine. They're not like us lot down here. They're a different breed. They're masters. We're servants. Naive to think owt else.'

Getting to her feet so abruptly that she scraped the chair legs noisily on the tiled floor, Florrie dug her balled fists into her hips. 'I've worked here all of my adult life so far, Thom, and maybe I'll spend the rest of it in service at Holcombe Hall. I've invested my blood, sweat and tears into this place, and that counts for summat.' She jerked her thumb repeatedly against her chest. 'I'm part of the fabric of this house. We all are. And you might think your opinions count for nowt with the Harding-Bournes, but if I've got the ear of Sir Richard and I think I can do some good . . . it will have been worth it.'

Desperately needing a breath of air, she stormed out of the kitchen and fled through the tradesmen's entrance into the cold of the courtyard. As she allowed the icy wind to cool her down, she wondered grudgingly if Thom had a point. Was she being a naive idealist in thinking she was anything more than just another expendable member of domestic staff to Sir Richard?

32

Early spring passed for Florrie in a blur of sensible domestic decisions and the instigation of housekeeping economies. As May and Sir Hugh's marriage to Daphne le Montford approached, however, the cutbacks she'd been asked to make were temporarily forgotten. Holcombe Hall was to host a wedding to remember, and the finest champagne was back on order to appease a very discerning guest list.

'Are the guest bedrooms all ready for occupation?' Florrie asked the maids whom she'd tasked with refreshing the rooms in the East Wing, in advance of the wedding guests' arrival.

'Yes, Florrie,' they answered in unison.

'Good. I'll inspect them shortly. The first guests are due to arrive by lunchtime, so I want you to get cracking with this checklist I've drawn up.' She handed out a list of last-minute jobs that were required to get Holcombe Hall looking its absolute best. 'I don't want to see one fingerprint on the brass door handles. I want to see every privy gleaming and smelling fresh as a daisy. And get the Ewbanks on the rugs.'

'I wish we had them electric vacuum cleaners,' Gwen said. 'Ewbanks are such hard work.'

'Well, money doesn't grow on trees.' Florrie

double-checked her master list. 'And a little elbow grease goes a long way.'

When the housemaids had been dispatched to buff and beat the Hall into gleaming submission, she turned to Sally. 'You're with me, supervising the set-up of the banqueting hall and the ballroom for the reception.'

She looked the ten girls from the village up and down to see that they passed muster in their borrowed uniform. Fidgeting nervously, they all looked terribly young. 'Right, you lot, you've been drafted in as extra help specially for tomorrow. You're all getting decent pay, and what I'm expecting from you in return is top-notch standards of service.' She pointed to Sally. 'Me and Sally here are going to train you in silver service. On the day, I don't want a single pea dropped in any guest's lap. I don't want to see scruffiness or slouching, and if I see bad manners or hear bad language, you'll be asked to leave immediately. Do I make myself clear?'

'Yes, Miss Bickerstaff,' the girls answered, some of them curtseying.

Florrie couldn't help but smile. 'You curtsey to the nobility, not me. And no flirting with the footmen.'

She led the group through the warren of claustrophobic below-stairs corridors and into the kitchen. Trooping past Cook, Florrie overheard an argument between her and the tiny, moustachioed Parisian chef who had been drafted in to oversee the wedding breakfast catering.

'Are you telling me how to make a gravy, when I've been cooking since I were old enough to hold a wooden spoon?' Cook snapped. Towering over the chef, she cut an intimidating figure.

The chef, however, was suffering none of Cook's territorial ways. He spoke English fluently but with a heavy French accent. 'If the Harding-Bournes were so enamoured of your stodgy English "gravy", madame, they would not have paid me handsomely to put the menu together for this wedding and to oversee the cooking.' He patted his tall chef's hat.

Noticing Florrie, Cook cried, 'Hey! Have you heard this nonsense, Florrie?' She jerked her thumb towards the chef. 'Have you heard this jumped-up little frog ordering me about in my own kitchen, telling me "zis" doesn't go with "zat", and "zis" is "peasant food", while his foreign muck is haute cuisine?'

Just about able to hear the cockerel crowing outside over Cook's diatribe, Florrie already felt like she'd been on her feet for an entire working day, rather than two hours. She puffed air out of her cheeks, feeling slightly dizzy through lack of sleep and the hustle and bustle of wedding preparations. 'Look, it's a society wedding. Sir Hugh and Miss le Montford wanted a French menu, supervised by a Paris chef. It's their big day and it's not our money, so it's not yours or my place to argue.'

'She called me a little frog!' the chef complained, his pencil moustache rippling above his top lip with undisguised indignation. '*Mon dieu!* Is this how you treat visiting craftsmen in your household?'

Florrie could see his point. She had no option but to chastise her friend. 'Apologize.'

Cook shook her head. 'Over my dead body. This is *my* kitchen. He's the interloper, here.'

'*Apologize!* That's an order.' She turned to the chef. 'And you, sir, kindly show some respect to a highly valued, senior member of the Holcombe Hall domestic staff.' She wagged her finger from one to the other. 'I know emotions run high whenever there's a wedding or banquet at the house, but you two need to work together, or Holcombe Hall will be the laughing stock of British high society. It will be all over *The Times,* the *Telegraph,* the *New York Times, Tatler . . .* you name it, they'll be printing stories about our incompetence.'

The Parisian chef shrugged. 'I am the great Monsieur Barbier. The affairs of Holcombe Hall are not my concern.'

'If this wedding breakfast is anything less than perfect, your reputation will be in tatters, same as ours, Monsieur. You take a Harding-Bourne commission, you tie yourself into this household's fate. Think on that, and *both of you*, find a way to work as a team. I'm too busy to referee your childish quarrelling.'

'Sorry, Florrie,' Cook said, biting her lip.

'Until this wedding's over and we're all back to normal, I'm Miss Bickerstaff to everyone. All right? We're an army with a domestic battle ahead of us, and me and Mr Arkwright are your captains. So it's Miss Bickerstaff . . . even to you, Cook.'

'Yes, Miss Bickerstaff,' Cook said softly.

The chef merely laid his hand across the bib of his pristine white chef's jacket and bowed.

Florrie didn't have enough time to feel guilty for pulling rank on Cook. She ushered the temporary serving staff and Sally into the banqueting hall, where forty round tables and a long head table at the far end of the hall had been set up to accommodate the wedding party and almost five hundred guests.

She marched over to a table in the middle of the room and slapped the tabletop which was entirely bare but for a wooden box of cutlery. 'All of these have got to be covered with fresh table-linen and set with the correct cutlery. I'm going to show you all how to set a table for a ten-course meal.' From her pocket, she took out the menu that Monsieur Barbier had given her. 'We need butter knives for the side-plates, a spoon for the soup, knife and fork for the starter, fish knife and fork for the fish course, then there's sorbet *before* mains . . .' She laid the cutlery for each course out in order, so that the village girls would understand what knives and forks went where.

'Do the toffs really have so many courses?' one girl asked. 'I thought they'd just have soup, mains and a pud.'

Sally laughed dryly. 'You're joking, aren't you? *That* lot make everything extra complicated to bamboozle *our* lot and remind us that we're not welcome to a place at their table. We're just fit to serve them.'

'Sally, I don't think that's helpful.' Florrie almost winced from the sting of Sally's razor-sharp observation. Ever since Sir Hugh had ridiculed her, and Thom had reminded her to *know her place* and keep her opinions to herself, Florrie had been agonizing over her perceived value as a lowly housekeeper in this rarefied world. The truth hurt. 'Let's just focus on helping these girls to do a professional job, eh?'

She left Sally with additional instructions to show the girls how to silver-serve, balancing platters along the inside of the left arm while they dished out food with serving implements in the right hand, and stacking dirty plates in the crooks of their left arm, using their right hand to gather in the used crockery and scrape leftovers as they went.

'Not one spilled pea, remember?' she said.

She was just about to make her way back below stairs to find out how far Arkwright had got with the name cards for the guest tables' place settings, when one of the footmen passed on the message that she was to attend to Lady Charlotte in her room as soon as possible.

Florrie checked her watch and frowned. 'She doesn't usually get up for another six hours. Did she say why she wanted me?' she asked the lad.

He shook his head and hared off before she could grill him further. Irritated that Lady Charlotte should demand her attention at such a busy time, when she already had a perfectly competent new lady's maid, Florrie climbed the stairs to the family's bedrooms.

She knocked softly at the door, wondering if Sir Richard was still asleep, even if his wife was awake.

'Is that you, Florrie? Do come in!' Lady Charlotte's voice lacked its usual chirpiness. She sounded weary. 'I'm in the bathroom. Out in a jiffy.'

Florrie entered and noted that the bed had only been

slept in on one side. There was no sign of Sir Richard. There was the sound of Lady Charlotte flushing the toilet. She emerged from the bathroom dabbing at her mouth with a hand towel. A sickly sheen of perspiration on her forehead shone in the dawn light, giving her a ghostly glow.

'Are you quite all right, my lady? You look a little drawn. Are you unwell?'

'Just an upset stomach,' Lady Charlotte said, placing a hand on her belly. She was only wearing a silk slip. 'Honestly, I've hardly slept a wink. It's nerves, you see.' She opened up her wardrobe and took out a dazzling, floor-length, black and white sequinned gown. 'Florrie, I don't know what to do. I bought this bias-cut Schiaparelli piece in New York and knew right away that it would be perfect for the wedding, but . . .' She thrust it at Florrie. 'Just help me to put it on, will you? You'll understand what I mean.'

'Of course, my lady.' How could Florrie hope to assert any housekeeper's authority with Sir Richard's wife? 'Tell me, are you satisfied with Doris, your new lady's maid?'

Lady Charlotte waved a manicured hand dismissively. 'Yes, yes, yes. She's perfectly fine. But this is a delicate matter, and I needed you, dear Florrie. I knew you'd be awake at this hour on such an occasion.'

Stifling a long sigh, Florrie tried to fasten the dress but could barely get it up and over Lady Charlotte's hips. 'Ah, I see. It seems the fastening mechanism is faulty.' Though she could see there was not, in fact, anything wrong with the fastening, she wasn't about to ask Lady

Charlotte if she realized she'd gained a good couple of inches across the hips since Christmas. 'Why don't I ask my mother to come and take a look? She's a dab hand with repairs and alterations as well as laundering. I think she could . . .' *Whatever you do, don't say "let it out"!* '. . . remedy this in no time.'

'Marvellous.' Lady Charlotte unexpectedly hugged her. She had tears standing in her eyes. 'See? I knew you were the right woman for the job!'

Florrie patted her gingerly on the back. She reflected that she had always found Lady Charlotte vain and silly, and she loathed the way this earl's daughter used her as the punchline to too many jokes, just to vanquish her own feelings of inadequacy. Being married to a man like Sir Richard and calling Holcombe Hall her home clearly wasn't enough for the girl who had everything. But wasn't Lady Charlotte just a free-spirited young woman, trapped in an apparently loveless marriage to an older man – a marriage that came with so many expectations, including having to live under her mother-in-law's roof and abide by her in-laws' rules? *Poor Charlotte,* Florrie thought. *I might be poor, but I'm free in ways she could only dream of.* 'There, there,' she said, as Lady Charlotte started to weep in earnest. 'What's all this about?'

It was then that Florrie realized what lay at the root of Lady Charlotte's erratic behaviour: her burgeoning middle; her refusal of alcohol since her return from New York; these unruly emotional outbursts. Lady Charlotte was pregnant.

Florrie stiffened and gently pushed Lady Charlotte

away. She thought about the fountain pen she still hadn't given back to Sir Richard and his affectionate note which she had hidden in a shoe, taking it out only to read before bed at night. She realized that her mother had been right all along. Lady Charlotte was carrying the heir to Holcombe Hall, and Sir Richard's overtures towards Florrie were nothing more than idle flirtation with a maid. Of course they were! How could they be anything more? Florrie had spent more than a decade of her life pointlessly pining for a man who belonged to another woman in a league entirely out of her reach, and now his bond to this spoiled daughter of a minor royal was fixed in perpetuity with a child. How young and foolish she had been!

33

'What God has joined together, let no man put asunder,' the Anglican priest said solemnly, surveying the huge gathering in Holcombe Hall's Wren chapel. The May sunshine was streaming through the stained-glass windows on the south elevation, hitting the marble floor in rainbow-coloured shafts of ethereal light. 'Blessed are you, O Lord our God . . .'

Florrie and Arkwright had slipped in together at the back of the chapel just after the ceremony had started, content that the reception preparations back at the Hall were complete. Now, Florrie craned her neck to catch a glimpse of Daphne le Montford, with her vibrant red hair and her exquisite ivory silk wedding gown. When several guests parted to reveal the couple kneeling at the front, Florrie watched with amazement as Daphne looked over her shoulder and seemed to bat her eyelashes at Sir Hugh's best friend, Walter.

She nudged Arkwright. 'Did you see that?' she whispered. 'That was a knowing look she gave him.'

He nodded in silence, his eyebrow raised. A few seconds later, he whispered his reply. 'Cuckolded before he's even wed. Common knowledge.'

The wedding continued, yet it felt positively funereal to Florrie. When Thom and the other gardeners slipped in towards the end of the ceremony, her heart lifted.

'Have I missed much?' Thom whispered to her, standing so close that she could feel the warmth from his body.

She shook her head. 'Just another sham society marriage.'

'They wouldn't know love if it slapped 'em in the face with a bunch of glads,' Thom whispered.

Florrie felt his little finger seek out and entwine with hers. She let his finger linger there a while, and squeezed it affectionately before breaking loose. He looked down at her with smiling eyes and a flush of pink in his cheeks. Had she been right to encourage him?

'I'd better get back,' she whispered.

A grand marquee had been set up in the grounds, only a few elegant steps for the illustrious guests from the tall French doors of the banqueting hall. In a bid to keep a watchful eye on her maids as they wended their way through the throng of guests, carrying platters laden with canapés, Florrie stood by a supporting pillar of the marquee, which had been swathed in white fabric and festooned with long garlands of late spring flowers. The heady scent of the peonies mingled with the expensive perfume of the guests.

Among the guests, she spotted Sir Hugh's 'bright young things', who had until recently been written about in all the papers as fearsome intellectuals, who happened to indulge publicly in a bacchanalian blowing off of steam. She wondered if the journalists would be quite so forgiving of their antics now that poverty was beginning to bite in earnest in Britain. There was certainly no sign of austerity measures in the marquee, as the Duke of Westminster rubbed shoulders with Lady Charlotte's royal relatives, and Oswald Mosley held court among the other politicians who had been invited. The wives of industrialists tittered at each other's witticisms, while comparing their hand-embellished gowns that they boasted had cost more than the price of a Ford Model A.

For the second time that day, Arkwright came to stand at her side. 'Look at them gliding among the guests: my lads and your girls. For all our differences, Miss Bickerstaff, we run a tight ship here.'

Florrie looked at Arkwright, blinking hard. 'Are you extending me an olive branch, Mr Arkwright?'

A smile twitched at the corners of Arkwright's mouth. 'Just for today, Miss Bickerstaff. Just for today.' He leaned in further. 'Say hello to your lovely mother for me, won't you?'

He strode off into the throng of guests before she could respond. It suddenly occurred to her that the true love in the air that day belonged to those below stairs. The thought warmed her.

As the day wore on, Florrie started to flag, running between the kitchen, to see that the various courses were being cooked and dished up to perfection, and the banqueting hall, to ensure the maids were serving correctly.

Once the sorbet dishes had been collected and before

the main course was served, she made her way swiftly down to the kitchen to find that Monsieur Barbier was yelling at Cook.

'You have burnt the dauphinoise! You stupid woman!' He raised his hands up in obvious frustration.

Cook pointed to the steaming dishes that she'd just taken out of the oven. 'That's not burnt. That's browned nicely.'

'*Non! Non, non, non!* It is burnt to a crisp and dry.'

Florrie clapped her hands together. 'Hey! What's all this? I turn my back for ten minutes and I find you both bickering while the chicken gets cold?'

'You must see this,' Monsieur Barbier said. 'I am going to take another dauphinoise from the second oven, and you will see. The liquid inside has curdled, *je crois*.' He went to the large storeroom where the additional ranges had been fired up – a solution Cook always deployed when she was required to cater en masse for a Harding-Bourne banquet.

'How dare you! You're just looking for a reason to belittle me, you jumped-up little bully!' Cook marched behind him. She was even redder in the face than usual.

Florrie followed them both into the adjacent room. 'Look, I know five hundred is a lot to cater for, but you two just need to get along and work as a team. You've got kitchen staff working beneath you that need to see you present a united front. The potato dish looks fine to me, and that lot above stairs are so drunk, I doubt anybody will notice.'

Monsieur Barbier took out a fresh batch of

dauphinoise and stuck a spoon into it. He wagged his head from side to side. '*Comme ci, comme ça.*' He flared his nostrils dramatically and regarded Cook from the corner of his eyes. '*Oui.* It will pass.'

'Oh, *thank you*, kind Monsieur!' Cook said sarcastically, tugging deferentially at her mob cap. 'Thanks a bundle.'

'For heaven's sake, you two,' Florrie said, 'use your initiative. If something gets a bit burnt, cut the burnt bit off. As long as we get the dinners out and they look nice and taste fine, that's all that counts. You can't expect Michelin starred grub when there's five hundred to cater for and only a handful of kitchen staff. Talented, you both are. Miracle workers, you are not.'

Despite the fact that tempers were running high below stairs, exacerbated by the claustrophobic labyrinth of corridors being clogged with sweaty wine waiters, who were running back and forth to the cellars for replacement bottles of wine, above stairs, the staff all seemed to be serving the guests with cool professionalism. Florrie felt proud that they were efficient enough to be almost invisible.

Once the dessert was finished and the petit fours were being served with coffee and port, Florrie decided she would approach Sir Richard before the band struck up in the ballroom, to check that he was content with how the event was being run. Waiting patiently behind him, she watched him exchange pleasantries over the merits of strawberries dipped in chocolate with one of Daphne's bridesmaids, seated next to him. On his other side, Lady Charlotte was laughing at something Walter

Knight-Downey had said. Florrie waited for a natural pause in their conversation before stepping forward.

'Sir Richard,' she bent over to speak softly in his ear. 'Are you happy with everything? Is there anything you need me to provide or arrange before you move to the ballroom?'

When Sir Richard met her gaze, his eyes, normally so sharply focussed and clear, seemed glazed. 'Florrie, dear.' He grabbed her hand and kissed the back of it, speaking slowly and slurring. 'You have done *such* a wonderful job today. You are a marvel, Miss Bickerstaff. I would like to take you for a turn around the dancefloor, if I may. Dance with me, Florrie.'

Florrie snatched her hand back, horrified at the unabashed and inappropriate display of affection. She was not the only person at the table who had noticed that Sir Richard had uncharacteristically relinquished some of his usual control.

'Florrie, do you have a moment?' Dame Elizabeth leaned back on her chair, shouting along the line of family members and waving her hand. 'Florence! I say!'

Relieved to walk away from Sir Richard's wine-fuelled request, Florrie moved to Dame Elizabeth's end of the table. 'Yes, Your Ladyship.'

'Kindly help me up, will you? There's a good girl. I feel that when the band starts its infernal din, it is time for me to retire and leave the celebrations to those whose knees are rather more robust.'

'Of course. My pleasure.'

Dame Elizabeth took her leave from the wedding party, allowing Florrie to escort her back to her rooms.

'At last, some peace and quiet,' Dame Elizabeth said. She kicked off her shoes. 'Do help me get out of this jolly uncomfortable garb and into my nightgown, there's a good girl. I've eaten far too much, and the whalebones in my corset are conspiring to squeeze out what little life is left in me.' She chuckled, seeming in good spirits.

Florrie unlaced her corset with nimble fingers, stifling a yawn. 'It was a wonderful wedding. Many congratulations, Your Ladyship.'

'In no small part thanks to you, my dear. You and Arkwright have excelled yourselves.' The old lady groaned with relief as the corset was loosened. 'Please pass my highest praise on to Cook and that funny little Frenchman that my son kept raving about.'

'Monsieur Barbier?'

'Indeed.'

'It was tense below stairs, I can tell you,' Florrie said. 'Cook's not one to share authority in the kitchen. But as long as everyone enjoyed themselves and was none the wiser . . .'

Dame Elizabeth allowed Florrie to help her out of her underskirts. 'Ah, the difference between the world below stairs and that above stairs. And never the twain shall meet. Ha ha.'

Florrie took the underskirts for the laundry and passed Dame Elizabeth her nightdress, sensing that her comment was loaded. 'Yes. Holcombe Hall is like an elegant swan with its flippers going ten to the dozen beneath the water's surface.'

'Quite.' Dame Elizabeth's smile faded. She rested her

hand on Florrie's arm. 'In fact, I wanted to speak to you about such matters. I suppose a swan is as good a metaphor as any – that which glides above in stately fashion and the frantic propelling mechanism that hides in the murk below.'

'Oh?' Florrie could guess the lecture she was about to be given. Her blood started to heat before Dame Elizabeth had even said a word.

'Yes. You and my son. I can see there is a familiarity between you that, while hardly uncommon between a master and one of his maids, is not something I personally wish to encourage. Not under my roof.'

'Your Ladyship?' Florrie's blood came to a bubbling simmer.

Dame Elizabeth locked eyes with her. 'I'll put it plainly, dear. I can see that there is something between you and Sir Richard.'

'I can assure you, there's nothing—'

Dame Elizabeth gave Florrie no opportunity to defend herself. She merely raised her voice. 'He is your employer, your elder and your better, and he is married to the daughter of an earl who has elevated my family's standing from common industrialists with a minor baronetcy, bestowed on my late father-in-law as an afterthought, to minor royals with heritable titles worth having. Their job is to produce an heir, so that Holcombe Hall remains in our family, our family increases in prestige and our business interests continue down the line. Your job is to know your place, which is below stairs, and to keep the domestic side of Holcombe Hall functioning smoothly.'

'But I—'

'I will not countenance *anything* or *anyone* jeopardizing the union between my son and his wife, regardless of whether or not he's taken a shine to you or if you've already coaxed him into a proverbial roll in the hay.' She delivered the last sentiment with a lashing of curled-lip disgust. Then she turned to sit at her dressing table and started to take pins out of her hair, flinging them into a glass bowl. 'You may leave me now, but do think on what I've said.'

Florrie stood rooted to the spot, aghast at what she'd just heard. She knew if she blurted out her response straight away, she would say something she regretted. *Bite your tongue, Florrie Bickerstaff. Think of your job and Mam and the kids.* The words had other ideas, however, and her blood was now truly on the boil.

'How dare you!' Florrie said. 'How dare you cast aspersions on my good character, insinuating that *I've* been trying to seduce your son.' She didn't try to keep the righteous rage out of her voice, and the unexpected and fearless battle-maiden inside her was pleased to see Dame Elizabeth balk. 'I've given this family the last ten years of my life. My best years. While other women my age are getting married and having children, I've been scrubbing your floors and dishing up your meals and changing your beds.' She poked herself in the chest. 'And I'm a respectable church-going woman; a spinster, at that, with the highest of moral standards, so if your *married* son has taken a shine to me, don't lay the blame at *my* feet. Saying that, though, Sir Richard has never laid a hand on me or said one improper word to me. Had that occurred to you? That platonic friendship can occur between a man and a woman?' Florrie ran out of breath. She stared at Dame Elizabeth, waiting for her outraged retort. 'Or does that only apply to Lady Charlotte and Sir Hugh? Or maybe you judge every woman by Daphne le Montford's standards?'

Dame Elizabeth gasped and clutched her hand to her throat. 'You dreadful girl! How dare you speak to me like that, when I am a Dame and you are a . . . common little *nothing*?' She pointed at Florrie. 'I see the way you hang on Richard's every word and follow him around the room with puppy dog eyes; how you ingratiate yourself with him so that you have become indispensable. You are full of secrets and dastardly plans. I see it!'

The voice of reason and doubt still called for Florrie to keep her opinions to herself, but by now, ten years of pent-up resentment was fermenting inside her. It all bubbled to the surface before she realized what she was saying. '*I'm* full of secrets? That's rich, coming from a woman who's being blackmailed.'

The old woman inhaled sharply. 'I have no idea what you're talking about.'

'Miles T. Brooke Esquire, your pen pal? That's right. I found the letters from him in the Chinese bedroom. They slid out from under the desk when my nieces and nephew were playing hide and seek, so I know all about—'

'Stop!' Dame Elizabeth clasped her wrinkled hands to her eyes. She shook her head. 'Stop. I beg you. It gives me no pleasure to pay that man for his silence, but pay him I must.' She narrowed her eyes. 'How much do you know? Did you read them, you nosy girl?'

Florrie opened her mouth to respond, but decided silence might be the best way to encourage Dame Elizabeth to say more. She merely shrugged and folded her arms, raising her eyebrow archly.

The old lady's shoulders sagged and she wedged those papery, veined hands between her knees. 'If it ever got out that Miles is Richard's real father . . .'

Blinking hard, Florrie wondered if she'd misheard. It had been clear from the correspondence and clandestine visit that Dame Elizabeth had been harbouring a great secret, but to hear a scandal of *such* gargantuan proportions issue forth from the woman's own lips was unexpected.

Dame Elizabeth continued to speak softly, full of contrition. 'There was a time during my marriage to Lord Harding-Bourne when I could find no happiness. Ours was never a love match.' She smiled sadly, looking at a framed photograph of her late husband that stood on top of a tallboy. 'Women in my situation . . . we are married out of convenience and strategy. If love blossoms subsequently, it is an unlooked-for boon.'

Florrie sat close to Dame Elizabeth on the edge of the bed, so that they almost touched knees. 'I understand.'

Dame Elizabeth stroked her wedding and engagement rings with the tip of an arthritic finger. 'Miles was an old friend of George. They'd been up at Oxford together and he visited regularly, though he was never

341

part of quite the same social milieu as we were. But after I had James, George lost interest in me for a long while, and I felt so alone.' She met Florrie's gaze at last. 'Do you know what it is to be lonely to the core of your very being, even though you are in a house that is constantly abuzz with the movement, chatter and petty dramas of other people?'

Florrie searched deeply inside herself and found the memories of first moving to Holcombe Hall imprinted there. An aching, echoing chasm of loneliness that took a year or more to fill; the emotional bruise of the four thousand nights she had since spent alone in her single bed, with no man to hold her, to promise there would be a happy ending. 'I'm no stranger to loneliness.'

Dame Elizabeth nodded. She choked back a sob, touching her lips. 'Miles and I . . . George was away a lot on business. I suspected he was . . . inconstant with his physical affections. While the cat's away and all . . . And I'm afraid I sought solace in his charming, attentive friend.'

'Did Lord Harding-Bourne know Sir Richard was another man's son?'

'No. I lied about the date of conception, and he never questioned it. I broke off my affair with Miles, once I knew I was with child.'

Florrie thought about the implications of Sir Richard having a different father. 'So, with Sir James killed on the battlefield in the Great War, Sir Hugh is actually the rightful heir to Holcombe Hall?'

'Shush!' Dame Elizabeth grabbed Florrie by the wrist.

'Keep your voice down. Nobody can know this terrible secret!' She loosened her grip. 'My younger son . . . I love him unreservedly, but Hugh is impressionable and childish. He is not suited to responsibility. If he had inherited the house and the reins of the business, we would have been bankrupt within a year. And Richard is so fiercely intelligent and temperate and honourable. Harding-Bourne Enterprises and Holcombe Hall are flourishing under his stewardship, even in these tumultuous times. My late husband may not have been his flesh and blood, but I still see so much of George's statesmanlike nature in Richard. There is more to fatherhood than just fathering a child.'

'Sir Richard *is* a wonderful man,' Florrie said, her wrath giving way to empathy. 'A true gentleman.'

Dame Elizabeth met her words with a pained expression. 'See? There you go again! Your affection for him is evident, but I cannot have the closeness between you threaten his marriage and plans for an heir, Florence. And this controversy over his father can never see the light of day. Do you hear me? If the newspapers get wind of this . . . How much will it take to guarantee your silence on the matter? Name your price.'

'There *you* go again,' Florrie said. She stood abruptly, feeling the room spin. 'I'm not blackmailing you, Your Ladyship. I think Miles T. Brooke Esquire is already doing a good enough job of that. I've done nothing to warrant such disdain and mistrust.' She sighed and shook her head. 'It's been a very long day, and it's not over yet. I'm going back to my post.'

'Wait!' Dame Elizabeth said. 'I'm truly sorry. You're

right.' She held her hands out to Florrie. 'Please. Can we forget everything I just said – those despicable accusations?'

Florrie stared down at the old lady's trembling, out-stretched hands. She ignored the gesture. 'No. You can't unsay any of it. You say you're sorry, but I know you don't mean it. You'd given those accusations plenty of thought for a long, long time. And to add insult to injury, you offered me money to keep my mouth shut, like I was trying to extort you.'

'How can I make things right between us, Florrie dear?' Dame Elizabeth rested her hands on her knees. Normally such an imposing figure in her widow's weeds, her hair decorated with arching ostrich plumage so tall that it almost touched the threshold of the doorways, now stripped of her voluminous skirts and the elaborate curls piled atop her head, she looked utterly forlorn and small. 'Please say there's a way.'

Florrie knew she might never again find herself in a situation where she truly had the ear of Dame Elizabeth. 'Look, you've already been right kind to me and my family. I'm forever indebted to the Harding-Bournes for saving my mother and my sister's children from a terrible fate. And I love working here. It's my home. My colleagues are as good as family. I know I'm lucky. But there's so many that are down on their luck.' She drew breath and balled her fists with determination. 'Forgive me for being so forward, but remember I talked about the people laid off at Harding-Bourne mills and pits and that? Folk what are now living on the breadline . . .'

Dame Elizabeth exhaled hard and nodded. 'Yes. I remember the conversation.' She pursed her lips. 'You wanted us to help them. Save them from destitution and fascism.'

'Aye. Continue your father-in-law's legacy of philanthropy, like.'

The old lady bowed her head and closed her eyes. 'How about I see to it that a charitable foundation is set up?' She opened her eyes and smiled resolutely at Florrie.

Florrie gasped with delight and clasped her hands together beneath her chin. 'Really?'

'I give you my word.'

34

'My dear, you are positively glowing,' the well-dressed man said to Lady Charlotte at the launch of the charitable foundation.

Three months had passed since Dame Elizabeth had committed to helping the poor who had lost their jobs at Harding-Bourne-owned mills, mines and shipyards. While the infrastructure had been set up by Sir Richard, Florrie had dedicated herself to maintaining Holcombe Hall and overseeing the care of not just the Harding-Bourne family but also her own. George had finally been registered at the local school and was attending daily, hitching a ride in with the lad Arkwright sent into the village on daily errands; collected in the afternoon by Thom. Nelly was due to start at nursery on her third birthday, which was only two months away. Now, Florrie found herself at the grand launch of the charitable foundation she'd conceived of on the back of a dismal trip to Manchester. She could hardly believe it.

The well-dressed man's voice snapped Florrie out of her reverie.

'Many congratulations to you both,' he said. He turned to Sir Richard and shook his hand. 'Let's hope you're blessed with a boy, eh?'

As the three of them laughed, Florrie watched Lady

Charlotte smooth her fingertips over her newly round belly that showed beneath the simple black Chanel dress Mam had let out for her. Her smile was indeed luminous, though Florrie suspected Lady Charlotte was more enamoured of being the centre of attention than with the prospect of motherhood.

'I can't *wait* to give birth,' she'd confessed to Florrie that very morning when Florrie had been styling her hair in advance of the charitable foundation's grand opening. 'I do miss champagne, and I *hate* being fat, and a nanny worth her salt will be able to bottle-feed while I sleep in.'

'Yes, my lady,' Florrie had simply said.

'And I hate having to wear sack-like clothes. I look like a frumpy old maid! I mean, I could be one of your girls.'

'I'm sure that's not true, my lady.'

Lady Charlotte had caught her eye in the mirror. 'Oh, do lighten up, Florrie. I was *joking!*'

'As you wish, my lady.' Florrie had forced a smile.

'Are you quite all right? You seem terribly glum these days.'

'I'm fine, thank you.' She'd set the comb down on the dressing table. 'But I do have housekeeping duties to attend to. Will that be all?'

Since the pregnancy had been announced and since Florrie's revealing conversation with Dame Elizabeth, she had finally acknowledged that her over-familiarity with both Lady Charlotte and Sir Richard wasn't serving her well. Lady Charlotte would have to look to her new sister-in-law for a confidante and the easy punchline for her jokes, and Sir Richard would have to look to his wife for idle flirtation.

'. . . haven't you, Florrie?' Sir Richard's voice jolted Florrie back into the moment.

'Sir?' Florrie looked up and remembered she was not in Lady Charlotte and Sir Richard's bedroom at Holcombe Hall, but standing in an office in the Harding-Bourne headquarters in Manchester, from which the new HB Charitable Foundation was to be run.

'You've been the driving force of this new charitable foundation.' He turned back to the guests in attendance, which included wealthy donors, Harding-Bourne directors, journalists from various newspapers, Mam, who had left the children with Cook for a few hours, and Thom, who had driven them all the way there. 'It's Miss Bickerstaff's brainchild, to help people like her delightful mother, Matilda, who was sadly made redundant from a Harding-Bourne mill some years ago. I am very proud to now have both women on the domestic staff at my family seat.' He pointed to Florrie and her mam. 'With Miss Bickerstaff running the show in exemplary fashion, obviously.' He saluted Florrie and everyone in the room laughed. The flashbulbs from the *Manchester Guardian* and the *Daily Telegraph*'s photographers started to pop.

'Smile for the camera, Miss Bickerstaff! Put your arms around your mother! Say "cheese and crackers"!'

Florrie put her arm around her mam and smiled awkwardly. She squinted and blinked in the sudden harsh light of the popping flashbulbs, feeling like a startled deer.

349

When the photographers had finished snapping away, Sir Richard continued. 'Before I allow Miss Bickerstaff to say a few words, let me preface her speech by saying that businesses will always have to expand and contract their workforce to remain competitive, depending on which way the economic winds are blowing.' He looked down at his brogues, wearing a thoughtful expression. 'Such flux is a regrettable but an unavoidable part of commerce. But at least now, we can provide some measure of financial relief to those who find themselves joining the ranks of the unemployed.'

The newspaper men were no longer interested in Sir Richard, however. They only had eyes and pencils at the ready for Florrie. 'Tell us why you wanted to do this, miss.'

All eyes were on Florrie. She swallowed hard, wishing she hadn't let Dame Elizabeth talk her into coming to the launch of the endeavour. She could feel her cheeks flaming and a nervous rash itching its way up her neck. 'Er, well, er, actually, it's not just my mother that put the idea in my head. It's my aunty and all the people I saw queuing for a hot meal in Manchester, back in the spring.' She watched the journalists scribble her words down. 'I've heard and seen some terrible things lately. Fascism. Poor people blaming recent immigrants for their own empty cupboards and hungry bellies, rather than the Wall Street Crash or the Depression, or whatever it is they're calling it in the papers. I just think, if we lighten the burden that our poor have to carry . . . you know, we can hopefully turn away from the path they're going down in Germany. It's about putting food on people's tables and giving them some dignity and choice.'

Everyone in the room applauded enthusiastically, with the notable exceptions of Sir Hugh and his new wife, Daphne le Montford. Florrie could see them whispering to one another, both wearing scowls sour enough to curdle milk. She hadn't intended to say anything political – who was she, a humble housekeeper, to tell anybody what to think? She failed to see, however, how the grinding poverty of Manchester's working folk could be separated from the changes in political leaning she had observed of late, where the beliefs of ordinary men and women were being polarized; pulled to the right by fascism and to the left by communism.

'That was some speech you gave,' Thom said, appearing by her side, when everyone was celebrating with tea and biscuits. 'You'll be running for parliament next! I'll be very proud to chauffeur such a brilliant mind back to Holcombe.' Gone was the winter ruddiness in his cheeks, replaced by the deep tan of a gardener in the summer months. His hair, unadorned with the Brylcreem that other men had started to slick their hair with, was streaked with gold from the sun and fell in his smiling eyes.

Florrie chewed her lip. She pressed her palms to her burning cheeks, wishing she could get some air on the stifling summer's afternoon. 'Brilliant mind!' she scoffed. 'I'm just a simple woman, me. I know good from bad and right from wrong.'

'Well, I'm a simple man who would like to ask a simple question.' He looked at her expectantly.

'Go on.' Florrie felt butterflies take flight in her stomach.

'Do you fancy going to the flicks with me when we get back? *No Exit*'s just started showing. It's supposed to be good.'

'Are you asking me out on a date, Thomas Stanley?'

Thom started to laugh. He locked eyes with her. 'Aye. It's seven months since you turned me down under the mistletoe. I was wondering if the heat of the summer might have softened you up a bit.'

'Like butter in the sun?' Florrie liked the way his Adam's apple jiggled in his muscular neck when he laughed at her suggestion. 'You look right smart in your Sunday-best suit, by the way. Scrub up nice for a man who spends the rest of the week caked in soil.'

'I sustain life from what I grow in that good, honest soil, Florrie, so I'll take that as a compliment. And you are more beautiful than any rose in the garden. Is that a yes to the pictures then?'

Florrie entwined his little finger in hers. 'Butter me up a bit more, and we'll see.' She winked, barely able to believe her flirtatious daring.

'Where are the children?' Mam asked on their return.

Cook was sitting at the kitchen table, writing menus for the week. She rolled her eyes. 'Them three? They drove me mad so I baked them in tonight's pie.' She laughed at her own joke then clearly saw the dismay on Mam and Florrie's faces. 'Only joking. They're with Arkwright.'

'*Arkwright?*' Florrie said.

'I'm no good with kids, me, and I couldn't be doing with them under my feet all day. Sorry, ladies.'

Cook pointed to the corridor that led to his office. 'I think they're still alive, judging by the noise. Go and have a look for yourself.'

Leading the way, Florrie marched down to Arkwright's office with a thudding heart. She heard a tremendous banging, some tuneless singing and the sound of George excitedly shouting, 'Yeehah! Giddy up, horsey!' before they'd even reached the threshold.

Mam pushed past her and froze at the sight that greeted them. 'Mr Arkwright! I asked Cook to watch the children. I'm so sorry she imposed on you.'

Florrie stood behind her on the threshold of the butler's office, flabbergasted by the sight of him in his shirtsleeves, bent double while he held Alice up by the hands. The tiny girl strutted forwards on her stiff, chubby legs, babbling with glee.

'It was no imposition at all, Matilda,' Arkwright said. 'She'll be walking soon, this one. Good job it was a quiet day, else we'd have all been in trouble.' He inclined his head towards Nelly who was sitting inside a make-shift tent he'd fashioned from two chairs and a blanket. Wearing a red belt around her head as a headband, she was banging a wooden spoon on an upturned sauce-pan and singing. Meanwhile, George was rocking back and forth in a frenzied fashion on a wooden rocking horse that looked at least a hundred years old. He was wearing his full cowboy regalia, pretending to shoot his pistol into the air. 'The Arizona Kid over there thinks his sister's Hiawatha, and she hasn't disabused him of the notion.'

Mam scooped Alice up and kissed her silky curls. 'Has Mr Arkwright been nice to you? Yes!' She smiled at the butler. 'Hey, you're a dab hand at this.'

Arkwright grinned. 'They're lovely children. A testament to your excellent mothering.' He bowed slightly. 'I hope you don't mind that I brought that old rocking horse up from the basement,' he said to Florrie.

'Not at all,' Florrie said. 'It's a brilliant idea, as long as the Harding-Bournes don't object.'

Tapping the side of his nose, Arkwright said, 'What they don't know won't harm them.'

'You must let me make you dinner by way of thanks,' Mam said, shyly looking over at Nelly.

Arkwright started to roll his sleeves back down. He glanced nervously at Florrie and then cleared his throat, turning back to her mother. 'I should like that very much.'

'I'll leave you two to make your plans,' Florrie said, feeling suddenly like she was intruding on something more than just idle chatter.

Making her way back to the kitchen, Florrie marvelled privately in the change she'd seen in Arkwright since she'd become housekeeper. It was almost unconceivable that the tyrant who had all but killed Mrs Douglas with his belligerent ways was now trying on surrogate grandfatherhood for size, like a new pair of shoes in a style he'd hitherto eschewed. She chuckled to herself. 'I wish Bertha could have lived to see that,' she muttered beneath her breath. 'She'd never have believed her own eyes.'

'You quite all right, Florrie?' Cook asked. 'Only you're nattering to yourself and grinning like a fool. You been at the booze at that charity thing?'

'Not a bit of it,' Florrie said. 'I'm just happy. I've got an evening to myself and I'm off out to the flicks.'

Cook's eyes were wide with curiosity. 'Who with? Is it Thom? It's Thom, isn't it?'

Florrie tapped the side of her nose. 'Never you mind.'

'Tell us! Go on! Is it Thom?'

Cook's interrogation faded as Florrie climbed the back stairs.

After she'd freshened up, relishing the cool breeze that the balmy summer's evening brought through her window, she dressed in the only other lightweight dress that she had – one of Lady Charlotte's cast-offs. Looking in the mirror on the back of her door, she decided she was satisfied with what she saw. She reached back into her wardrobe and pulled out her spare pair of shoes. Sir Richard's note fell out on to the floor.

Feeling a pang of regret and misplaced longing, she re-read the note. Christmas felt like a different country; a lost world. She remembered pushing Thom away underneath that mistletoe, still privately hankering after the untouchable Sir Richard – a nobleman behaving ignobly; the knight who belonged to the Earl's daughter.

'It's time,' she said.

Florrie took the pen in its box out of the top drawer of her chest of drawers, where she'd hidden it among her stockings. Sliding it into her handbag, she made her way downstairs using not the servants' back stairs, but the grand staircase itself. She relished the feel of the polished oak banister beneath her rough hand. She drank in the smell of beeswax from the wood panelling. She paused to appreciate the creak and crack of the old house's timbers, ever-expanding and contracting, as though Holcombe Hall was a living, breathing thing. The portraits of ancestors that hung on the landing seemed to glower down at her for daring to tread a staircase that was never meant for her, but that evening, she didn't care.

With the Harding-Bournes remaining in Manchester for the night so that they could entertain their new charity's trustees, the house was quiet, the reception rooms unoccupied. It was easy to walk into Sir Richard's study unobserved. The July evening sunlight still streamed in, turning the dust motes on the air into shafts of gold dust. Florrie paused to drink in the smell of Sir Richard's expensive sandalwood cologne and cigars. It was a good smell, a comforting smell, a smell she would always love, but tonight, she realized, it was just the lingering scent of the wealthy man who paid her wages – nothing more.

She walked over to his leather-topped desk and placed the pen box down carefully in the middle. She took a piece of notepaper from a pile that was neatly stacked

in a purpose-made walnut box and she used a pencil
to write.

*Many thanks for this, but I think it's too grand a gift for a woman
of my station. I hope you can find a more fitting home for it.*

Peering down at her words, she wondered if he would
be insulted. Was she doing the right thing?

'Get on with it, girl,' she told herself.

Exhaling slowly, she placed the note beneath the box;
pushed the pencil back into the pencil pot. Allowing
herself to take one last, lingering look at the gift that
had signified so much but delivered so little, she slid
her hand into her handbag and retrieved Sir Richard's
rolled-up missive from between her purse and handkerchief. Opening the top desk drawer, she found the
cigarette lighter that she had seen Sir Richard use count-
less times. Sparking the lighter into life, she held the
merry flame up to the note, allowing it to lick its way
along the paper's edges. When it caught fire in earnest,
she dropped it into Sir Richard's ashtray and watched it
blacken and disintegrate. It was as if it had never existed.

'There,' she said. 'That's that.'

Florrie loved the way the scent of honeysuckle, jasmine
and flowering tobacco that Thom had planted beneath
the windows found its way into Holcombe Hall on a
summer's evening. Each silent, sun-filled reception
room that she passed seemed to thrum with memories
of the past year: not just the Harding-Bournes' family

drama, but also the woes and triumphs of the domestic staff who served them.

'This is my home,' she said. She stopped at the foot of the grand staircase and spun around slowly, looking up at the galleried landing, imagining Sir Richard standing there, flanked by Lady Charlotte, Sir Hugh, Dame Elizabeth, Lord Harding-Bourne, all of the staff, including Mrs Douglas, Mam, the children and Irene. In her mind's eye, they were all smiling benignly down at her. 'This is *my* home. *I* am the housekeeper of Holcombe Hall.'

She came to a standstill and giggled at her own silliness. Yet it felt good to remember all that had come to pass under that roof since she had arrived at Holcombe Hall, a bedraggled and nervous girl of fifteen: ten years of trials, tribulations, laughter and jubilation. Florrie wondered what the new decade would bring. Would the Depression pass soon? Would prosperity be just around the corner? Or would Britain be gripped by either fascism or communism and descend into authoritarian chaos?

'You coming, then?' Florrie's thoughts were interrupted by Thom, shouting to her from the main entrance. He tapped his fob watch. 'Film'll be over if we don't make tracks.'

'Sorry. On my way.' Florrie left her memories and reflections at the foot of the stairs and walked towards the here and now.

'I've got the car round the side,' Thom said. 'Thought we could travel in style, like. His nibs won't be any the wiser.'

'I won't tell if you won't,' Florrie said. 'Just don't let Arkwright see.'

'I'm not daft.' Thom held his arm out for her. 'Right. Is the housekeeper of Holcombe Hall ready to start her evening off?'

Florrie smiled up at her handsome date. She linked him and stood on her tiptoes to kiss him on the cheek. 'I feel I could take on the world tonight. But how about we start with Holcombe, eh? Take me out, Thomas Stanley. The housekeeper of Holcombe Hall is quite ready to start a whole new chapter.'

Acknowledgements

The Housekeeper of Holcombe Hall was a joy to write. The 1920s and 1930s were fascinating decades in British and European history, featuring such political and economic churn, that it didn't take me long to decide on a brave new heroine, enduring much struggle in her life, but all in a picture-perfect setting that I felt confident would appeal to readers. I hope you enjoy reading this first book in my new Lancashire-set series as much as I did writing it!

Books don't appear magically of their own accord on bookshop shelves, however. It's a team effort to take the first draft of a manuscript, polish it until it gleams and wrap it in a beautiful cover. So I must thank the following people for their support and input in that process. Thank you:

To my darling family, for putting up with me when I'm 'in the tunnel' and chained to my laptop for seven days per week, week in and week out, during the penning of a first draft. Their encouragement spurs me to keep on writing, so that ordinary people's stories from bygone eras are not forgotten.

To my agent, Caspian Dennis, for being my biggest champion as well as a terrific friend, and to all the others in the crack team at Abner Stein – especially Sandy, Jasmine, Rebecca, Tom and Ray.

To my editor, Hannah Smith, and the excellent team at Penguin Michael Joseph. Thank you for believing in Maggie. Thank you for loving Florrie as much as I do! This first book wouldn't be the page-turning read it is without the additional editorial machinations of Beatrix McIntyre and Sarah Bance. Thanks to Phillipa Walker for looking after the pre-publication stage. Thanks also to Hattie at Penny Street and the sales, PR and rights people at Penguin, (whom I haven't even met yet at the time of writing these acknowledgements!) for their role in getting Florrie into shops and into the hands of readers. Teamwork really does make the dream work.

To the lovely librarians who will buy in copies of *The Housekeeper of Holcombe Hall* for their historical saga-loving readers, and to the book-bloggers who read early copies and champion Florrie on social media.

To my amazing readers, who have followed my writing from my *Nurse Kitty* trilogy to this new series all about Florrie Bickerstaff and the gilded world of her employers, the Harding-Bournes of Holcombe Hall. I really hope you've enjoyed this first story and will stay tuned for the next instalment . . .!

Reading Group Discussion Points

1. What sort of a lead character do you think Florrie is? She is regularly reminded by other characters, from both above and below stairs, that she should 'know her place'. Do you think she gets involved with the lives of her employers, the Harding-Bournes, in a way that is justifiable, or is she behaving inappropriately? How different might Florrie be if the novel was set in the present day?

2. In the slums of Manchester, Florrie's family is fighting to survive. What do you think working-class life and expectations were back in 1929, compared to the present day? Do you think the gap between the rich and the poor is any wider now, or roughly the same as it was then?

3. Florrie left home at fifteen to begin service at Holcombe Hall, with infrequent prospect of returning to visit her family, many miles away. What would you have liked/disliked about being in service in 1929? If you'd been poor, would you have sent your own child away to work at the age of fifteen, or would you yourself have wanted to leave home at that age?

4. *The Housekeeper of Holcombe Hall* is set at the end of the 'Roaring Twenties', on the cusp of the Wall

Street Crash and the Great Depression. What do you think were the positive aspects of the Roaring Twenties and 1930s (if any), as depicted in the book, and how might life have generally been better back then, compared to nowadays?

5. Sir Richard Harding-Bourne is a nobleman with a conscience, and Thom is a plain-speaking gardener with a big heart: Who do you think is the stronger, better man and why?

6. In the novel, Arkwright the butler is bossy and cold towards the female staff, Danny the valet is lazy and rude to the girls, and Sir Hugh is self-indulgent and arrogant, belittling Florrie in public. Yet Sir Richard and Thom are both gentlemanly in their own ways. Do you think that men were more respectful of women in the 1920s and 30s than they are nowadays? If so/if not, why?

7. Lady Charlotte is dressed by Coco Chanel herself, the Harding-Bournes are driven around in the finest cars, and Holcombe Hall is a well-maintained stately home from the 1700s, set in landscaped grounds. Can you make a case for the luxurious living standards of landed gentry in the 1920s and 1930s? And today? Do you think it's better that houses like Holcombe Hall are kept within a family and passed on from one generation to another, or do you think all should be owned by the National Trust and open to the public?

8. What similarities can you see between the political events in *The Housekeeper of Holcombe Hall* – the rise of fascism, and the ill-treatment of recent Jewish immigrants, who have fled the pogroms of Eastern Europe – and those unfolding currently? How do they differ? Do you think history offers a solution to today's issues?

9. Who is your least favourite character and why?

10. What was your favourite bit of the story and why?

A Conversation with
Maggie Campbell

Your first series of 'Nurse Kitty' books were set in Manchester at the end of World War Two. Why did you choose to start a new series set in rural Lancashire in 1929?

My own mother was a cleaner-cum-housekeeper for many years, struggling to make ends meet as a single parent. We lived in a tiny, terraced council house on an estate that was very close to the old raincoat factories by Manchester's 'Strangeways' prison – factories in which my own grandparents, aunts and uncles had worked. Pre-war, my family lived in the Victorian terraces of Higher Broughton/Cheetham that were cleared as slum dwellings and demolished by the council in the 1960s, if they hadn't already been bombed during the Blitz.

Our family story before that is one of migration and hope at the turn of last century, borne out of danger and destitution – typical of Manchester, which by 1929 was already something of a melting pot.

I felt that after three 'Nurse Kitty' books, telling Kitty's story from the start of the NHS to the start of the Cold War in 1950, I was ready to move on. I knew I wanted to write about the north-west again, but the question was where precisely? I cast my mind back to my youth. Not only did I spend the school holidays happily accompanying my mother to those cleaning jobs in 'big' houses, but I also visited Holcombe Village with my father, who had divorced from my mother and had settled in Ramsbottom, Lancashire. I have great memories of climbing the wild, almost desolate but beautiful Holcombe Hill, with its foreboding Peel Tower. Those memories, that family history, and my childhood love of the TV series, *Upstairs, Downstairs* got me to thinking: what if I wrote a story about the housekeeper of a fictitious stately home called Holcombe Hall? What if my young housekeeper came from the slums of Manchester? And what if I set the book at the end of the Roaring Twenties, just as the Wall Street Crash, the ensuing Great Depression and fascism really started to bite in England? I had the foundations of a heart-warming story that would hopefully appeal to historical saga readers as well as fans of TV shows like *Downton Abbey*!

How did you come up with Florrie Bickerstaff's backstory?

I had originally imagined Florrie to be a young widow, but then, in the course of researching the era, I read that staff were expected to remain unmarried and childless or else leave service. I consequently adjusted Florrie's age downwards and then thought about her extended family. I knew that the slum housing in Manchester was damp, poorly ventilated and prone to infestation, and indeed, I remember my own mother complaining of cockroaches in such numbers that when she rose to pee in a bucket in the middle of the night, she would have to throw a shoe into the middle of the room to frighten the carpet of cockroaches away! My infant uncle tragically died from gastroenteritis, consigned as he had been to a back bedroom in a freezing cold, damp house. Life was hard. Premature death was common. I consequently thought it fitting to have Florrie lose her sister, Irene, to lung disease. It made sense that the Bickerstaff men were all either dead or gone (as many of the menfolk in my own family were). It was a flight of fancy to assume Florrie's Mam, nieces and nephews might move to Holcombe Estate's gamekeeper's cottage, but Holcombe Hall and its grounds and outbuildings feel like an extra main character, so I set out to explore everything within the estate's boundaries, just as I would explore all the facets of a key protagonist's personality.

What inspired you to include real-life celebrities and historical events in the story?

While researching, I was intrigued to read about the entrepreneur Clarence Hatry, and the events that led to the Wall Street Crash. I had already imagined that the Harding-Bournes would be wealthy industrialists, so it made sense that Sir Richard might have invested in the big steel merger that Hatry was trying to broker. It also occurred to me that a high-society designer like Coco Chanel, who, for a time, was the mistress of the Duke of Westminster, likely would have befriended the likes of Lady Charlotte – a close relative of King George V. Given appeasement was the order of the day in Britain until 1938 and given antisemitism was rife, wouldn't it be fitting, I reasoned, if Chanel visited Holcombe Hall and espoused some of those nasty antisemitic views she was infamous for, whilst picnicking in the grounds? Why wouldn't Sir Hugh's friends be 'Bright Young Things' like Evelyn Waugh, and why shouldn't impressionable, arrogant Sir Hugh be influenced by and rub shoulders with the likes of Oswald Mosley, who was not only part of the political establishment in 1929, but also an aristocrat? So I believe that showcasing real celebrities in the story lends authenticity to the fictitious characters, and real-world events lend a believability to the goings-on at Holcombe.

Which is your favourite bit of the story – the romance or the politics?

This is a historical saga, so the faithfully historical aspects of it will always be coloured by the human story at the heart of the novel. I knew I wanted young, idealistic Florrie to be embroiled in a love triangle, and for her to experience unrequited love for a married man, who seems beyond her reach, as well as encountering something far steadier and attainable, with a down-to-earth man from her own social class. Who knows where Florrie's heart will lead her in the next book?! Importantly, though, I also wanted to foreground her ties to the other women around her: her mother; her sister; Mrs Douglas, the original housekeeper; Cook and the other maids. Nowadays, the younger generation have a notion of 'chosen family' – i.e. good friends whom you love as much as any blood relatives. It is this idea of the staff below stairs becoming akin to family that I wanted to explore in *The Housekeeper of Holcombe Hall*, just as much as Florrie's sense of duty towards her blood relatives.

Do you have a routine when you write a book?

Yes, I most certainly do. I'm very focused and I write fast. Many of you will be surprised to hear that I also write crime fiction as Marnie Riches, and since the beginning of my career as a published author, I've been writing two books per year, minimum. I've had eleven crime books published, with a twelfth – a cosy murder-mystery called *The Gardeners' Club* – due out in April 2025. I've penned six children's books under the pseudonym Chris Blake, as well as the three Nurse Kitty historical sagas, penned as Maggie Campbell. When I'm not writing, I teach academic and creative writing for the Royal Literary Fund and New Writing North. I've even taught creative writing at Cambridge University! This means that I generally have to work seven days per week, which earns me less money than you'd think and wreaks havoc on my gardening schedule. As I write, I am late taking my dahlias up for the winter, and we've had some hard frosts. I do hope they survive.

I digress! I wake at around 7 a.m. and down a full

cafetiere of coffee while I read the papers from cover to cover until 9.30 a.m. This is the luxury of growing older, after years of doing a fraught school-run with my children, and I like to see how social trends, significant events and political drama around the world enmesh to create the history of tomorrow. If I've a writing deadline, I will then sit and write a chapter each day – around two thousand words – until I'm done. Some days, that can take three hours, others, ten hours. I'm often still writing at 9 p.m., and then I'm zonked by 10. I read for twenty minutes and then put the light out, mentally exhausted! Normally, I dedicate a month to full-time research before I plan, and only *then* start to write. I research fine detail as I'm first-drafting, especially the etymology of spoken language, to ensure my dialogue's historically accurate. I fit in my teaching and admin where I can.

I believe that to be a good, prolific writer, you have to be incredibly disciplined. To write two books each year, you have to be one of those lucky people who can 'get into the tunnel', and I suppose I am. Most writers only pen one novel per year, but I'd be getting into all sorts of mischief on social media if I didn't write two each year. The devil finds work for idle hands . . . When I eventually retire, I will exercise more and my garden will be immaculate, all year round. There. I've said it now, so I'll have to be true to my word!